La Maga

A Story about Sorcerers and Magi

by Soror ZSD23

ISBN-13:978-0615687223
ISBN-10:0615687229

Cover art: Gustav Klimt 1862-1918. Hygeia, detail from painting title
Medicine

Cover design: Dee Rapposelli

Leaving aside those principles of magic that play on the superstitious and that, whatever they be, are unworthy of the general public, we will direct our thoughts only to those things that contribute to wisdom and that can satisfy better minds.

—from *On Magic* by Giordano Bruno (born 1548; burned at the stake February 16, 1600).

Chapters

1
The Conus Magus Maneuver

"**P**ass and photo ID. You can't get into the class without an admission pass and photo ID: student ID, license to practice magic, magical association card. Did you not receive the notice?" the hall guard croaked. And she was frog-like—small and bloated with a thick, jowly face and bloody, popping eyes; matronly. Like all school hall guards, she gobbled up whatever little power over others she could muster.

"No one ever gave me a hard time about being a walk-in," the man protested. "I promised my son that I'd take the class with him."

"*This* is a closed class," the hall guard snapped, firmly affirming in her gravelly voice: "You cannot be admitted without an admission pass and a photo ID."

"Where do I get a pass?" the man asked.

"You don't. The class is filled," the froggy character said.

The man stormed away. The hall guard continued barking at students and adults about the entrance requirements as they congregated at the threshold of a small lecture hall. There, a controversial celebrity lady mage—a *maga*, that is—would be presenting a class called Lost and Found: Mystical Codes and Keys. It would be the first time such a class was ever presented at the H. Trismegistus Mystical Arts Academy. The maga, who was also a new professor at the school, would be teaching this class on Tuesday and Thursday mornings and also teaching several other classes at the Academy. She herself was once a student there, and her name was Sofia La Maga.

Leonard and his buddies, Anil and Bertrand, presented

the appropriate documents and were admitted (their other friend, Cary, didn't make the cut). Leonard's father, whose name was Leo de Lux, followed them. Leo de Lux was a sorcerer, which was like being a mage but different in the same way some persons are Conservative and some Progressives, some Democrats, some Republicans, some Catholic, some Protestant, or Jewish or Muslim, or, Hindu. You get the idea.

This Leo de Lux was one of the top rulers of the North Atlantic Sovereignty in a country called Terra Novit in the Inner Plane. He was accompanied by an older smartly groomed man named Victor and a masculine-looking woman. Victor was de Lux's personal assistant, and the woman was a staff-bearer—that is, she belonged to the police squad.

"Pass and ID. No one is admitted without an admission pass and photo ID," the hall guard rattled. Upon realizing who she was now talking to, though, she froze. "You can go in," she rasped to the Lord Consul Leo de Lux. He was, in fact, the equivalent of a governor in the North Atlantic Sovereignty.

Consul de Lux huffed and rolled his icy eyes. He could hear a woman behind him muttering, "What's he doing here? Goddamn thought-police."

Someone shushed her.

"I don't care," de Lux heard the woman protest. "I'm tired of being victimized!"

The consul's two companions bolted toward the woman. They hauled her away to give her a security check and a none-too-friendly warning about her attitude. de Lux himself avoided looking at the woman even though he could've fried her in her shoes if he cared to bother.

The lecture hall was a dimly lit semi-round room with a half-dozen rows of slightly sloping bucket seats. The ceiling was tin-molding speckled with whirling fans that made a person dizzy if she stared up that way too long. The leaded windows were heavy plated, stained or mottled to block out the sky or the trees or passing birds so the mind couldn't fly outside to daydream. At front and center of the room were a podium, a desk, and a chalk board illuminated by a bare bulb hanging from a wire. The professor hadn't arrived yet.

Leonard de Lux Junior made quick work of setting up a prank while his father chatted with some people from the Royal Conservationist Party. He figured he'd get away with it, and his dad would get a mean laugh from the escapade. Leonard would feel strangely proud of secretly giving twisted mirth to his father, who had been on the rag about this new teacher.

With sleight of hand, he dropped a stink-bomb on the professor's chair. When she sat at the desk to study the seating chart and call the roll, she would, you know, make a smell. Leonard twitched his eyebrows and sneered to appear daring and shameless to his buddies. They all sniggered and sputtered so that their pimply, adolescent faces turned reddish and even gawkier.

These fellows, who at the age of 16 were nearly men, thought that they were making a bit of fun for all — except the new teacher, of course. But she was supposed to be a good sport. If she were, she would have to regard the indignity as a required razzing — a kind of initiation.

She was supposed to have had lots of initiations in her relatively young life — or lots of initiations for someone still relatively young, but what was supposed to be so, what people said was so, and what really was so could be completely different. That's what Leonard's father said whenever the subject of Sofia La Maga came up.

As mentioned, the father, Leo de Lux, held the esteemed and very powerful position of consul within the Senate of the North Atlantic Sovereignty. And, as mentioned, this meant that he was the governor of that sovereignty. He was a mere 43 years of age when he assumed the role 2 years previously. His rise to the position, earned at such a young age, suggested that his family was high class and had a lot of influence.

Consul de Lux was vehemently against Sofia La Maga's teaching appointment. He fought it in league with several other parents who were members of the Royal Conservationist Party. As consul, he should have had the final say — and would have in times past — but now that the democratic process was in vogue, with its hyperbureaucratic checks and balances, his influence had eroded.

Although vocal, the RCP (that is, the Senate's Royal Conservationist Party) was in the minority about whether Sofia La Maga should be allowed to teach at the Academy. Its petitions were countered by petitions from the populist Expansionist Party whose members argued that the maga's appointment to the prestigious H. Trismegistus Mystical Arts Academy Secondary School would be a quantum leap in the advancement of magical sciences. The consul could have vetoed the ruling, but doing so would have heightened and prolonged the media circus surrounding the return of Sofia La Maga to Terra Novit. He consoled himself with the notion that the uppity maga was sure to cross the line again and ruin herself for good. Figuring that he ought to stay in character, he released a livid statement to the press in which he said that the ruling reflected a loss of values and a sign of contempt for the patrician class.

Of particular concern in his tirade were comments suggesting a return to the caste system, which pigeon-holed people according to social status. de Lux caught flack for his comments, but it was not as if he didn't expect it. In the end, he was forced to issue a tightly worded apology in which he insisted that he in no way meant to suggest that

Inner Plane societies reinstate the caste system. He nevertheless showed how two-face he was by adding that the tradition had encouraged "social stability and gentility."

Anyway, Leonard (Junior) and his buddies, Anil, Cary, and Bertrand, had gotten a glimpse of Sofia La Maga the day before. They gloated like the spoiled-brat junior elitist patricians they were that the hype about the professor was nonsense. It was just as Leonard's father had insisted. Professor La Maga was nothing but a bedraggled kitchen witch.

She didn't seem at all like the stories told about her. In fact, she roamed through the secondary school's second-floor corridor as if she were roller-skating with three left feet and had the mental disposition of a hedgehog.

She was a tall, slender but robust woman with the rough-and-tumble appearance of someone who had weathered hard climbs in exotic lands. Her clothes were rustic, quaintly worn, and embellished with savage jewelry: jangling bells and sashes of bone and fur, claws, shells, and spike-studded pods. Her Medusa-like mane was haphazardly plaited here and there and cluttered her face, blinding her as she toddled along. She was gripping a mass of overstuffed folders, and from her arms dangled plastic bags filled with items that were heavy. The bags swung like pendulums in the wake of her clumsy pace. The heels of her worn leather lace-up boots alternately caught on the frayed hem of an ankle-length skirt. It caused her to wobble pathetically as the heavy bags alternately beat against her ribs.

No one offered assistance. They were busy gawking at her and probably thinking the same as Leonard and his pals were. *This* was the prodigy who had been gallivanting across exotic lands and speed-reading through mentorships with wild wizards, shamans, and hermits?

Leonard reported the observation to his father who smirked and lectured him about how the Inner Plane was going to the dogs. He blamed immigration and student exchange laws and especially the prohibition against the caste system—even though it had been nearly a century since the prohibition had been in effect.

As far as de Lux senior was concerned, the discontinuation of the system undercut the privilege of the privileged. It made for circumstances whereby the child of the lowliest peasant spell-caster (that is, Sofia La Maga) could become a prestigious mage—all because she had spent 12 years spelunking through some caves on the Inner Plane of Katmandu or Machu Picchu or . . . some place.

Leonard's father repeated that Sofia La Maga was a fake. He said that the heroic tales about her were hoaxes. He stressed that she was the bastard spawn of a wayward woman who had died under suspicious circumstances. He reminded Leonard and his friends that this one Sofia La Maga also had been kicked out of the H. Trismegistus Mystical Arts Academy School of Graduate Studies in her junior year of college. She was a trouble-maker who almost took the school down because of her political extremism. A *terrorist*, Leonard's father insisted. Furthermore, rather than applying herself to unusual scholarship in the Terra Mysticus as was claimed about her, she had been running some sort of silly "New Age" cult among the Commons in the Outer Plane for the past 15 years . . .

The stink-bomb that Leonard had placed on the professor's chair resembled a lovely little seat cushion. It was a thin satiny, plush red cushion that had a violet-colored lace crocheted hem. It was doily-like: about six inches square and would let out a methane cloud if a heavy-enough weight—like that of a human body—sat on it.

But Leonard wasn't the only one in the class who

apparently had a foul message for the new teacher. A floppy, sad, and weedy-looking bouquet of basil, tansy, and hellebore was plopped on the podium. Leonard knew from his father's horticulturist that the message hidden in the mysterious symbolism of these particular herbs and flowers was to "fuck off and die."

The students were in their places, and because this was a special, advanced-training program, a small group of adults were allowed to attend. They sat in the back and side tiers of seats within the small lecture hall. Some adult attendees were participating to earn continuing magical education credit. Some were attending for personal enrichment; and some, like Leonard's father, were attending to gather ammunition to petition the Academy to discharge Sofia La Maga from her teaching post and send her packing back to the Inner Plane of Mogao . . . or . . . Sedona . . . or . . . wherever.

At a point in which the fraternizing, the fidgeting, the adjusting of desk stands, and the swiveling of bucket seats came to a lull, Professor La Maga made her entrance. She was oddly dressed in a blousy white petticoat over which was a long, red shift that was loudly embroidered with images of elephants, eagles, and crocodiles. Her wild, voluminous hair was haphazardly plaited and affixed with jewel-studded clips. Somewhere in that baubled mass of bronze and umber tresses, peered a small, sweet face that was wind-burnished and somewhat swarthy. She had yet to make eye contact with anyone, but it was hard not to notice that her almond eyes, the color of molten chocolate, glistened with an intriguingly fiery gleam.

"Hello, boys and girls!" she chirped. When she smiled, which she did often, the right corner of her mouth turned up and the left corner turned down. It was a soft and shy smile, but the sight of it caused a kind of giggle to run through a person. It drew out a gleeful, alright feeling.

Momentary. Hard to put one's finger on when it happened, like déjà vu that leaves a slight pinch of perplexity. That should have been Leonard's first clue not to mess with the professor. She was sly, loose, and wide-ranging about magical acts. But it was too late by then.

She swiped the nasty "fuck-you" bouquet from the podium and strode directly to her desk chair. She grasped the stink-bomb and flung it into the air so that the corners of the lace hem whirled like a pinwheel. She aimed her staff at it as if she were hunting ducks with a rifle. The staff was nothing more than a stick of petrified wood topped with a crystal skull and a jangling girdle of red ribbons, beads, shards of shells, and bones. A soft blue spark shot out of it. The professor comically stumbled back into the chalk board as if off balanced by the force of the shot.

The class erupted into giggles and applause that turned into mean laughter. Upon bursting, the stink-bomb rained confetti and pink flower petals on the prank's culprit—Leonard de Lux, Junior.

Professor La Maga let the students snicker as she studied the seating chart. "Alright, honey-bunnies," she muttered. The students watched her glance at Leonard and then past him to the consul, who was sitting almost in line with his son but five rows back. The right side of the professor's mouth curled up, but the left side stayed the same. Leonard guessed the expression was a sneer of an annoyed and vengeful sort. The youth flushed hot with shame and dread. He dared not turn to see what his father's reaction to all this was but he could feel the man's mood as if it were a brush fire scorching his back.

Leonard watched the professor's brow pinch. He examined how her gaze toggled back and forth between him and his father. In a voice tinged with false astonishment, she said, "Junior Mister Leonard de Lux. You picked the day." She eyed Leonard as if both she and he should be amused by what had happened. She told him that he had to stand up.

His father still made no comment, and so Leonard slouched upward until he was somewhat vertical.

He was a tall, lean but strongly built young man. His head was lowered so that his amber eyes peered sullenly from the tops of their orbits through a wispy fringe of dark auburn hair.

"Junior Mister de Lux, you're kind of young to be tripping over your own balls, don't you think?" the professor declared in a booming voice.

The room fell silent because no one dared make a sound after that in the presence of the consul. He was a severely attractive and overgroomed fellow, befitting his patrician status and high political rank. He was, like his son, relatively tall and robustly lean. His complexion was fairer, and his hard eyes were strangely pale and piercing. Although he otherwise always looked very dignified, his bejeweled right hand was now pressed against his brow as if nursing a massive headache.

"In my beneficence," Professor La Maga announced, "and because I'm such a good sport, I'm going to give you the opportunity to redeem yourself, impress your father, and all that etcetera by demonstrating your academic prowess."

She turned her attention to the seating chart that was on her desk. On the seating chart was a color-coded note about each student's grade point average. The professor gazed, pan-faced, at the chart for a while. Leonard knew she was staring at an orange-yellow grade point code that was pretty bad on a prismatic scale of red to violet. She was probably wondering how Leonard had gained entrance to the class besides that he was the consul's son. She was probably also wondering what the hell to do next.

Leonard didn't know whether the chart said what a

delinquent fuckup he was. He wasn't good at anything except orchestrating pranks, which he actually sucked at, considering how often he got caught. He was an ace at the Phaeton maneuver, though. The Phaeton maneuver was an illegal and really dangerous sport that Inner Plane teenage boys played anyway.

If he was interested in anything having to do with school and magical studies, it was lost codes and keys, but those things were usually only covered in special graduate programs. Whatever Leonard knew about these topics, he learned on his own. So even though the supposed reason that he was attending Sofia La Maga's class was to help his father discredit her, the real, secret, very personal reason, regardless of his bad behavior off the bat, was to receive instruction in mystical codes and keys.

"Stand up straight and meet my gaze, Mister Junior," the professor announced.

The prickles on the back of Leonard's neck were saying that his father had risen from his chair. The young man, however, was paralyzed in the grip of the professor's eyes, which felt like snuggles and warm chocolate pudding.

"What is she doing?" he heard his father hiss and bang his staff on the floor.

Leonard wanted to say that the maga was mesmerizing him, but he also wanted to just let it happen. It felt too pleasant. All was lost so why not just lose it.

"Don't belabor the point, Reverend Lady," the consul's voice commanded. "The boy is clearly a moron. Come away, Leonard. It is time to *go*."

But Leonard remained unmoved without concern and watched the professor blink.

"Really?" she said. Her face lit up with relief. She grinned.

"Excuse me, Professor?" Leonard whispered.

"That's very interesting," she said to herself. She

smiled widely as if Leonard had told her something utterly fascinating. Meanwhile, Leonard's father had again barked that Leonard should excuse himself from the classroom. Everyone else was either giggling or feeling very nervous.

Leonard could now clearly hear his father griping to someone that the "folk-woman" ("Reverend Lady" Professor La Maga, that is) was in for it and that Leonard should be told to join his father in *Dr. Bruno's* office on the other side of the pavilion. Dr. Giordano (Danny) Bruno was the dean of the graduate school and chief administrator of the secondary school.

Then, as if beaming with pride, Professor La Maga announced: "Mister Leonard de Lux, Junior. Can you explain to the class the origin of the term the 'Conus magus maneuver'?"

As if awestruck, Leonard uttered, "Yes." He had spent the summer studying its legend and swimming in fantasies about how he had discovered its lost key.

"Go ahead, then, Leonard. Please tell us," the professor coached.

"In common parlance, the term 'Conus magus maneuver' means that a sorcerer or mage has pacified a foe, but the meaning, mostly among sorcerers, is that the sorcerer has paralyzed his opponent—that the opponent is too mystified to act," Leonard began.

"It's an insult," the professor announced to the class, "mostly uttered by 'sore winners.'

Continue," Professor La Maga requested.

"It's a figure of speech," Leonard said, "about a hostile magical practice—the Conus magus *charm*—which involves striking and then absorbing energy from an opponent."

"And when is this hostile practice typically used?" questioned Professor La Maga.

"All the time, but no one ever admits it," Leonard responded.

"Indeed, it's rampant even among Commons in the Outer Plane," the professor confirmed. "Go on, Mr. Junior de Lux. We're waiting to hear about the legend."

"The term 'Conus magus charm' refers to the *legendary* charm of the same name, which is much more intense than the charm used today," Leonard said. "According to legend, the original charm was discovered by a sorcerer named Mare Maré who lived around 250 BCE. He was a Melanesian sorcerer who was very familiar with venomous cone snails of the South Pacific, particularly the snail that millennia later would be christened 'Conus magus' by Outer Plane marine biologists," Leonard explained.

"He was a sea-charmer," Professor La Maga interjected, adding that sea-charming was how Mare Maré "managed to cross great expanses of ocean long before the invention of luxury cruise liners. The name Mare Maré means 'Nightmare of the Dark Sea.'"

The professor magically materialized the tapered shell of a cone snail. Grasping it between her thumb and forefinger, she held it out so all could see how harmless it looked: white with brown and tawny bands and dapples. Red, needle-like claws jutted out of the shell's opening.

"But this is only the tip of the proverbial iceberg, isn't it, Mister de Lux, Junior," she said and lobbed the deadly creature into her audience. Students ducked and screeched, but the snail vanished in midair.

Leonard glanced at Bertrand, wondering whether his buddy was as awed by the professor as Leonard was. Bertrand, an athletically built youth with ginger hair and sullen eyes, made a subtle but enthusiastic nod. Indeed, he pouted and raised his brows as if to suggest that he, too, thought the professor might be pretty cool.

Leonard finally turned to see whether his father was still in the room. The man was coldly glaring at him. Then he made a slight nod of the head and flashed his eerie pale blue eyes. Leonard took it as a gesture to continue his performance.

"Mare Maré had a rivalry-thing with a mage named Corno," Leonard explained. "Mare Maré absorbed Corno completely the way venomous cone snails paralyze and eat their prey."

"Corno Magus was absorbed into Mare Maré Sortiar," Professor La Maga announced. Here she identified the legendary rivals according to their magical titles. Corno was a mage. Therefore, he was addressed by the title "Magus." Mare Maré was a sorcerer. Being so, he was referred to by the title "Sortiar." In the same way, Professor Sofia La Maga's formal form of address was Sofia La Maga *Magus*. Lord Consul Leo de Lux's formal address was Lord Consul Leo de Lux *Sortiar*. Eventually, Leonard Junior would get to tack the title "Sortiar"—if he ever managed to become one—to the end of his name, too.

Professor La Maga paused and grinned at Leonard. The youth gripped the desk stand affixed to his seat because the event triggered an upwelling of woozy heat. No one—not father, mother, nor any other relation or person close to him—had ever smiled with such affection in any memory he could recall. It was awesome as in frightening, and terrific, as in terrifying.

"And why aren't sorcerers, magi, and other what-not running around absorbing each other out of existence anymore?" Professor La Maga questioned.

"About 800 or 900 years after Mare Maré, they were," Leonard exclaimed. "Mare Maré's followers had grown exponentially so that all the different groups of them began attacking each other. In this one book by an historian—Gustav Galeorhinus—he said they killed each other off."

"Gustav Galeorhinus. Now there's a sleep remedy for you. You've read Gustav Galeorhinus, Leonard?" the professor asked incredulously.

"Yep," he boasted. The material, dry and written in quaint and very wordy Victorian English, was interrupted here and there with passages that were in Coptic, Greek, Hebrew, Latin and Sanskrit. Leonard had made a point of figuring it all out because he was *that* interested.

The professor's brow pinched. Her smile seemed partly amused and partly confused. She went back to glaring at Leonard's poor academic ranking on the seating chart and then glanced at Leonard's father, who also seemed puzzled. "The demise of the charm led to what?" she finally asked.

Leonard fell silent.

"Anyone?" Professor La Maga asked the students. "Grownups back there?"

She was about to deliver the answer when Leo de Lux announced in a direct voice slightly tinged with contempt, "The end of the Dark Ages among the Commons and the advent of the Renaissance — the Age of 'Enlightenment.'"

Leonard watched the professor flash the sweetest smile at his father. "Thank you, Lord Consul," she said. Leonard glanced back to see the man curl a corner of his mouth into a faintly sneering smile.

As mentioned, Leo de Lux had peculiar eyes. Now, it was very common for sorcerers, magi, shamans, sadhus, yogis, and others like that to have a lot of personality in the eye. The more character in the eye, the more a person knew he or she was dealing with impressive magical talent.

Sofia La Maga Magus had warm, dark, fathomless eyes that glistened like the moon on water. Leo de Lux Sortiar had eyes that were like the palest, iciest, and most remarkably prismatic blue gem. They had turned that way from a deeper blue during his youth when he had survived a dark act of magical warfare.

His critics, those who feared or who had been attacked by him, and even some of his admirers referred to him as

Leukoculi—"White-Eyed." In certain magical traditions (such the family line of Sofia La Maga), pale eyes like those of de Lux were unlucky. They were a sign of wickedness . . . of being an absorber . . . a sapper . . . a vampire—not unlike the infamous Mare Maré.

Besides the strikingly pale eyes, de Lux had severe but attractive features. His closely cropped hair was dark auburn. He had a smooth, fair, unblemished complexion; strong, intense brow; a perfect nose; and thin expressive lips that moved along with his fierce eyes to pout, wince, sneer, and tediously sigh.

The man looked bored or exasperated most of the time. He saved his smile for either indulgently bawdy or awe-inspiring moments. He was not easily impressed, but he was easily annoyed.

He was finely focused on the power of appearances. He had a knack for materializations. This was not a particularly profound feat, but a noteworthy and entertaining one. Not only could he materialize all sorts of precious objects, he could, for the entertainment of friends, materialize whole holographic theatrical performances, concerts, and sports events.

For his enemies, he made annoying and sometimes forbidding thought-forms that tended to be nearly impossible to get rid of. Indeed, his ex-wife's scandalous fall from grace had something to do with her having had an affair with a thought-form that de Lux had conjured to incriminate her, although this was not at all true.

The former Lady de Lux, a senator during the time of her marriage to Leo (who himself was a mere senator at that time), had had a kind of mental breakdown some years past. She abandoned Leo and their son to join a fringe magian commune on an island in the South Pacific. The idea was so nasty to Leo de Lux that, instead of the truth, he told everyone that he had dismissed his wife because she preferred having sex with a thought-form instead of him. Although an odd story for a man to admit, it got him a lot of sympathetic ass from women who very much wanted to fill the vacancy left by the rude departure of ex-Lady de Lux.

Consul de Lux never officially replaced the consort who had abandoned him and a child for religion, but being a severely handsome, wealthy, and highly influential person, he had no shortage of female companions. He was not a particularly warm or involved parent, though. It was unclear whether he even "liked" his son, especially that the young fellow was growing up to be a troublesome — and embarrassing — ne'er-do-well.

"Gustav Galeorhinus Magus was a little bit of a revisionist," Professor La Maga told the class. "But assuming he was correct, what was the flaw that led to the demise of the Conus magus charm? You can sit down, Leonard. That was great. Anyone? Am I going to have to make Junior Mister de Lux the assistant teacher for the day?"

A girl raised her hand. With a quick look at the seating chart, Professor La Maga announced: "Miss Thetis Mirabilis. Go ahead."

"The extinction of the Conus magus charm and the Mare Maré lineages are examples of the function of the Chaos Principle," she asserted.

"The Chaos Principle. That's a good topic for discussion," said Professor La Maga. "We'll be talking about that a lot this semester."

Another adult piped in. "The legend is fabricated — made up. It's meant to be an allegory about the Chaos Principle."

"That's an interesting view. You may be on to something," the Professor replied.

And what was the Chaos Principle but a kind-of

religious belief that was often used to explain how society worked. Namely, it was the name for the observation that conservative social patterns tended to slowly advance to tyrannous extremes before rebellion caused public policy to embrace more progressive views. Once becoming the predominant norm, the progressive social atmosphere had the potential to advance to anarchy before folks started tightening the screws and rebelling again. From Chaos to Cosmos to Chaos and back again. This was how the Universe worked.

"What else? Students? Anyone under the age of 17 have any ideas?" Professor La Maga coaxed.

Before any teenaged students could get a word in edgewise, Consul de Lux declared that Gustave Galeorhinus's account of the Conus magus charm was completely made up and had nothing to do with the Chaos Principle. He insisted that no special or lethal key to the charm existed beyond the one used "rampantly in polite society."

"Galeorhinus Magus fancied himself a sea-charmer. The villainous Mare Maré Sortiar was nothing more than a fictional alter ego that allowed Galeorhinus to express his aggressive tendencies through fictional reveries," de Lux remarked. He went on to say that the practice of the actual Conus magus maneuver was so rampant that a moralistic legend—engineered by a mage (he felt compelled to drive home this point)—was made up about it, but that it had no special origin. It was nothing more than natural magic. "As mentioned by the esteemed professor, even Commons do it as a matter of course," he sniffed.

After making his point, he paused in the attentive silence given him and then sat down.

"And there's no Santa Claus or Easter Bunny either," Professor La Maga announced.

Giggling and hushing sounds followed this exchange.

The consul flecked his eyes and slightly grinned almost as if he were amused by the professor's guff. Professor La Maga then announced that she was in agreement with the consul...sort of.

A strange, peeved silence took over the classroom. Leonard's heart sunk. Everything he had read that summer had convinced him that the Conus magus charm was real. If he could rediscover the key to the Conus magus charm, his father would have to treat him a lot more nicely than was customary.

"A number of legends about the origins of charms and lost codes and keys were made up," said Professor La Maga. "Sometimes someone was just stretching his imagination and sometimes someone—such as, you know, some blowhard mage—was trying to be preachy, but there's another more common and important reason. We're going to get into all of these things this semester. What is that other important thing?"

Suddenly Leonard felt uncharacteristically inspired. "To protect the charm," he blurted out of turn.

Professor La Maga made more flower petals shower upon him. "And we have a WINNER!" she shouted. Tiny materializations of angelic creatures flashed momentarily like soap bubbles over him. "To protect the charm. How is that Leonard?"

"The stories make you think the charm is something else than what it is and only certain very specific people know what the charm really is, what it really means, and how and when to use it. The stories might even have codes in them that only they understand but that ordinary magical people—or Commons even—take at face value, so they think it's shi . . . not meaningful," he stuttered. "Or else they do something really stupid and weird with the charm, but someone secretly knows what it really means and it has nothing to do with the story."

"Excellent, Mister Leonard de Lux, Junior," the professor gloated. "I can't believe you're the same kid who stuck a stink bomb on my chair just moments ago."

Leonard couldn't believe it either. He didn't feel bad about the attention or the accusation. Everyone seemed to be having a good time.

When the class had ended and the students were filing from the room, Leonard found himself smiling at the professor. She smiled back and seemed about to say something before being interrupted by a flock of her friends who were struggling against the tide to get to the front of the lecture hall.

Leonard glared sheepishly at his father when he caught up with him. He waited to be stared down, but it didn't happen. The two men, junior and senior, didn't speak. In fact, Leonard's father, rather than vindicated, seemed pacified. It made Leonard wonder whether they both hadn't been mystified.

II
An Apprentice

Sofia had a book she wanted to give Leonard. It was called *Sticking It to Grandmother and Her Stories*. It discussed the myths and legends behind certain popular but questionable magical beliefs and practices. Included were essays on the true origins of the Illuminati, the real meanings of various codes and keys, and how the caste system was still being practiced in Terra Novit.

Leonard was bewildered. On the one hand, he very much wanted to approach Sofia and engage her in conversation. On the other, the youth was obligated to withdraw to his father's side and exit the lecture hall.

Sofia felt her gaze gravitate to de Lux senior. She found his scary pale eyes, the disdainful air, and the side of his face that habitually sneered both disturbing and as fascinating as the curls of smoke of a snuffed candle or the intricate anatomy of the inside of a flower.

She remembered the story of how the consul's eyes got that way. The then 20-something Leo de Lux allegedly ambushed and killed a mean character who had been his family's archenemy.

The actual event was never proven, but the enemy, a sorcerer named Antonius Maymon, had mysteriously disappeared, never to be seen or heard from again. He had been involved in the deaths of all but one of de Lux's brothers and a couple of extended family members. Whatever happened during the alleged fateful confrontation between de Lux and Maymon caused de Lux's eyes to be sapped of color. They became pale blue, nearly white. This was a frightful thing for people like those from the La Maga clan. In folklore dating from antiquity, eyes like those peering from de Lux were considered *malocchi* — "evil eyes."

Now he was the ruler of the North Atlantic Sovereignty. "Good for him," Sofia sourly thought. She felt sad about what a hard life such a privileged person had to bear and how the cold, bitter thing he had become was now everyone's problem.

She turned her attention away from curiosity about the de Luxes and yelped with glee as her best pal from her high school days pushed through the exiting crowd to embrace her. The friend's name was Elizabeth Anne Raphael. She was a tall, robust, bubbly woman with cherry cheeks and long, wavy reddish hair. Her brother, Alan, also was there. He was looking saintly in white pants and a tunic. This outfit was the distinctive every-day wear of so-called "white-coat magi" — magi of a very orthodox and pious bent. He had become a big-shot magus doctor and mediator. He was trying to pull another friend, Juliet Vetiver, away from conversations with people in the exiting crowd.

When Elizabeth got close enough to her old friend, her face took on a sly expression. She quickly glanced back in the direction that the de Luxes had gone and mouthed, *"What are you doing? I can't believe you did that! You're such a sorceress."*

Elizabeth, like Sofia, was a bit of a renegade. Her parents had expected her to study magianism at the H. Trismegistus Mystical Arts Academy Secondary School and become a proper, nunnish, and contemplative kind of lady mage, perhaps married to some stiff, priestly and well-heeled magian academic. But she did not want to study magianism; she wanted to be a Druid. Her parents disapproved.

She and Sofia clicked as friends in their first year at secondary school. Elizabeth's parents weren't happy about this. They blamed their daughter's wayward spirit on her friendship with Sofia, the dangerously untamed and orphaned ward of folk practitioners.

Elizabeth's parents confiscated all the sorcerous tools and knickknacks she had been collecting and were about to send her off to be "rehabilitated" and "deprogrammed" at a half-way house affiliated with the Balthazar Institute, which was a psychiatric hospital. She ran far away and ended up in the Britannic Sovereignty of the Terra Principalis on the other side of the sea. There, she joined the Order of the Lady of the Lake and entered the Heritage Druidic Academy. Her parents didn't speak to her for 5 years. Her brother Alan paid her tuition to the Druid academy. He also ended up performing a mystical operation called the Lux Clarus Rite to encourage his parents and sister to reconcile.

Elizabeth's fortune was to become the founder of a Druidic fellowship as well as the founder of a few witch covens even further away from home in Outer-Plane Australia. Alan, on the other hand, held a Magus Celestus degree and a couple of doctorates. He was a fellow in the Royal Order of Sorcerers and Magi and was a department head at the Balthazar Institute. Their other friend, Juliet Vetiver, became a career student at the H. Trismegistus Graduate Academy. She acquired a professorship and had been teaching subjects such as esoteric anatomy in the secondary school and cosmogony and advanced astrology in the academy.

So they all had done well in their own way even though Sofia had yet to earn any graduate-level academic degrees. She had been forced out of the H. Trismegistus Graduate Academy years ago, as Leo de Lux had said, but the reasons were complicated.

She had taken youthful political activism too far. If Dr. Giordano Bruno hadn't expelled her and arranged for her passage into the Terra Mysticus, she most likely would've been disappeared on the orders of a certain industrialist named Hipparchus Gorgon Sortiar. Hipparchus Gorgon really ruled the roost in much of Terra Novit. Disappeared magical persons—those who weren't assassinated old-fashioned Conus-magus–style—tended to turn up later, completely fried, as residents of Outer-Plane psychiatric care facilities.

"What am I missing here?" Juliet said, wedging her way between Elizabeth and Sofia.

"Sof' just pulled the Conus magus maneuver on your Lord Consul de Lux. Weren't you watching?" Elizabeth snickered.

Sofia protested that it wasn't so. And Juliet, looking bewildered, said, "You know, I thought something odd was happening. Was that kid doing that himself or were you making him say those things?" she asked Sofia. "Because, I have to tell you, he's a complete idiot, that kid."

"I don't know about that," Sofia muttered astonished. "But he's definitely got issues."

"The kid gives a new meaning to the word 'issues.' A little tip, Sofia: don't mess around with the de Luxes," Juliet cautioned. She hugged her friend. "It's so good to see you. You look great. Goddess! You look the same as before you went away. Look at me." Juliet had gotten a little chunky and her hair was graying already.

"He's evil and he hates you," Alan cut in. "And I don't mean the boy." He snatched up the noxious bouquet of basil, tansy, and hellebore from the floor.

"I think he's fascinating," Sofia teased. "Especially with that *malocchio* thing going on." She gestured toward her own eyes even though she was referring to de Lux's. She watched Alan place the rude bouquet on a piece of parchment. With a few quick mutterings and the tracing of a sigil or two in the air, he made the bouquet disintegrate into soot and ash.

"The 'evil eye' is the least of it. Worry about the rest of him," Alan said. He folded the ash and soot into the parchment. "He and Hipparchus Gorgon are in each other's pockets—and each other's pants. He finds populists threatening and people of 'folkie' upbringing—like you—crude and deserving of censorship. He also doesn't tolerate political dissidents, even rehabilitated ones. He's made of ice, and he's nothing more than a boorishly randy, self-serving patrician sorcerer. He got a sack of balls to show up for this class after the ruckus he kicked up all summer about you coming back here."

"You're just jealous," Sofia teased. She told Alan that his warning was duly noted and tried to swipe the parchment envelope from him. "C'mon. You never know when I'll have to fix up a dark brew," she bleated.

Juliet said that patrician sorceresses went crazy trying to get time with de Lux. She added that "the only woman he played house with ran out on him—with a thought-form—a mirage—that he created, and not as a sex toy . . . allegedly. That says a lot," she snipped. "The wife supposedly didn't know that she wasn't doing it with a real person. Sick."

Sofia and Elizabeth begged to hear the juicy gossip.

Juliet related the tale of de Lux's (ex)wife's unfaithfulness and how embarrassing it was for her when it was discovered that she was fooling around with—not a real man—but a thought-form—an illusory entity manufactured by de Lux to trap her. Such tawdry intrigues were run-of-the-mill among patricians and were trivialities among sorcery circles, anyway. Sorcerers tended to be libertine and polyamorous. The scandal was that de Lux's wife had allegedly fallen in love with a mirage—or at least preferred the mirage to de Lux. He sent his wife packing when all was said and done.

"He used the incident as an excuse to get rid of her," Juliet said. "Who knows what even sicker things were going on. No wonder the kid is screwed up."

Alan raised an eyebrow and announced that the story was not true. "Disinformation," he announced.

"What do you know?" Juliet challenged.

"*Ex* Lady de Lux had an interest in magianism," Alan said.

"*No way*," the women gasped.

"So believing that this alternative path would redeem her from whatever her pathetic circumstances were, she took a large sum of de Lux's money and ran off to take shelter with a notorious fundamentalist magian cult communing on an exotic South Pacific island," Alan stated.

"No *way*," the women squealed again.

"Yes, 'way,'" Alan replied. "And de Lux did nothing except concoct a cockamamie story about cuckoldry and his extraordinary powers of materialization to cover up the truth."

Alan winked at Sofia and handed her the parchment envelope filled with the ashes of the nasty flowers that had been gifted to her for her first day of class. Then he hugged her. He lingered with his lips pressed against her forehead until a tear leeched out of the corner of her left eye. Elizabeth yelled at her brother to quit it.

Heat and an electrical sensation radiated from Alan's chest into Sofia's. The same thing was happening the other way around. Some in the sorcery set called it the "Sweet Surrender maneuver." They regarded it in the same way as they did the Conus magus maneuver. The recipient was considered to be, at least temporarily, disempowered.

In any case, Alan and Sofia had been fond of each other. More than fond, but that was complicated, too. Whether and how that was going to play out wouldn't have mattered if Alan hadn't married someone else and had children during Sofia's long absence. If he had been a sorcerer, it would have been alright for him and Sofia to have started in where they had left off. Alan could've had multiple partners without blame. This sort of lifestyle was not accepted among very high-level orthodox magi, though. Many of these magi were celibate or otherwise held strict disciplines and ritual observances about sexuality even if they were married.

As for Sofia, she had developed a unique understanding of herself as a personality and a projection of karmic momentum. This was the result of the disciplines and austerities that she had engaged in and the attainments she had achieved in the 15 years she had been in exile.

Many of those years were spent studying with mystics in the Inner as well as Outer Plane of the Indus and the Himalayan Range in the area of the Terra Mysticus. Working her way back to "polite society," she went on to travel into the most remote inner regions of the Terra Origens, which corresponded with the Middle East and Turkey.

Even though she hadn't earned any academic degrees—so important among her peers in the Terra Novit—she had accumulated initiations and empowerments from dozens of illuminated beings operating within the Inner and Outer Planes.

Her beginnings were tragic. The fellow who had fathered her was in question, and her mother had gone missing within a month of giving birth to her and a boy—twins—which were separated and taken in by different households. Sofia had been adopted by folk practitioners and the boy . . . Sofia's adoptive kin were paid good money and given a vineyard to keep quiet about his fate.

As for her birth mother, the evidence suggested that she had inadvertently *aportated*—that is, disappeared into—

another, deeper, better Inner Plane after having decoded an encrypted message in a medieval magic book. In other words, the woman read something in a magic book that was supposed to be very secret and "got it." Becoming illumined, she transformed into a rainbow and passed into another dimension of existence.

It was a rare happening. It was said to otherwise only occur among advanced adepts in the Terra Mysticus. It also supposedly happened, on occasion, in Tibet. But in places like the Terra Novit and Terra Principalis, it was spoken of in the same way as, say, spontaneous combustion — or the Conus magus charm. Whether it was mere urban legend or not, what had allegedly happened to Sofia's mother in the way it had happened was said to have occurred at least four times in the past 500 years.

The document was called *The Beauteous Consorte of the Mirour of Luna*. It was a page of sigils, tiny pictures, hatch marks, and glyphs that resembled a magical alphabet stamped out by something like the feet of a cockatiel or a canary. The original owner of the document, a fellow named Tomas Ladon, was burned at the stake in 1522 on charges of practicing magic among a list of other abominations that included the suspected murder of his wife. But the wife, according to history lessons within the Inner Plane, was the first person ever to have turned into a rainbow and disappeared, never to be seen again, after laying eyes on the document.

Little was known about Sofia's mother. She was thought to have been a highly educated patrician and not from Terra Novit. She was last seen doing research in the rare books section of the library of another local academic institution called the Bythos Academy of Magical Sciences. An incomplete copy of *The Beauteous Consorte of the Mirour of Luna* was kept there.

Sofia had followed in her mother's scholarly footsteps,

but instead of antiquities and mysticism, she had dedicated her sophomore and junior years at the H. Trismegistus Mystical Arts Academy to research on the abuse of inhabitants of the Outer Plane — or Commons, that is. She explored everything from guru cults to bad labor and marketing practices to political tyrannies. Then she began to scheme ways to expose the perpetrators and force them to make amends for what they had done.

The number one person who was out for Sofia's head for her rabblerousing back in her collegiate days was Hipparchus Gorgon Sortiar. His placement of associates in various entrepreneurial, judicial, and political positions in countries within the Outer Plane was responsible for immense suffering through phenomena that Commons took for granted: famine, poverty, social and political strife — all the forces that divided and conquered. Hipparchus Gorgon's signature magical tool was a staff made of iron that was encrusted with diamonds set in platinum inlay. The object was meant to bespeak his power and relentlessness.

In her time away, Sofia had proved that she had become apolitical and, as mentioned, she had accomplished many achievements that were considered beneficial to magical and mystical societies. Hence, the word went out that she was rehabilitated; if she so wished, she could return to normal relations in her homeland.

On her first day back, she was entertained at the palatial home of a certain ambassador whose wife's teenaged nephew had died by misadventure. On her second day back, she performed the Lux Clarus Rite for the ambassador's wife and the mother of the boy who had been killed. She spent the third and fourth days in conference with Dr. Bruno, who in fact was her very first mentor even though this was a very well-kept secret. On the fifth day, with the help of her adoptive mother and a lady who specialized in translocation, Sofia was able to simultaneously visit several relatives who lived in various distant places. By the sixth day, she was beginning to move her belongings into a tower-like high-rise called The Magistrar. It was where many of the professors of the H. Trismegistus Academic Pavilion lived.

She settled in; she got her bearings. By the twelfth day, even though she had no academic degree besides a basic secondary school level 1 magian license to practice magic, she walked into a classroom and began to teach graduate courses to secondary school students.

Dr. Bruno, Professor Waite (who was the associate principal of the secondary school), and a female student from the Graduate Academy had entered the lecture hall. Professor Waite and the student remained toward the back while Dr. Bruno strode up to Sofia and her group of friends.

He addressed Alan. "You know, if you could have managed to endure getting through that Sortiar Theoreticus degree, I could've gotten you in as assistant dean at the A. A. Uriel Boys' Academy, but you had to be a magus egghead."

Alan smiled bemusedly. In an innocent and respectful voice, he informed Dr. Bruno that he had grown up to become chair of the Department of Transpersonal Healing at the Balthazar Institute.

"Balthazar Institute," Dr. Bruno exclaimed in surprise. "Did I help you get in there?"

"You wrote a stunning recommendation letter, Dr. Bruno. There was even some controversy, if I remember correctly, about whether the recommendation was laced with a coercive charm," Alan replied, even though this wasn't true.

"Really?" Bruno seemed as perplexed as gratified. "I guess I didn't think you were such a big magus egghead after all. How do you like that?" He turned to Sofia and

29

said, "You're not here for . . . what? . . . a week and a half? And you're making trouble." He cringed and shook his head.

Sofia shrugged.

"The parent-alumni reception is tomorrow night," Dr. Bruno told her. "If I tell you it's very important to be there, you'll blow it off. So, don't come. I don't want to see your face there. It's a completely trivial event. And I know for a fact that your new archenemy, His High and Mighty Lord Consul Leo de Lux Sortiar, won't be there; so, there's no reason for you to show up. By the way, that was a pretty ballsy Conus magus maneuver you pulled on him—and the old Sweet Surrender thing with the kid. Precious." Dr. Bruno chuckled sinisterly, turned on his heels, and strode away.

"K," Sofia asserted, calling after him.

"Don't let me see you there," Dr. Bruno reiterated.

Sofia sent a miniature materialization of a very sexy winged nymph after him. Dr. Bruno was nearly out the door when the phantom nymph caught up to him. He could be heard bashfully laughing about it.

"Dr. Danny . . . he's a piece of work," Elizabeth muttered.

Professor Waite, who by then was in Sofia's face, turned an appalled glance at Elizabeth. Recognizing her, Professor Waite rolled her eyes and grimaced.

The associate principal was a nervous, brittle-looking, and sweaty woman who had had many a disciplinary run-in with Elizabeth Anne Raphael in days gone by. She was clad in nunnish magian attire. Her outfit consisted of a pastel blue-gray dalmatic—a type of gown with wide sleeves—and a matching turban. Acting all sewn-up and serious, she ordered Alan, Elizabeth, and Juliet to leave so that she could speak confidentially with Sofia.

They wandered out, smirking impudently in

reminiscence of youthful days under the rod of Professor Waite. "Remember. The Phoenix and Harp Country Club. Tonight," they reminded Sofia.

When they had gone, Professor Waite turned to Sofia and said almost incredulously, "They tell me you performed the Lux Clarus rite for Lady Hrasvelg and her sister Lady Whiting."

"Well, I did it for the dead kid, not the ladies," Sofia replied. She was referring to a young fellow who was about Leonard de Lux's age. He had "bought it" during an illicit Phaeton maneuver match. The boy's aunt was the wife of a high-ranking foreign diplomat.

Professor Waite glared and waited for Sofia to give the details. When the new professor didn't, the senior one uttered that Lady Hrasvelg and Lady Whiting must have been much relieved that someone of Sofia's celebrity and expertise should do such honors. Then she bristled and pointed to the young woman at the back of the room. "Her name is Mirelle Soleil. A *Deeple*," she hushed, which was slang for *Dimidium Pleb*. A Dimidium Pleb was a person who had recently transitioned from the Outer to Inner Plane. That person was considered a citizen—like a plebeian—but of very lowly status. Deeples were sometimes also called Half-Commons, because even though they were in the Inner Plane, they really were from the Outer.

"She comes from a family of Hoodooins . . . displaced from the Louisiana Delta to a major midwest city called Chicago," Waite continued. "What they haven't done to get one of their own into the Inner Plane," she sighed and wagged her head. "She has a special history and was granted special privilege to attend H. Trismegistus," the woman hushed in a pedantic sing-song. "We all thought her placement here was completely inappropriate, but Dr. Bruno insisted. The file is classified."

Sofia eyed the girl. There was something strikingly and unnaturally familiar about her, considering that Sofia had been a world away in the Mysticus for nearly the whole of this girl's life. She was about 18 years of age, an Academy freshman. She had the tawny complexion of a mulatto Creole and was tall and lithe, with a doe-like face that was delicate but also rather sour and intense. Her hair had carelessly grown out into thin matted strands that reached down her back, and her eyes were an eerily light grayish green. That Danny Bruno had perhaps selected her to play into one of his many secret schemes was extremely intriguing. Sofia quietly bristled with suspense about where this conversation with Professor Waite was leading. She watched the girl slightly smile and tilt her head. When she did that, her eyes flashed white.

Sofia cringed. A low repulsed noise eked from her. She abruptly pivoted, turning her back to the girl. With fingers close to her mouth, she made a sound like, "Peh" in a ritual spitting gesture.

"Professor La Maga!" Professor Waite gasped in an appalled but muffled screech.

"Why are her eyes are fucked up?" Sofia growled.

It was the *jettadura;* the evil eye; the wanton, sapping, vampiric eye. The girl and that pompous patrician sorcerer, de Lux, both had it. Two in one day! Sofia fumed over Danny Bruno's sick wit.

"Mirelle has ocular albinism. Had she remained in the Outer Plane she would've been legally blind by now. The nerves in her eyes are palsied for lack of melanin. It's a genetic disorder, Professor La Maga; not a curse. I'm surprised at you!"

"What am I supposed to do with her?" Sofia sighed impatiently.

"She's a special student," Professor Waite lilted and abruptly turned toward the girl, who was poised to back out the door. *"You stay right there!"* she screeched and made the doorway become a solid part of the wall.

"Why are you showing her to me?" Sofia reiterated.

Waite sneered meanly at getting an eyeful of the big-shot celebrity maga going loopy about a girl with funny eyes. "Medea Sarin Sortiar has been inquiring about her, and it would behoove us all if the girl were mentored by you instead of that particular sorceress," she explained.

Sofia didn't know who Medea Sarin was but the *esses* in Waite's enunciation of the word "sorceress" hissed in her ear.

"Really," Sofia muttered.

"Yes," Professor Waite said.

Sofia reminded Professor Waite that she had no academic credentials and was, therefore, not allowed to mentor.

"Paradigms change over time, Professor La Maga, and this is no longer the rule. In any case, a special committee was called to discuss an arrangement between you and Miss Soleil. You should feel privileged," Professor Waite said.

Sofia's eyes bulged and nostrils flared at the audacity.

"Professor La Maga," Professor Waite began in a huffy and chastising tone. "This is a security issue. You have been chosen to mentor this Deeple Commons immigrant to keep her from becoming a dangerous threat to herself and the rest of us. I do not know the specifics of her special circumstance. It is classified information. You have a debt to this society. You are here in Terra Novit at this moment because amnesty has been extended to you after your many long years in political exile. Step to the plate, Professor La Maga. Put your folkie superstitious nonsense behind you if you want to be taken seriously as an academic," she added bitterly.

The tirade sobered Sofia. Tears even itched in her nose

and swelled in her eyes. They were of frustration no less than remorse. Professor Waite took one of Sofia's hands into her own and sympathetically caressed it while Sofia sighed long and nodded a few times.

"Dr. Bruno convened the committee in which all this was discussed," Professor Waite quietly stressed.

Sofia grimaced and rolled her eyes. "Alright," she sighed again, and said it a few times as if mustering resolve. She slipped her hand from those of the associate principal and thanked her for the tough-love talk. Professor Waite appeared surprised and perhaps flattered by this gesture.

"Alright then," Professor Waite replied. She patted Sofia's shoulder and smiled as if gratified to be the famous maga's counselor. Then she departed, putting the classroom doorway back where it belonged. Sofia and Mirelle Soleil were left alone to speak in confidence.

"Do that white-thing with your eyes," Sofia demanded after Professor Waite had gone her way.

The girl, still standing yards away, looked perplexed.

"That white flash with the eyes," Sofia grilled her.

"I don't do it on purpose," the girl huffed defensively.

"Do you know who I am?" Sofia asked.

"Of course," Mirelle said.

"Wouldn't you rather be an apprentice of that other woman, the great and powerful Medea Something-or-Other?"

"I want to be your apprentice," Mirelle replied.

"If you become my apprentice, you'll be at my beck and call and have to put up with me and do everything I ask no matter how stupid and humiliating. Forever. Or until I say so. And you can't be flashing white, bad eyes at me."

Mirelle simply repeated that she didn't do things with her eyes on purpose and that she wanted to be Sofia's apprentice.

"*You* have a choice, but I *don't*," Sofia declared.

The girl scowled. Sofia waited for her to back out the door now that she could, but she remained waiting.

"I'm going to hone that edge and take your head right off with it," Sofia announced.

"Yeah. *You do that,*" Mirelle snapped.

Sofia found the punchy response humorous. "Are you a sorceress or a mage?" she asked.

"Whatever," the girl replied.

"Alright," Sofia smirked. "We'll get along." She gestured for the girl to approach.

Sofia knew her. She strongly felt that she did. She couldn't remember from where and thought it very strange not to be able to place someone with such strange eyes. But, again, how could Sofia have known her.

"Have you ever been in the Mysticus?" she asked.

The young woman was about to speak. Then Sofia remembered the time — the clock-time.

"I'm so sorry, sweetheart," Sofia exclaimed. "I gotta go. I'm really late. Really really late." And she was quite late for an appointment with a publisher who wanted her to write a book about her exploits in the Mysticus. After that appointment, she was to rush back to the H. Trismegistus before rushing off to the Bythos Academy, then to a reception at an art gallery, and finally to the Phoenix and Harp Country Club where Alan and everyone would be eagerly waiting for her.

All this stuff, and now an apprentice with evil eyes. She hastily told Mirelle the date and time that she was to come to her apartment for initiation and gave her instructions about bathing, dress, and other preparations.

"Go to some store in town and pick out a staff and a stone. It doesn't matter if the stone's rough or polished or faceted, just that it's right for you. If you also want a wand or any other ritual junk, get it. Put the cost against my name. Have them put all the stuff aside for you. I'll present them to you when you come to see me. Okay?" Sofia told Mirelle.

"How much will I owe you?" the girl asked. "Besides for the staff and stone?"

Sofia bristled in response as if she didn't understand the question.

"What's the offering?" Mirelle said. "How much does it cost to be initiated by you?"

Sofia blinked. "The cost doesn't come from a wallet," she said testily. "*You're* the offering. Don't forget it."

III
Magus Celestus

Sofia La Maga entered the banquet hall in the company of the dean, Dr. Giordano Bruno. Reggie Solaris noticed. He nudged Leo and snidely uttered, "Who says time doesn't stand still?"

Leo sniffed just as disdainfully and turned his back to the woman. He was 8 years Sofia's senior, but he remembered the gossip about her from bygone days even before she got into trouble with the Sovereignty. Leo not only had been privy to the gossip about her and Dr. Bruno, he himself had witnessed the girl's conspicuous familiarity with that particular sorcerer, who at that time was a young assistant dean.

Back in the day, Leo had the opportunity to observe the adolescent Sofia coming and going from Bruno's apartment all throughout her latter years of secondary school. Leo had been on the cusp of his appointment to the Senate and was working as an assistant to a praetor. The praetor's office and The Magistrar, where Dr. Bruno then lived, were directly across from each other, with the Mercury Gardens in between.

The Mercury Gardens was a beautifully sprawling urban park. Meandering through the Gardens were wide promenades and labyrinthine walkways weaving among flower patches, flowering trees, lawns on which peacocks preened, and two large ponds with fountains and too many swans and loons. A snack bar and bistro or two melded into the scenery. Gazebos and benches were placed here and there.

It was the place to while away time between tending to government business, or high-end shopping, or going to school in the heart of the capital of the North Atlantic Sovereignty. Its southern perimeter abutted the H. Trismegistus Campus Pavilion. You didn't have to sit there long to see everything in the world go by.

Yes, Leo had noticed Sofia's comings and goings. He had been curious about them and what she was all about or would turn out to be. He had heard a curious story about her birth mother. Something about allegedly transfiguring into a prism of light and disappearing out of sight, leaving two babies to be parceled out like puppies.

As he remembered it, Sofia was a sharp, adept, and precocious young woman who might have been too bright for her own good. In Leo's unspoken opinion, he didn't think Bruno—despite his reputation for being a player even among his bright-eyed and infatuated students—was having an affair with that particular underage maga. He suspected, from certain subtle signs that everyone else was too lazy or dull to notice, that Bruno had given the young Sofia the Pyr Sacra empowerment and had adopted her as his "magical child": his magical heir . . . his lineage-holder. In Leo's mind, that was more provocative than carnal relations.

Still, it was difficult to know whether a mentorship or an affair or both was between them. Of course, it was more entertaining to imagine that Bruno and Sofia were lovers. But if Sofia La Maga Magus were the lineage-holder of Dr. Giordano Bruno Sortiar, being so would be a serious and peculiar matter. It meant that Sofia knew and could do all of the wily and threatening things that Bruno could. It was hard to believe looking at her, especially now. She was a disheveled, wind-blown, gypsy lady mage who had been reared by folk practitioners and was given to bleeding heart politics and Eastern mysticism.

The thought that Sofia La Maga was Dr. Bruno's lineage holder was as sour as it was intriguing to Leo. Were that Bruno was Leonard's mentor. If Leonard hadn't turned out to be such an underachieving delinquent, Leo could've arranged it. Leonard would've grown up to be someone then. As it stood, Leo would have to produce additional offspring in midlife with "girlfriends" if he wanted a suitable heir to maintain the dignity of his family line. The implications were not appealing, but Leo knew he had to get on with it rather soon.

Leo was torn between observing and ignoring Sofia La Maga during the parent-teacher alumni reception. Something itched in him about it. He hated when that happened. He blamed it on amateur coercive magic and almost griped to Reggie about the obnoxiously conspicuous smile enchantment the maga had pulled on her students the day before. Like pausing to gape at a train wreck, Leo gave in to observe how bubbly Sofia and Bruno appeared in each other's company. They must've been thrilled to be reunited. Bruno had saved her life after all, even if she did have to live 15 years of that life in exile.

She was clad in a belted alb and matching dalmatic of unbleached raw silk gauze. It was gossamer and had an off-white coral hue. Overlaying these gown-like ceremonial dresses was a rosy red cape on which was embroidered a flower sacred to magi: the rose. Amulets made of coral, azurite, malachite, and other sacred stones embellished her chest, and instead of a turban, a zucchetto–a type of beanie—rested on her head. Affixed to the zucchetto was a long, red veil of lace netting that obscured her face. Bruno himself was clad, not in sorcerer's garb, but a dapper dark gray three-piece suit.

Leo watched Bruno lift the veil from before Sofia's face and fold it back over the zucchetto. An odd feeling struck him. He expected to see the Bruno and Sofia kiss like bride and groom after the exchange of vows, but that didn't happen. They simply continued to kid and chat. But the maga did look rather heavenly that night in contrast to how disheveled and savage she had looked since her return to Terra Novit. She was cleaned up for this event and dressed in proper magian attire.

RCP treasurer Lucas Marcus, who had sidled beside Leo, commented that the maga finally looked more like a woman and less like a wild thing. "She is kind of *'cumly'* when she's all cleaned up," Marcus said.

Leo studied all the details.

"I saw the maga nuzzling up to the good doctor Raphael Magus at the Phoenix and Harp yesterday evening," Reggie muttered slyly.

Leo commented that he wondered whether the maga and Alan Raphael were an item again. "Or perhaps she's making up for lost time juggling beds with Bruno and that blustery boor," he said

Reggie Solaris, a polished and stocky man with neat, dark hair, very blue eyes, a seductive smile, ruddy skin, and a gift for gab, was Leo's closest friend. He reported that a slew of persons were in the company of Raphael Magus and La Maga Magus at the Phoenix and Harp Country Club the night before. He added that he hated it when magi invited their folkie, plebeian friends to the Phoenix and Harp. Leo mentioned, in turn, that the place was going downhill and that the Orion Club was much better. It catered to patrician sorcerers and discouraged the patronage of the riff-raff. The men then agreed to stop frequenting the Phoenix and Harp and make the Orion Club their new haunt.

Reggie had been Leo's long-time buddy in important activities such as womanizing and carousing. The man's household was something of a polyamorous tribe. He had three wives, each of whom shared affections among themselves as well as among extramarital liaisons. Through these, Reggie had a healthy lot of children who may or may not have been expressions of his gene-pool. Leo also had seen the man in action with a male playmate or two. Reggie was juicy like that, and he could not understand Leo's selectivity and caution in intimacy.

Leo's own father had had four bitterly competitive wives and no time to know too many of the 11 persons — four sons and seven daughters — he had sired from interacting with them. Two of the man's sons had died, though. They had been victims of a magical attack launched against the de Lux clan. The attack had almost claimed Leo as well. The other surviving son, Leo's eldest full brother, who was 12 years his senior, was left unscathed, but he had been long disowned and considered a renegade with whereabouts unknown.

This elder brother had adopted a fatherly role when Leo was very young. He was doting and supportive for a time, but something went wrong when the action and adventure yarns he spun to amuse his younger brother became his reality. His stories were tales about apocalyptic wars that smacked of echoes of the Book of Enoch in which the archangels Michael and Lucifer duke it out. Instead of angels, Leo's brother's stories were about sorcerers and magi, and young Leo was both rebel and hero quashing the reigning power structure.

After white magian clothes and politically charged writings about an uprising that would overhaul the aeon were found in his living quarters, the brother was sent — or rather exiled — far, far away, across the sea. Although the family told all who asked about the brother's where-abouts that he was studying abroad, he actually had been committed to a sanatorium in the snowy northern hinterlands of the Terra Principalis.

Leo was 8 years old at the time, the same age that Leonard was when his mother decided to lose her mind and fund some offshore fanatical magian religious cult with

Leo's money....

The brother, whose given name was Emmanuel, had escaped the sanatorium to become a shadowy figure at the helm of a secret and virtually untraceable illuminist society called the Lions of Light. The father was left to groom Leo, the youngest child of the litter, for a cut-throat political career. When Leo considered his own predicament in regard to his own son, he wondered whether his own birth was a mere matter of practicality—his father's last and overdue shot at producing a suitable vessel to carry on an agenda.

On account of his childhood environment, Leo avoided collecting spouses. Having women was one of the few pastimes that made life worth living, Leo would say, but accumulating them would be like nurturing song birds in a cage. The idea was charming, but small, caged birds, if not meticulously house-kept, were putrid-smelling, and they made a mess.

Leo had had his share of affairs. They were too easy to come by. Complicating matters was that he was the constant target of love charms, most of which he had become immune to. Unlike the situation with Reggie Solaris, however, consorts—that is, wives and heart-felt lovers—were few and far between. He was in a quandary about what to do, because he imagined that having the right companion would take the edge off the banality of his work-a-day rut in a way superior to debauchery.

"I desire high magic and fuel from between a woman's thighs," Leo would pine. Reggie would laugh at him and say that he sounded like a teenaged troubadour in love with his best friend's perimenopausal mother.

Reggie was a praetor—a kind of judicial enforcer and arbitrator. He also owned a few Outer Plane factories that manufactured widgets for Commons. In addition, he had a 16-year-old son who was a bit of a bad seed, like Leonard.

That boy was Leonard's buddy Bertrand.

Leo nudged Reggie upon spying the arrival of Alan Raphael Magus at the reception. How could anyone not have noticed the mage? He was conspicuously dressed in a blindingly white and gold dalmatic, chasuble, and matching cope. His head was wrapped in a relaxed, rakishly-styled turban with a long tail that ended in a large, spun-gold tassel, and he wore white stockings and white and gold slippers that had long toe boxes that curled into decorative whorls.

"*By Jove,*" Leo growled and materialized a pair of sleek, mirrored sunglasses to mock being blinded by the "white." Ceremonial vestments were, like among some Outer Plane Christian clergy, modeled after late Greco-Roman attire. The first layer was the alb, which was a belted, long, straight gown with long, fitted sleeves. Over or in place of this was worn the dalmatic, which was a knee- or ankle-length smock with wide sleeves. The chasuble was an embroidered, sleeveless piece of apparel that slipped over the head and draped over the shoulders, like a fancy poncho. It was worn over the dalmatic. Finally, the cope, which was a richly decorated, hooded cape, might be worn.

Magi almost always wore vestments that were some variation of white accented by gold thread and, occasionally, they included a layer of apparel that was either bright red or some light to brilliant shade of blue. For headdress, they wore turbans or else zucchettos, earning them the disparaging names, among sorcerers, of either rag- or beanie-heads. The women often pinned gossamer veils to their headgear.

Sorcerers were freer about the color schemes of their ceremonial clothes. Purples and brilliant to dark blues or greens were popular, as was black, of course. They preferred the miter — a squat, five-sided hat — or else tall conical hats for head wear.

Although Leo and Reggie took pleasure in scoffing at Raphael Magus's ostentation, they, too, were clad in voluminous whorls of flashy fabric. Leo himself was clad in as many layers of apparel as Alan Raphael. Not shining white. His costume was a mélange of opalescent purples, greens, and blues with blood red accents. The fabric was weighted with heavy brocaded mosaics of gem beads. Leo's bejeweled miter had long ear flaps and a high cone-like top. It and his cope forebodingly jangled with jingle bells.

He would've much preferred to wear a dapper three-piece suit, like Danny Bruno had. Being who he was, Leo had to endure wearing this mass of regalia when he showed up at these kinds of events. He often wondered whether the pomp and circumstance was meant to help high-level dignitaries maintain their miserable and menacing attitudes while in public.

Raphael Magus was in the company of his wife, Gloria, who was a petite, falsely smiley woman who also was donned in very formal and very white attire that was so layered and voluminous that she seemed lost in it. Leo suspected that Raphael and his wife were obscenely monkish. High-level magi were supposedly stinting and sublimated about their sexuality: dickless and frigid boors. Leo made special note of Raphael's reaction to Sofia's presence at the gala. He imagined that the mage was overwhelmed with wanton, throbbing lust beneath his piously white costume. The thought oddly felt like a distastefully personal insult to Leo—as if Alan Raphael had no right to feel that way about Sofia La Maga if he, in fact, was feeling that way.

He shook the concern from his mind and tried to spot a good distraction. He would've gone to linger by the bar if two hedonist babes in his circle of associates, Gwen Goldenlance and Marina Sarin, weren't loitering there. He would be expected to engage in suggestive conversation with them. He wasn't in the mood. He thought about whether threatening Professor Vetiver about Leonard's poor grades might be mildly entertaining.

He found himself chatting with the RCP treasurer Lucas Marcus, when he overheard Sofia speaking with Professor Vetiver and a magian couple named Cosmo and Celeste DiCosmos about an audience she had had with Ambassador Gregory Hrasvelg and his wife.

"She was very gracious," Leo heard Sofia say of Lady Hrasvelg. "And the Ambassador. They treated me very nicely. When I heard they wanted to see me, I had reservations because, you know . . . patricians." Sofia's voice dropped off, but Leo could hear her, Lady DiCosmos, and Professor Vetiver speaking in hushed contemptuous tones before Celeste DiCosmos gasped, "What a shame about the nephew. Who would think a kid from such a family would be doing that."

"And how did the rite go?" Cosmo DiCosmos asked.

"I think it went well," Sofia replied thoughtfully.

A wave of surprise washed over Leo. The gist of the eavesdropped conversation came to light. Sofia La Maga had performed the Lux Clarus Rite for the nephew of Ambassador Hrasvelg. The youth had been a casualty of the Phaeton maneuver, a particularly dangerous—and illegal—adolescent amusement.

No one ever thought his child participated in Phaeton maneuver matches. This was precisely why Leo continued to campaign that the blame for such mischief should fall on the parents—all of the parents of participants in Phaeton maneuver matches that came before the law. He would impose heavy fines and even incarceration of these parents and quite remedial rehabilitation for the participants.

Such measures would bring a very abrupt end to the ritual, but too many members of the Senate thought that they were draconian. Reggie also had cautioned Leo that, although everyone liked his fire-and-brimstone bit, it was well known that the Phaeton maneuver was an illicit pastime of *patrician* youths. Were the ritual more aggressively exposed, elite persons in government and business in the North Atlantic Sovereignty would be singled out and held accountable for the crimes of their sons.

He approached Reggie and asked him if he knew anything about the purpose of Sofia La Maga's audience with the Hrasvelgs.

"What rock have you been sleeping under?" Reggie snorted. "You need to get out more." He motioned toward Gwen Goldenlance and Marina Sarin. They were still at the bar.

The women were ogling the men and touching each other. Gwen brushed her hand over Marina's breast and pinched a nipple. Marina overdramatized her enthrallment. Leo and Reggie were left focusing on the mark the now erect nipple made through the woman's clingy blouse.

It was apparently too much—or perhaps just enough—for Reggie. He caught the gaze of the youngest consort within his pride, who was loitering some yards away. Leo watched her join Reggie as he approached the two other women. The temptresses proceeded to fondle the younger woman while Reggie salivated on the bacchanalian eye candy.

Another fellow sidled up to the group. Then a mediator with whom Leo also was in the habit of having interludes, Vinca Blanco, brushed passed him—a raven-haired pixie with a big personality. She widened her eyes and batted her lashes. "Join the fun, Lord Consul," she purred. "You are the best altar for a girl to get sacrificed on."

While Leo was deciding whether to leap in, another

gentleman grasped Vinca's arm as she went skipping toward the lusty amassing.

Leo watched the clique bristle and grope but averted his gaze from Marina's. Although both Marina and Vinca were regular sex-mates of his, Leo was not taken-enough with either to go play house. He also wasn't up for an orgy. The scene was getting old, or maybe he was.

The group began to make its way toward the exit without him. They looked back at Leo in hopes he would follow. Reggie's voice finally rang in his ear despite that the man had left the hall. "We'll be at Marina's place if you change your mind, buddy."

There was the impulse to go, but indifference as well. It would have been crazy for Leo to admit to Reggie Solaris that his interest in that sort of thing had waned. In the moment, it was intoxicating, but it was also banal. Leo lusted, for sure, but he lusted for another kind of experience. Something transcendental, and it wasn't happening with the old crew. Vinca did have advanced skills in sex magic, but Leo had concluded that, even though she was adorable, her key wasn't all that great. He himself occasionally used thought-forms or multiple partners to dabble in sex magic, but something eluded him so sourly that the thrill was gone.

He wandered to the bar and got a tumbler of bourbon. The aura left there by his sometime friends was as steamy as a midsummer day; the kind of day that is so hot and languid that it makes a person mildly oxygen-deprived because the breath is shallow and labored. It was a groggy sensation that Leo experienced as a cloying pressure in the joystick of his pelvis — his cock — the anatomical site where so much of one's personal energy sunk, dissipated, and squandered itself on banalities.

Only a few years ago, Leo would've relished this feeling and gone off to select a consort wannabee or two for an exhaustive reverie. It was annoying now. It was like a dull earache or a cramping hunger pang that couldn't be sated. Leo observed it as if it were a discipline to do so.

He doffed his heavy miter and freed himself from the cranky weight of his bejeweled and bell-lined cope. He whipped the scapular from his shoulders and loosened the layers of cord belts that gripped his waist.

The music had stopped. Dr. Bruno was smacking his staff against a microphone at center-stage of the band shell. He was a tall man with thick black hair and a swarthy, meaty face that expressed a sly joviality. Although he had been lanky — almost willowy — in his youth, he had become rather husky with age. He was always dapper, though, standing there in his slick, satiny, gray suit accented by a flashy, bright-red satin handkerchief. He gripped a serpentine staff made of silver, gold, lead, and yew in one hand and a tumbler of scotch and soda in the other.

"I'd just like to say that it's great to have you all here as we begin yet another academic year at the Hermes Trismegistus Campus Pavilion," he began. "The Graduate Academy has been repeatedly cited as a top-tier institution for magical studies, and the Secondary School is also very distinguished. And now we're really pushing the envelope with the professorship of our very own prodigal child, Lady Sofia La Maga Magus who has just begun presenting some advanced training courses at the Secondary School."

Mild applause interjected Bruno's speechifying.

"In response to requests, we'll be sponsoring a program in the near future in which the esteemed maga will entertain us with her exploits in the exotic planes of the Mysticus and the Terra Origens. Isn't that right, Sofia?" Bruno exclaimed.

Sofia shyly acknowledged him by smiling and fidgeting.

"Indeed, she received training from the legendary

Mattheas Magus in Inner Plane Cypress soon before returning to our own territories," Bruno boasted.

Leo never quite understood that story of Sofia La Maga's meeting with Mattheas Magus. Mattheas Magus was centuries old if he were alive. The story implied that Sofia had taken an intoxicant-guided dream walk to communicate with Mattheas Magus, who likely resided within a Deep Inner Plane. The Deep Inner Plane, of which there were many levels, was what the ordinary Inner Plane was to Commons. It was not a place that was easily accessed. A person's body was not made to enter that other world, unless that person had the special ability to take on the appropriate form and slide in and back.

"Apologies if I'm boring you about this woman. It's just that the Academy is taking this occasion to award her for her achievements with . . . *an honorary degree of Magus Celestus!*" Bruno exclaimed, as if announcing a grand prize to a game show audience.

Leo watched surprise alight on Sofia's face. Her entourage, which included Alan Raphael Magus, took turns embracing her.

Some people applauded and toasted the honorary confirmation. Others turned their backs in contempt and went back to their cocktail-partying and networking. Leo observed a gaggle of associates from the RCP shake their heads, smirk, and rudely laugh.

Bruno had to beckon Sofia twice before she approached the band shell to accept her degree confirmation. She stumbled on her way. Her stride seemed unwieldy in those fancy red stilettos she had on her feet.

Leo watched Bruno speak intently to the maga off mike as if in conference. He showed her a new staff. The wood might have been linden, holly, or a combination of both. It was coated in a lattice of gold, brass, and silver and had a rose-shaped finial made of red coral and carnelian. It was difficult to detect, but Leo observed a small gold glyph of a Sanskrit term—a sacred syllable—mounted on the tip of the central bud of the finial. It was not the prosaic Om, but the mantra *hrim*, which was a mystical sound associated with a Great Goddess of Hinduism called Bhuvaneshvari, The Lady of the Spheres.

Bruno cupped his hand on Sofia's head so that his thumb pressed against her brow. At that, Leo imagined he saw a luminous glow descend on her. Perhaps Bruno was bestowing an empowerment that was oddly and namby-pamby displayed for all to see. The maga neither winced nor gasped. She merely twitched as if goosed. Her gaze was turned upward as if toward a vision. It was as momentary as it was momentous. A magian-style initiation. It was soft and mushy by Leo's standards.

The woman didn't display any confusion or expression of awe or surprise in the aftermath of the empowerment. She cheerfully embraced Bruno and toddled away from the band shell to accept more congratulations from her friends. Within minutes, however, she was briskly walking past the bar to the rest rooms. Leo observed how her pace had changed. She was no longer clumsy in her shoes. She glided with determination. Leo snorted at the silly affectations so many magical persons felt compelled to adopt—even this Sofia La Maga, acting like a clownish bumble-bunny in one moment and a gazelle the next.

Upon returning from her bathroom break, she approached the bar and began quizzing the bartender about the wines that were in stock. The bartender found himself lining up a rainbow of goblets for a wine tasting exercise.

All that was lacking was a spittoon. Leo materialized one. To express his ridicule of Sofia's noxious and confounding glamour, he spit a stream of bourbon into it for the entertainment of RCP treasurer Lucas Marcus and some other RCP folk loitering at the bar. Then he sauntered toward the maga and grasped a long, slender goblet of a pale yellow wine. He shook the glass to make the wine swirl and aerate. He examined how the "legs" of the wine washed against sides of the glass, and he inhaled the aroma. He passed his hand over the goblet's mouth and handed it to Sofia. "Now try it," he said.

She glared at him. With an uneasy smile, she sipped the wine and seemed pleased.

"Oh yes," she exclaimed in mirth. "*This* is what a Riesling tastes like. Not *flat soda.*" She held the goblet out to the bartender and gestured that he take a sip. The fellow gaped at Leo as if he hoped the consul might reprimand the woman for her guff. Leo simply smirked. He was slightly amused.

"Austrian Rieslings are superior to the German these days," he muttered. "The industry became a victim of the Chaos Principle several decades ago. It was really more of a media hoax."

Made wistful and chatty through the magic of strong drink, Leo explained to the maga that a handful of producers had been caught adding a sweetener—a glycol derivative—to their vintages. "I knew the sorcerer who engineered that. He made a bundle," Leo remarked.

The press sensationalized the questionable practice, reporting that the additive, *diethylene glycol,* was a component of antifreeze. As damage control, Austria imposed upon its wine producers the strictest rules and standards ever anywhere. "Rendering more recent Austrian wines the purist you'll ever experience outside of the barrels in your father's barn, Lady La Maga," Leo exclaimed.

"Ah. Well, I didn't know that," she simpered. Leo grimaced and rolled his eyes because he was sure that she did. She had grown up on a vineyard, hadn't she? He nevertheless congratulated her on her prestigious honorary degree and told her that she now had to aspire to acquire the degree of Sortiar Excelsis.

"I have to go back to school for that," she griped. "The Sorcery Oversight Committee isn't giving anything away to the likes of me. What do they know..."

"What *do* they know?" Leo replied, amused by her exposed edge, but the woman just laughed to herself as if conversing about it were ridiculous.

"Accelerate the process and take on a mentor," Leo suggested. "I could put in a recommendation for you with Medea Sarin Sortiar. I'm in the habit of having 'relations' with one of her relations," he snickered and called to mind such a provocative image of Medea's cousin Marina that his eyes rolled up and his skin flushed. "I can't think of anyone more challenging for a person who is as distinguished as you as Medea Sarin Sortiar."

"Someone mentioned that name to me the other day," Sofia said uneasily.

"She might be a little too *dark* for you," Leo clucked. "But then I heard you were involved in some dark practices in the Mysticus. Feeding demons and cavorting with infernal deities. "

"*Fierce* deities," Sofia corrected him. "I wouldn't call those practices 'dark.' They were something different. I did almost do something with a corpse once, but I chickened out."

"Animating a corpse," Leo tsked.

"But I couldn't do it. I mainly did meditations on and emanations of deities, mostly the Lunar Goddess cycle," she stuttered.

"Mmm-hmmm," Leo muttered. Word was that the maga had become a goddess-worshipper. The term "quaint" came to mind, but he didn't utter it. Another tumbler of bourbon or a magical goblet of wine from the array before him? He couldn't decide. He also didn't know whether to be on his way. Then Sofia, in a warm and chatty voice, announced that one of her great grandfathers was a sorcerer.

"The grandsire of the folk practitioners who adopted you or another great and grand sire?" Leo wistfully replied.

That must have struck a nerve. The maga turned silent. Looking sad and disappointed, she pulled away from the bar and retreated. "Thanks for speaking with me, Lord Consul, but I ought to go back to . . ." Her index finger lamely gestured toward Raphael Magus and the lot of friends who were still mingling on the main floor of the banquet hall.

"But I'm not ready to let you go," Leo lilted. Feeling particularly wicked, he launched a lusty Sweet Surrender maneuver of the sorcerous kind on the maga. "Stay and tell me a story about this great grandfather of yours."

The maga stood wavering. She seemed smitten by — or at least assessing — Leo's magic against her. Her breath billowed high in her chest and her skin flushed dewy.

"I'm not a folk practitioner; I'm a mage," she plaintively said.

"Of course, La Maga Magus. You've proved yourself a curious credit to your adoptive family and society. Of this, there is no doubt," Leo replied.

The maga nodded thoughtfully. Then, smiling brightly, with the juiciest spark in her midnight eyes, she deflected Leo's Sweet Surrender maneuver back on to him. The ricocheted rush of sex was so intense that Leo messed himself with ejaculate underneath the layers of ceremonial garb he was wearing. And he didn't even care because the ecstatic headlessness of orgasmic effacement sort of reverberated for a while despite that he had shot the wad. He should've been very piqued at having the tables turned — and would be later when he recovered — but he couldn't help but indulge in the sensation that gripped him.

"*Lady La Maga, we should have done that together, I think,*" he gasped. His hand drifted out to paw at her.

"Yeah, well, if you weren't such a nasty ass," she replied and immediately went on to babble that her great grandfather was a *fattucchiero,* a "fixer." "He specialized in coercion and binding spells. He was busy making money casting evil eyes, and my great grandmother was busy raking in dough for lifting them."

In the moment in his entranced condition, Leo thought that was the sexiest thing he had ever heard. He seriously wondered who he was, in fact, dealing with. Then she reminded him that he was dealing with his *own* magic, not hers.

"You don't want me to sober you up do you?" she asked.

He was oddly impressed—with himself or her, he couldn't decide.

What else did he know about Sofia La Maga? He knew that her adoptive family, for generations, had been immigrating and expatriating from the Inner Plane. Except for an anomaly here or there, they had never academically applied themselves to the magical or mystical sciences. They were folkies with questionable magical fluency. If Sofia was a prodigy, she got it from her natural relations: her birth mother, who must have been a mystic if she had transfigured into a beam of light, and her father, whoever he was.

Leo's ancestors, on the other hand, had fled from the Inquisition to the Inner Plane during the late 15th century. Over the generations, they had distinguished themselves as gifted sorcerers in the Inner Plane and influential powerbrokers in both the Inner and Outer Planes.

Given that fact, Leo was concerned about his son Leonard's fate. The boy was pretty much useless. Leo already had resolved to set him up in a cushy do-nothing job in the Outer Plane where he probably would oversee one of Hipparchus Gorgon's enterprises. Leo did not relish the thought of his son joining the ranks of Gorgon's demonic minions. Given the boy's track record, though, unless he founded some kind of religious cult in the Outer Plane (and Leo didn't see that happening), Leonard's options were limited.

But Leo had already secretly softened about Sofia La Maga. His feelings had changed just a tad after seeing her treatment of his son during that first codes and keys class. She could've humiliated the boy—and Leo by extension—but she turned it around. Leo thought that, regardless of the coercive enchantments that she had brazenly expressed that first day of class, she had been rather tender and encouraging toward Leonard. In response, the youth revealed to her—and everyone else, including Leo—that he was not an idiot.

Danny Bruno stepped up to Leo and Sofia and asked the maga whether she was ready to depart. He turned to Leo and told him that a group of influential folks would be gathering at his place. "The beach house, not the apartment," he said. "Ambassador Hrasvelg is planning to show up around 10. So, if you want, you can still grab a quick lick at the Sarin orgy and then swing by."

Bruno pivoted on his heels and strode away. Leo was left feeling dumbfounded. He was burned by the insinuation about his agenda, he was confused about the sincerity of Bruno's invitation, and he wanted Sofia La Maga to stay.

Abruptly making off after her escort, Sofia uttered, "Have a nice night if I don't see you, Lord Consul. Enjoy your lust charm."

IV
"She Who Will Become Fierce"

The consul didn't show up at the "beach house," which was not to be confused with a wind-worn cottage or cabana. It was a McMansion: a garishly triangular-sort-of-rectangular architecturally space-aged kind of building. It has been constructed on a cliff overlooking the sea. It had very high ceilings made of glass panels. The walls were polished aluminum, and the floors were marble so that every move made a sound that reverberated and was meant to be musical. The opulent austerity of space was offset by bold pieces of American abstract expressionist art. Danny Bruno had gotten a few pieces through Leo de Lux, in fact: a Pollack, two Motherwells, a Gottlieb, and a Kline. He had a Roethko, too, that he had intended to give to Sofia someday . . . maybe . . . except that he liked it too much.

Not attending Danny's soiree, Leo missed out on networking with an impressive gathering of dignitaries. Not all were Expansionist Party sympathizers. Danny Bruno was adept at playing both sides of the fence—and even places above and below it. Few dared cross him, but every once in a while, perhaps for entertainment purposes, Danny would form a misbegotten alliance with a character who had grown one too many testicles. Then he would crush the smart ass good when he or she tried to pull a fast one.

Danny had the ability to lead people to the Netherworld, an ability he had been known to use on occasion. He had put a few people into psychiatric care as well. And even though he often came off as a goof and as a rakishly jovial type, he was particularly challenging to apprentice with precisely because he set people up. His art was to slice into the underside of a person's consciousness, forcing profound transformation (if not madness). Great insight, humility, guile, and power were the prize.

Hipparchus Gorgon didn't know what to make of Danny and left him alone. He did summon the doctor for consultations now and then when he was trying to figure out how to best manage certain persons—such as Sofia La Maga—whose existence had become problematic for him.

Gorgon and Danny obviously had an "understanding" about Sofia. She got to stay alive and sane and progress in her magical training—but in remote places on the other side of the world. Danny knew that all hell was going to break loose with her return regardless of whether she had been "rehabilitated." He liked that.

While his guests were socializing and networking, Danny was vetting a racketeering scheme or two with some fellows in his library. When he emerged from his conference, his company had thinned. A small group of Sofia's closest friends: Elizabeth and Alan Raphael, Juliet Vetiver, Cosmo and Celeste DiCosmos, and a few others, were huddled by a fireplace in the grand house's sunken den. Ambassador Hrasvelg had gone his way, but his wife had lingered. She and Alan Raphael and Alan's wife Gloria sat primly on the leather sofas while the others lounged on pillows strewn over the plush area rug. Sofia was sitting on the rug with her back against Alan Raphael's knees. His hands were on her shoulders and were subtly wriggling themselves into her curls and skimming her neck. Alan's silly smiley wife simply sat there looking dignified and intentionally clueless.

The ladies were making tiny materializations that had the life spans of bubbles. Influenced by orientalism, Sofia created angelic creatures that resembled characters from the murals of the Caves of a Thousand Buddhas in Mogao,

China: apsaras, gandharvas, dharmapalas, and bodhisattvas. Elizabeth, who was visiting for the week, was more interested in mythical creatures: griffins and dragons, sylphs, and mermaids.

Gloria produced Old World angelic creatures that looked as if they popped out of early Renaissance paintings, and Celeste DiCosmos, who was shy about the endeavor, made images of little children that were supposed to be cherubs. Juliet Vetiver displayed finesse in producing celestial bodies, and Lady Hrasvelg impressed everyone with two-foot high, glowing images of the archangels of the four directions: Michael, Uriel, Raphael, and Gabriel. She placed them in their respective quadrants and set them in scenes corresponding to their respective elements, times of day, and seasons: dawn light in dew-laden spring, high-noon in the wheat fields of summer, a blazing sunset over an autumnal sea, and the starry night glistening on winter frost.

Lady Hrasvelg announced to Danny, when he joined them, that a book had been written about Sofia. She held it up. It was an Outer Plane product, a paperback titled Secret Teachings of the Wisdom Queen. Elizabeth had shown Sofia the same book the night before when they were socializing at the Phoenix and Harp Country Club. She had made Sofia sign it.

The author didn't mention Sofia by name, but a pencil sketch of a person strongly resembling her, with her long wild hair, sparkling eyes, lopsided smile, and sweet but impish expression, appeared as Plate 3 in the book.

Sofia said that she didn't know the author, but the publisher she had met the day before knew about the book. "She called it 'Fluffernutter.' I didn't know what Fluffernutter was, but I kind of got that I didn't want to be compared with it," she said.

"Peanut buttery marshmallow goodness," Elizabeth

quipped. "An Outer Plane delicacy."

"For 4-year-olds and fetishists," Cosmo DiCosmos added.

A gooey salty sweet ick of an odor happened then as Alan materialized a gob of the stuff. Sofia wrinkled her nose at the frothy white and ochre mush ungainly embellished with a grape jelly swirl and smeared on a slice of white bread. In fact, she squelched a gag and felt that the evening had soured. Between that, the secret caresses she was receiving from Alan as she sat too close to him, and the dodgy attention she had gotten from Leo de Lux at the reception, things had gotten bleh.

Danny soberly caught on to her mood. He quietly brooded. He had grown weary of the company but let it linger, fascinated — but only slightly — with his guests' well-meaning but boorish treatment of his star apprentice Sofia. They wanted her to think up reasons why her picture was in the Outer Plane book. Sofia told them that the author obviously had had communications with the anchorite with whom she had studied while living near Lake Manasaravar in Tibet.

She reasoned that the likeness of her, rather than that of the anchorite, appeared in the book because the anchorite "didn't like having her picture taken. So, she used mine. Shot into the Commons lady's head."

Sofia explained that the anchorite never spoke and allowed only three people to ever see her. Those three people were her apprentices. She only communicated with them while they were asleep or otherwise out of their normal minds.

"But besides getting into our heads, she used to be up all night listening to Commons who were, you know, praying to whoever because of their 'problems,'" Sofia explained. "She used to comfort them...give them little teachings. She told me I was going to have to do that someday, but I don't know if I have the patience. I ignore them when they show up," Sofia confessed.

Danny watched a stunned look come upon her when she said that, as if she suddenly remembered something very important.

"It's called the Misercordia maneuver in our tradition," Alan said, but Sofia's gaze had frozen on Danny. He nodded reassuringly and formed a picture in his mind of the student Mirelle Soleil. The "classified" information about this young woman, which was documented in her immigration papers, was that she had had communications with a person matching Sofia's profile when she was a child living in the inner city of Chicago and Sofia was a political dissident living in exile in the Inner Plane of Tibet.

"I knew a mage who became sensitized to praying Commons," Juliet said. "Man, if you never want to sleep or have an uncluttered thought, do that—listen to Commons and respond to them," she laughed. "It got so bad that this guy couldn't work anymore. It took up all his time and all his mind. I don't even know if he ended up in the Balthazar Institute, he got so crazy."

She turned to Alan to ask whether the case sounded familiar at which the friends got into a loud discussion about oddities involved in communications between Inner Plane denizens and Commons. Sofia remained silent in her weariness. She was sleepy, a little tipsy, and in awe about how she knew Mirelle. Danny just carried on with the rest of the guests, announcing that he was in agreement with Alan who, although boorishly overbearing, made the point that magi who run into problems with the Misercordia maneuver have "Fluffernutter" for brains.

"They become egotistical and sappy and insinuate themselves into the lives and concerns of Commons. Erroneously identifying with them, they believe their whining has substance," Danny said. "I'm in agreement with those Conservationist buttheads who say that there shouldn't be any of this transplanes communication crap going on because it messes everything up. People should stick to their own planes."

"That's what sorcerers say, but they're the first ones to go meddle. At least magi have good intentions," Celeste DiCosmos argued.

Danny just wagged a hand and scoffed. He told her that it was far better, magically speaking, to do something for "naaasty" reasons than for deluded ones.

"They call it Mahamaya in the Indus," Sofia yawned. "The 'Grand Illusion.'"

"The 'Divine Comedy,' is more like it," Cosmo DiCosmos laughed.

The party of friends finally asked Sofia whether anything relevant was written in the Outer Plane book about her.

Sofia said she had paged through it and that, from what she could tell, it was patent chatter about not thinking too much and being "one with God."

"It's basic Commons pop-culture Hermeticism with ting-tong cymbals and prayer flags and saris floating in the breeze," she said. "Why the author felt compelled to stick my picture into it . . . Whatever," she yawned.

A lull fell upon the group. It seemed time to call it a night. Lady Hrasvelg then turned to Sofia and said in a chipper voice, "So, did your teacher—the one from the Himalayas—give you a name? Isn't that the custom after initiation in the Mysticus?"

Sofia explained that the idea of naming things—or that things had names—was not part of that particular teacher's consciousness, but another teacher of hers had given her a special name. He was a holy man with whom she had studied while residing in the Inner Plane of Benares, India. "His name was Prakash Shaami. He was so old he should've been in the Deep Inner Planes," she laughed. "He spoke in conversational Sanskrit—which is like speaking in conversational High Latin—except he did it with a Bengali accent, with o's for a's and shhhes instead of ess sounds.

"He used to call me '*Chandibhavishyati*,' which means, 'She Who Will Become Fierce.' He used to say to people, 'Treat that one right; *chun-DEEM bha-VISH-yo-tee*': 'she will become fierce.'" I didn't know if he was teasing people that I had a bad temper; or that I was going to become a really kick-ass sorceress; or if I was going to 'become' the goddess Chandi, who in Hindu mythology is the embodiment of the power of all the gods and is famous for killing a bunch of demons to restore the order of the universe."

"Oh, yes, that's you. Definitely," her friends laughed. They interjected other sarcasms and let her carry on.

"Did he tell you when you were going to 'become fierce'?" Celeste asked.

"Yes," Sofia asserted. "When I have a son . . . Missed the boat on that one," she griped and conspicuously shooed Alan's discreetly fondling fingers off of her.

Danny reached out to hand Sofia a tumbler of vodka that had a lemon wedge in it and a rim coated in pink sugar. He patted her head gruffly before sitting back in his place. He knew the word was that he had been banging her from the time she had sprouted breasts. He probably would have if he wasn't her mother's first cousin and if their mutual great dame of a nut-cracker great grandmother hadn't appeared to him in an impressively menacing royal-bitch transfiguration and threatened to put him a perpetual state of blue balls if he sexually diddled with the girl.

The matriarch had instructed Danny, in regal Esperanto—which he didn't understand but got the gist of anyway—to protect and mentor Sofia and, of course, keep it all very secret for very secret reasons. So no one, not even Sofia, knew that she and Bruno were related. But, in fact, he felt proud and privileged to be Sofia La Maga's mentor, because she was extraordinary. He thought of her as his child — his daughter, now all grown up and having had it with this bunch of really boring people who were overstaying their welcome. He slouched back with sleepy eyes and pointed sighs that took on a furious note when he heard the women tell Sofia that she was still young enough to procreate.

"Sofia is going to have Leo de Lux's *incubus*," Elizabeth joked.

"His *next* incubus," Juliet added.

"Quit it!" Sofia blushed. She played along; her lips smiled but her eyes dulled. Her fingers reached into her tresses to nervously rub her scalp and yank her hair.

"He materialized the best glass of wine for me at the reception tonight," she said. Then she boasted that he and his kid were surprisingly easy to charm.

"Chip off the old block," Danny muttered.

"If Sofia can pull a Conus magus maneuver on de Lux, he can't be all that tough," Juliet announced.

"He tried to Sweet Surrender me tonight," Sofia confessed. "I pushed it back on him. I think he came in his pants — or whatever he wears under all that fabric and bric-a-brac."

"*Gah!*" The ladies whooped and cajoled on that for quite a while. They chided her for not indulging herself on his Sweet Surrender attack.

"Stay away from him. He wants to bind you and throw you overboard," Danny scolded.

"*I'll give him a run for his money,*" Sofia avowed in embittered breath.

"Get your life back together. Never mind him," Danny said.

The night was through, ending on a bit of an awkward note. Danny stood up and made a half dozen tiny images of

Mickey Mouse scurry into the room to sing the Mousekateer farewell anthem in squeaky, speedy voices so that they sounded more like The Chipmunks in a rush.

As everyone was filing out, Danny pulled Alan Raphael aside and told him to keep his compromised, white-coat magus hands off Sofia. Then he set to pulling off a charm to take the wind out of de Lux for a while.

V
The Son

Leonard couldn't care less about whether the guys were confused about it; he wasn't missing class. He didn't have to explain shit to them. They all suddenly seemed like a bunch of assholes.

"You said your father wasn't going to that class today, Lenny," Bertrand growled.

"I don't show up for class just because my father's taking it!" Leonard snapped.

"'Taking the class.' *What the fuck are you talking about?*" Bertrand hollered. Cary and Anil were hanging by his side and looking just as confrontational.

"You're punking out on a Phaeton maneuver match. That's, like, traitorous," Cary said.

Leonard went silent but held his ground. The guys laughed, they teased; they cajoled; they didn't "get" that Leonard was serious. He did not want to play. He did not want to miss the lost codes and keys class. It was the only class he ever took that he liked and did well in and that made him feel as if he weren't doomed.

"*C'mon!*" they insisted.

Leonard was well aware of why they were pressuring him. His participation in the match was vital. He had the key to the Phaeton maneuver. He always won. In doing so, he kept everyone else well-entertained and mostly out of harm's way.

In another era—before the game had been outlawed—Leonard would've been a Phaeton maneuver pro-athlete. He would've been rich and famous and retired by the age of 32, with a sprawling estate populated by beautiful nymphomaniacs. That was never to be, though. If it were ever learned that Leonard was involved in Phaeton maneuver matches, his father would definitely kill him and probably have to kill himself afterward because his political career would be blasted and the whole family plunged into disgrace.

The Phaeton maneuver involved the conjuration of an explosive, luminous orb. The orb was meant to represent the sun. Thus, it was called the helios, after the sun-god of early Greek myth. Helios had a son named Phaeton.

Phaeton was permitted by Helios to drive the sun-chariot across the sky. Phaeton, however, proved not strong enough to control the solar steed-drawn chariot.

He veered up and away from the sun's trajectory, causing the Earth to freeze. Then he dipped until the chariot was so close to Earth that the sun scorched great swaths of its surface. Back and forth, here and there, all over the place, wreaking havoc with the seasons, the tides, and terrain.

Just as the boy totally lost control of the chariot and was about to smash, with the sun in tow, into the Earth, Zeus, the king of the gods, hurled a lightning bolt at Phaeton. The boy was mortally wounded, but the act saved Earth from destruction.

The morning star that fades as it is overcome by day — that was Phaeton now. He was just a boy who wanted his father's admiration and whose father was overindulgent instead — a combination that led to ruin....

After conjuring the helios, participants in the Phaeton maneuver would take turns playing chicken to see who could come closest and remain the longest near the suspended orb. Levitation and aerial stunts were two of the magical powers used. The ultimate goal was to dissolve the helios before it blew up.

Leonard thought he was good at the game because he could identify with Phaeton's father-issues. Leonard was

Phaeton: a young man who had miserably failed to prove himself to his prestigious father and whose father would not let him find his own rightful place where he could shine.

Two considerations had sobered Leonard about participation in the matches. One was the death-by-misadventure of the son of a foreign ambassador—a big shot named Hrasvelg. The incident caused a political stir that landed on Leonard's father's desk. Good thing Leonard's team was not in on that particular match—but if it were….

The other sobering consideration was the serious danger of the game, which was becoming more apparent to Leonard the more he matured and the more he observed Phaeton maneuver dynamics.

To up the ante, some of his buddies and their opposing team mates were showing up high for matches and cavorting like Viking berserkers. Leonard could be as reckless and as big a stoner as the next guy, but it was no good being two sheets to the wind while playing chicken with an incendiary device. Leonard began to understand what his father meant when he griped about the glut of mindless diversions that magical persons lost themselves in

"They complain that they don't want to be controlled, but they deserve to be if they're going to make themselves as dense and vulnerable as Commons," he would argue. Then he would threaten to figure a way to migrate out of that social morass and into the Deep Inner Plane. This kind of talk always angered Leonard because a person of his father's ilk would have aeons of incarnations left before he could ever hope to transcend to a deeper plane of existence. But that was all stupid, fluffy "religious" stuff anyway— stuff his absentee, whack-job fundy magian mother believed in—not his ruthless player dad.

"Lenny's got a hard-on for the folkie maga," Cary

hollered and squawked with Anil and Bertrand: "MAGA-maga, MAGA-maga!" (That's what they had been calling Professor La Maga.) They had taken to mimicking how she drunkenly tottered and limped, arms laden with bags and books, through the second floor corridor almost every day. "MAGA-maga, MAGA-maga!" They squawked and leaped in circles around Leonard while flailing their arms like a flock of raptosaurs.

Anil punched the butt of his hand hard into Leonard's shoulder. "Maybe she'll give you the Pyr Sacra empowerment," he said. The youth shuddered spastically and howled like some persons did when they got empowerments — or orgasms.

"Fuck you," Leonard responded.

It was getting about time for Leonard to draw his wand. He regretted having met the guys in the courtyard behind the Sigils Archive. It was a secluded and overgrown section of the campus pavilion. It made a great hangout and was a secret-enough place to get high and create lewd thought-forms and all that — but things had gotten out-of-hand that early afternoon. All because Leonard wanted to go to class instead of — literally and figuratively speaking — play with fire.

"You're a waste," Bertrand finally said. "Get outta' here. Maybe La Maga-maga will make you her boy-toy."

"Yeah. Maybe she'll teach you all that Tantric stuff she learned in the Mysticus. Won't that be special?" Anil said.

"Maybe you can have a three-way with her and her boyfriend, The Crazy Professor," Cary chimed in.

"That's right. She likes retards," Bertrand added. "And he's a freak, too."

Leonard stomped away. "Assholes," he muttered.

The Crazy Professor they were referring to was a strange, spaced-out sorcerer who looked like he belonged in a rock band. He taught philosophy at the Bythos

Academy. He was heavily involved in charitable work for Deeples and also "Deevees," the utter dregs of magical society, lower than folk practitioners.

Leonard's father thought The Crazy Professor was a terrorist. It did not surprise him in the least that, within weeks of the H. Trismegistus parent-alumni reception, Professor La Maga was seen cavorting with him. His name was Aurelio Zosimo.

"She's found her match. How touching," the father had acridly snipped, but from what Leonard knew, The Crazy Professor was just too weird to be "doing it" with anyone, most especially not beguiling Professor La Maga Magus. Leonard hoped they weren't. He couldn't stand to picture it. No, the two of them were probably just scheming up radical, liberal, anarchistic things.

Leonard's "friends" continued to bait and insult him as he retreated. He wished he could disincorporate them all, Conus magus style. That would show them. He was pretty sure he could do it. As he seethed on the wish, one of the three other youths lodged a magical attack on him.

A partial faint seized Leonard. He went breathless as if the wind had been punched from his lungs. Vertigo. His stomach scrunched up into his throat as if threatening to turn inside out. Colored clouds blinded his eyes as his blood pressure plummeted, but he did not black out. He slumped and teetered, clinging to the thought that a grown sorcerer would not falter. He was sure that his father would remain unmoved no matter how badly hit.

He found himself wearing the idea of his father like protective armor, envisioning notions of his steeliness and resolve. The image of a lightning bolt came to mind. Zeus: that was Leonard's dad. Royal, no-nonsense, self-righteous, detached, and filled to the brim with guile and undeterred passion. In that moment, on the one hand, Leonard felt like such a fuck-up in comparison to the root from which he had sprung. On the other, a notion about true power descended on him.

But he did fall. His hands clutched the lawn and his nose became crammed with the odors of grass and dirt. The guys were laughing riotously and insisting that all would be forgiven if Leonard would just come to the match.

Having gotten his bearings, Leonard stood up and zapped all three of his former friends with a spell that knocked them out for about a half-minute.

"Hey! HEY!" voices hollered in alarm as two witnesses within the Sigils Archive translocated from somewhere within an upper story of the building to the site of the assault. Their staffs were poised in menacing stances. They cornered Leonard and the other boys, who were reviving. Two school staff-bearers also instantly appeared. Now Leonard was in for it. Now his day—and the rest of his life—would be a total hell. Staff-bearers pointing their weapons at the son of the consul of the North Atlantic Sovereignty! Holy crap.

Leonard was tempted to fly away, but he squatted. He placed his wand on the ground and his hands behind his back. He was hoping the staff-bearers would behead him or something right then and there.

All four boys were dragged, hemmed in by the staff-bearers, to Professor Waite's office. Dr. Bruno was there. While they were being reprimanded 1) for hostile behavior and 2) for using magic during hostile behavior, the school nurse-practitioner fretfully examined them. She checked their pulses and blood pressures and examined their eyes and auras.

"This is what is called 'magical warfare,' boys," Professor Waite screeched. "It's ILLEGAL. It won't be tolerated on the school grounds."

They all were suspended for 10 days. By hook or by crook, they would have to make up missed school work.

They were not allowed to be seen together for the remainder of the semester, and community work would be assigned.

The incident would go down as a first offense (even though it would be the third "first offense" for all of them on top of a slew of warnings that they had received about their bad behavior.) A second offense would earn them a criminal record. A third offense would be the impetus to ship them off to The Archangel Michael Young Men's Reformatory in the upstate regions of the North Atlantic Sovereignty. There they would learn the meaning of the word "rehabilitation." Additional offenses, depending on the severity, would land them in jail, and, ultimately, if worse came to worst, they would get the Lock Penalty, which consisted of being frozen in paralytic stupor.

"You hoodlums can clear out now," Professor Waite announced.

"And I don't want to hear any bullshit from your *fathers* — especially you, Solaris and de Lux. 'Cause you'll be out of here for good," Dr. Bruno roared. "Let your big-shot dads get you into the Bythos Academy of Magical Sciences. If it were up to me, you would've been in the reformatory straight out of primary school. Now, *get the hell out of here.*"

The antagonists slunk out of the office, turning hateful glances at Leonard, who lingered behind.

"Professor Waite," Leonard softly uttered. "I'd like to attend my codes and keys class — Professor La Maga's class. Then, I'll go. Will you let me?"

Professor Waite's eyebrows pinched together. Leonard could tell that her jaw was clenched as if wholly dismayed by his request. She glanced at Dr. Bruno, who looked almost as stunned.

"Let him go," Dr. Bruno said gruffly and flecked the back of his hand toward the boy.

Leonard watched how genuinely agitated they both

appeared when a grateful smile burst on his face. He thanked them before rushing out to class.

He was very late, of course. He trudged to his seat, demoralized, head lowered, eyes defiant but flickering up to gaze at Professor La Maga. Waiting. He was waiting for her to say something crass about his delinquency.

She was about to comment, eyes fixed, mouth poised for an utterance, but she suddenly cancelled her thought and went on with her speechifying.

Someone had asked her about her time in the Mysticus when she was living by a certain famous lake in Tibet at the base of a Himalayan peak called Kailash.

"There's a good lake and a bad lake," Professor La Maga was saying when Leonard came in. "The good lake is shaped like the sun, and the bad lake is shaped like the moon. People believe that if they take a dip in the good lake, their sins will be washed away, and they'll be fit for enlightenment. As for the bad lake, they think nasty serpent-like creatures live there. To its shores venture only serious adepts and sorcerers."

The students, of course, wanted to know what disciplines Professor La Maga practiced at the bad lake. She smiled softly. Without speaking about herself, she mentioned that adepts could be found in the dead of night practicing how to overcome fears and realize the nature of reality and illusion.

"In one rite, they would offer their bodies as feasts for the spirits inhabiting places like that," she said.

"Is it some weird form of necromancy?" asked Kestrel Silvestri. She was someone Leonard would've liked to Sweet Surrender. She was petite, prim, and blond. Her aerial maneuvers were the quickest and most graceful of all the girls in his grade who knew how to fly.

"No," Professor La Maga replied, and the new assistant teacher, a snotty folkie Academy freshman named

Mirelle—who was rumored to really be a low-life *Deeple*—smirked as if such an idea were utterly stupid.

"Believe me, there's plenty of necromancy going on in the Mysticus, but what most of these adepts were doing was different. On the one hand, the ritual of which I speak is an act of compassion for hungry fallen spirits. On the other, the practitioner experiences the illusion of the physical self during the ritual. He or she also experiences the assailing spirits as self-limiting aspects of his or her own consciousness. We have similar practices in our own tradition. Depending on where you are in your Hermetic studies, you may get into them," Professor La Maga said.

"Where's the power in this Mysticus rite?" Kestrel wanted to know.

"Well," Professor La Maga replied, "when a person gets past the idea of 'self,' the power is quite limitless." She smiled and, changing the subject, began to talk about a hypnotic love charm that had something to do with the Sweet Surrender maneuver, a form of Venus called Morpho, and a Latin American butterfly of the same name. It explained why the room was swarming with the insects—most of them iridescent shades of indigo, blue, or heliotrope.

Between the flittering butterflies and what had happened so far that day, Leonard couldn't focus. "Why can't we keep on talking about power instead of bugs," he exclaimed. Other students and adults in attendance griped and mocked Leonard's behavior. "It's the de Lux kid," a woman whispered. "Piece of work," a man replied.

"What do you want to tell us, Mister Junior?" Professor La Maga countered. Her face was turned away in a grimace, but it didn't faze Leonard. He was used to such responses, especially from teachers.

"I want you to tell us. Finish what you started before," he said.

The professor stared off into space and brushed a whorl of her hair against her lips. Then she said, "First of all, what is defined as power has a slightly different meaning, depending on whether we're talking about mysticism or magic. Are we talking about mysticism or magic, Leonard?"

Leonard didn't know what to say, but it didn't matter. The professor grasped an ornate staff that was different from the savage rattle stick that she normally carried around. This one was gilded and had a rose-shaped concretion of red stones at the knob. Brandishing the spiffy new staff with flair, she went into a rant as she paced the floor in front of the podium.

"Here we get into the difference between personal and transpersonal power," she said. "Practical magic — sorcery — is more concerned with the practical and personal. The idea of ego-transcendence might be somewhat undesirable to a sorcerer's goals, but I have met several high sorcerers who have the key to that. All grand masters of illusion. Master materializationists. Dr. Bruno, for instance. Don't be fooled by his cheeky glamour. The man's magical activity cuts like a surgeon's scalpel," she admonished and wagged her staff at the students. "So, you guys, you've got to think about this.

"Now," she continued, "magi, on the other hand, are more focused on the mystical. They focus on identification with the source of their power and reality, which they believe is something that transcends the idea of themselves as egos or personalities."

"The Pleroma," a girl's voice blurted. She was referring to a Gnostic term for the divine totality, which one could say was "God." The girl quoted a Gnostic slip from St. Paul in Acts 17:28: "In him we live and move and have our being."

"Thank you. Who said that? Thetis Mirabilis?" The

professor acknowledged the young woman and turned to Leonard, "Where's your buddies, Bertrand and Anil? Taking the day off?"

"They're not my buddies," Leonard replied.

Professor La Maga nodded and flexed her eyebrows.

"Okay. In the transcendence of the ego-personality and the identification with a transpersonal reality, an adept can derive great power. Why?"

Thetis piped in again: "Because he or she isn't hindered by the limitations of the personality, which is formed by certain limiting circumstances and experiences."

Thetis was another wild-looking folkie type: a girl who the boys hadn't yet noticed was filling out nicely after a gawky puberty. She was lanky and all limbs and feet. Her head was a mop of shimmery nearly cork-screw ringlets, and she had the tremendous green eyes of a lemur. She was a nerd who wore odd clothes and jewelry, just like Professor La Maga. It was obvious that she did so on purpose to ape the famous professor. Leonard's (ex) buddies called her "Thetis La Magette," which soon slurred into "Thetis the Maggot."

"Very excellent, Miss Lady Mirabilis," Professor La Maga commented and smiled sweetly at the quirky apple-polisher.

When a gong sounded, which was the cue that the class had three more minutes to wrap it up, chairs creaked as they swiveled and desk stands squeaked as they were folded away.

Professor La Maga reminded the students, once again, that Mirelle was the person to address if they wanted to plan an extra credit project and that, if they needed assistance or had any issues, they should approach Mirelle. If any student wanted to have an audience with the professor, they had to go through Mirelle . . . (Leonard thought the protocol sucked. No one liked Mirelle. She was nasty and, as mentioned, word was that she wasn't a folkie; she was a bloody Commons-immigrant Deeple who made it into the Academy as part of some weird social experiment or magic mindfuck of Dr. Bruno.)

"Grown-ups, you can just send a mind-mail if you want to go over points made in class, but please don't mind-mail or send rude vocalizations insisting that I do something for your kid. Mirelle is the interface for that. It's part of her apprenticeship, so be good sports about it please."

This was another bug up Leonard's butt. Mirelle was Sofia La Maga Magus's first apprentice. It figured she'd pick from the dregs fresh out of the Outer Plane. She was a liberal, anarchist social reformer after all....

Leonard had been fantasizing about being Sofia La Maga's apprentice. It was an absolute impossibility, of course. He felt increasingly bitter about it, but who could he blame? He was a fuck-up, after all.

Impossible fantasies about becoming her apprentice gave way to dreams about being her sexual friend. How weird to have a crush on that woman, but, man, was he filled with a strange fire when he jacked off to the thought her. Part of the thrill was desiring someone who his father hated.

Now Leonard would have to slither home and wait for his father to notice that he had gotten into trouble again. The wrath that de Lux junior would incur from de Lux senior would be silent and seething. Leonard was trying to figure out how the rigmarole would go without admitting that his "crime" was related to a dispute about participating in a Phaeton maneuver match. That would be a monster. That would be a lot more than what his father could endure, even if the moral of the story was that Leonard had come to his senses about it.

His father hadn't been feeling well anyway. Whether

his condition was related to burnout or caused by a hostile charm was in question. In any case, Leonard's father hadn't attended Professor La Maga's class in two weeks. He hadn't attended to his Outer Plane businesses for quite a while, either, and when he attended the Capital building, he did so only for an hour or so and took to delivering jurisdictions by proxy.

Leonard didn't go home after the codes and keys class. He did not leave the school premises. Rather, he skulked around the second floor corridor, keeping clear of hall guards and teachers.

He was waiting for Professor La Maga to wander by in her usual way, limping along with a burden in her arms. He was braced for a bold act, considering that he would not be able to see the professor for another two weeks. Or perhaps he would never see her again, depending on what his father did to him when he found out what had happened and why. So it was important for Leonard to find the professor and make an impression on her before departing to be crushed by fate.

At about a quarter past three, moments before the close of school, Leonard up with her. She was carrying a huge stack of overstuffed hanging file folders and limping along as if hoping that the awkward toting of heavy, slippery things would at last lead to calamity. Leonard emerged from a hiding spot in an alcove and sidled beside her.

"Professor La Maga!" he uttered robustly. She turned slightly. The folders flipped out of her grip and splattered yards across the floor. Both he and she placidly watched this occur. Leonard even slightly nodded when his gaze met the professor's.

"You do this on purpose, don't you, Professor?" Leonard said.

The professor looked away at the mess and seemed to

distantly smile. What folks around her—even other professors—were too dumb to see, was that she was engaged in a magical act. It was a set up—this behavior in the halls. It was a deliberate link in a chain of events related to the activation of a magical spell. That's what Leonard thought. He had helped her accomplish a magical act. That must've been worth something to her.

He took to helping the professor gather the files. He didn't know how to get into what he wanted to say—or even know what he wanted to say exactly; so, he just opened his mouth to see what would happen.

"I know I'm supposed to be talking to Mirelle, but I just got suspended and I'll be out for 10 days but . . . um . . . maybe I can get my grade point average up if I have an extra credit assignment or maybe you could . . . ."

"You need a tutor big time to get your grade point average up, Mister de Lux," she said. "Can't 'Daddy' shell out for one? Or maybe you can dip into your drug-money budget?"

Leonard lost his voice. He could only watch the professor fuss with the folders. He was sad that she was not kind and cordial with him. He found himself becoming angry at his father because of it.

The maga smelled like orange and lavender, patchouli and pine. Leonard closed his eyes for a stolen second to disappear into the refuge of the scent and the delectable melancholy of his hapless love for his teacher.

They were squatting and, therefore, close to the white and gray-blue checkered tiles of the corridor's floor; their backs were rounded and their heads were inclined toward each other. Leonard was hiding his face from passersby and getting dizzy from the pattern in the fabric of the professor's garishly striped dress, which was something Bhutanese. A long necklace made of vertebrae carved into skulls dangled from her neck.

She glared at him and finally gasped, "What are you doing, Leonard?" and hushed in an urgent tone, "Listen. Your father will get you pushed through the graduate school despite your grades but then what? The only job you'll be fit for is as a genocidal tyrant in some God-forsaken Third World Outer Plane country where you'll end up being the puppet of some evil Illuminati sorcerer. Then you'll probably land yourself in a war crimes court and go down in history as a maniac who did crappy things because he had syphilitic dementia or drug psychosis, fetal alcohol syndrome or something. Is that what you want for yourself?"

"You're the only one who can help me, Professor La Maga," Leonard blurted. "Even though they say you're a folkie and all, you're the only person who kind of acts like she gives a shit—I mean cares, even though today wasn't so great," he stuttered. "I know everything is messed up. I know everyone thinks I'm a waste. I'm as good as dead and a menace, but I know a lot of stuff, and no one knows, and no one cares. But I think you care, Professor La Maga—or could. Just please care and help me," he pleaded.

"I have to go home and tell my father I'm suspended now," he continued. "My friends are shitheads, and they'll all be out zapping me now. I don't want to end up in the Outer Plane doing shit for Hipparchus Gorgon. I want to be a key-holder. I know I can do it. If . . . if I could . . ."

The professor bowed her head. She appeared to be very moved—even weepy—because of Leonard's plaintive outburst. She grasped his hand and tenderly placed it against her forehead. She mournfully nodded and let out an abashed laugh when she smiled. They stared at each other for what seemed like a long time. The professor smiled sweetly and uttered reassuring words before asking Leonard whether he would be interested in receiving a Pyr Sacra empowerment.

Leonard's jaw dropped and his heart popped.

"DO NOT tell anyone," she said pointedly, "especially NOT your *father*." (She didn't say "father" exactly but mouthed it as if the word were taboo.) "It'll be the end of me, as you well know."

Leonard nodded sincerely.

"And then you can bet they'll cart you away to be 'rehabilitated' into a mule for some devil, like Hipparchus Gorgon. It'll be all over for both of us," the maga hushed and turned edgy. "So think about what is happening right here right now—and don't cross me. Because, honey-bunny, I can blow everything sky-high."

"You'll never regret giving me refuge, La Maga Magus. I swear it. I'll be your son before I'll be my father's," Leonard avowed with a fervor that startled and elated him.

An astonished look came over the professor. Her face flushed and her eyes spilled tears. She lowered her head to hide in her mop of hair.

"I mean it. Really," Leonard implored. "Are you alright?"

The professor made a small, breathless laugh and muttered "thank you" a few times. She went back to scraping the spilled documents into folders and the folders from the floor. Leonard followed suit and stood up with half the folders in his arms. "Where do they go?" he asked.

The professor looked around. "I don't know," she sniffled. "Give 'em to me. I'll dump them somewhere." She took the monstrous stack of folders back, now balancing them with ease. "Can you get out of here without being seen or should I go with you?" She winked as if quite aware of what had gone down behind the Sigils Archive building two hours earlier. "Your friends aren't out there waiting to zap you, are they?"

Leonard shrugged. "They're probably still playing the Phaeton maneuver." He had no qualms about admitting as much.

The professor huffed out another laugh. She made her watery eyes look mean for a second and shook her head. "Well, you better get out of here before you end up getting into trouble for being *in* school. And no more Phaeton maneuver stuff now. Stay alive for a little while."

Leonard agreed with a nod.

"I won't let anything bad happen," she said.

Leonard didn't know what that meant exactly, but he believed her. He was awash in relief. "Professor," he said as he started away. "You were serious about the empowerment, right?"

"Do you not want it?"

"Of course I want it," he exclaimed. "But when?"

"Oh, you'll know," she said and bid him to get going.

VI
The Pyr Sacra Empowerment

The de Luxes—father and son—lived elegantly but modestly for their means. Curiously, their home wasn't manor-like. It did not have boxy architecture and heavy lintels and columns in the style of what Outer Plane folks called "McMansions." It was a nouveau Tuscan-style abode, with large beige quarried stone walls, red tile roofs, arch-shaped windows and portico, promenades, and patios. It was nestled in a rolling landscape of maple, dogwood, and willow trees, forsythia, rhododendron, and azalea shrubs, and informal gardens full of flowering sage, lavender, and thyme, puff balls of ornamental onions in bloom, roses, mums, and other flora common to the North Atlantic Sovereignty.

Stepping-stone paths were coated in moss and trailing roses clung to the stone walls and roofs of the porticos. The home had big wooden doors and was built in a square around a large courtyard within which the tropical garden paradise was magically kept.

de Lux senior furnished the interior of his home with Victorian effects, stained glass accents, and functional design: sliding doors and inset cabinets, bookcases, and shelves. Footsteps trod over the stone floors made musical sounds as they tippy tap reverberated over the stone walls and wooden ceiling rafters. Woodwork was dark, distressed and ornately etched. Masterpieces of fine art were stationed here and there, and the scents of aloes and galangal were heavy in airways quietly saturated with the angelic Baroque chorals of Tallis, the richly laced concertos of Geminiani, and the spirited works of Handel. It was why Leonard junior was sequestered away in his own wing of the house—on the opposite side from where his father mostly lived. There, he could make a racket and do whatever he willed without disturbing his father too much.

He had a bedroom that he could climb out of into a tree house built into giant sea berry tree that loomed from the tropical garden in the home's central courtyard. He also had his own den and a studio that was supposed to be for magical practices but where Leonard kept his sound system because the echo off the copper ceiling was very cool. Leonard spent most of his time there.

In turn, Leo spent his free hours in his own den or one of the four floors—from dungeon to turret—of a tower that was annexed to the house. Else, the elder de Lux could be found sunning in his courtyard, which was, as mentioned, a magically tropical haven within which grew giant balsa, sea berry, fig, and coconut palms. The tall trees shaded a pond and waterway around and within which grew spiked bromelia, phallic- and flame-like-flowered caladium, heliconia, and anthurium. Orchids, begonia, passion flowers, bougainvillea, and various other flowering vines, and posies with heady perfumes abounded. Blue neotropical butterflies and brightly colored birds also flitted among the foliage.

This was where Leo held his social events: on a spacious, marble patio around which his Eden thrived. He also kept some of his more decorative magical worts there, but most were tended to in a greenhouse further back on the property. Behind greenhouse was a thicket and then a lake that caught the moonlight. Leonard junior would get high there but only during the day because his father sometimes visited the place at night.

Three days passed before de Lux senior noticed that his son hadn't been to school. He walked a half mile from his manor house to a rolling field speckled with shade trees and cottages that housed his servants: his housekeepers and groundskeepers and a driver who doubled as a repairman. Leo was looking for the driver and found him building a pond in the field where the cottages stood.

"My son hasn't been to school this week. Why is that?" Leo asked.

The man shook his head and shrugged. "Said the school told him to stay home."

"Excuse me?" Leo grimaced.

The man jumped back. "I'm just telling you what the kid said."

Leo did not have the energy or the desire to pursue the matter with the driver. He walked away. He could barely remember the fellow's name—Langsdorf—no, he was the horticulturist. The driver's name was . . . Lazar—Mister Fullbright Lazar, a bit of a slacker.

Hours passed until the weekend came. Leo did not confront his son. Rather, he kept to himself, fed up and brooding in seclusion in an upper compartment of his tower. There he wallowed in feeling assaulted by fate and uncharacteristically monkish. He had been more selective than usual about attending political and legislative functions because of his health. It was fatigue. A sickly pain throbbed in a space above his left eye. Indigestion, bowel upset, aches and pains, and wheezing. His physician said it was stress but de Lux imagined that it was the effect of a spell.

He had been the victim of a magical attack many years before. It had been sudden, nearly fatal, and inflicted by an archenemy of the de Lux clan. Leo's success in avenging himself and his kin made him someone in his father's eyes. It proved that his father hadn't spilled his seed in vain like he maybe thought he had with all the offspring who had come before Leo. This victory dramatically changed Leo's destiny. Whether for better or worse was the question. His current illness was nowhere near the same caliber as that past one, though. It was a moderately draining nuisance, but it went along with a particularly restless and sulky mind.

"Maybe you're pregnant," his buddy, Reggie, had kidded.

"If only," Leo sourly muttered. He found himself thinking about Zeus, who swallowed his pregnant wife Metis so she wouldn't birth a son who would ruin him like Zeus had ruined his father, Kronos, and Kronos his own father, Ouranos, and like Leo was sure his own son was going to ruin him. Instead of dull aches and relentless fatigue, Zeus had gotten a massive migraine, which heralded the birth of the child his devoured wife was bearing: Athena, the goddess of guile and wisdom. She was born from Zeus's head. Cloned. That was the trick.

Son or daughter. Leo didn't care, as long as the being could grow up to step up to the plate and carry on for him better than Leonard could ever manage to. And if Leo could accomplish that without having to put up with the ramifications of impregnating someone, that would be a big plus. Odd ideas about creating a homunculus or golom itched at his brain, ultimately putting him in a panic that the hex on him was now making him insane.

Leo imagined that Marina Sarin, in a fit of unrequited desire, had cursed him. Either she or her cousin, Medea, had done it. He didn't think Marina had the expertise—but Medea. Even he kept his distance from her. She was a power vacuum and a ruthless bewitcher. Her sorcery was relegated to a world of petty intrigues and to escapades involving Commons who were dabbling in the dark arts.

Leo would endure the condition a little longer because 1) he felt sorry for Marina, she being so overwrought with him, and 2) Marina was too lusty and dramatic not to attach herself with as much enthusiasm to another man. Leo was sure his sickness would subside once her attention shifted elsewhere.

Monday came. Leo had still yet to confront his son about his absence from school or vice versa. Indeed, father and son had not seen each other for days although they both had been brooding about the grounds of the estate and wandering amidst signs of the other's presence.

In preparation of the inevitable confrontation, Leo had written Leonard's name on a desk calendar. He had written "Leonard" in plain blue ink in the Monday slot on a line that said 4:30 PM. He arranged for a light supper to be served 4 hours later, assuming that his stomach would be churning and head aching even more than usual when he got through extracting a confession from the boy. But he learned the details of Leonard's status earlier in the day. Dr. Bruno, the chief administrator of Leonard's school, made an unexpected visit to the consul's home. Bruno claimed that he had telephoned the de Lux residence twice after Leonard's most recent behavioral snafu and that Leo had failed to acknowledge the calls.

"Who took the messages? Had they been delivered to me, I would've responded immediately, of course," Leo sputtered in a tone that bespoke his indignation over being humiliated.

Bruno simply grunted. He and Leo had a diplomatic relationship that was, in a way, cordial and familiar, but in another way, as paranoid and testy as proverbial pissing contests could be. In a word, it was impassioned. The two men held each other in awe. They wanted the other to be on his own side but had no qualms about flinging wrenches into each other's gears when they couldn't see eye-to-eye.

Leo had the head housekeeper, Lady Poinsett, deliver espresso and a bottle of cognac and its snifter paraphernalia to the den where Leo and Dr. Bruno went to conference. "And lemon peel please — and some figs and almonds and what not," he ordered. " — and those little biscuits."

The housekeeper nodded without expression.

The men settled into antique, leather-upholstered chairs. They reveled in sunlight streaming through mottled, cathedral glass into the wood-paneled room, sniffed their warmed cognac, and sipped their espresso from dainty cups. They popped almonds into their mouths and ripped open dried figs with their teeth to sensuously rub their tongues into the gritty jellied meat beneath the fruit's leathery skin. They chatted about their side businesses and Bruno's desire to acquire a piece of art from a contemporary Outer Plane artist whose forte was mobile sculptures. Leo said that he would look into it and then finally uttered, "I need to get that boy into a very specific mentoring program. Leonard." And admitted, "It's long overdue. A heavy-handed approach is out of the question. I need a specialist and a discreet setting for my son."

Bruno nodded. "I'll see what I can do," he said. "But you have to put something toward keeping that kid in line. He's going to end up doing something very compromising. He's a hair's breadth away."

Leo nodded gravely. There was no point in getting his back up about it; it was true. "He needs a constructive pastime," he said. "Perhaps I can get him into a sea-charming program. Send him off to the Aegean for the summer. He likes marine biology. Spends my fortune on collector-grade cone snail shells. Fascinated with venomous cone snails, wherever that is leading," his voice ominously trailed off.

"Now there's a plan," Bruno exclaimed with fake enthusiasm. "Sea charming. But the kid's fate is in your hands, not mine. Don't sell him out, Leo. You know what I'm saying."

The consul bristled. "Isn't that the point of this conversation," he said heatedly. "Yes. I want to 'do' something. The boy has serious behavior problems. They are going to bury me and my career. But he's bright enough underneath it all. That noxious pet of yours, La Maga Magus, seems to bring it out. I'll give her that much. But why haven't any of his other instructors in all these years accomplished the same? I've entrusted the education of my son to you. So who has been remiss?"

"Do you want me to give La Maga Magus free reign to straighten him out?" Bruno asked. "'Cause I can do that."

"Hah!" Leo scoffed and twitched. He managed to let out an edgy laugh. Bruno chuckled along with him but meanly.

When Leo composed himself, he said, "To be frank, I want you to train Leonard personally. Mentor him."

Bruno bristled with an air of ridicule.

"What's it worth? Let me negotiate something then," Leo bargained. He blurted that he really wasn't up to impregnating Vinca Blanco—and certainly NOT Marina Sarin—or one of his other "regulars" on the off chance that the event would produce someone worthy of maintaining the family line. "I want to rectify this situation with Leonard for my own well-being and his. I'm offering you a shot at control of my lineage and life. Why are you laughing, Danny?"

"You're messing up my good suit with your spilled guts, de Lux," Bruno snipped.

"Well?"

"I'll see what I can do," he reiterated and winked reassuringly in such a way that Leo sorely regretted having said a single word to the man. Mean mischief would now be afoot. A magical repartee between him and Bruno—if it came to that—would be insidious and messy. Leo didn't have the time or energy for such nuisances.

"That Vinca Blanco might be OK to knock up," Bruno quipped. "Probably mess up her figure. When they're short like that . . ." Bruno scowled and wagged his head. "And that Marina Sarina." He wrinkled his nose. "High maintenance, although I hear she's the very doting mother of a 4-year-old girl. The kid isn't yours?"

"No," Leo said sharply and shook his head. "Marina was involved with," he fumbled for the recollection and how to word it. "Some prehistoric praetor—the name escapes me. The old fool supports the kid and Marina's shopping binges, but the sire of that child is probably the fellow who cleans her pool or some other tool." Leo rolled his eyes.

"It wasn't Gwen Goldenlance, was it?" Bruno chuckled.

"I'm sure that it is not a complete impossibility," Leo sneered.

"There's some pressure for Sofia to get on with that. Reproduction," Bruno enunciated. "Sure you don't want to hook up and create a 'moonchild' with her or something?"

Leo simply twitched his brows and scowled, peeved that Bruno sought to bait him another time with mention of the woman. "A 'moonchild' to 'immanentize the eschaton' and usher in a 'new aeon,'" he grumbled smartly. It was catch-phrase jargon, spewed by both Inner and Outer Plane counterculture types: blasted Thelemites, Chaotes, and Illuminists—including his renegade brother's Lions of Light ilk—about a magically conceived person whose appearance would initiate the end of this world and the beginning of another.

"Now that would be an amazing journey," Bruno quipped.

"Is that where this woman's head is at now?" Leo questioned gruffly, not that he expected Bruno to level with him about it. Word was that she had ditched Alan Raphael and was now hanging around with a very crazy and disheveled hippy sorcerer who was a professor emeritus at the Bythos Academy. The character was involved in social reform projects for the Dimidium Plebs and Dimidium Vulgaris — "Deeples" and "Deevees" — society's outcasts. *Aurelio Zosimo Sortiar* was his name. He had a bunch of anarchistic young followers who referred to themselves as Inchaotes. Put it all together, and he was on the Sovereignty's "watch" list a few names away from his new girlfriend, Sofia La Maga Magus.

"I think she wants to adopt," Bruno replied.

"I mean, her designs on bringing about the end of the world with that freak 'The Crazy Professor' from the Bythos Academy," Leo said.

Bruno's eyes bulged before his jaw broke into guffaws that made him fumble for a pocket handkerchief to wipe his face. *"You're a riot, de Lux,"* he exclaimed, and stood up to depart. "How've you been feeling these day, anyway?" he asked. "Word is, not so good."

"I've been preoccupied," Leo murmured off-handedly and stoically glided through a shooting pain that strangely hammered at his knees, his asshole, and a space behind both his ears as he walked Bruno to the front door. The man robustly grasped Leo's hand in a parting handshake and said "OK, Leo. Good to chat. Please see what you can do about the kid."

As Danny Bruno wandered away, Leo rued being unable to combat and counter the man's wiles and realized that instead of getting his back up about Sofia La Maga, he should have used the tone of the little chat with Bruno to satisfy his curiosity. What was the relationship between her and Bruno and what did Bruno have to say about what was going on in that classroom of hers and her liaison with crazy Zosimo Sortiar? And if she wanted to play house and rear a bloody dark horse to end the age, why wasn't Bruno sticking it in and accommodating her?

Leo fitfully rested until, at 4:30 PM sharp, his son was summoned to his den. There the youth was obliged to confess his misadventure. Leonard, seemingly prepared, took a full breath and boldly admitted that his pals wanted him to participate in a Phaeton maneuver match and that he had refused.

"So they started ragging on me and hit me in the back with an attack charm while I was walking away to go to class. When I got up, I pulled a spell on them that put them all down with one shot."

Leo nodded. He seemed pleased with the very last part of Leonard's story, but then the critical question came. "And why were these boys—your best friends—pressuring you into a Phaeton maneuver match, Leonard?"

Leo knew what his son would say. He dreaded it as if it would make his skin dissolve from his bones. The shame. The shame on himself for being so blind to his son's reckless mischief. He was quite sure Danny Bruno knew that part of the saga. Were the news made public, de Lux would be a laughing-stock among the citizenry. It would end his career.

Leonard was no less horror-stricken at the prospect of coming clean, but he intended to do so in his resolve to turn over a new leaf. He would have to watch his father's eyes burn like rock salt on ice when he did so. The punishment would be to endure the man's abysmal and smoldering disappointment along with a barrage of weird spells meant to punish him: hobgoblins over his shoulders reminding him of how shameless he was and the refusal of every device in the home to work for him, including the refrigerator and his sound system. That meant no lights, no social media, no music, no hot food unless some household servant had pity on him—and none did—until his father relented.

"I've done it before," Leonard confessed.

de Lux senior shut his eyes and clamped his jaw.

"I gave it up," Leonard exclaimed. "That's how I

ended up getting into trouble."

That was the end of the conversation. de Lux senior said nothing more. He looked away and raised his hand as a cue that Leonard was dismissed from his presence.

Leo didn't speak or look at his son for days. There were no hobgoblins or lock-outs on appliances for de Lux junior, though, only alienation and solitude. The days were long and filled with listless diversions that soon became just listlessness.

Professor La Maga would give him an empowerment, though. She would make him an apprentice—a secret apprentice at that. She would not let anything bad happen. She had said so. Leonard thought he would hardly hold onto his sanity if he hadn't that promise to cleave to. A little light, a little redemption, a little something that resembled affection.

Leonard mounted his Vespa and ventured into town only three times during his suspension. That wasn't like him. He tended to loiter in the streets nearly every night. He would hang around the greens or the cafes and shops in the more chic and shady districts of the capital, such as the notorious neighborhood dubbed Limbo, where he and his buddies overheard music and ogled provocatively dressed girls. It was there that the best music, wacky worts, and sexual escapades could be found and where Phaeton maneuver memorabilia and gear could be bought and sold.

No. Leonard steered clear of Bertrand and the others and stayed clean and out of the red light districts. He went to a movie and moped around Mercury Gardens where he tried to make time with Kestrel Silvestri. The Mercury Gardens was the social venue for people of means who had tamer entertainment needs. They lolled about in the cafés or enclaves in this or that plaza where events might be featured. Even though he wasn't supposed to, Leonard told Kestrel whose apprentice he was going to be.

"Yeah, right, de Lux," she snorted and rolled her eyes.

"I'm telling you, it's true," he insisted.

"Stop being a jerk," she replied and told him that she always thought he was cute but that he was a troublemaker and a waste. She said she had her sights set on someone more put-together — a friend of one of her brothers who was a senior at the Bythos Academy Secondary School.

Yes. That conversation was why Leonard hadn't gone into town much.

After Kestril dissed him, he remained in the Mercury Gardens all night, having come upon a formation of orchid-covered boulders that contained a shallow recess in which to hide. From there, he watched some middle-aged ladies get topless and drum and dance in the moonlight. He crossed planes twice to take trains to New York City where he wandered, drank coffee, and totally messed up a creep who mistook him for a hustling waif ("You want to see my wand?" Leonard winked and then zapped what went for brains in the wingnut Commons).

At a loss of patience and faith, Leonard got stoned and remained that way for most of the second week of his suspension. Meanwhile, de Lux senior had retreated to his tower, moving from one studio to another trying to figure out how to banish his sickness and clone offspring.

On the night of the Saturday before the Tuesday that Leonard was to return to school, the youth was holed up in the room that was supposed to be his studio. It had a copper ceiling on which were embossed orbs and stars that incandesced in the dark to resemble the night sky.

The acoustics were great in that room, but Leonard was sitting in silence. He was so bored and downhearted that he thought he might disintegrate. What would turn him away from his misery? A hit of fine blue wacky wort and a set of pornographic materializations. He could only make small ones, the size of people on a television monitor.

Girls with humongous tits and guys with really big dicks. Leonard would materialize the forms and watch them play while he wanked himself. He regretted that he was too magically stupid to make life-sized thought-forms to amuse and abuse himself with, like his father did.

He had his hands in his sweatpants and was thinking about his options. Maybe just a joint of lesser-grade wort would do. He contemplated a box that contained a few wacky worts harvested from a wing of a greenhouse that Langsdorf, his father's horticulturist, idiotically thought Leonard hadn't discovered.

Those were his choices. He could hardly get himself to move, though. He was pretty sure that Professor La Maga had forgotten about him. He was ready to conclude that she was jerking him off with her glamour — the girly cuteness, the familiarity, the sappy, stumbling false vulnerability. It was a complex ruse to undo Leonard and his father. Leonard had fallen into the trap. Stupidity.

He was in the kind of mood in which a person questions why he was born and whether staying alive was worth it. He pricked his finger on a splinter of wood gouged from the floor. He wanted to feel the sting and watch a bead of blood well up.

A black hole, a dark night. Leonard felt a tingly sensation fizzle over the left side of his body. It became especially strong when it reached his cheek and then his ear. A heat, as if he had taken a shot of hard liquor that ignited his insides, swelled in his stomach and leeched up.

This heat and a tingling pressure pent up at his neck. It forced Leonard's spine to elongate as if he were a marionette tugged on a string. As the sensation burst into his head, he was enveloped in a scintillating flood of light. Thunder, like the sound of a furious tide, roared inside his ears. His heart beat hard, and his breath rhythmically billowed in a way Leonard could not control.

Arrested in terror and elation, his eyes fluttered and teared to the vision of vast light and stroboscopic effects. He uttered an amazed sound as if gazing upon something magnificent—an entity of breathtaking beauty and hospitality. He could neither see nor hear it, but he witnessed it nonetheless.

Everything about his life and circumstances—and everything about everyone else's life—suddenly seemed incidental and pathetic. Reality, on the other hand, seemed to be pure happiness, and it was in his grip.

The seizure subsided. The thunder resolved into sheer calm and the strobing into radiance. The episode was probably much briefer than it seemed. It left Leonard refreshed and full of breath like he might have been at the moment he was born.

The room seemed illuminated. Leonard himself seemed illuminated. He could only laugh however disoriented, because it was as if he didn't know himself. He pressed his thumbnails into his fingertips and examined his hands. They seemed to be glowing. He had to find a mirror and look into it. He hardly recognized himself.

His eyes ran with tears. Tears of laughter, tears of awe. It seemed all the same, and then of gratitude when he pulled himself together enough to realize what had happened.

Lady Poinsett was calling him. She was rapping on the door.

"Leonard, are you in there? What are you doing? Your father's on the phone. He wants to talk to you. I know you're in there, Leonard. I can smell you," the housekeeper said. "Open the door, Leonard," she impatiently insisted. "Don't get your father mad. He'll take it out on me, damn you."

Leonard hastily composed himself and opened the door to his studio.

"What are you doing in there, Leonard?" Lady Poinsett scolded. She peered past him to inspect the room.

"What?" he said.

"Your father." The woman thrust a phone at him.

"Hello?"

"Are you alright, Leonard?" de Lux senior wanted to know.

"Yes. Very."

"What does that mean?"

"It means I'm alright. What did I do now?"

"That's what I'm trying to find out," his father replied.

"I've been sitting in my room doing nothing," Leonard griped and took a breath; he didn't want this conversation to spoil his excellent mood.

"I can imagine," the father said tersely. Leonard sensed a smoldering pause. He let the man enjoy it.

"Nothing bad is happening," Leonard assured him.

"Hmmm," the man huffed. "Because I feel like something is going on, Leonard. I won't be fooled. I've had enough with you."

"Well, maybe something is happening, but it's not bad," Leonard said.

"And what exactly is this thing that's going on, Leonard? Can you tell me? Can you tell me at all? I can't bear this, Leonard. I am trying to level with you. What can I do?" His father was actually pleading. He sincerely sounded concerned.

"I don't know!" Leonard gasped, because he didn't exactly (and, of course, he was not going to tell his father that he just got Pyr-Sacra empowered by *Sofia La Maga*). "I don't know what's going on if something's going on, but it's not bad. I promise."

"Nothing peculiar is happening in that house?" de Lux senior asked.

"Everything's really okay over here," Leonard insisted.

Another pause, and then the man said. "Can you find — not Langsford; he's pathetic. The other man . . . Lazar . . . No. See if Victor is around. Find Victor and go look around the house with him — including my rooms in the tower. Take my staff — the long thick one with the onyx Ea at the top. Hold onto that staff and use it if you see anything strange. Can you do that, Leonard?"

"Sure," Leonard replied.

"Alright. Do that and call me back," the father instructed.

Leonard knew nothing was askew in the house — only he was, but as he had told his father, whatever it was, it wasn't "bad."

He found Victor. He was the head of his father's personal cadre of staff-bearers — his bodyguards. He lived with a wife and a pack of boxers on the property in a nice-sized stone cottage apart from the nestling of cottages in which the household help lived. He was a husky man with a strong but calming demeanor. He took his role as a chief attendant to the consul with unwavering and ungrudging solemnity and faithfulness. Leonard found him at home, where he was propped on a sofa, watching a movie, and savoring pretzels and oatmeal stout while his wife was gardening in the moonlight.

He and Leonard and the canine guard skulked around. The dogs sniffed here and there, but neither the dogs nor Victor were willing to descend into the dungeon of de Lux senior's tower.

It was gloomy, with a single low-volt lighting fixture with which to illumine the shelves housing artifacts, worts, potions and props, organic materials, and metal plates and parchments of wicked sigils and defensive glyphs. The room had a well and a pit with a flue that took fumes of burned things through a tunnel in the ground to the outside away from the house. Nothing unusual seemed to be there.

In the ground floor studio, Leonard found the big staff. His father didn't tote it around in the way too many magical persons did their own staffs. The man could summon it through the aethers and into his grip on demand.

Wands and staffs typically had a wood core, generally oak, yew, holly, ash, rowan, cherry, or willow. They all had specific magical properties. Oak was commanding; yew bridged the here and hereafter; holly commanded the energies of the element of fire as ash did those of water; rowan was mercurial, cherry good for love magic, and willow for moon magic and healing.

The wood would be sheathed in a full coat or lattice of metals: iron, silver, platinum, gold, copper, bronze, nickel, etc. and studded with special stones. The staff that Leonard's father had asked him to retrieve was made of oak and hawthorn sheathed in a serpentine design of iron and tin, spotted with chips of black and red stones. An onyx finial of the sea-goat Capricornus—the zodiacal sign under which Leo de Lux had been born—was mounted on a jewel-crusted girdle of platinum on the top of the staff.

Oak for majesty, hawthorn for the power of lightning, onyx for smiting magical attacks, and the metals of Mars and Jupiter. Capricorn: the sea-goat; the southern gate of the sun; the Babylonian Ea, god of wisdom; Grecian Aegipan, restorer of Zeus' might in defeating the Titans; saturnine, mercurial, and spanning the heights to the depths. This staff was a martial and lethal weapon but not because it made a good cudgel.

Victor jumped back when Leonard grasped the staff. The dogs barked and whimpered.

"What are you going to do with that, Lenny?" the man nervously asked.

"My dad told me to get it," Leonard replied, "to protect myself, I think."

"Watch where you point it, son," Victor cautioned. "Are you in some kind of trouble?"

"Nothing bad is happening," Leonard said as if the phrase had become a mantra.

The only peculiar thing Leonard came upon in the ground-floor studio—his father's place for ordinary practical magic—were the remnants of a Morpho potion. Leonard could tell that it wasn't a love charm exactly. Scraps of black and indigo butterfly wings and ocelli—the eye-shapes on butterfly wings—were scattered on a plate. It was as if de Lux senior had concocted the potion in haste. Morpho potions were usually blue, the brighter the better for love spells. Here the butterfly used in the potion seemed to belong to a species of the dark *Morpho* subgenus *Iphimedeia*.

Leonard, before his Pyr Sacra episode, might've looked upon all this with contempt, but he found it tender and sweetly revealing at that moment. His father, at age 45, had concocted a spell to repel a lover.

Leonard ascended to the second floor, where his father conducted more esoteric practices and refined studies. Then he climbed a spiral staircase to the turret. Leonard didn't know what his father did there, but the site felt holy. It opened to space filled with the scents of flowering trees and the sky-dome of constellations. The only furnishing on the turret was a stone pool lined with crystals in the style—but appearing quite different—from the well in the dungeon.

Leonard was still feeling good. He felt content regardless of circumstance. Indeed, there was hardly a thought in his mind.

His father was attending a benefit at the Phoenix and Harp Country Club. The benefit was a gala in which charms to fix this or that crisis were donated for the benefit of Commons. Such functions had become fashionable among some patricians. Of course, government dignitaries had to act as if they were socially engaged in these programs. de Lux senior, however, had little patience or interest in the trials and tribulations of Commons.

Because he was the consul of the sovereignty, Leo had to show his face at these benefits. He had to give speeches about the value of such programs and donate precious charms for preventing or else softening the effects of draught or famine or saving victims of other calamities otherwise preventable through the faculty of foresight, which Commons sorely lacked.

Leo had taken Marina Sarin as his escort. He had done so to smooth things over and to slip her a reverse Morpho charm. It was a potion made of the wings, including the ocelli, of dark species of Morpho butterflies, which were not really blue, indigo, brown, black, or any color really. The butterfly wings were composed of tiny panels of tinier mirrors that reflected light. Orion Lumiere Sortiar, Leo's childhood mentor, had been in the habit of stressing that point. The blue in the butterfly wing was a reflection, not the thing in itself, the same as love was the reflection of a fantasy that was projected on a moving and often insensible target.

"The Morpho is short-lived — taking three and a half months only to flourish. It does not eat solid foods but sucks the sap of rotten fruit through a nose-like structure. If you should ever play with this Morpho love charm, remember these facts as metaphors," Lumiere Sortiar had instructed.

Leo had sacrificed the butterflies to Ares, a war-like deity who was two-timed by Venus who was making time with a young mortal named Adonis, according to legend. Leo made a fine powder from the butterfly wings and from pistachios, horseradish, dried lemongrass, and lilies. In the old days, the blood or viscera of some animal — a toad or a cat—would go into the concoction—but there were restrictions on blood-letting in the new era. Besides, Leo didn't have the time to be so particular. In any case, it was not so much the ingredients or even the rite in working a spell, but the strength of intention. After all, Leo was brewing a charm, not a recipe.

He did not need to get the potion "in" Marina, only on her. She was a honey-blond with warm and bubbly breasts, a sharp and sinewy curve from her waist to her hips; lips and kisses enchanted with seasonings: vanilla and sugar, citrus and chocolate. He managed to pour the potion into her cleavage anyway. He massaged it into her buxom chest during a lusty embrace in the back seat of his Bentley Arnage as it neared its destination (Lazar, the driver, was accustomed to such romps).

No sooner had they entered the reception hall had Marina lost interest in her escort. She was nowhere to be found when Leo gave his speech. In fact, he didn't spy her until he was on his way out after calling Leonard.

She was traipsing back from the club's rolling golf course, illuminated by lampposts and the moon. Appearing blissfully disheveled, she was arm-in-arm with an assistant mediator named Donald . . . something . . . Sortiar (Leo couldn't remember his name).

It was as if Marina didn't recognize Leo as he crossed her path to summon Lazar. He comported himself as one does when seeing a familiar but unwelcome face in a crowd and acts as if he doesn't. He left the benefit without her. It wasn't as if she had a right to mind.

That much settled, he moved on to resolve a peculiar stirring. It first occurred while gazing at a scallop wrapped in bacon during his repast at the benefit. "How 'Commons,'" he thought of the hors d'oeuvre, and then realized that the cuisine had an appalling theme: mushroom caps, crab cakes, mini-quiche, and wieners (Leo was asked to choose from salmon, filet mignon, or palliard of chicken over rice for an entrée.) The refreshments were supposed to celebrate Commons cuisine. He chose not to indulge, requesting an un-Commons bourbon straight up in a tumbler.

But it was while he was gazing upon this gustatory pairing of a pig and a mollusk that he felt something distinctly shift in his consciousness. It was as if the world had tilted. He could not define the quality of the sensation, but it was striking and sudden, and, therefore, caused alarm. He became suspicious of Marina's activities that she was gone from his sight. Then he called Leonard, feeling as he spoke, a rare and ferocious desire to protect him.

He arrived home at about 1 AM. A waxing half-moon was tiny, icy, and high in the sky. Leo found Leonard alone in the courtyard. The youth was serenely sitting on one of the gilded divans situated along the edge of the patio. His eyes were closed, but he was not sleeping. His hands grasped the Ea staff, and he was glowing an elegant, rosy light. Bright blue and heliotrope butterflies that were supposed to be sleeping and camouflaged in the mulch of the atrium floor at that hour were flitting about and perching on the young man.

"That's an interesting trick, Leonard," Leo remarked. (It seemed like something that would impress young ladies.)

"They all woke up when I came in, so I just sat down," Leonard replied.

"Hmmm," Leo sighed. "And nothing bad is happening?"

"No," Leonard said. When he opened his amber eyes, light came out and met his father's ice-blue gaze. The sight was curious to Leo. It was curious because it had happened at all and also because the youth seemed unaware of it.

"What have you been doing, Leonard?" he asked, but

kindly. "Something's changed."

"Yeah, I know," Leonard laughed agreeably. "And how've you been doing, Dad?'

Leo felt that shift again, and he finally realized what it was. He laughed because it was so simple: his illness had passed. "I'm feeling much better now," he told his son and found himself saying, "thank you."

VII
Peace and Illumination

Some persons carried worry beads. Sofia had been carrying a brass nut and bolt fortified with a copper brace. The brace looked as if it held the nut in place. It moved with the nut along the grooved shaft of the bolt. The widget was about three fourths of an inch long and was obviously something that had popped out of a piece of heavy machinery.

Sofia kept the nut and bolt in a pocket of a worn, ruddy red jacket that was made of Peruvian fabric. It was richly embroidered with flowers resembling roses, but the lining was ripped, the seams and weave were coming undone, and the cuffs were frayed. It was a once impressive but now raggedy piece of apparel that Sofia seemed reluctant to part with. Mirelle was pretty sure that the nut and bolt were related to a secret magical working. Perhaps the old jacket was a magical tool as well. Sofia wore it whenever she took long strolls in the woods.

There were various routes to take, each with their own character, guideposts, and attractions: ruins, majestic trees, caves and rock formations, ponds, a stream, and nests or lairs of wild creatures. The place where Sofia walked was a wild wood. It was a parallel plane where Commons often accidentally wandered in and out without even knowing it. Sofia mostly stuck to the path that ran along the stream. She walked a straight line at a moderate pace that sometimes slowed as she foraged for edible plants and magical botanicals and greeted certain trees and other structures that she seemed to be friendly with.

As she walked, she would twist the nut and its copper brace up and down along the bolt's shaft and study its parts as if perpetually fascinated by some new element: the way the copper brace hugged the top and bottom of the nut, the wear on the metal, and the digits on the head of it:

ARA
EL
36 SOL
7 169

and the letters "AN" and "A" in tiny circles.

It could've been a cryptic magical message. It probably was. Mirelle wallowed in the frustration of knowing this and knowing that she was too lowly to be told outright or given the tools to work out the puzzle. She would have to labor and suffer and jump through a myriad of hoops first.

She wasn't allowed to talk during her walks with Sofia, anyway. In fact, she had to walk on her own, alone, with her own silence. At first, she seethed, wondering whether Sofia made Lenny walk like that, too—or whether she talked to him while they walked.

If it wasn't that he had done a 180-degree turn since Sofia had made him her special project, Mirelle would've become completely discouraged. She had to trust the method. She had to trust that a wonderful transformation was in store for her too. Even if Sofia kept her as an assistant forever and never let her take wing on her own, it was okay. Mirelle could've had a far worse fate.

Medea Sarin Sortiar would've had Mirelle doing all kinds of weird things if Mirelle had apprenticed with her. She would've been learning magic straight-away, though. The magic would've been dark and chaotic but magic nonetheless. There had yet to be magic or thought-forms, keys, or rites in Mirelle's apprenticeship with Sofia La Maga. So far, the only things that had happened were these long silent walks and hours of sitting meditation in which

Mirelle felt the weight of time and the racket of her mind and brooded.

She kept at it. She hoped that if she dealt with her situation gracefully, she would be taken seriously by La Maga Magus who would then teach her something.

Emptying the mind is a dangerous thing precisely because it's purgative. One sits expecting stillness that tames the tedium of time only to find that time is nothing more than the succession of thoughts. Even if they are muted, they persist nevertheless, like TV-screen static that hisses and scintillates annoyingly and is made of ions from the beginning of time.

The noise goes on. Mundane thoughts give way to visions that seem like communications but are deceptions, more junk from the depths of consciousness: random archetypes and convoluted wonders, mixed up impressions of stimuli complicated by one's human senses. Emotions without thoughts soon follow. These are realized as things best forgotten that are disguised as nightmares and neuroses emerging from an abyss: a Pandora's Box called contemplation. One knows oneself then or goes insane.

Resolve, resting, the thoughts do not cease; they go far away, as if they were someone else's property. That's when serenity emerges as a sense of balance awaiting the next wave.

In the Outer Plane, Mirelle was a wan and fragile little black girl with weird eyes and seizures. She had been the subject of a clinical case study called "Ocular Albinism and Absence-Type Epilepsy in a 7-Year-Old Female of Creole Descent." The doctor who had presented the case at an annual meeting of the American Epilepsy Society was attempting to draw a connection between damage in the eyes caused by a genetic flaw and electrochemical misfirings in the brain.

Mirelle's type of illness was called "absence seizures."

It had nothing to do with flailing limbs and frothing at the mouth. She would have a blank and distant expression, her lips would brood and grind, and her fingers would mindlessly wriggle even though she was not conscious. She was, in a way, absent.

Inside herself, she would become wavelike, as if floating on a choppy sea. The sensation was the sign that a seizure was coming. She would momentarily be shaken by the panic of breathlessness before ejecting from her body and flying off to completely unfamiliar places. There, her sudden ghostly presence would startle any persons in the realm into which she had landed. She would be like a ghost among beings living in another dimension, which was kind of cool.

But the kids at school called her a vampire, and boys would say things like, "Suck me." They did this because she wore dark glasses to protect her fragile eyes from the light and hide the palsied things they would do. They jiggled left and right and gleamed white and mirror-like if bright light hit them a certain way. Between that and the seizures, she was a target of repulsion and fear.

"My aunt exorcised me about 10 times before my mother took out a restraining order on her," Mirelle had remarked. "My ma and granny kept telling me to bide my time. They were trying to get me into the Inner Plane since I was 10. They were so afraid I'd get retarded from the epilepsy because, when you have a seizure—especially if it lasts a long time—your brain gets fried. If they hadn't thought I was special, I don't know where I'd be now." A thoughtful sadness brooded behind Mirelle's prickly composure. "They sacrificed a lot for me. They gave me up to save me."

Mirelle had described Sofia when she spoke with Professor Waite and Dr. Bruno about her childhood illness. She claimed to have seen Sofia when she was a child given to fits that ejected her from her body and into the Inner Plane. Thus, Sofia had been asked to mentor Mirelle.

It all came to light when Mirelle sought refuge with Professor Waite while trying to avoid Medea Sarin's designs on her. A week into the start of the fall semester at the secondary school, Dr. Bruno and Mirelle had stood by the big window near the staircase of the second floor corridor to observe Sofia bumbling about with her bags and books. Mirelle recognized her and was filled with pity.

"What's wrong with her?" she asked Dr. Bruno.

He shrugged with an expression that was sly and amused. "She's having a little fun," he said. "I think she's hunting."

Mirelle cringed. "Hunting for what?"

"A wild cat," Dr. Bruno said.

Mirelle didn't understand the riddle, but now she did. The wild cat was a lion cub named Leonard de Lux, the son of one of the most powerful and intimidating persons in the sovereignty. Whenever Mirelle recalled that scene, she was filled with reverence for the patient cunning of her mentor. Mostly, she felt tenderness for Sofia — and Dr. Bruno, too. Thus, she submitted to their whims even when the tasks imposed were tedious and annoying. Sofia and Dr. Bruno were kind to her. They treated her as if she had promise and as if she — a lowly immigrant — was destined to be an equal.

Mirelle's transition to the Inner Plane was arranged by a specialist who faked Mirelle's death. Mirelle's epilepsy diagnosis made it easy. "Sudden Unexpected Death in EPilepsy" — or SUDEP in short doctor-speak — was the official cause of her premature demise.

So at age 14 years, Mirelle "died" in her sleep, stricken by a seizure that lead to an arrest of breath, an inflammation of the lungs, suffocation, and death. That was how her Outer-Plane existence was covered up to move her into the Inner Plane.

Her Outer Plane schoolmates, upset by her sudden (faked) death, went through the motions of being sobered about her demise. They attended her wake to bask in the drama of it, looking weepy and remorseful as they gawked at a magical phantom of her cradled in a casket.

But Mirelle was relieved to be free of the world of Commons and the limitations it imposed on her body. And she was not lost to her loved ones forever. She could infiltrate their dreams and appear in visions, and if she applied herself to exceling in magic in the Inner Plane, she would learn how to cross planes in body as well as mind at will.

Mirelle thought of her childhood troubles when she walked along the stream in the woods. She thought about school and about relatives who shunned her, slights and abuses, all those sorts of things, but her eyesight was fine in this realm; her eyeballs hardly twitched. Their spooky washed-out color and ability to flash white light were enviable among sorcerers precisely because they seemed sinister. She had even freaked out Sofia La Maga Magus with those eyes, hadn't she?

When Mirelle did break in the course of her walking meditation training; when the thoughts became too tedious to sort through and the presence of the present stretched out like radiant space, her pace slowed and became full of her footsteps touching the loam, the smell and sway of trees, the wind and the stream, and the twists and turns of the path: the patterns of bark, the hallowed crevices, and altars of stones.

Mirelle knew she was getting somewhere with her training when Sofia stepped onto a certain flat boulder that was one of the many that sat in the stream. It was Sofia's favorite sitting rock. She would meditate there and gaze at a shallow waterfalls that lay a few yards ahead while

Mirelle kept walking.

Sofia broke the silence. "Mirelle, did you ever see the waterfall from my rock?"

Mirelle didn't know whether she was allowed to speak. The invitation—the sound of a human voice in what had been the natural quiet—seemed annoying.

Sofia gestured for Mirelle to approach. "I like to watch the mist," she said. "If you stare without blinking at the horizon where the air and water meet, your eyes make you see holes into other worlds."

Mirelle still didn't speak but gazed at where the stream narrowed and funneled over a five-foot drop and continued flowing.

"What is that thing you have in your hand?" Mirelle finally asked.

"It's a screw," Sofia replied. She showed Mirelle the widget.

"It's a nut and bolt that popped out of something," Mirelle told her.

"You think so?"

Mirelle shrugged. "It could be anything you want, I guess."

"I think it's a metaphor," Sofia grinned.

"Between Raphael Magus and the Royal Order of Sorcerers and Magi, I think you're getting screwed just fine," Mirelle quipped.

Sofia's grin grew wider so that even the part of her mouth that turned down when she smiled curled up. "Yeah," she replied, as if she liked that response.

Alan Raphael was a weasel as far as Mirelle was concerned. According to Sofia, he had gotten a "warning" from a "high sorcerer" (Dr. Bruno probably) to keep his distance, but he had been dogging-around anyway.

Everyone thought that Sofia had turned her attention away from him to a professor from the Bythos Academy,

Professor Zosimo Sortiar, but that was just friendship. Professor Zosimo was a genius and a space cadet. Some people said he had a mental disorder or maybe he was on drugs, but Mirelle thought he had everyone snookered with his kick-ass weirdo glamour.

He was tall, dark, and slender, with a thick mop of long, ratty ringlets of hair, perplexed black eyes, a goofy smile, and a wistful Italian accent. He and Sofia might've made a nice couple; they looked alike in the way well-matched couples often do.

Mirelle liked Professor Zosimo. He was a good person. He led educational workshops for Deeples and the lowlier DeeVees. He was sincere and thoughtful, even childlike. Alan Raphael Magus, on the other hand, wore a holier-than-thou blessedness in his white clothes and wordy airs that Mirelle found as effeminate as insincere. She did not think his manner was real; she thought it was a badly launched glamour. She couldn't imagine what Sofia saw in Dr. Raphael and wondered whether he had (a dick and) a different, more authentic self when he was alone with her . . . Probably not, considering Sofia had just confided that she was in the habit of meditating on a screw.

As for the Royal Order of Sorcerers and Magi, its members had been debating, from the time Sofia had received her honorary Celestus degree, about whether she was eligible for fellowship. Testy questions were being volleyed. Did her degree legitimately reflect her fitness to be a Celestial Magus? Was she genuinely rehabilitated or would she begin ticking-off patricians who did business in the Outer Plane? Would she get antsy about the treatment and rights of folk practitioners, Deeples, and DeeVees in the Inner Plane? Furthermore, besides acquiring an informal education in the Terra Mysticus and Terra Origens, what exactly had she contributed as a magical citizen of Terra Novit?

The debate had made the local news; or rather, the local news aired sound bites of the debate. The repartee typically consisted of two blowhards who verbally sparred for a moment or two when real news was either scarce or being censored just like in the Outer Plane.

Sofia never watched the news, but Mirelle had seen clips of Sofia accepting her Magus Celestus degree at least 15 times. A running footer would accompany the news clip that read such things as: "'Prodigal child'?" "But what has she done for Terra Novit lately?" or "How do you spell 'rehabilitated'?"

Dr. Raphael—out of chivalry or who knows what—got himself caught up in the debate. His face-time, during a televised news commentary, consisted of the rebuttal, "I disagree," after which he was cut off. The camera cut away to the news anchor moderating the commentary.

"It's perfectly understandable that you would defend her, considering your intimacy during college years," the news anchor said. "How lovely it must've been to reunite after more than a decade, but can you really be trusted to have an unbiased perspective on this, Dr. Raphael?"

Dr. Raphael dropped his jaw to speak when the person chosen to deliver the opposing view—a sorcerer, of course—announced that Sofia La Maga had no advanced degrees or affiliations recognized in Terra Novit except for the questionable honorary Celestus degree.

"It would give the wrong message and set a bad precedent if fellowship to the Royal Order of Sorcerers and Magi were extended to her. There's nothing more to say," the sorcerer spokesperson concluded. And there wasn't anything more to say because the anchor announced that the time was up for that section of the news.

"Doesn't that make you angry?" Mirelle asked Sofia as they dawdled on the rock in the stream and recalled the incident.

The maga shrugged.

"Sometimes I watch those things on the news to help me get my glamour on," Mirelle confessed. By her glamour she meant her nasty attitude.

"It suits you — the glamour, I mean," Sofia replied.

"You think so?"

"I always wanted to be intimidating. I figured out how to be devious instead," Sofia quietly said. She related her story about the Bengalese wise man, Prakaash Shami, who told her she would become fierce someday. She paused, seeming thought-filled. "Isn't there a word for when you fidget with objects — a doctor word?" she asked Mirelle.

"It's called 'punding,' but punding is more of a mindless habit," Mirelle replied. "People with autism and Parkinson's disease and some other problems that mess up their brain cells do it."

Sofia squinted as if vexed. "Do you think I'm doing it? With my screw, I mean."

Mirelle shrugged. "Punding is much crazier and it looks stupider than what you're doing with your nut and bolt."

"It's a metaphor," Sofia repeated quietly, almost sadly.

"It's something that makes you think of tender things. Even you," Mirelle consoled, and then she knew what going on. Sofia La Maga was in love. Mirelle suspected that she knew with whom. It was impossible and perverse, but Mirelle tried not to pass judgment. It wasn't Professor Zosimo or Dr. Raphael; it was someone else. She knew how and why these things happened and that they were far more ordinary and reasonable in their own way than they were crazy. "Maybe it puts you in touch with a thought that's full of longing that you have to work with."

Sofia nodded like a child absorbing a lesson. She thanked Mirelle and told her that she was probably going to start telling her things.

"Yes?" Mirelle asked.

Sofia paused before saying, "Magic is activated when the self is overcome by pleasure or pain, terror or bliss." She closed her eyes and stopped talking. Mirelle gazed at her for a while before growing anxious about what was to happen next.

She listened to the babble of the stream and, bored, closed her eyes. It was then that Mirelle felt Sofia's breath in her ear. The sound stretched into a nasal drone. Hitting Mirelle's heart, it made her jolt and created a flip-flopped upward feeling in her gut that rose dizzyingly upward. Inside or outside of herself, Mirelle couldn't tell, but she was facing a field of golden light from which, like movie credits, words began to scroll. She heard a chorus, made of her own voice, reciting a line from an old Hindu book called the Ashtavakra Gita:

Salutations to that which is happiness in and of itself, which is peace and illumination and upon the dawn of knowledge of which all wandering in the world becomes dreamlike.

Mirelle then disappeared into an undertow of utter absorption unlike sleep or seizure-addled loss of consciousness. She was aware, but aware of what? Not of time, space, or the relationship between one thing and another. Nor was she aware of herself. She was aware of sheer awareness.

When she came to, she heard the sound of the stream and remembered her vision. She was shocked to open her eyes to dusk light. Her body shuddered from the damp cold. She was alone and mildly concerned about how to get home. She wasn't yet practiced in translocation. She wondered whether she could bear the chill all night and whether she could retreat back into her mind.

She heard thrashing over leaves. She thought it was an

animal in a rut, but it was Sofia running toward her with a quilt in her arms. She cloaked it over Mirelle.

"That was a long nap," she exclaimed. "Did you go anywhere?"

"I disappeared," Mirelle muttered bewildered.

"Did you meet anyone?" Sofia asked.

Mirelle shook her head and looked puzzled. Then, with her nose and eyes pierced by prickles—the kind that come before tears--she finally blubbered, "Why don't you remember me?"

"The little vampire-girl who used to visit me when I was holed up in caves in Nepal?" Sofia quipped.

"I'm NOT a vampire," Mirelle exclaimed in a flood of tears, which were really tears of relief now that the truth about her connection to Sofia La Maga was completely out.

"Oh, no, no, no, Sweetness. I was just teasing," Sofia cried. She took Mirelle into her arms. "You were a goddess. I always thought you were—and you are."

"Why is life like this?" Mirelle whined.

"What is it to wake up from the idea of yourself?" Sofia asked cryptically.

Mirelle kind of knew what Sofia was asking, but didn't know how to reply.

Sofia told her that the realization she was in the throes of felt bad at first but would become freeing and sweet. "You're upset because the dream was no fun, and you're still startled by it and angry for having had it. It's natural."

Mirelle took a deep breath and felt greatly reassured. Indeed, things felt very loose and light, almost unfamiliar. They were glowing even though it was the gloomy night.

"Do you know how to get back in the dark?" Mirelle asked Sofia.

"Maybe," she replied. Sofia gripped a corner of Mirelle's quilt so that the girl would be in tow. She began singing a song in Hindi or some such foreign tongue. Her tone was lullaby-like at first and then, as they followed the rivulet back through the descending darkness, it became hollering, accompanied by the jangle of her old bone-rattle staff, as if to keep scary things away.

VIII
The Sun

Leonard was anxious. It would be the first time he was to sit for meditation with his mentor. He wanted to shout to the world and boldly in his father's face and in the faces of all his rotten, derelict, ex-friends that he was under the wing of the infamous folkie abomination, Sofia La Maga.

He felt privileged and special. He wasn't sure whether not being able to tell another living soul about his circumstance made it more special or irrelevant. He wondered, nearly obsessively, about what people would think when the truth finally came out. He hoped to someday be the center of gossip like Sofia and Dr. Bruno were.

Unfortunately, Leonard would not be alone with his mentor during meditation practice. He had to share Sofia with that girl, Mirelle, who *did* turn out to be a Commons immigrant—a Deeple. Leonard was sworn to secrecy about it. Consorting with immigrants was considered defiling for someone of Leonard's social class. The forbidden-ness of what he was doing was so better than any Phaeton maneuver match. Still, Leonard wished he had Sofia all to himself.

She had spent weeks into months going over Leonard's sorcery practices, his general school work, everything that had gone cockeyed in the past 16 years of his life. Catching up left little time to go forward.

While Sofia was managing that with Leonard, she was forcing Mirelle to meditate for long hours daily. The girl was completely pissed off about this at first, but then she got into it. Having come from the world of Commons, she was impatient about magical training. That's what Leonard thought. Maybe she thought she had a handle on things because her family was into some kind of half-baked Commons sorcery. But having entered the Inner Plane . . . . well, now she was facing the real deal. All of her paradigms had to be overturned, and she had to be very humble. Leonard would have told her that, but he feared Sofia would get mad at him for flexing his patrician muscle on the girl.

Sofia must've decided that Mirelle had gotten somewhere in her practices very quickly, though, because arrangements had been made for her to gain entry into immigration camps and even prisons to counsel people there. Her official title for this work was Place Adjuster. To say she was a Place Adjuster was just a frilly, less snotty way of saying that her job was to keep people in place and adjust their attitudes in a way different from, say, a staff bearer.

Transplanes immigration was a major social mess. New immigrants were always getting into trouble because they refused to know or keep their place. In their drive for empowerments and magical mysteries, they tended to become the pawns of psychopathic wingnuts like Medea Sarin Sortiar.

Like the Devil, Sarin and her kind promised these hapless ex-Commons dominion over the world if they would serve them. All they got for their efforts was a criminal record. In fact, the parts of prisons reserved for characters receiving the Lock Penalty for their crimes were overwhelmingly filled with immigrants, like Mirelle. Some facilities were so overloaded that the folks running them were supposedly stacking the inmates on top of each other instead of storing them in personal, tomb-like vaults.

Leonard's dad had never toured such hellish horrors or considered intervening to stop them. He thought that uppity misbehaving immigrants got their just desserts in the Lock Penalty, so he was a hard-ass with bleeding-heart Expansionist Party members and their programs to "fix" things.

Rather than subsidize educational programs like the ones Professor Zosimo Sortiar hosted or else fund more Place Adjuster outreach, the consul's solution, driven by the Conservationist Party, was to build special facilities, resembling warehouses, to store the surplus of people doing Lock-Penalty time. Other efforts included the tightening of immigration laws and the nearly daily passage of some new rule about what an ex-Commons was and wasn't allowed to do or become.

They didn't know what they were getting themselves into when they crossed over. If they didn't fall into mischief as the gremlin of some dark sorcerer until time caught up with them, they became the servants, toys, or tools, or, if they were very lucky, the life-long junior apprentices and assistants of ordinary magical persons.

But Sofia was not treating Mirelle in this way. She was treating her as a regular apprentice, complete with the special community-service job of "adjusting" people like herself. Still, it took a while for Mirelle to figure out how really privileged she was—at least that was how Leonard saw it.

When she was her relaxed self, she was kind of fun to be around. She even had a sense of humor—and interacting with her was cool and edgy for Leonard precisely because he was in no way supposed to be interacting with a Deeple. But when she was in class or going about her public business, she was icy and sharp. Leonard figured that she was trying to be dark and edgy, like most other magical persons her age were trying to be.

She rarely spoke or looked at Leonard in class, especially if his father was in attendance. It was not proper of her to be addressing high-ranking patricians, even if she was La Maga Magus's teaching assistant. When she did address Leonard in that setting, she was sharp and direct and looked past him when she spoke. Leonard would try to make her laugh in class, but he had yet to succeed.

Having arrived at The Magistrar, Leonard parked his Vespa in Sofia's parking space, fitting it tightly behind the tiny black hatchback she got around in. Then he snuck past security (just for the heck of it) to get into the building.

The Magistrar was a tall, cylindrical tower where everyone lived in the round. A quarter of a pie. That was the size that made up Sofia's unit. It was on the seventh floor and had a west northwest exposure. It was one of the less desirable units because it didn't provide a good view of the moon. Nevertheless, the view of the sunset was particularly charming. Golden light spewed through lead glass, rearranged shadows, and then warmly dimmed.

It was a duplex that consisted of a loggia below which was the rest of the apartment: a living room, kitchen, sun room, studio, and secret chamber behind the kitchen where magic and mysticism were practiced. The loggia; that is, a structure like a large, indoor balcony, was Sofia's sleeping space. Its outer wall was lined with thin, horizontal stained glass panels placed high near a ceiling of rafters. Squat book shelves, low tables and cabinets, and giant pillows were strategically positioned for a person who was either a midget or intended sit on the floor or lie down a lot. A thin mattress was austerely placed on the wood panel floor. From the loggia, was a view of the living room where, directly above the entrance to the apartment, was a display of antique weapons arranged in a great, big circle: swords and daggers, hatchets, tridents, clubs, and spears. The weapons corresponded with those in the hands of a dozen statues of weapon-wielding goddesses that were on display throughout the apartment.

The kitchen was situated directly below the loggia. A small sunroom was on one side of the kitchen, and a studio full of books and curios that Sofia had collected from her travels was on the other side. Behind the kitchen, was a secret chamber. It, too, was an austere room full of shelves that stored scriptures and magic books, mandalas, and yantras; statuettes; prayer beads and shawls; candles, resins, herbs, oils, lustral waters; cloths of various colors; the weapons of magic: swords, wands, daggers, staffs, patens, goblets, crystals; and bones of men and beasts as well as claws, hooves, and horns.

When Leonard got to her door, he noted how heavy the air was with the aroma of sandalwood, galangal, and cinnamon. It was the incense leeching from Sofia's apartment. He thought to knock but the door clicked open. Leonard lifted his arm to shield his eyes from radiant light leeching from what was inside. He gently pushed on the door and entered. Sofia and Mirelle were sitting on cushions amidst the goddess statues. Mirelle was emitting a plain golden light and Sofia was sitting in a phantasmagoric spectral mandala of luminous archetypal structures and letters and glyphs.

A cushion lay to Sofia's right on which a thin, silken shawl was folded. Leonard wrapped the cloth around his shoulders and sat on the cushion. He tried to "be" where the women were in their meditative poise, but he was mostly distracted by Sofia's incensey body smell. It and her buzzy energy tugged at his groin. Eventually though, when he relaxed into it, he was swept away into a strange but intoxicating stillness. All he sensed was the billow of his breath. It felt like warm chocolate brownies in the way totally mismatched things seem somehow the same in dreams.

They sat for more than an hour, but it seemed like no time. Then Sofia dissolved her galactic mandala. The room dimmed into mid-evening. Mirelle yawned and stretched; she lit dim lights and served tea while assembling a meal made of things that could've been foraged: asparagus, mushrooms, wild leeks, and fern heads.

Mirelle put a heap of quinoa in everyone's plate. She topped the mound with the vegetable sauté. A platter of batter-fried squash blossoms and cauliflower florets, smelling of crunch and lemon and salty cheese, was near Sofia. She pushed it and plates of olives and a white-bean mash to the center of the table and poured wine that was so purple it stained Leonard's teeth and left a mustache on his upper lip.

Mirelle placed her hand over her glass when Sofia went to fill it. "It messes with my meditative glow," she said.

Sofia grimaced and mocked her. She and Mirelle snickered, but no one spoke much at first. It was serene, eating food that could have been plucked from the wilds and drinking country wine from tall water glasses. If Leonard's father could have seen him, he would have been appalled but by what Leonard wasn't sure.

"Do you know what a siren is, Leonard?" the man announced when he learned that Leonard's academic transformation (at least) was on account of Sofia's influence. "A siren is a creature of feminine mien that seduces men with wisdom of such caliber that they are stupefied and waste away." Then he recited a passage from Homer's Odyssey:

Now pay attention to what I will say.
Heaven itself will make you remember it.
First, you will come to the Sirens who enchant all who near.
For the man who unwarily comes too close
and hears the Sirens' song,
He is never welcomed home by wife and offspring again.
For those Sirens sit in a green field

And, with the sweetness of their song,
serenade that man to death.
Indeed, there lies a mighty heap of dead men's bones
With flesh still rotting on them.

"The Siren maneuver is a malicious ruse perpetrated by a sorceress with an ax to grind about men," Leonard's father bitterly claimed as if speaking from experience. "She'll give you teaching you can neither grasp nor apply and through it, coordinate your ruin . . . teaching you can neither grasp nor apply . . . Remember that, Leonard."

Leonard's dad acted as if he were annoyed even though he should've been glad that Leonard was catching up. But then, Leonard had overheard his father tell Bertrand's dad that Professor La Maga's intercession was nothing more than a perverse magian ruse to shame the consul for otherwise having reared a troublesome moron. A *moron.* That's what Leonard's father had called him . . . .

After a while, Sofia and Mirelle began to chat in a jaunty, sing-song. They were mostly agreeing with each other's observations, suspicions, and snide remarks about other people. Leonard never thought Mirelle was so chatty or that she and Sofia were so chummy. He also thought it strange that they were so catty.

"How's your 'meditative glow,' Lenny? Waned yet?" Sofia remarked. *"C'mon, I need a drinking buddy."* She splashed more wine into the youth's glass. Then she and Mirelle cracked up because Leonard had a wine-stain mustache.

"A picture of this would make good blackmail," Mirelle quipped. She made a nasty comment about him and Kestrel Silvestri. "You could do so much better than her, Lenny. Jeez-Louise. Pining over that pris."

"Len could have any girl he wants," Sofia remarked.

"He could have every girl all at once. Yeah, right,"

Mirelle cackled.

"He likes those girly-girly types, just like his daddy," Sofia said bitterly. "With their beauty-shop hair-dos and matching accessories."

"So Commons," Mirelle snipped.

"I don't know why my father doesn't like you, Sof'," Leonard said. (He didn't know why or how that slipped out. He actually had a message for Sofia from his father. He was too ashamed about what he had just said to say what he was supposed to.)

Sofia and Mirelle gaped at him. Then Sofia nudged Mirelle and said, "When I took him on, I specifically told him not to tell anyone that I did, because I'm gonna' get my head cut off if anyone finds out. Right? So who does he rush off to tell?"

"Kestrel Silvestri," Mirelle replied.

Sofia nodded.

"That little bitch," Mirelle griped as if Kestrel—not Leonard—were at fault.

"But instead of getting a blow job for it, he got blown off," Sofia announced.

Mirelle apparently thought this news was incredibly funny. She smacked her hand on the table and laughed in huge, snorting, and unattractive guffaws.

Sofia had risen from her chair and, in drunken ebullience, hugged Leonard. "But you're adorable! I LOVE you!" she told him.

There was more irreverent banter to the effect that Leonard would be better off making time with Thetis Mirabilis, but then Sofia voiced concerns about such a pairing. She said, soberly now, that she was going to initiate Thetis into apprenticeship very soon.

"It would be too close for comfort. The two of them would be all distracted during their practices. Why don't you like her, Lenny? She's kind of goofy when she's not in class," she blurted. "You like me, and I'm just as weird as she is."

Yeah. Leonard knew that Thetis was goofy when she wasn't being an egg-head and apple-polisher in class. And she was just as "weird" as Sofia La Maga because she was trying too hard to be Sofia La Maga. It was obnoxious. Maybe initiation would straighten her out. He wasn't going to get into it with Sofia and Mirelle. He remained silent.

"You know, if I were 16 years old, he wouldn't give me the time of day, this one," Sofia complained. "He'd be scorning me and calling me things like 'Sofia The Maggot.'"

"I'd NEVER say that!" Leonard loudly protested, even though that was what Bertrand Solaris (and Leonard at first) was calling Thetis. Bertrand and the other boys started out calling the girl "Sofia La Maguette," but that name very quickly slurred into "Sofia the Maggot."

Sofia pointed a finger. "I know you made her cry the other day because you told her that she *wasn't* me." She pursed her eyebrows and growled, *"What-the-fuck was that about?"*

Leonard's jaw dropped. Sofia had turned on a dime. She was scolding him and even using expletive deletives. Without comment and as if brooding, she retired to the kitchen to rattle around with pans and cabinets like a wife in a tiff. Mirelle jumped from her seat to get in gear about clearing the table. Leonard slowly rose, waiting for a directive.

"Don't be running off anywhere. I have a new practice for you," Sofia hotly told him.

Leonard sulked. He wasn't sure how things got so sour so quickly. Sofia told Mirelle not to fuss in the kitchen. "Just leave it," she insisted in a bothered tone.

Mirelle quickly grabbed her jacket and knapsack and, with a sneer, unkindly quipped, "Good night and good luck,'" as she intentionally slammed the door behind her.

Quiet time passed. It was long. Leonard realized that the time was for reflection. Sofia had plopped into a lounge chair near where he stood staring at the door.

"What was that all about?" he finally said.

"All what?" Sofia questioned in a tone that was her regular self.

"All that fucking up the 'meditative glow'—and grilling me about Mirabilis. I know I shouldn't have done what I did, but I was putting her in her place. And I'm not going with her," he insisted. "I don't need a *you* substitute."

Sofia blushed about that. It made Leonard bold.

"I didn't like that thing at dinner between you and Mirelle," he said. "I don't know what the big teaching in all that was supposed to be for me. Like: Don't react to guff from Deeples or maybe just don't get drunk and be an asshole?"

"Just having a little fun," she replied.

"Really? It's not right for her to act that way," he insisted.

"It's very right. Understand what is happening," she replied, but Leonard hadn't a vague glimmer about what she was babbling about.

"Know what?" he said. "I'm waiting for when you and me are going to have a little 'fun,' seeing how obsessed you are about my—and my father's—sex lives. I don't want to be passed off on Thetis," Leonard announced. "You know what I want."

"That would be incestuous," she said.

That caught Leonard off guard. He didn't know what the come-back to that was or what it possibly meant.

"Yes, yes," she clucked as if she was now just gently amused about what he had said. "Do you know why the world has treated you so badly up 'til now?" she asked.

Leonard rolled his eyes to hide that he was utterly mortified by her reaction to his advances.

"It's because you're good and the world isn't," Sofia said.

"Yeah, well, that's not what my father tells me," Leonard shot back.

"You're a threat to how it operates," Sofia continued. "What does the world do with threats? It does its best to destroy them right out of the box. Some people take it and say, 'the world screwed me over so I'm going to screw it back hard.' Some people think they must've deserved their hard luck because of something they did that they can't remember and that maybe happened when they were a different person in a distant past. They spend their lives putting up and shutting up and trying to figure out how to not be bitter about it.

"Other persons," she continued, "regard their experiences as ways to help them realize the plight of the human condition. These folks have big hearts. They have empathy, compassion, keen perception, and they know the difference between being a nice person and being good one. They realize that the grand illusion of life is pain and that the reality behind the illusion is gratitude and joy."

Leonard didn't know where Sofia was going with all this. Because he was expected to respond, he rambled about how much he had changed after his Pyr Sacra empowerment. He said that before it occurred, he was groping around a world where everything was a big "whatever." Aimless with no wherewithal for forethought.

His empowerment was a door. It opened to a light that burned up monsters. Everything was mostly clear and easy now, he said. He didn't feel mean or spiteful toward anyone anymore — not really. He felt moved by the angst he saw oppressing others (like his father, for instance — or Thetis trying to "be" Sofia, or Sofia and Mirelle getting catty over dinner, even). He could see where it came from as if he could see a string of causes and effects reaching to the beginning of time. He could see that the momentum was grounded in hapless and arbitrary circumstance. Nevertheless, he felt something very tender and manly for Sofia. But what could he do about it?

Sofia nodded reassuringly without further comment. She led him through the studio full of books and oddities to her hidden magical room. They sat on the cushions and faced each other. Only a small candle and city lights glowing through stained glass panels illuminated the room. Leonard closed his eyes and waited for whatever Sofia intended to do to him.

He smelled her; he felt her. He couldn't resist fantasizing that she had embraced him. He felt the luxurious kiss and the excitement of attained conquest. Her straddling him. Him locking his eyes into hers. She giving in to his violently ardent caresses. He startled when he penetrated her in his vivid imagination. A rush went straight to the head on top of his neck instead of the one between his thighs. Then he felt as if he were expanding and gliding and full of delectably fiery juice.

His eyes shot open. Sofia was not on him. He was not in her. They were sitting on cushions each in their own place. She blushed and snickered and motioned for him to close his eyes again.

Leonard braced himself for more sexy images, but nothing like that happened. He felt two fingertips tap his breastbone and heard a sweetly sonorous droning sound. A tiny gold seed emerged in his inner vision out of which little glyphs of Sanskrit, Greek, Hebrew, and Orphanic words and letters popped along with symbols of angels and planets. Sofia touched Leonard low on the abdomen near the root of his cock but instead of getting hot, he felt radiant. The droning got deep and howling like an autumn's gale wind. More glyphs from sacred garlands of letters emerged in his mind and began to arrange themselves in a complex multidimensional polygon that enveloped him and was him as much as it was the vast Cosmos. Every place that he felt Sofia's fingers tap as they ascended up the column of his body released a glowing seed of unique sounds, words, symbols, and calling cards that shot out into web-like lines and planes of a hyperpolygonal shape that was the container of Reality.

Sofia uttered a passage from an ancient Hindu scripture called the *Brihadaranyaka Upanishad*: "'As a spider moves along its thread, and as glowing embers fly out in all directions from a fire, so from the Self emanate all forms, all worlds, all gods, and all beings. Its secret name is The Truth of Truth.' Now you know it," she said.

Upon hearing it, everything in Leonard lit up as if another Pyr Sacra empowerment had been ignited. He felt vast and small, grand and tender. He glimpsed the transparency and interconnectedness of all things and approached the realization of his true essential nature.

He sat rather poised in that for an hour. When he emerged from it, Sofia was gone. He meandered through her apartment to find her huddled in blankets in a giant green bean chair in a drafty alcove adjacent to her kitchen that was full of leafy tropical plants. It was her sun room. A small stained glass lamp dangled from a chain attached to a ceiling rafter. She was drinking port and eating warm flourless chocolate cake. It was about 10 o'clock.

When Leonard approached her, he placed his hand on her head.

"It's normal for apprentices to have erotic feelings for their teachers," she said. "It's only natural, but it's best to leave it to the realm of dreams. Do you understand what I'm saying?'

"You don't want to have sex with me," Leonard said flatly.

"Yeah, well, Danny Bruno never laid a finger on me,

either," she remarked in bitter commiseration. "It made me feel rotten, especially because he was such a rake. But we had a little chat, too, he and I. And I'm more intimate with Danny than anyone he's ever stuck it in, apprentice or not. I can do all the great and nasty things he's ever done if and whenever I want. No one knows that," she grinned. "He loves me intensely, like blood."

"My Dad always suspected you had something going on with Bruno," Leonard grinned. "I promise not to wreck the big mystery."

Sofia flexed her eyebrows and impishly smiled as if she and Leonard had just shared yet another sinister secret. Then she asked whether he was feeling okay after coming back from his flight into the Ground of Being.

"Superbly mellow," he said.

She gave a little nod and smooth smile. "Well, now you're my lineage-holder, honey-bunny — my spiritual child, my son," she said. "That makes Dr. Bruno your magical grandpa. How would Daddy feel about that?"

Before Leonard could comment, Sofia stressed that he (technically) could do what she could and that, instead of being a rake and a juggler like Bruno — or a mean and brittle bastard like his father — he should be a healer and a savior.

"I want you to be my solar deity," she said. "My *sun*."

Leonard blinked. It was a tall order. "Alright," he said.

Sofia got up and readied herself for Leonard's departure. She doused him with a protection charm for the ride home and loaded him up with a bag of home-baked biscuits, the leftover squash-blossom fritters and nuggets of fried cauliflower, a tin of tea, a wand that she had made, a bag of magically charmed gems, and various other trinkets and edibles. Then she added a bottle of wine to the bag. "For your father," she said pointedly.

"He's inviting you to a party he's having — my father,"

Leonard finally blurted. That was what Leonard was supposed to tell Sofia.

"Really?"

Leonard shrugged. It was true. "You can invite your tutor," de Lux senior had quietly told him while speaking with Lady Poinsett about the event.

"I didn't say anything about it 'til now 'cause you seem pretty mad at him," Leonard said.

"I'm not mad at him," Sofia shrugged. "I'm frustrated." She reached into the air and materialized a bouquet of yellow tulips. "You can give this to Daddy, too."

Leonard took the bouquet and told Sofia that he would see her in his dreams. Then he went off to pollute the peace of night with the putter and zip of his Vespa.

He sped away from the state houses and the nearby H. Trismegistus academic complex and carried on though the suburbs and into the winding, hilly roads of the patrician neighborhoods of sprawling lawns and mansions guarded by formidable iron gates and stone walls.

His father was perched on the turret of his tower when Leonard arrived home. *"'Do not give your soul to a woman for her to trample on your strength,'"* the man announced as Leonard walked up the drive.

"That's a good one, Dad," Leonard quipped. "Ecclesiastes nine, two."

"You weren't with that woman all this time 'getting tutored,' were you, Leonard? Is that the new name for it among young people these days?"

Leonard pulled the wine bottle from his satchel and hollered, "The 'woman' told me to give you this. She crushed the grapes with her very own feet so it should be . . . whatever . . . ."

Leonard plunked the bottle along with the yellow tulips onto a small stone table in a garden area at the front of the house. He proceeded in the direction opposite his father's tower toward the rounding of a corner that would lead to the entrance of his own wing of the home.

"Is she coming?" Leo's voice anxiously echoed.

"Yeah, yeah," Leonard muttered but hardly and slunk around the bend.

IX
Elephants, Eagles, and Crocodiles

On the night of the soiree, Sofia arrived at the house clad in the red elephant, eagle, and crocodile shift that she had worn for the first day of class. Her outfit was embellished with amulets and ornamental ritual weapons.

She brought Leo two bottles of wine. He graciously accepted them, remarking that the previous sample was "exceptional." Leonard watched his father smile with warmth and hospitality as he led the professor into the courtyard. Heads turned, especially those of the ladies, who gave Sofia a once-over. They muttered among themselves about who she was, how Leo had despised her, and why she was in his house now.

Sofia's face lit up when she recognized Leonard sitting has he had been that night his father came upon him after his Pyr Sacra empowerment. "Butterflies at night?" she grinned.

"My son's mere presence wakes them. Did you teach him that trick?" Leo asked.

"I don't think so," Sofia replied. "It looks kind of girly. *Leonard*," she hollered across the room. "What *is* that?" She waved her hand around to mean the butterfly swarm that had enveloped him.

The youth shrugged and briefly incandesced, which he had been doing a lot—mostly involuntarily, since his Pyr Sacra empowerment.

"I don't think he's doing it on purpose," she assured Leo. "But he has been giving off a very bright light, hasn't he?" She winced as if perplexed.

"You've noticed as well?" Leo muttered.

Sofia inquired about one of Leonard's troublesome friends. She stuttered recalling the student's name. "You know . . . The one who dropped the class."

"Bertrand Solaris," Leo grunted.

"Yes. That one." Sofia mirrored Leo's disdain.

"He seems to be out of the picture. The overwhelming majority of Leonard's associates these days seem to be ladies — young . . . and grown," Leo said.

"Well, he's a nice-looking boy," Sofia exclaimed.

Leo did not know how to respond. A pause ensued before he turned his attention to Sofia's attire.

"You have an interesting sense of style, La Maga Magus." He coaxed her to pirouette. "Lovely. Is that an 'athame' you have in your belt?"

She blushed. "I don't know if I should unsheathe it here. It's a stiletto. Fifteenth century." The grip of the dagger was a twist of a dark wood and gold. "Maybe one day you can see my collection. I think you'd appreciate the pieces."

"Ritual weapons," Leo mused. His ice-blue eyes glistened with fascination. He eked out a subtle laugh and assumed the attitude of someone unexpectedly pleased. "Leonard mentioned something about a wall in your apartment."

"My collection," Sofia nodded.

"And how do you collect weapons without a means of income? I mean," he faltered, "with minimal means while in hiding all those years. You were a bit of an anchorite, weren't you?"

"Well, I wasn't a nun," she blurted.

"I'm just saying," he stuttered.

"Some were gifted; some materialized — things have a habit of materializing in the Mysticus" she jabbered, "and I wasn't completely without funds . . . so . . . ."

"So you did have support in your time away," Leo

acknowledged.

"My family — and I had a benefactor," she said.

Leo paused and wryly smiled. Others had eared in on the conversation. He scoffed: "Raphael Magus supported his sister through school and you while in hiding?"

"What a guy," the interlopers chuckled.

"No, not exactly," Sofia muttered.

"Well, who is he?" a woman questioned, hardly knowing about what she was asking. She turned to Leo as if awestruck, "Is she the maga — the folkie one from the Mysticus?"

"Which mage took you under his wing, La Maga Magus? You must know that this has been an intriguing topic for some time," Leo said.

"He's a high sorcerer," Sofia boasted.

"I knew it," Leo exclaimed victoriously. Hangers-on muttered "Bruno." Leo winced. Despite satisfaction, his tic-like facial feature was tinged with acidity. "And what else is he? I've always wanted to know," he asked.

"He's been my mentor for the past 20 years," Sofia uttered.

Leo smirked as if vindicated but not appeased. *"But do you screw him?"* he wanted to say, but contained himself. "Your mentor," he mused instead, because he was alighting on the implications and glaring at Sofia.

Leonard then approached, grasped her sleeve, and yanked her away.

"Where are you taking her, Leonard?" his father called.

"I want to show her something," the youth replied.

They escaped into Leonard's private quarters. Leonard showed Sofia his electronics and how they all worked. He pointed out how the ceiling of his studio glowed and revealed the case of dark Belgian ale that he had stolen from the party. Sofia was pleased. She liked dark Belgian ale — with flourless chocolate cake, she said.

Leonard showed her his cone snail shell collection and also how he understood the alchemical metaphors about metals. He made a small holographic display of a Phaeton maneuver match, with a tiny replica of himself as the star-player. Because the ceiling in his studio was high enough, he showed Sofia how well he could fly. Then he begged her to bilocate to check out his father's dungeon and talk to him about it at the same time, but she wouldn't do it.

They settled into drinking the ale and headily discussing whether God was impersonal or not and whether It was a function or an entity.

Lady Poinsett rapped on the door: "Your father wants you and your guest to join the rest, Leonard. You and the professor. Come out of there."

Sofia tousled her hair and pulled at the shirt beneath her shift to appear suggestively disheveled. She sidled past the housekeeper. The woman cringed. Sofia winked.

Comically but not without brittle annoyance, Leo was explaining to one of Leonard's aunts that the youth had been sequestered in his room with his grown-woman teacher for most of the evening. "Here he is," he seethed and glowered at the boy. Sofia followed, saying, "He was showing me stuff."

"Yes. Well, the size of Leonard's 'stuff' gets bigger every day," Leo remarked.

A wide, giggly grin broke out on Sofia's face. It made Leonard laugh. Leo was unnerved, although the caliber of their giddiness suggested that nothing exceptionally provocative had gone on between them. He fumbled but went on to lead Sofia to a trio of ladies: Patricia Whitehead Magus, Ceres Pagano Sortiar, and Cosmina Noumen Magus.

"I was told you were quite stylish," Lady Pagano said and grasped a handful of the skirt of Sofia's shift. "This is gorgeous. Frayed, but eloquent."

"I've collected some interesting things in my travels," Sofia remarked. She told the women that her shift was a gift that was handmade. "The embroidery refers to a Hindu myth that I find meaningful. Well, actually, it's the prayer that mentions the myth. I always cry when I say it."

The ladies glanced at each other as if the admission were adorable and quaint.

"And what are these creatures on your dress?" Lady Whitehead inquired and waved to Leo and a man who seemed to be Mister Whitehead. "Come and listen. The maga is going to tell us a story about her dress."

"Alright then. Let's see it in color—the story, I mean. Leo, you're the expert," the gentleman said.

"An illustrated tale?" Leo mused.

"Do you want to see Leonard do it?" Sofia smiled. "Lenny. Come here," she anxiously chanted.

A group converged around Sofia and Leonard in the center of the patio to hear the story.

"Okay. Now make it nice. Nothing cheesy, Leonard," Sofia said.

"First tell us what these creatures are, La Maga Magus—the ones on your dress," Lady Noumen requested.

Sofia answered, "Elephants, eagles, and crocodiles." Then she began: "Once, there was an elephant."

With a fidget of fingers, Leonard created a handsome-looking, scaled down elephant, the size of a chair. It had big, winnowing ears and long, thick tusks and was floating in space.

"We need an Indian elephant. That one's African," Sofia said. "Sorry, Lenny."

The ears had to shrink, and the tusks had to be much thinner although Sofia told Leonard that they could longer and curly.

"Make the scene junglely with a watering hole," she instructed.

The elephant began to plod in place while the flora within the courtyard grew denser and more enveloping. The creature reared its trunk and let out a squeak.

"So, once there was an elephant," she stuttered again, with her usual goofy bravado. "And it went to go soak in a lake when a humongous crocodile—not an alligator, Leonard, a *crocodile*—caught the elephant's leg in its jaws."

The ladies screamed. A creature heretofore resembling a rock jumped out and gripped the elephant's right hind leg. Bellowing and thrashing began. The ruckus spilled beyond the magical mirage's boundaries, causing the walls and pillars within the courtyard of the de Lux villa to shudder and the trees to bend and sway. Quelled swamp water doused everyone and made a mess.

"*Good show, Leonard!*" the impressed guests cried. They blotted their mussed hair and attire.

"The crocodile was going to drag the elephant under and have a tasty meal, but in that moment, as the elephant faced its death, it remembered that, in a past life, it was a human king who was very devoted to the Divine Pervading Principle of the Universe, Lord Vishnu. I'll do that one, Lenny," Sofia interjected and went on: "The elephant prayed to Lord Vishnu but nothing happened. So then he prayed again, and nothing, 'cause gods are like that."

The thrashing and splashing, rumbling and roar continued with heightened violence. Sofia hollered her story above it: "Finally, just as the elephant was about to be overcome by the crocodile, its heart filled with the desire for redemption, nearly with its last breath, it called out one last time to the Divine Lord of the Universe. Then, the deity finally showed up, wafting around on his mighty giant eagle."

With hands swirling in the air, Sofia materialized an image of a white eagle astride which was a handsome pale blue deity bejeweled, garlanded, and clad in orange-yellow fabric. A pack of arrows was strapped to his back. With his four arms, he held a conch shell, a discus, a gilded club, and an ornate archer's bow.

The eagle and the deity placidly soared in loops overhead that Leo—inspired—doctored into a luminously endless galactic sky. Indeed, he had obscured the boundaries of the courtyard with a wave of his hand to create a jungle. Startling caws of birds and small primates, moisture, heat, and smells of musk, detritus, exotic flora, and loam enveloped the audience. Wild creatures lurked in the distance.

"Although on the brink death, the elephant plucked a lotus from the lake and held it aloft as an offering to the deity," Sofia continued. "Acknowledging the gesture, Lord Vishnu whirled his discus to stun the crocodile. He dismounted his eagle, and—this should be good, Len—grasping the crocodile's jaws, he tore the creature apart."

Guts spattered across the room and doused all who were near. Squeals, grunts, and laughter resounded.

Quietly amused, Sofia wiped her forehead and picked bloody bits of grizzle from her hair. Lord Vishnu, spotless despite the grisly conquest, flew on his eagle into the sky's galactic radiance. The elephant, showered in flowers, trumpeted and kneeled. Sofia recited the last stanza of a prayer:

"In the early morning, I praise that great god who holds the conch and the discus with which he tore apart the crocodile to relieve the elephant's great distress. He who removes all fear, him I praise so that the sins committed by me in previous births may be destroyed."

Sofia placed her hands over her face because the words still made her cry.

"That was very sweet," the ladies said. The men

heartily applauded and pat Leo on the back because his son was so clever.

Fortunately for all, Leo was as expert in dissolving thought-forms as he was in creating them, so clean-up was easy. Blood and guts and swamp sludge dissolved. The guests tidied whatever else had gotten disheveled. It was all a lot of fun.

It was in the early hours of morning when the party thinned. Leonard lurked in the doorway while his father walked Sofia out past the front patio. "That was A LOT of fun, Lord Consul," he heard her say.

"No need to be formal, Lady La Maga — Sofia," Leo replied. He paused and quietly muttered that the attention and progress she had made with his son were "remarkable. I often wonder what the motive is. I . . ." his voice dropped off as if at a loss for words.

"Leonard is great," Sofia exclaimed. "He's got so much going on. He just needs . . . He needs someone to know him. Let him shine. I don't think he ever had the opportunity so things got strange," she stuttered. "I think he could have a lot of power. I think he has a lot of power." A moist-eyed sentimentality arrested her face.

"You're the key-holder. You would know," Leo sighed.

She thanked him again and started on her way.

But a thought needled him as he watched her depart. "La Maga Magus," Leo uttered. His voice turned sharp. "Did you give that boy the Pyr Sacra Empowerment?"

A lull ensued. Sofia lost her voice. Leo put his hand to head as if massaging a pain. "All these revelations this evening, Lady La Maga."

"It's...what it is," the maga muttered and backed away.

Leo exhaled weightily as if to empty the burdensome storage of air in his lungs. (Bruno, he fumed. Dealings with him were always peppered with a vile and spiteful twist.)

"The audacity!" he exclaimed. A big staff popped from nowhere into his grip. He watched the maga startle. Her posture sunk. Despite the dark, Leo could see that her lips were pursed as if something bitter had been forced on her.

Leo nodded slightly without words to speak. He inhaled, again with a sound like a gasp and said, "Do not move, La Maga Magus. I promise not to hurt you right now."

He examined her. He did so perhaps in the way that she had examined Leonard on that first day of class when she had asked him to look her in the eye. Leo glanced back toward a rhododendron that was buttressed near the main entrance of the house. It was a sight unseen, but Leo was fairly certain that Leonard was lurking there. Leo glared in that direction until he was satisfied that the youth knew that his presence was no secret.

He approached the maga. "Yellow tulips," he scoffed. A thick bed of them sprouted and bloomed around her. Leo trammeled those in his path as he neared. "'Hopeless love.' I wouldn't have thought your choice of flowers was deliberate had I not seen how efficiently you dispensed with your lovely bouquet of basil, hellebore, and what-not on that first day of class. You have an amusing and flip sense of humor. It's one of the reasons I've grown tired of being ill-disposed toward you, frankly," Leo shrugged.

"And why should I act dismayed about your latest transgression? It was so predictably obvious that you would violate my son as an expression of your 'hopeless fondness' for me." The words were drenched in biting sarcasm. "As if it were all that simple," he griped and added bitterly, "Why you?"

"He asked me," Sofia whispered.

"Who? Bruno Sortiar?" Leo snorted. "It wouldn't have been the first time he's manipulated your messianic inanity, thrown you to the wolf pack, and treated you like a piece of meat—but it might be the last time."

"Leonard asked me," she confessed.

"How dare you," Leo grimaced coolly. "You *seduced* him, and now you're *blaming* him."

"Blaming him for what?" Sofia gasped. "He's a top-grade student instead of a 'moron.' Overnight. You're welcome. I guess giving the kid back his brain and soul spoiled him for *Hipparchus Gorgon.* Did I fuck things up or what, Lord Consul?" Tears began to ooze from her eyes and her nose got runny. Her left hand was rigidly folded into a gesture meant to avert the "evil eye." Her right hand seemed poised to summon a weapon.

Leo stopped himself from further comment. He placed his hand on the maga's folkie hand gesture. Gripping it firmly and with a gentle twist, he drew it up into the space between them so that she was forced to look at it. Sofia sniveled and blanched. It was a sad and aggravated way to end what had been a remarkably pleasant evening.

Leo glanced back at the rhododendron to find Leonard in plain sight. He was sitting on a step of the main entrance. Several of the few remaining guests lingered there as well. They were watching and no doubt hearing the heated repartee. Leonard stood up and conspicuously did his incandescing thing. The maga anxiously looked at the youth. Leo's gaze simply shifted back and forth between the two.

The hand remained in Leo's grip. He was averse to releasing it. The hand was tense and resistant, but it was also hot and soft and sent a feeling through him that was mildly intoxicating. Leo let his thumb caress it. He found himself wondering how he could use the maga to draw on that energy, avail himself of it, control it for his own indulgence.

"You are remarkable, aren't you," he muttered ironically, realizing that she, in fact, actually might be.

He released the hand and finally said, "I'm prepared to tolerate the circumstance if you can manage to exercise allegiance to me in regard to my role as a head magistrate and as the father of that young man. The record is against you, La Maga Magus, but we're in dire debt to each other now. Do you have it in you at all to desist from plots and intrigues and further secret and meddling behaviors?"

The maga nodded.

"Tell me some words, La Maga Magus. Let me hear something," Leo taunted impatiently.

"I've no interest in the futile endeavors of the world machine," Sofia blurted. "I'm only interested in my light and the light I find in others. I'm not going to interfere with your politics or patrician imposition on the order of things. But I can't allow Leonard to be thrown away and destroyed because of," she grasped the words and spit them out with a flood of tears, "meanness and neglect. He asked for my help, and he needed it badly. He's not what you, *his own father,* or everyone thinks."

"'Meanness and neglect,'" Leo muttered. A condemnation. He was poised to ask her about what she supposed he and "everyone" thought Leonard was "not," but whatever she said would be true, and her plaintive emotionality was unsettling in its sincerity anyway.

"No more tears, Lady La Maga," he muttered. He materialized a rather gossamer and delicately embroidered handkerchief. She daubed her eyes and blotted her nose with it.

Leo reached to brush his hand against her cheek. Her eyes bulged and teared as the hand made contact. Leo laughed. He wasn't sure whether it was satisfying to be so threatening.

He caught one of her tears on his finger and mindlessly transformed it into a small diamond. He rolled the stone between his thumb and fingers the way persons handle scabs picked off wounds or castes of snot from their noses. Then he displayed it to her playfully and pressed it against her forehead where it disappeared. It lightened the tone between them.

"I had asked Danny Bruno to mentor the boy," he said in a quiet and thoughtful voice. "Will he pick up where you leave off?"

"I don't think that will be necessary, but I'll talk to him about it," Sofia said softly, adding, "Can I go now, Lord Consul," and stiffly uttered, "I sincerely thank you for the evening, which was really nice, and your thoughtful leniency in these circumstances."

He nodded agreeably. "Do we have an understanding?" he asked her.

"Of course," she asserted and sniffled. In a respectful and sincere tone, she thanked him again.

"Let's sort this out, Lady La Maga," he said.

She nodded, faintly smiling. Her eyes continued to leech dewy tears. Leo looked at the hanky thinking it might be good to have it back. A little rag soaked with Sofia La Maga's tears might be a potent magical ingredient, but then he thought it probably would be best to make the item disappear when she was done with it.

"Alright," she muttered, as if the word were the conclusion of their exchange. She draped the soggy hanky over his index finger and watched it dissolve. Then she winked and smiled lightly as she started away.

Leo remained in place. He glanced at the main entrance and then back at Sofia. Her pace was rather hurried. Back and forth he wavered until he called to her.

"Sofia, have you ever met Justice Janus Magus? He's going to be speaking at the Orion Club next Sunday. It's down the road from the Phoenix and Harp. You might appreciate meeting him. He's an avid social reformer. Very big on immigration law reform." Leo said it as if each word were a stab wound. "The event is for sorcerers, but I could get you in. Would you like to go?"

Sofia, already some yards away, seemed dumbfounded about the invitation.

"With me, I mean," Leo called out. "Would you like to accompany me? Give it some thought. We can talk when we meet for class next week." He smiled lightly and turned back toward the entrance to attend to his other departing guests.

X
A Very Reluctant God

L eo spent a great deal of time on the turret of his tower. He needed the quiet. He needed the holy peacefulness and took solace in gazing into the shallow, round, crystal-lined tank that he had installed up there.

Sometimes the water within it was clear and still. Sometimes it was rippled by the wind. Sometimes it was marred by leaves, drowned insects, pollen, and dander. Sometimes raindrops plunked into the tank to make designs before merging with its contents.

Whatever the condition, the tank was a source of fascination and mental calm for Leo. It helped him know his mind, the contents of his mind, and the difference between the two. Magical prowess depended on sharpness of mind. It depended on thriftiness of thought, unambiguousness of motive, and unwavering momentum.

It was this presence of mind that made Leo a master of materializations. Unless he specifically willed it, his thought-forms were not affected by instability or decay. They were creations like those of an artist—or like those of a god.

But the person who could create things of substance on a whim and with ease was tasked with maintaining sobriety and self-restraint. For this reason, Leo was a subdued person, although his subtlety went unnoticed and unappreciated, as already mentioned.

As he matured, however, he increasingly wasted his gift on small entertainments and the manufacture of collectibles coveted by Outer Plane folks. Whether because he enjoyed the extra income or taking advantage of Commons and their vulgarities, his manufacture of objects precious to them had become a robust hobby over the years.

Was that newly discovered van Gogh by van Gogh or Leo de Lux? A slew of Tiffany lamps, Venetian glass and Goebel Hummels, Mesopotamian seals and Mayan gold, Black Madonnas from Romanian grottoes, excavated Buddha icons from jungle ruins—even dinosaur bones.

When Commons marveled at such objects and muttered that they were "out of this world," they might have been right. Unlike replicas and forgeries crafted by Commons, the true origins of things materialized by Inner Plane people and planted in the Outer Plane were virtually untraceable. Hence, stories (woven with fascination charms) given about their history were unchallenged.

True masters of this art, like Leo de Lux, engaged in high-end antiquing and lucrative museum acquisitions. Amateurs and mischievous young adepts deposited supernatural phenomena in the midst of Commons: sea monsters in lakes, neo-cavemen in snows, and little green men that went bump in the night, not to mention mermaids and unicorns, and various other apparitions. Unlike entrepreneurial schemes, mischievous materializationalism in the Outer Plane was outlawed but hard to enforce.

It, like Phaeton maneuver offenses, fell into Leo's jurisdiction. This meant that he had to engage in public lectures and news briefings in which he spoke on the danger of introducing inexplicable phenomena into the world of Commons. It confused and perverted their cultural and spiritual beliefs, he would say.

"Such sadistic practices result in long lapses of instability, conflict, hardship, and intellectual decline among these lower peoples. We are tasked, as a more evolved race, to treat these peoples with tenderness rather than disdain, for their plane is valuable to us and the eventual home of those who live in the Outer Plane is with us," Leo would say. Meanwhile, placard-carrying college students and Expansionist Party sympathizers would protest outside wherever he was giving a speech. They continually accused him of hypocrisy and double-dealing and also demanded an end to the entrepreneurial oppression of Commons.

This was Leo's lot as a resident and magistrate of the North Atlantic Sovereignty, Terra Novit, Inner Plane Regions. It was wearing on him.

In addition to his job, another heavy burden was parceled with his gift. It was another element that demanded flawless control. Being an entity who could create anything, Leo had the power to destroy anything as well—not merely his or another's thought-form, but all forms, any entity.

Although the tale of the legendary Conus magus charm was probably made up, Leo de Lux could do what Mare Maré did. He could make beings completely disappear, and he could absorb their vital essence. He, his mentor Lumiere Sortiar, and a small group of old, retired politicians who were his father's cronies were aware of this talent. In his youth, Leo, like the Grim Reaper, had practiced the Conus magus charm on animals and a few dying persons. He used it once on a rival.

It was a power best not transferred; hence, Leo had never taken an apprentice. He had even kept a distance from his own son because of this. It was an act that had backfired. Still, he sometimes thought of his decision and his difficult circumstance as atonement for the violence he had perpetrated in his youth. It was a respect for the Clarus Principle, which was something like the Chaos Principle but more about the wisdom of proper behavior in maintaining the natural balance of the universe. Whether the Clarus Principle existed or not, whether it was an essential underlying "truth" of Existence or a manufactured paradigm, Leo had decided to observe it in his own way (he was, after all, a principled and discreetly mystical man . . . in his own way . . . .) In any case, a person had to champion order over chaos if it were within his capacity. That was all there was to it.

Leo had much to worry about when it came to his son. He was concerned about the youth's obsession with marine cone snails and the fascination he had with the possibility of "disappearing" rivals. Leonard's latent abilities—if he had any—would come forward in his liaison with Sofia La Maga, but would she temper them? Would she direct and transform them? Leo felt increasingly confident that she—more than any other magical adept—would. How could he fault her?

The fellow who Leo had done away with Mare-Maré style was an industrialist like the then young Hipparchus Gorgon. His name was Antonius Maymon Sortiar. He wanted to break the de Lux political dynasty, which meant quashing the family's key political heirs.

Maymon tried to win over young Leo, who was known to have a cold and pressured relationship with his father, but de Lux didn't go for it. It was then that Leo and a number of his siblings and cousins began to suffer militant attacks. The first attack lodged against Leo was the spontaneous combustion of his pet, a regal Belgian sheepdog. The last was a seizure that threw the then 22-year-old man into violent convulsions and make every nerve fiber spark and sear. The same type of attack struck at least eight of his cousins, a half-sister, and two half-brothers. Beside himself, only three cousins and the half-sister survived.

What was Leo to do but ambush Maymon and destroy him? The act made Leo great and favored in his father's eyes. It was why Leo had become who he was now: the ruler of the sovereignty destined to become a ruler of Terra

Novit itself.

Because it was easy to commit and because it figured into particularly sinister magic, murder crimes carried strong penalties in Terra Novit—at least on paper. Getting away with murder hinged on a person's level of influence, and so the brunt of enforcement mostly fell on renegade immigrants and folk practitioners.

Punishment for the crime of murder would not be death or incarceration per se. Those judged guilty would be paralyzed and placed in suspended animation. In that state, they would be "locked" in the pit of their own minds—the subconscious, the place of monstrous twists and turns, nightmares, and incoherent thoughts. For this reason, this form of punishment was called the Lock Penalty, because the penalized person was locked in himself.

If the criminal could not sense the lights dimly beaming in the upper atmosphere of his consciousness and ascend, so-to-speak, to more reasonable planes of awareness, he would eat himself alive in the terror of the predicament that was his own mental chaos. Those persons who spontaneously recovered from the Lock Penalty were considered to be rehabilitated and were paroled, but very few managed to do this.

The antidote to the Lock Penalty was the Lux Clarus rite. It was performed by certain State-appointed specialists. The locked-in person would be called back to normal reality and sent on his way after serving his or her time.

Despite his reputation, Aurelio Zosimo Sortiar was one of these Lux Clarus specialists. He had recommended Sofia La Maga Magus to the task, but she had yet to be notified about it. Leo de Lux had been sitting on the recommendation, but he probably was going to let it to go through. The maga's very large dossier was taking up most of his desk. He shuffled through it nearly daily, dithering about what his public attitude toward her should be and how he could best use her to his advantage.

Now that he knew she was an apprentice of Danny Bruno, Leo was vexed with the question of whether she was his primary apprentice—his lineage-holder. It was an important question, considering that no one had yet come forward to claim that role. Bruno was crazy and repulsive enough to do that—secretly give it all out to a folkie, mage woman. But that folkie lady mage was an alluring prodigy, and she was now mentoring—and perhaps sexually diddling—Leo's son. That was something that could be juiced. It had to be. Leo had to draw Bruno's prowess out of her for himself and for Leonard.

When Leo gazed into the tank on his turret, he laughed mournfully at the irony of circumstance. He had to figure out how to play and not get played by that notorious folkie maga Expansionist Party sympathizer who he, in truth, wanted to ride. The woman, after all, was poised to transform his only son into a worthy heir.

In addition to the tank on his turret, there was a pond in a thicket behind the greenhouse that Leo liked to gaze into. He liked to focus on the flashes of light bouncing off the water. If he could skim off the cares and worries clinging to his mind he would reflect on the Lock Penalty and then of his mortality and the Afterlife. How to recognize the difference between reflections of light and light itself? Leo would have to know this when his time came to pass from this life. How to migrate to the Deep Inner Planes—even while still vitally alive? If he discovered the right lights, could he get there? Was there such a light in the evening sky or a dim orb beyond his mind's reach? He often imagined that the world he was in was really a kind of Lock Penalty—a dark pit buried within another state of being that he could climb out of if he could only find the right guideposts.

Many Inner Plane persons believed that when they

died, they would be reborn or else transmigrate in completeness to another plane of existence. Ideally, a person aspired to transmigrate to one of the Deep Inner Planes. They were thought of as ascending orders of heavenly realms. They had different names and glosses about what to expect in one or another, but Leo didn't concern himself with the fine print. To him, they were just the generic Deep Inner Planes.

Of course, it wasn't as if Leo had done the slightest thing to merit transmigration to a deeper Inner Plane. Quite the contrary, but Leo secretly aspired to this destiny. Being a jaded sort, he wondered whether he would be treated like a dog by the inhabitants of a deeper plane in the same way he treated folk practitioners, immigrants, and plebeians. All these thoughts pressured him in midlife and were riled even more so by the appearance of Sofia La Maga.

She reluctantly agreed to attend the function at the Orion Club. They had discussed it in the doorway of the lecture hall where she delivered the Codes and Keys class. Students sauntered past them as they conversed. Leo had presented her with a tight and neatly ribboned handful of spearmint, jasmine, and blue scilla. He added a few sprigs of fruited wild strawberry to give the bouquet more festivity and color. It was a peace offering and a flirtation. It was meant to convey warmth and atonement. It felt quite strange to be wooing Sofia La Maga in this way. It felt subversive. Dirty. Thus, however coy, it was hot and exciting.

"It might be awkward," she said while nibbling the spearmint.

"In what way?" Leo inquired, staring down gawkers who filed past.

"Well, I know we've had our moments, Lord Consul, but word is we're not such best pals," she said.

"If you've been listening to the gossip, the 'word' has

quite changed," Leo replied. "I'm extending myself to you," he said gently. "I'm sure you've been entertained with vicious anecdotes about me, and our rapport for the most part has been volatile. However, I thought we ultimately dealt with our last exchange in an honest and tender manner, don't you?"

"Yes," she murmured undecidedly.

"Are you at all interested in me as a man?" he asked straight out.

"Yes. Very much so," she grinned. Her eyes sparked.

Leo was unprepared for the response. For a moment, he, strangely, could not speak. "Well, there you have it, then," he said. "I'll come around with the car, and we'll go together . . . unless you really don't want to attend this function, and we can revisit this development in another way."

Sofia simpered. She made a gesture with her hands that seemed to express that she was okay about the outing to the Orion Club.

When the time came for the "date" and Leo came around to The Magistrar to retrieve Sofia, he did so in a stately but very sleek Benz Schnitzer. Sofia was waiting at the curb for him. She went to the front passenger side to board the vehicle but was taken aback at the sight of Lazar.

"Ma'am?" Lazar said languidly

Sofia glanced to the backseat to see Leo's ice-like eyes flash. She fumbled to in beside him.

"That's my driver, Lazar," Leo muttered and added stiffly. "He should have been at the ready to open the door for you, of course."

"It's alright," Sofia said in a sing-song voice. "Hello, Mr. Lazar."

"Ma'am," Lazar said again.

She smelled of her usual intoxicant: an infusion of benzoin, orange, lavender, patchouli, and pine — as if she had spent the day being ritually fumigated in a Hindu shrine. She commented that the car sounded like heaven, but it actually sounded like Francesco Geminiani's Concerti Grossi adapted from Corelli's Opus 5 sonatas for strings. This was the same thing as "sounding like heaven" as far as Leo was concerned. That Sofia recognized as much was a good sign.

He illuminated the cabin of the car to take a look at her: her dress, her attitude. Most of the ladies would be in suggestively fitted black cocktail dresses, but not Sofia. Her silk dress was fitted on top, flounced at the waist and imprinted with cool pastel colors of lavenders and blues, heliotropes and swatches of hot violet here and there. A small papery gold bindi dotted with amethyst and citrine bits was glued to her forehead high up where it met her hairline.

"Specks of gold," Leo observed. They lightly dusted her face and shoulders. It was a reason to touch her collar. "Hair's not too mussed," he added, to which she impishly confided that she had combed it that day especially for him.

They continued with light conversation: upcoming class topics, Leo's collection of upscale cars, wine, and then some background on Justice Janus. He was involved in immigration and cultural asylum issues, Leo reminded her.

"Word is, he works with the Underground—the people who 'fix' things to get unsanctioned people over to this side. It has come to my attention that that young-woman apprentice of yours has been doing some counseling work with immigrants, including incarcerated ones. Mind-training meditation practices and what not. If some kind of coordination could be worked out between you and the girl and this justice perhaps it would keep various political complications off my desk and the both of you out of trouble and controversy—as much as you are want to avoid it, that is," Leo explained. "You're not turning that girl into another you at age 19, are you?"

"I'm turning her into herself, Lord Consul."

"Yes, but what are the implications?" he winced.

Sofia took a deep breath and collected her thoughts. "Mirelle's taken on something that has a strong civic impact. Preparing transitioning people for successful, law-abiding lives in the Inner Plane. It's hardly threatening to the Sovereignty or anyone's enterprises."

Leo grunted. He was well aware that Mirelle Soleil was not of the folk-practitioner class but was herself an ex-Commons immigrant Dimidium Pleb. She had no right to be a student at the H. Trismegistus or to be taking on supervisory roles. He let it slide. He had a vested interest in keeping the conversation with Sofia La Maga reasonably light and amiable. Being this close to her was like having the opportunity to pet an exotic wild animal or like tasting a peculiar delicacy for the first time.

"I already told you that I don't fuss with these things anymore," the maga snapped. "They're treadmills for gerbils." She complained about how frustrating it was to be measured and abused because of the ghosts of her past.

"Now that I'm back, things fit strangely," she confided. "I'm treated as if I were in suspended animation. I am in a way," she added. "I don't have a recognized academic standing; I'm criticized for that. Instead of a consort, I've got Raphael Magus crawling through my back door window like a profligate priest . . . people either idolizing me or beating me down because I was that nasty person who tried to shift the paradigm way back when. It's so unbearably banal." She bitterly sighed and then laughed, "I'll be out of your hair soon enough, Mister Lord Consul. Not to worry."

Leo did not belie emotion, but he could feel hers in his bones. Her angst was not so different from his own. It was not his place to confide or commiserate, though. He preferred to let her ramble and rue.

"I'm sorry," she muttered in an abashed and airy laugh. It was as if she had come to her senses about how inappropriate is was to be baring her soul to the consul. Leo felt the odd closeness intriguing. Some quiet time elapsed. Leo placed his hand on Sofia's. She let it rest there motionless.

When they arrived at the Orion Club, Leo asked a favor of her, hoping she would comply. "The glamour," he winced and shook his head. "Sorcerers can be catty and spiteful persons . . . Royal Conservationists." He nodded as if he didn't have to spell things out. "You're a sheep among wolves, and they're going to get an eyeful seeing you in my company. It's going to be outrageous. Behave demurely. Don't play into baiting. Do you understand what I'm telling you?"

She nodded solemnly. He gave her a light hug for encouragement and brushed his lips against her brow.

"Alright," he sighed windedly and forged on with the endeavor.

The Orion Club was a sprawling, dimly lit atrium. Slate paths wove among miniature palm trees and other tropical fronds, tikki-type gazebo bars, and carp ponds with arched footpaths spanning them. Persons mingled festively among lounges couched within the primeval environment. That would be for later for Leo and Sofia. They made their way directly to the salon where Justice Janus would give his presentation on immigration reform to a bunch of patrician sorcerers and their progressive affectations.

Leo stood close to Sofia, eyeing all with a severe gaze. He made note of who sneered or pursed their eyebrows. Sofia, for her part, stood very tall, taller than she actually was even in heels. She glided while walking. The skirt of her dress swished seductively, and her hair fluffed out in voluminous curls. Her demeanor was regal and detached.

A faint light beamed from the bindi glued to her forehead.

They entered the salon. It was a comfy lecture hall with padded seats and armrests that held drinks and plates for hors d'oeuvres. Justice Janus was at the podium with an entourage of fawning high-level magi: white-coat magi in their ceremonial white albs, dalmatics, chasubles, and turbans. Leo cringed at the sight . . . infiltrating the milieu of sorcerers and, worse, putting on pedagogic airs. Bile seethed up. Raphael Magus was among them. Leo watched a flash of surprise cross the mage's face when he recognized Sofia. She smiled and waved at him.

"Did you not know that your paramour also knows Janus?" Leo asked brittlely.

"We haven't been speaking actually," Sofia wistfully replied.

"He looks like the unbearably-banal-in-the-sack sort, if you ask me," Leo quipped. "Despite your rant in the car ride over here, word is that you ditched him for that rabid-looking character from the Bythos Academy, Zosimo Sortiar. How is that going?"

Sofia responded with an odd smile and another abashed and airy laugh before taking her seat.

"Is it not so?" he pressed, but she would not answer.

Leo tried not to imagine her and The Crazy Professor at it. Nor her and Raphael Magus. Leo eyed him disgustedly. The man would be chatting with Sofia later. He would pull her aside into a secluded corner, perhaps out onto the outdoor patio, to the far end of the poolside. There he would ream her about the company she was keeping and plead to visit for a romp in her bed. The thought angered Leo.

"Raphael Magus and 'The Crazy Professor' terrorist," Leo clucked. He shook his head and rolled his eyes. "Can't a 'big celebrity' maga like yourself do better?"

"I pop men's fuses," she muttered. "He can manage

it." She motioned her head toward the mage and faintly smiled.

"What does that mean?" Leo questioned.

The maga grinned bashfully and made her fiery eyes flash.

"Tell me," he persisted. The curious utterance had worked him into a sexual urgency, but Janus had begun his oratory. Leo had to desist, but he was feeling hot.

The beaming, prissy magi brigade sat facing the audience. They were in chairs arranged behind Janus—whatever that was about. Between that insult and Sofia's fuse-popping remark, Leo could not focus on a thing that Janus said.

When the presentation was over, there would be milling from the room, the insufferable pausing to chat with this one or that, and the introduction of persons whose names would escape Leo faster than they had been uttered. Over and again, Leo would be forced to introduce his companion, saying, "Professor Sofia La Maga Magus," and she would have to utter "Yes, from the Mysticus" and say something fascinating and brief about the place.

Back to the atrium. Leo had been requested to attend an impromptu assembly of senators gathered there. He positioned Sofia in front of Janus and left her to commiserate, chat with Alan Raphael, and do whatever she needed to bide her time while he made haste in attending to matters of State.

Even there, his concentration was muddled. He was anxious to be done with this business and interact with that maga. But when he emerged from the conference, he had lost sight of her. His usual cohorts—Reggie Solaris, RCP treasurer Lucas Marcus, the Praetorate of Finance, and some other good old boys—drew him into their conversation. He continued to chat but was growing in restlessness and languor. He wanted to be doing something else! Something sexy and interesting.

He spotted a few infiltrators from Hipparchus Gorgon's camp in the room. They were big supporters of relaxed immigration precisely because it meant more persons here in the Inner Plane as well as "there" in the Outer to corral into the vicious wheel of servitude and consumption. Contractors were already building "training camps" for the slew of new denizens filtering in through the Black Magic Market and the Underground as well as the presently lax immigration system itself.

It wasn't enough to let them in; they needed refuge and the keys to the self-actualization that would redeem them, Leo heard his mind jabber as if delivering a double-faced speech. But he felt the truth of it. He realized how much better, more productive, and fulfilled everyone — from the elite to the lowly — would be if mutual support among different strata of peoples could be orchestrated. It was disorienting. He realized how things otherwise worked, though. Right then. He was in the mouth of a shark. Indeed, he and most everyone in that room were the shark's teeth. Their existences were bent on grinding down other, lesser beings. There was little that was magical or mystical about it. No wonder his life, however privileged, seemed so dull. It was a treadmill for gerbils.

The revelation sprung on him with such force that he thought he might, right then, pop out and reappear in the Deep Inner Planes. But how would Sofia get home then?

"Taking a walk on the wild side, buddy?" Reggie Solaris grinned. "You got some major kink going for mage women, don't you?" He pointed to Sofia. She was some yards away, speaking with the dark sorceress Medea Sarin. The sorceress's brassy coiffure was wrapped so high and her head was so large atop her sinewy body that Sofia appeared dwarfed in her presence. Leo watched the sorceress step closer to Sofia. The gesture caused the maga to slip back on her heels. Reggie and his friends laughed at the sight.

"They say she's got a loopy glamour. She pulled all the stops out for us tonight," Reggie smirked. "You missed the cat fight between her and your girlfriend Marina."

"What do you mean?" Leo questioned.

"Like son, like father," the men snickered. "Moving onto graduate studies in your sex-magic dabblings, de Lux? Bring her around. Maybe she can conduct an intensive."

Leo simpered and sneered for a moment. "What did she do that I missed," he hissed.

"Look at her! She's freaking looped!" Reggie cackled. "Could you imagine gang-banging her in that condition? She must be a rip in action."

Leo watched Sofia search frantically for an allied eye in the crowd while he listened to Reggie mindlessly ramble about what it would be like to rape her. She managed to catch Leo's gaze. He flashed a quizzical look. She responded with a magical attack. The icy pang that pierced Leo's gut and scintillated through his limbs was rather delectable, though; like lovelorn loss — something he wasn't sure he had ever felt before.

A riot of hoots and laughter seized his companions. The only thoughts that Leo could muster, though, were that Sofia La Maga was likely in love with him, needed to be rescued, and popped men's fuses.

He materialized his Ea-topped staff and aimed it at Reggie. *"How dare you insult my escort!"* he growled. With that, the mirth of his compatriots went riotous. He jabbed at Reggie and backed away.

The mirth abruptly soured as the men realized that Leo was truly piqued. He was defending the lady. They gasped aghast protests.

Leo just glared at them before storming off.

"What the fuck did she do to him?" he heard Reggie

say.

Persons gaped askance at the consul. He strode up to where Medea Sarin and Sofia La Maga were facing-off. Without acknowledging Medea, he grasped Sofia's hand and in leaned in to say, "Are we having fun yet?"

Sofia's brow wrinkled, and her eyes misted in response. Her bindi and sparkles were gone and her eye makeup was a little smeared, too.

Leo hurried her out, as if the two were fleeing, which they were. Leo was strangely flushed with indignation about his peers. He also was elated to be free.

He couldn't wait for Lazar to respond to his page. "Let's fly somewhere," he said.

"I don't know how," she replied.

"Never learned how to fly? Even in the Mysticus?"

"Translocation," she said.

"That's no fun." He drew her arms over his shoulders. "We're going to get very light and spin—whirl—until we're caught in the wind," he explained. There was a term for it in the Mysticus: Vayu gaman siddhi, the power of going in space.

"But I don't want to go with you," she whimpered.

"Yes, you do," he insisted and lifted off, spinning, becoming very light and making Sofia weightless too.

They set down in Leo's backyard by the lake behind the thicket. He had built a sitting area there. The seats were beveled marble arranged amid flaming red bush and dogwood heavy with lotus-like blossoms, huge white moon flowers, spikes of fox-glove and delphinium, voluptuous pastel and purple iris blooms, and carpets of violets and pansies. The moon wasn't full, but Leo made it seem so. He tucked the orb into a cottony skirt of clouds that made moonbeams and radiance.

"Bring the car around. Yes. Bring it home. I'm here. She's with me. Just drive it back." Leo clumsily reasoned with Lazar to get the Benz Schnitzer back into the garage. He slid his phone into the inside pocket of his jacket. Why was he using a cell phone or any such communication device anyway? "Worse-than-Commons," he muttered to himself about the contraption. "I could just shout inside people's heads if I want to tell them something, shouldn't I?" he questioned, but it was as if he were asking Sofia for permission. Then he said of Lazar,

"The man wants me to let him go and does his best to provoke me."

"Which is why you keep him and let him drive that really cool car instead of yourself," Sofia remarked.

Leo could only wince at the irony. Why wasn't he driving his own nice cars? Why did Lazar get the privilege?

He materialized two goblets made of thin, sonorous crystal. The stems of the goblets were encrusted in pimply concretions of gold. Leo dipped both goblets into the lake.

"Do you like drama, Sofia? No," he answered his own question. "A little mischief, a little amusement. You put on a veneer of tolerance and grace and play with a ridiculous glamour, but your patience with people is actually thin, and your glamour is the slyest poison."

She smiled deeply, as if very flattered at being found out.

"I want you to be authentic with me. You've impressed me," he said sternly. "That is no small feat, La Maga Magus."

"Was that a test over at the Orion Club? 'Cause I really wasn't on my best behavior. Things were too screwy," she confessed. "How are you going to get back at me for it?"

"Maybe I wanted to cross the line, taunting my droll social circle with the likes of you. Shake things up," he replied. Fearsomely in the dark about the extent of her misbehavior, he wasn't sure whether his statement was true. In the moment, he wanted it to be. "Mission accomplished," he added smartly and displayed the ornate goblets full of brackish water. "Would you be very impressed if I turned water into wine?"

"It would depend on what it tasted like," she replied.

He transformed the liquid into a dry, light, yet slightly fruity ruby-colored draught and told her that he was "pretty resilient to women's spells; but if you've done something, I don't mind it so much for now."

She huffed out a laugh. "Why would I be working on a tyrannous patrician sorcerer who has the evil eye on me?"

Leo made the same breathy chuckle that Sofia had. It was a pained, uncertain, rueful sound masked in wistful humor. "My eyes are my most distinguishing feature. Sorceresses find them irresistible," he replied.

"You're an attractive and intriguing and very influential man," she said. "You're smart to be paranoid about the ladies if all you're looking for is a little fun."

"Real intimacy has been elusive, but I'm not averse to it," Leo told her. "Most all of my interactions seem like ruses. And here we are, you and me, of all the disparate couplings. Does this sensation come from myself or is it being imposed on me through magical mischief?"

"Doesn't a 'big-shot' high sorcerer like yourself know his own true will?" she asked in the same snippy tone that Leo had used to ask her if she could do better in her choice of male companions. Leo paused. He was just very recently coming to terms with what his will was, which was quite different from what it was expected to be.

"Nothing bad is happening," Sofia muttered and relaxed to admire the sky, the moonlight, the shadows on the water, and the perfumed breeze as if it and their conversation were a familiar repast. Leo recalled her saying that phrase before, but no; it wasn't her. It was Leonard on the night he had changed.

"Bad things are always happening and for no good

reason," he declared. "You seem to have had a night of bad things happening, and I suspect you're anxious about how this present moment will go despite your mooning at the moon. What I want to know," he pressed, "is how you intend to turn yellow tulips into red ones. Hopeless impossibility into something worth it?"

"I think you've taken on that task, Lord Consul," Sofia replied. "But, really, you're the last person I should want to be with."

"The sentiment is mutual. Very," Leo said, but the banter was just coy play. It was time for it to break. "But am I the last person you want to be with?" he asked.

Sofia didn't respond. She simply placed her hand on his.

Some quiet time passed. The two sat leaning against each other. Their hands were clasped. They focused on the billow of each other's breath and how it became entrained, rising and falling in unison. The experience was both strange and new and oddly familiar as if the two of them had been reunited after a long and pining separation. Leo nuzzled his head against hers. He kissed her. He submerged himself in a so-called Sweet Surrender.

The heat and electrical sensations radiating from the maga were unique among the magical women with whom he had been—even Vinca Blanco. Leo scarcely knew what to do with these feelings or whether they were coming from him or her or were a mutual combustion. He craved to have them persist.

The term "popped fuse" echoed in his mind. He feared that he had been out-witted by strong magic and would be seeking vengeance when the spell broke. On the other hand, his gut was full of roller coasters at the thought of being romantically aligned with someone so insidiously potent. He continued to embrace her, familiarizing himself with her body's terrain.

"You hold the key," he said somewhere in there. He felt her hold on him tighten and her passion flare. He would've said anything to maintain the relief he gleaned from embracing her. If she could suspend him in it, then let the world and its scandals go to oblivion; they would be consorts, he concluded in his lust-addled delirium. "What went on between you and Marina tonight at the club," Leo asked during a lull in their escapade. "I heard there was a confrontation."

"She told me that you were going to sexually vampirize me and then empower her with my juicy juice the next time you did it with her. So I gave her a condom."

"Mmm," Leo muttered, not knowing how to interpret that or what the next question should be. He tried to act as if her confession made perfect sense.

"Then I spilled some wine on her, and Alan dragged me outside to talk."

Leo did not belie perplexity or pique. Rather, he continued to nod knowingly. "He brought you out to the far end of the poolside," he stated.

"Yeah."

Leo's gut twisted because he simply didn't want her to be liaising with that fellow. He leaked out another thoughtful "Mmm" sound. "He bad-mouthed me and tried to seduce you," he said.

"Yeah," Sofia grinned.

"Why didn't you leave with him?" Leo asked.

A perplexed grimace wafted across Sofia's face. "I was supposed to be with you," she said.

Leo mulled over the response. It suggested that Sofia maybe was a faithful sort. He went on to ask about what Medea Sarin had to say.

"She's angry because I got Mirelle. I don't know what she was saying. She wants me to give her something to make up for it," Sofia breathlessly replied.

"Give her what?"

"I have no idea. Did you ever stand near her?" Sofia grimaced. "She has a smell."

"I don't acknowledge Medea," Leo stammered. He mouthed some words about his liaison with Medea's cousin, Marina, while Sofia stressed about a nasty smell.

"I don't know if I actually smelled her with my nose, but my stomach was coming up when she got within two feet of me . . . and this jiggly, haywire feeling." Sofia fretted her arms around as if tracing the woman's form.

"She's dark," Leo said. "Best to pretend that she's not there. More than once, I've been asked to participate in plots to make her disappear," he confided.

"Really? But I'm the one who had to disappear to not get disappeared. That's called irony," she said.

"I make a point not to participate in disappearing persons, believe it not, La Maga Magus, unlike another one of your liaisons, Dr. 'Danny' Bruno. And what could be so grievous about being able to have extraordinary experiences in other realms and returning to the Fatherland as a celebrity," Leo taunted. "Besides Medea Sarin is not a political threat or a threat to the community, only to persons whose perversity leads them to seek out the wrong kind of mischief. For that, they should pay. What use is that girl, Mirelle, to Sarin Sortiar anyway? What is she?"

"She's received empowerments from many entities from the Deep Inner Planes," Sofia told Leo.

"She's a bloody immigrant," Leo scoffed.

Sofia froze with mouth agape and then began to laugh. "You know everything, Lord Consul," she exclaimed impressively. "Just like Santa Claus."

"It's my business to know," Leo stuttered.

"You're great," she exclaimed. "I'm so glad that you're not as clueless and hard-ass as everyone thinks. I was really *really* hoping you weren't."

"Clueless hard-ass," Leo muttered. "It is my business to deport her and bring down Bruno and that school for what is going on with that girl and any other immigrants being unlawfully schooled there. You do know that," he calmly said. "I've chosen to be derelict in my responsibilities, La Maga Magus. I may use it as a leveraging point in the future. You and your mentor owe me," he said. From his perspective, that was true, but far more important at that moment was that Sofia La Maga thought he was "great." He nevertheless turned a sharp glance at her. He did not mean to be harsh, but he did want to set her straight about who he was. "Now tell me," he uttered in an officious tone, "how could she have *possibly* received 'empowerments' from Deep Inner-Plane entities?"

"Epileptiform seizures," Sofia replied. "She used to pop out during fits when she was a little girl. She doesn't remember too much of the really Deep Plane or know how to use what she got from being there. My job is to help her know herself and protect her from people who want to use and twist her up—like that Medea Sarin woman."

"So you're telling me that this immigrant is full of wondrous potential that could be rendered into a time bomb in the wrong hands," Leo uttered.

"Yes," Sofia asserted. "Exactly."

Leo nodded thoughtfully, content with the ease of communication. "And is Leonard also full of wondrous potentials that you feel compelled to draw out?" he asked.

"Yes. Very," she grinned with eyes lit up.

Leo smiled with deep satisfaction at the response. "But my son is now mixing with a 'Deeple' under your mentorship," he countered.

"Yes. They are in the same room together sometimes," Sofia replied. "Do you want me to keep them separated?"

"My son deserves respect, La Maga Magus, from you and especially her. She seems a bit bitten around the edges when I see her in that class of yours," Leo said.

"She is bitten around the edges, but so are you. Let's try to find a way to fix that that works for everybody," Sofia responded.

Leo grunted, unsure of whether to be annoyed or thoughtful. Then he asked, "What do you see in me besides a 'hard-ass,' vampiric evil eye then?"

"You? I'll tell you later" she smiled.

"I would like you to tell me now," he coaxed, but she wouldn't discuss it. It wasn't until they were absorbed in another feverish embrace that he plaintively asked her again in a hot sigh.

With eyes welling with sentiment and a grip on him that nearly popped his fuse, she whispered: "A very reluctant god."

XI
Syzygies

"From hell to heaven in three hours flat. I think that's pretty good," Sofia joked. "It usually takes three days, doesn't it?" She was lounging in a reclining chair in Danny Bruno's office. Her feet were propped on a window sill. She had a good view of the H. Trismegistus Pavilion from the window and could see straight through to the Mercury Gardens.

She imagined that she could see Consul Leo de Lux heading toward the Capitol building among the ant-like meanderings of persons. She caught the speck that could be him between her thumb and index finger and held the person there as he walked. Nothing about him could be seen; he was just speck, but Sofia imagined that the speck was a regal fellow in a sleek dark suit. He had a well-manicured cap of dark ruddy hair and the face of a Roman god. She imagined that the speck adjacent to the one she "held" was Leo's debonair attendant Victor.

She was exhausted but her chest and head were flooded with the radiance of elation. She hadn't slept. She felt wired however weary. She was drinking strong tea but would crash into listless good-for-nothingness at about the time her afternoon class rolled around.

"I don't trust that guy," Danny snapped. He was sitting behind Sofia at his amoeba-shaped chrome desk. It was a specimen of Italian futurist design. He was spiking his morning triple cup of espresso with anise liqueur. An exquisitely ethereal mobile-like sculpture that resembled a hybrid fish, sea-craft, and flying saucer was suspended directly overhead. Fins, mesh, panels, and beads of eyeballs strung on translucent fibers pricked at space. It was a specimen of post-modern art. Danny had acquired it through Leo de Lux of all people. It was exquisite. Sofia assumed that Bruno knew it was as forgery, though.

"Yeah, well, the romance would've been here and gone already if he wasn't sick for two whole months. You're crimping my momentum over here, Danny," Sofia whined.

"You think I made him sick?"

"Yes."

"I wasn't making him sick; I was trying to take him out," Danny blurted and traced an index finger across his neck.

"You lie," Sofia cackled.

"So he's got a set of nuts," Danny huffed. Then, he relented. "de Lux is alright. He lets me jerk around his 'spiritual crises.' He's good like that. But that other one—the white-coat magus. He's a dick, sneaking around like some bourgeois Commons. All those white-coat magi. They're a bunch of hand-jobbers. I don't like people being undiversified. It's divisive."

"Life would be so boring. You wouldn't have anyone to be on the rag about," Sofia told him.

"I'd have no trouble," Danny griped.

In the moments between the banter she shared with Danny, Sofia recalled the previous evening as if it were a dream one keeps falling back into between waking up too much.

She felt very much adrift when Leo abandoned her to the company of Justice Janus at the Orion Club. The judge addressed Sofia in platitudes and sound bites and was not about to comment on his involvement with the Underground. He did imply that he was a supporter of a program that suspiciously sounded like the caste system.

Sofia finally asked him whether he was a liberator or a slave trader (she figured that he wasn't listening anyway). In response, he asked her whether she was a maga or a sorceress or both. "It's like being a wise man and a wise guy at the same time," Janus said. He uttered the comment as if he were talking about himself and thought his comment was subtle and witty.

Sofia forced a smile and turned her back on the dignitary. She walked away as if closing a door behind her, but she was feeling at a loss of her staff, her wand, her stiletto, her sword, even her nut and bolt. She missed having some kind of magical item to hold onto to feel safe.

Gwen Goldenlance was propped up, as usual, at one of the little bars scattered throughout the atrium. Why did she always have to be at these stupid events? Marina Sarin was with her but wouldn't acknowledge Sofia's presence. It wouldn't have mattered, but Gwen decided to make a scene.

"Love your dress, Sofia," she said.

"Thanks," Sofia demurely replied.

"So what are you doing here?" Gwen huffed.

Sofia strained to find Leo in the crowd but couldn't. "I got an invitation from the consul to meet Justice Janus," she replied.

"That was nice of him. Because, you know, magi aren't supposed to be here. Leo would be the first to get his nose out of joint about it. So . . ." Gwen ended her jibe there and tried to get Marina to comment. The woman grimaced as if the endeavor were impossible and went on chatting with a nearby fellow.

"I heard there were a bunch of white coats sitting on the stage during a presentation in one of those rooms where they have conferences," Gwen said. She ribbed Marina. "Did you know that, Sweetie? That must've been the freak show that Leo took La Maga Magus to see instead of you. But I guess she's become cordial with the consul now that she's tutoring his son." Turning back toward Sofia, Gwen asked, "Are you being paid for that?"

"Leonard's sort of my hobby," Sofia replied.

"Really?" Gwen snorted. She nudged Marina again. "She's doing little Leonard, not Leo, Marina. So, you can stop being so pissy." She again faced Sofia to sarcastically comment about her friend's behavior. "Isn't she rude?"

But Marina decided to pipe in. "Got to start somewhere."

"So, I guess Leo is really happy that his son finally found a teacher to pet?' Gwen remarked.

"Yeah," Sofia agreed. "But I think he's happier that he doesn't have to knock-up someone like your friend here on the off-chance that whatever pops out won't be a loser like Leonard used to be." She formed an "L" with her thumb and index finger and rapped it against her forehead.

Gwen didn't reply. She squinted at the maga whose manner was turning loose and unmannerly. Marina also turned to gape at Sofia who had gone on to accuse the bartender, in a barking voice, of not serving wines in their proper glassware. Indeed, she was trying to lift herself up and lean in over the bar to point out a certain goblet that was dangling from a rafter. Turning back toward Gwen, she said in wonder, "Did Leo ever make wine for you? He can make it just like Jesus did."

"Leo can make a lot of things," Marina snapped.

"Reverse Morpho charms even," Sofia exclaimed.

"You're gonna get it, La Maga," Marina snarled. "You think you're going to get in with the consul, but he is going to sap you and crush you and give all your saccharine magic and idiot glamour to me the next time he and I fuck."

"You should use protection then," Sofia replied. She materialized a large, brightly colored, polka-dot patterned ribbed and nibbed raspberry chocolate-scented condom fitted over an erect rod of space. While everyone gapped at the provocative balloon-like thing as it floated in air, Sofia made a large goblet of deep purple Chianti go sideways into a splatter spill in Gwen and Marina's direction.

Alan Raphael yanked Sofia away from the bar. She might have been insulted by Alan's intercession if it hadn't been so well timed. She listened to Gwen and Marina shriek and curse over having their dresses stained.

Alan glared at Sofia and then at the very irked and amassing sorcerers who were responding to Gwen and Marina's distress. With a firm grip, he hurried Sofia outside, through the bay doors to an outdoor patio, and continued walking, because the sorcerers milling out there began shouting at them as well.

Finally, he and Sofia were standing in the dark on the edge of a golf course near the very the far end of an Olympic-sized swimming pool.

"If this is your way of getting back at me, you're digging a hole for yourself," he said. "When the semester is over, maybe you should go somewhere else where life will suit you better." He went on to browbeat Sofia about how sorry he was about her interrupted life—all those years suspended in exile. But she had responsibilities to live up to now, he said.

"This dangerous liaison with de Lux is absolutely ruining your already fragile credibility. They're saying that you were at his house last weekend, being the entertainment after spending and hour and a half 'servicing' his teenage son? This is what is being said about you," Alan scolded. "And keep your distance from that Zosimo character. He's an *Inchaote*. A groundless, disheveled joke. That coupling is being called *Armageddon*. What are you doing? Despite the circumstances, I am here for you. And as a man, I'm here for you."

"We're not doing stuff anymore, Alan," Sofia told him. "We should've just left it with the dinosaurs. Now I feel like there's something icky about you even though I'm half of the ickiness."

"What are you talking about, Sofia?" Alan exclaimed. "We have a long history, but what is this crazy thing you're doing with de Lux and the other one?"

"Well, I must be immanentizing the eschaton just like people are saying, don't you think?" she quipped.

"I wouldn't put it past you," he replied. "I don't like this new glamour you're playing with. . . hanging around with that Inchaote sorcerer . . . Zosimo Sortiar. It's making you dark and jaded. Listen to yourself! And here I find you on the arm of Leo de Lux?" Alan shook his head in disgust. They both sulked before Sofia announced that the evening was a disaster and that she was departing.

"I'll take you home," Alan said.

"No," Sofia drawled. "And your friend Janus is a two-faced asshole." She said this way too loud and rushed away from Alan.

Her ankles wobbled and crimped from fleeing on high heels. If that weren't enough to turn heads in the way Leo de Lux had admonished her not to, she repeatedly hollered at her rejected paramour, "Don't follow me!" and told the sorcerers protesting her presence there that they should "fuck off" because she was a guest of the consul of the sovereignty.

She went inside to figure out where the front of the atrium had been and ruefully cursed Leo for setting her adrift in a sea of hostility. She indignantly muttered that he wasn't so smart thinking he had trapped her. No sir. She was about to translocationally "pop" out of there when Marina's cousin, that smelly bitch, Medea Sarin, accosted her.

But, in the end, it couldn't have been better. . . Leo de Lux . . . Sofia had been obsessing over him for months.

Repulsion is the flipside of attraction, and disdain is sometimes denial of something within oneself that is fearsome to face. Sometimes one extreme and its other are not poles apart but are more like a loop where the ends are confused because they run into each other. These were the facts over which Sofia was sure Leo was musing. The best part was the awesome sensation of the shift to a new attitude. It made you die and be reborn. It made you feel disoriented, then new, then (at least temporarily) free because you had dropped the burden of predictable behavior and belief, which could be very heavy.

Sofia was well aware that love of the erotic kind was a small compensation, a straw shelter in life's tempest. That was what all of her many teachers had drummed into her; but still, she couldn't take it to heart. It was a taste of something that was delicious because it was rare and fleeting.

She didn't go home until morning, artfully avoiding a run-in with Leonard. She had folded herself into a remarkably exuberant Leo de Lux, who did not walk or run—or even fly—but had instantly translocated himself and her from their lakeside tryst to his cavernous bedroom suite when their interlude at the lake had gone too far.

A tremendous and ornate poster bed, like the refuge of an ancient king, dominated his room. It was overrun with saprophytic orchids and bromelia. The air was heavy-laden with jasmine and honey-scented flowers, and the skylight overhead was lit up with a myriad of stars.

For a hidebound patrician sorcerer of the North Atlantic Sovereignty, Leo was remarkably attuned to the energetics of intimacy. Not the mere crypto-onerism of a penis in a vagina, a mouth in a crotch, a genital orgasm, a singular reverie in the overspent need of release, like a popped balloon that startles and is then just sadly gone. It might've been that they were simply well-matched but, gee, he had a knack for sensation, bioelectromagnetic pulsation, timing, entrainment, sublimity, and ecstasy that made the garland of nodes in Sofia's etheric body vibrate as well as it tingled her thingy.

She giggled out loud. To have cut through the mask of that man and have him lay his body and his presence over her and mesmerize her with scintillating ardor . . . . That luscious, fleeting thing spoiled the specialness out of every other experience.

When she returned home, she retrieved the nut and bolt from the pocket of her Peruvian jacket and held it gleefully. "Syzygies," she muttered again and again. The term came from Gnostic mysticism and denoted a divine dyad, a complementary pair auspiciously yoked as a unified whole.

She put the widget in a little jewel-encrusted box that she kept on her nightstand. She would treasure the widget until this love sojourn was over. She would have to retrieve the thing and use it in a ritual way to detach if and when the romance soured.

Heaviness lay behind her eyes for lack of sleep. Her heart beat too fast from the labor of sleeplessness, of love and sex, and of uncertain new moments that would seem very stretched out and unrelenting until the situation settled into a new habit, a new automation, with its own particular choreography.

Danny was prepping Sofia about a presentation he had planned for her as part of the Academy's Masters of Magic program. He had included a lecture and demonstration on ritual weapons in the schedule. He expected Sofia to display many of the implements she had acquired in her travels through the Terra Mysticus. She would lecture on their symbolism and perhaps give demonstrations about their use.

"Hello? Inner Plane to 'Lady de Lux Redux.' Are you listening to me?" Danny hollered.

"Yes," Sofia whined, even though she wasn't.

"Do you want to do it outside in the athletic field?

You'll have more space. But if you're just going to yak and B S—which is going to be a snooze—we'll do it in the auditorium and tell folks to bring pillows and sleeping bags."

"We'll do it outside. You can tell everyone who wants to sit up front that they should wear stain-proof plastic rain gear and bring umbrellas, because things could get bloody," she said.

"Good!" Danny replied. It would be on a Saturday afternoon—three weekends hence.

That having been decided, Sofia drifted to her 11:30 class—the codes and keys class. Leo was not in attendance. Leonard was. He looked as if he hadn't slept either.

Sofia had Mirelle direct most of the session, and she let Thetis Mirabilis talk a lot. Mirelle sparred with the girl. Sofia winked approvingly now and then over the repartee.

They were discussing the parallels between the gifts of the spirit, the alchemical planets, the sephira, and the chakras of Asian esoteric anatomy and how to alight on the common key. Sofia, as if sleep-talking, gave a compact dissertation on how these things were tied into the concept of emanation and summarily reviewed the positions on the matter according to Hermetic, Cabbalist, and Valentinian Gnosticism; Yoga-Tantra; and the ancient Samkhya philosophy. Her yakkity yak was interrupted by the gong heralding the end of class. Students lurched from their seats.

"Bye," she yawned as the students deserted her.

Leonard approached. He walked toward her with tall, manly strides as if he had become very resolute and regal. He continued walking until he had the maga backed against the chalkboard.

"Don't think I don't know where you were all night," he scolded in a bitterly subdued voice. "Making it with me is perverted—but not with *him*. That makes a lot of sense.

After all the shit he said about you and all the crap he has planned to mess you up."

"Lenny, you know something else is going on," Sofia replied too wistfully.

"No. Other things aren't going on. I live with him. I hear and see all the meanness and denseness and misery and shit!" Leonard vigorously tapped his fingers against his brow. "He's twisted! He's binding you—and trying to stick it to me. I don't want to pop your balloon. You want to get off like everyone else, but my father is not the guy. Okay. Never mind me," the boy added. "I'm a stupid-ass kid with a hard-on. I understand that. But my father is not the guy. He's going to fuck you up, and I don't want him to hurt you."

The youth made a shy gesture toward caressing Sofia's cheek. He repeated that his father's attentions were nothing more than the elements of a cruel binding spell and that Leonard didn't want Sofia to be victimized.

"You need to have more faith in me," she said but flinched. Leo, although absent from class, was approaching. The youth turned. He snarled at his father and stormed off.

"Well, I hope you win at trying to fuck each other over then, because after he eats the candy, he doesn't save the wrapper. That's all I'm saying," Leonard announced in a booming voice.

"'Wisdom from the mouths of babes'?" Leo shot back.

The youth lifted a hand to his shoulder and gave his father the finger.

Leo eyed him contemptuously until he had left the room.

"Is he heartbroken?" Leo asked Sofia. When she didn't respond happily enough to his epiphany, a hotly piqued composure took over him. He glared even more fiercely in the direction that Leonard had traced. He watched Sofia examine the straggling loiterers—mostly adults—who couldn't manage to leave the classroom, preferring to gawk at the exchange between the professor and the younger and now elder de Lux. Leo turned his threatening white eyes at the witnesses then. They stirred and moved along.

"'Nothing bad is happening,'" Leo murmured.

"It's not like he doesn't have a point," Sofia said.

"What did he say?"

"You know what he said," she scoffed. "He said you're a creep and that you plan to abuse me," she said, adding that she would be terribly disappointed but not surprised if their nice time together had just been a trap. Her face flushed a little bit and her eyes went pink and dewy for just a moment.

"I can't take back past things that you have heard about me, Sofia," Leo said in a windy sigh. "Negative behavior is founded in pain and habituation, you know that." Then he laughed, admitting that he could feel the "juiciness" of her thought waves all morning long. "I could barely focus during my meeting with the Senate Regulatory Committee on Transplanes Communications. Now you're all cold and sighing and muddled about whether you should feel regret because that vengeful *boy* has to compete with me."

Then in a sharp voice, Leo told Sofia that his son would have to abide it. He told her that there would be no more erotic interludes between her and the youth if there already had been. "And Bruno and Raphael are done—and that freak professor from Bythos," he snarled. "I've jumped off a cliff and decided on you, and I do not share. If your designs are to *own* me, the price is submission and sacrifice *to me*. A dyad is two, not a half-dozen. And they'll have to abide it. They'll all have to abide it!" Leo cocked his chin toward where onlookers had been. "Tell me now how you stand with this."

"Okay," Sofia said without hesitation.

After a mute moment to let her response sink in, Leo placed Sofia's hand against his chest and announced, "You are the white goddess of creative inspiration; I am the dark god of numinous being. May the redemptive sun, the light of life, be born from our eclipse."

He kissed her and then zapped her with such a sudden and intense Sweet Surrender maneuver that she lost muscle tone and would've collapsed into mush from the impact of a terrific orgasmic seizure had Leo not been holding her rather firmly. *"I can pop fuses, too,"* he hissed.

He told her to cancel her classes and go home and nap. He would be sending a car around in a few hours. They'd be going to the Outer Plane. Then he positioned her against the wall so that she would gently slide down into a seated sighing and giggling little crumble when he let go of her and went his way.

He *wanted* Sofia La Maga. He seemed to be in the rare love he aspired to attain. He did not care by what means he had been stricken by it. He had wanted something transformational to happen, and it had occurred. He strode from Sofia's classroom to that of Leonard's next class.

"Good afternoon, Lord Consul," the professor tending that class smiled, but he no sooner shrunk back in panic as the consul barreled into the aisles of student seats.

With a surly gesture, he forced a clear-out of those seats in the row directly in front of the one in which Leonard sat. Leo positioned himself in front of his son and leaned in.

"Do NOT interfere. I NEED this," he asserted in a crisp and direct tone.

Father and son glared at each other until Leonard's gaze softened. Leo gently nodded. He wanted to pat the boy's head reassuringly, but he didn't dare. He strode out of the room with the same heel-clattering and determined pace. He felt a breathless elation about what was happening. He didn't care how or why it was happening. He was in love.

The three-week interim between their first tryst and the Masters of Magic spectacle was as pleasant as could be. Leo didn't renege or waver about all that love- and dyad-talk. Rather, he took Sofia all around: to private parties at museums and private showings at art galleries in the Inner and Outer Planes where he hob-knobbed, wheeled and dealed, and comported himself rather seductively — especially among Commons in his mischievous efforts to prey on their desperations.

Sofia got to observe what gave him pleasure and what gave him aggravation and how he, like Danny Bruno, hooked into persons' vices and toyed with them for entertainment purposes.

It didn't take much scrutiny for Sofia to confirm that Leo de Lux was not a "bad" man; he was a bored man. He was a man who, fearing the breadth and impact of his potential, had engaged in things that were self-indulgent in meager, measly ways when they could've been truly eccentric and grand.

He asked Sofia if she thought his treatment of Commons was sinister — if it upset her magian sensibilities. Sofia knew that all the really good high sorcerers had an audacious streak. It was their key as catalysts of transformation. They were teachers but their method was to turn a person's soul on its end to make it violently squirm to aright itself.

Sofia told Leo that history, reality, and time were very fluid for Commons. They were all matters of belief and convention, not actuality. She admitted that it didn't matter that Leonardo da Vinci, for instance, had created less than 20 paintings in his lifetime. If 20 more were "discovered" and sold through Leo de Lux, reality would abruptly change and with it perception, time, and history.

The ruse would be the pleasure and prerogative of an Inner-Plane person to perpetrate. That was one of the quirky things Sofia had learned about the relationship between the Inner and Outer Planes. It had forced her to calm down about the ways of the world. It had made her philosophical and carefree instead.

"They're all mere intrigues, self-limited events occurring in a milieu where all purpose and meaning is artificial. Mere amusements," Leo said. "Occasionally someone I've toyed with 'gets it,'" he confided. "He or she has a realization. When that person reminisces on me, he calls me 'teacher.' I hear him, and it feels sweet; but it's not a very common occurrence."

He spoke about wanting to escape to more sublime realms and what an impossible ambition it was considering his role in making the North Atlantic Sovereignty the abysmal pressure cooker that it was. He spoke about how the realm in which they lived could be an enlightened place, but it was pretty much a replica of the Commons plane.

"We're the inside of that. What's inside us? Is it a rat race or something better?" Leo asked Sofia.

He asked her whether she saw the world in a different, better way than he or other persons in their realm did. Sofia said that she often reminded herself of the fleeting and fabricated nature of ordinary reality. She also said that, although she felt herself to be a person and a personality, she knew she was neither. She and all things were the activity of something greater that was the organism of Existence.

"The Divine Ground, Suchness, the Monad, 'God,' or one of your goddesses?" Leo questioned. "Define it for me."

Sofia shrugged. "All these words are metaphors for life, its power, and potential. People have to chock-a-block it into dogma. Just more gerbils in treadmills," she said. "Reality is reality regardless of belief. I could believe that the sky is green even if everyone else insists that it's blue. So what. Life goes on, and the sky doesn't care what color I want to think it is; it stays over me the same as over everyone else. I don't have to worry about what to aspire to or think or be or do; I just have to let life live as me. I think there's a lot of faith in that. Just trusting that existence is what it is and letting it be. A person doesn't really have a choice."

"A magical person does, though," Leo replied. "He manipulates the illusion of reality to his benefit."

"Take it a step further then, Leo," Sofia challenged. "Realizing the illusory nature of things makes you feel sour and groundless however much you exploit it, but it could make you feel very free and really powerful. If anyone has the ability, you do." That was the truth Leo de Lux wanted to hear. If he could swallow it, Sofia reasoned that not only him but the whole world could be saved.

They quickly became quite the magical couple. No one knew what to make of the pairing. There was talk about which one of the two was flummoxed by a heavy-duty binding spell cast by the other.

And yet the big things that made their pocket of Inner Plane society churn did not change so much. Leo continued to placate rich patricians and their designs on the social order. Sofia continued to rehash Eastern and comparative magic and mysticism in her academic appointments. It was the small and idiosyncratic things that riled and threatened people. For example, griping began when Leo summoned an oversight committee to draw up a document called "Critical Operational Guidelines and Protection-of-Rights Policies for New Immigrant Training Facilities." Then a petition calling for his resignation began to bounce around after he ordered strict enforcement of fines for violations of the magical emissions statute.

The media also had quite a few provocative hey-days after Leo had an "outburst" during an assembly of the Royal Order of Sorcerers and Magi in which he admonished the order for sensationalizing and delaying fellowship status to Professor Sofia La Maga Magus.

He and Sofia had been sitting on the edge of her mattress in the loggia of her apartment on the day the taped and close-captioned episode aired. They had been luxuriating after which Sofia tested Leo on the symbolic, mythical, and mystical import of each of the ritual weapons displayed high on the wall on the other side of the apartment. The phone had been ringing and hanging up on voicemail until, finally, the caller — Mirelle — dispensed with conventional niceties and sounded her voice in the apartment's space. "Sofia, PICK UP THE PHONE, GODDAMIT!"

"That's great!" Sofia laughed. "That's Mirelle," she proudly told Leo.

Leo nodded and muttered, "Strident" in an annoyed tone.

"That's very cool that she knows how to do that. Don't you think," Sofia mused.

"No," Leo replied.

Sofia walked across the upper compartment of her living space to a spot that was trashed with papers, books, artifacts, and magical supplies. She grasped the receiver of an antique cordless phone kept neatly in its cradle on a small, utterly cluttered table.

"Hello, Sweetheart," she said.

"Can you make a television over there for a minute?" Mirelle breathlessly asked. "You gotta' see this. You do."

"Make a television set?"

"A display screen of some kind. Just for five minutes. Can you pull out something from Sorcerers Network

News? It just happened. I don't know when they'll replay it," Mirelle said.

Rolling his eyes and shaking his head, Leo arranged Sofia in her low, little desk chair in the cluttered space of the study and made a small holographic image appear before.

"Do you see it?" Mirelle asked anxiously.

The image was the close-captioned telecast of Consul Leo de Lux Sortiar addressing an assembly of the Royal Order of Sorcerers and Magi. A runner along the bottom of the image read "de Lux appeals to ROSM for La Maga • Accuses Order of Commonsness."

There he was dressed in regal ceremonial vestments, including an indigo dalmatic fitted over a golden orange alb covered with a purple chasuble with green and gold linings over which, in turn, was a matching jewel-studded purple cope of richly arrayed shades or orange, aqua, violet, and purple. His high, matching miter was full of imposing bells. Even though the distinguishing feature of Leo's favorite staff was an onyx figurine of the sea-goat Capricornus, which he referred to by the Babylonia name Ea, the insignia emblazoned in gold thread and jeweled beads, on his miter and vestments was a glyph of the sun within which was the astrological symbol for Leo. This symbol was the de Lux family crest.

He was sneering in his perennially pissy public manner. His white eyes were as searing as laser scalpels. He was scolding the Fellows for their "shameless diversion of time resources" on "irrelevant partisan quibbles. For weeks with your testicles tied in knots over whether a maga who studied abroad should be able to join the ranks . . . . Meanwhile, such issues as the Order's position paper on magical emissions disposal are lost in the ethers."

He added that no matter what one's personal views about Sofia La Maga Magus were, the dossier on the matter—if anyone had bothered to read it—"clearly suggested" that she was qualified for fellowship status. "The behavior of the Order on this matter has been nothing more than—in fact, worse than—Commons," he concluded—which was a scathing indictment. Whenever someone in the Inner Plane thought something was insufferably perverse or banal, he or she would announce that it was "worse the Commons"—worse than what could be expected from Outer Plane folk, that is.

"When did this happen?" Sofia asked.

"This morning," Mirelle said.

"He actually makes sense sometimes," Sofia commented.

"Man, he lays it out when he talks," Mirelle exclaimed. She asked Sofia if there was a chance that the consul would ever look her in the eye and act as if she were a human being. "Like, at least in class," she said. "I mean, you know. He's like the evil step-father now."

Hearing this, Leo, thus, requested the phone receiver and spoke with Mirelle directly. He told her that her mentor, La Maga Magus, was continually carrying on about what a prodigy Mirelle was. "Plucked like the ripest rough-hewn gem hidden in a coal heap, dusted off, polished, and reserved as a crest jewel," he said. "I'm willing to offer some assistance in assimilating your refugees—your work with the immigrants, I mean. But this will be in the strictest confidence. Strictest," he admonished.

Mirelle asked Leo why he was extending himself. He uttered, "because I have no interest in being part of the 'machine.' It's not enough to avoid a dragon; you have to kill it. A little teaching for the day from a high and distinguished sorcerer. Treasure it, young Lady Soleil." He handed the phone back to Sofia, hollering, "Now, go away. We're BUSY," but Sofia and Mirelle kept on talking.

When Sofia hung up the phone, she told Leo that he

wasn't so bad.

He told Sofia that he wanted more from life than a snake swallowing its own tail. "'Gerbils in treadmills,' as you say. I'm tired of being a gear in the clockwork, operating under the false impression that being an eater rather than the eaten makes me free. I'm merely a mechanism in an automation. I don't want to be that.

"I've longed for a catalyst for redemption," he continued. "I did not know what it would look or feel like or what exactly I would be redeemed from. Now I do know, and I say we have not bound each other; we have found each other. Let the world and its arbitrary intrigues go on spinning. I will focus on the dyad that I have become. The yoke will be the binding quality of love, and the dizziness of the whirling and ravenous world will be kept at bay."

XII
The Glory of the Goddess

good-sized crowd showed up for Sofia's Masters of
Magic presentation. It would take place in the
school's sports stadium. The stadium resembled a
Greek amphitheater, with a deep arc of tiered seats that
hemmed in a dusty, chalk-lined playing field. The seats
were mossy, cobbled into a grassy hillside. Filing in and out
always had a festive feel about it.

Mirelle, Leonard, and Thetis Mirabilis, who had just
been adopted into Sofia's inner circle, stood at the gate that
led from the lockers to the field. None of the apprentices
knew quite what to expect. They simply stood by Sofia
while Dr. Bruno gave the audience an orientation about the
afternoon program from the kick-off line.

"The professor should be appearing any minute now,"
he said and anxiously glanced toward the gate. It wasn't
enough to simply walk onto the field, though; one had to
make an entrance. What that would be was not discussed
between Sofia and Danny Bruno. The man went back to
small-talking the crowd until it gasped in choral unison.
Bruno placidly turned to spy a Bengal tiger—about eight
feet long—leisurely slinking along the field's perimeter.

"Well, that must be her now!" he announced.

The crowd cheered. The great cat frisked. It romped
and broke into a trot before stalking Dr. Bruno. It paced
menacingly, roared, taunted, and sprung around the man
with whirlwind ferocity. Dr. Bruno then got the bright idea
to produce a hoop. Leaping through it, the tiger landed as
Professor Sofia La Maga Magus.

The crowd applauded robustly.

Dressed in a bright red halter and a matching pleated

skirt of Madras cotton held in place by a belt made of silver bells and clappers, Sofia resembled nothing less than a Dravidian warrior-queen. Ash and glyphs dusted her brow and the top of her head was sugared in ochre and sandal paste.

"Can you all hear me?" she asked.

The crowd roared.

"As Dr. Bruno Sortiar has explained, weaponry may be used as ritual tools that express symbols and metaphors. Being so, they are loaded with magical and mystical efficacy," she announced. "In spiritual and magical warfare, we don't cut into skin with a blade; we cut into momentum, into time, space, and causation. Moreover, in moving beyond desire and conflict and aspiring to transcendence, weapons become meditations that force paradigm shifts. The shift occurs in the microcosm of the self, which as magical people know, is how to get in gear with the macrocosm, which is the sphere of activity in which one exists. The hero-warrior in this melodrama is the higher self; the adversary is the lower.

"As you know, in the Terra Mysticus many-armed deities have been all the rage for millennia, but what do these forms mean? The form of the deity is a combination of symbols and metaphors. Each part, each symbol, is its own meditation."

She pulled a golden arrow from space. While stringing it in a weighty archer's bow, she recited a passage from the *Mundaka Upanishad:* "'Taking the great bow of Upanishad and the arrow sharpened by meditation, draw the bowstring with a focused mind. Hit the target, the Supreme Divinity.'" She launched the arrow into space. A magnificent burst of light exploded overhead. Scintillating sparks rained down.

As the audience reveled in the display, Sofia continued the recitation: "'The primordial creative vibration is the bow; oneself is the arrow. The Supreme Divinity is the target. Penetrating it unerringly, become one with it, just as the arrow unites with its target.'"

When the audience settled from its enthusiasm, Sofia joined her hands in prayer and chanted:

I meditate on She who embodies existence, the grantor of perfection, who is utterly luminous, whose eyes swell with tears of compassion, and who holds in her hands the net of unity, the scimitar of wisdom, the bow of determination, and the arrow of penetration.

She proceeded to sprout 10 weapon-wielding arms.

"The sword of discrimination, club of articulation, bow of determination, arrow of penetration, pike of attention, rod of restraint, axe of right action, net of unity, trident of harmony, and discus of revolving time. With these weapons," she announced, "the adept slays the mighty host of demons within himself." She began uttering the names of demons known to Hindu myth:

Mahahanu: The Great Deceiver
Parivarita: The Aimless One
Bidala: The Hypocrite
Kruddha: Anger
Ugrasya: The Savage
Durdhara: Given in to Temptation
Raktabija: Rampant Desire
Chanda: The Vicious
Munda: The Malicious
Shumbha: Conceit
Nishumbha: Self-deprecation

Armed, menacing, livid creatures, hairy and ogre-like, with snouts and tusks, claws and tails appeared. They amassed exponentially, charging upon the transfigured maga who glided about, dodging attacks and hurling weapons at the beasts. A whirlwind melee double-eighted the field until all the hobgoblins were cut to the quick. The field was rendered into a pit of bloody mud and grizzle. Severed heads, limbs, and entrails of monsters were heaped about. Sofia, winded and drenched in blood, resolutely stood in the midst of it.

She stretched her arms up, wrung them, and shimmied as if shaking off a chill. The grizzle that coated her dissolved. The field resumed its earlier, more pristine condition. The crowd cheered. Sofia produced a golden goblet of wine and sipped it. She smiled. While lingering in this manner, she explained that the phantasmagoria just witnessed was selected from a particularly important Hindu tale called the *The Glory of the Goddess,* "which relates three episodes of how the Great Goddess, who is the embodiment of the power of all the gods, battles demons to restore the order of the universe."

She was nearing the end of her speech when a giant water buffalo with a tremendous rack of horns sprung onto the field. It rutted and bellowed, threw up dust, and charged.

"'Yes, go ahead and roar! Roar and bellow while I finish drinking this wine,'" she told the creature. "'When I'm through, you'll be DEAD and the gods will be roaring in this very place!'" She egged on the audience to cheer, adding that "the worst demon of all that needs to be slain is the Great Ego, which manifests as the animal-familiar of the god of death. That demon is simply called the 'buffalo-demon,' Mahishasura."

The great animal charged. Sofia pranced around the beast's rut, racing and skirting over the field while dueling the creature's horns with a trident. Finally, she took a ferocious running leap at the creature as it charged. Skirting a head-on thrust, she stuck her weapon into the animal's side and pole-vaulted onto its back. She pressed her left foot onto the buffalo's neck and, although her weight on the beast had to have been slight, it sunk as if overwhelmed.

Collapsing, a fissure opened between the horns of the animal's head. From it emerged another livid ogre. The audience squealed. Sofia produced a double-edged sword and, with it, lopped off the ogre's head.

Cheers resounded. The grizzle dissolved. A rainbow flooded the sky from which flowers rained down and wisps of angelic creatures wafted about. Sofia thanked the crowd, curtsied, and made a run for the gate.

Leonard, Mirelle, and especially Thetis were wide-eyed with awe as Sofia galloped back to the sidelines where they stood. She was bristling and winded but nevertheless luminous. She leaned against Mirelle to catch her breath before cordially putting on gracious airs for all those who had followed her off the field to praise her performance.

"That was the most entertaining presentation in the whole Magical Masters series," one of the many justices in the audience applauded. "Better than Professor Vetiver's virtual reality sky show or last month's display of mediumistic zombies that they did over at the Bythos Academy."

"Thank you. Thank you," Sofia blushed.

Then, there were friends and relatives patting Sofia and telling her how surprised and impressed they were to see her display such feats.

Leo stormed in with Danny Bruno in tow. They appeared to be arguing.

"Marvelous," was Leo's last word. He spit it out as if nauseated on a piece of grizzle. He glared at Raphael Magus, who, having attended the program, had managed to immediately sidle beside Sofia. Zosimo Sortiar was there, too—or had been. Leo spied the mangy creature slinking off into the crowd. Then he eyed Sofia and Mirelle before his gaze seared toward his son who was standing way too close to the new apprentice, Thetis Mirabilis.

Pushing past Raphael, he whispered to Sofia that "demonstrations of prowess can be dangerous affairs."

He glanced accusingly at all around and announced, "Yes. The maga is marvelous, isn't she? Quite a spectacle but what of the substance buried in the bloodlust? In any case, the maga is quite late for another appointment. Thank you. Thank you. Come. Let's away." He corralled Sofia as well as her hangers-on to the parking lot.

Without question or protest, Sofia followed Leo, brushing through the swarming crowd in the wake of the consul's security forces. Sofia's apprentices and hangers-on followed. It might've seemed festive if it weren't for all the security personnel and something eerie in the air that was mixed up with Leo's mood.

"Yes. Just all come back to the house. Follow my driver," Leo announced to Sofia's entourage. "Raphael Magus, why not come along," he told the mage. "I can be cordial. We will need to talk at some point."

"I thought you and Sofia were off to another appointment?" Alan Raphael countered.

The consul glared at him for not "getting" whatever was mysteriously happening. But the gravity of the situation was such that these two fellows let down their guards.

"Ah," Alan exclaimed in recognition and joined the jostle to move things along.

They trailed off to the parking lot of the Academy. It was sparse with the fancy cars of people who, not needing mechanical vehicles for travel, used them anyway for the sake of display and because casually popping in and out of space was considered rude, at least in the North Atlantic Sovereignty.

While magical folk wheedled about that festive

afternoon, both government and corporate plain-clothes staff-bearers congregated in strategic spots in the lot and along the hilly embankment surrounding it. A trio of young women loitered in the distance. They were silhouettes to the right of a lone craggy myrtle tree upon the embankment beyond which the sun would set. Pointing fingers at Mirelle, they scowled and mouthed nasty things.

"My ex-friends," Mirelle muttered. "Medea Sarin's girls."

Sofia studied them. "Now, I get it," she said.

Mirelle let out a pained and exasperated sound.

"Where she is? There she is!" the girls jeered.

Leo was about to inform Sofia and the others that a threatening spectacle of political posturing was about to erupt right there and that Sofia would be targeted. He needed her to clear out. Before he could explain himself, a plume of red dust frothed up within feet of the Bentley that Leo had arrived in. Medea Sarin Sortiar was standing in the ruddy smog. Security personnel in Leo's service moved in.

"Ignore her. This isn't it," he told them. He anxiously ordered Sofia, Mirelle, his son, and the new girl, Thetis, to board the car.

Medea pointed her staff at Sofia. "'I'll get you, My Pretty'—and your little Deeple, too!" She zapped her staff at Mirelle. The shot missed the girl but put a gash in the finish of Leo's car.

Retaliatory flares from Leo's attendants were shot as Medea cloaked herself in the red-cloud bloom and disappeared. Leo quietly seethed. Victor asked him if the sorceress should be pursued.

Glaring straight on, Leo cringed and shook his head. "Get them back into place," he growled and gestured toward the diverted security squad.

"What about the girls?" Victor inquired. A squadron was poised to pursue them.

The consul merely lifted his left hand and made a subtle negative gesture. Something meant to be strategic apparently had gone very wrong. He glared at the plain-clothes staff-bearers in the distance. They were all tall, fit, cocky young men bent on the arts of coercion and domination. They were Hipparchus Gorgon's people, and they were having a good laugh. Leo barked at Lazar — his driver — to make haste in departing the lot. He leaned toward the front passenger side window where Sofia now sat. He nodded gravely.

"Now what did I do?" she pined.

Leo winced and grumbled. "It's not about you and it is," he said. "I don't regret it."

He then glanced toward the occupants in the back seat of the car. As if making small talk, he asked Mirelle if she had ever seen the movie *The Wizard of Oz*. "I believe they've been broadcasting it about twice a year for nearly a century in the United States." He asked Mirelle if she happened to have dropped a house on any witches when she barreled into the Inner Plane.

"No," Mirelle pouted.

"Well, you should have," Leo replied.

"I think I'll just go handle it," Sofia announced.

"Handle what?" Leo replied.

"I can do it. Just get the kids out of here," she said.

"What are you talking about? You have no idea what is going on," Leo hollered. "It's not about you. Lazar, MOVE. *You sit tight right there, La Maga Magus,"* he bellowed, but in a faint mist of light, she disappeared from the car to reemerge within a few feet of Gorgon's people. Leo, in turn, translocated the Bentley and its remaining occupants away to a safer place.

In subdued horror, Leo watched Gorgon's forces form a circle around Sofia as she strode toward a tall, dark, swaggering character with eerie sapphire blue eyes. His name was Tyrone Sauros Sortiar. Barely aged 25 years, he was Gorgon's protégé. Leo was known to refer to this kid as Rex, the Lizard-Boy or else just Tyrannosaurus — sometimes to his face.

"What is she doing?" Victor asked.

"Let us see," Leo huffed.

Thus, the makings of a mutiny or coup — a standoff between the consul's security forces and staff bearers affiliated with the corporatist Hipparchus Gorgon Sortiar — was at hand in the parking lot of the H. Trismegistus Mystical Arts Academy. Between the factions stood Sofia La Maga.

"Did you like the show?" she shouted at the entourage of Gorgon's staff-bearers.

"The phantasm was a rip but the encore in the parking lot with the wicked witch was lackluster, I gotta say," Sauros replied. "You were all set to be a good girl about those tricks you turned — I mean, learned — in the Mysticus, Lady La Maga, Right? Wasn't that the deal between you and the Lord Consul?"

"I've been a very good girl," Sofia remarked.

"I'm sure you're good. Very," he said wryly.

"You'll not get away with this, Sauros," Leo exclaimed. *"The audacity!"*

Gorgon's people laughed at him.

Leo was mulling over dramatic but not too devastating magical attacks to launch when Victor diverted his attention to the embankment where Medea Sarin's girls lingered. They appeared to be engaged in a rite. They were wildly dancing around a man who, though a speck in the distance, may have been that Aurelio-Zosimo fellow.

"They are not in their right minds, those girls," Victor uttered. The stuff of witches raising a cone of power, but no there was something forced and craven about their movements. They were neither in control of themselves nor in reverie, but oppressed by an enchantment.

Zosimo was gauntly clad in black leather. A drooping, black cone with jangling bells was on his head. He was gripping a thick, pole-like staff that was wrapped in black leather and accented with feathers and dangling spiked baubles that made the staff resemble a freaky cat-o-nine-tails. That and his feral hair whipping around in the breeze and the girls bounding around him seemed seductively diabolical. He was pacing rabidly, like an animal poised to pounce.

"Zosimo Sortiar conducts magical exercises with La Maga Magus. You do know that, Sir," Victor said.

"Mmm," Leo grunted affirmatively. Sofia had never spoken about him. Leo thought that the fellow was out of the picture, but then what was he witnessing? He watched Sofia raise a hand in greeting to Zosimo as he neared the slope of the embankment. The man bucked his head like bull in a rut.

Leo wasn't sure, but he had a premonition that something amazing was about to occur. He wanted to see it even if it was the very last thing he or anyone there ever did see.

"You're out of your league with her, Boy," he shouted at Sauros. "All of you. Step away. She will cut you down and all this will blow up into something Gorgon never bargained for."

"You are so done, de Lux," he heard someone holler. "You and your girlfriend should just walk away. Retire to a private island in the Outer Plane." But the voice did not come from Gorgon's side of the divide. Within the Sovereignty's own security forces, there were cadres that had turned against him. They were insidiously and strategically positioned in the H. Trismegistus parking lot.

Then the whir and putter of a helicopter overhead drowned out sound.

Leo watched Sofia gaze up toward it, raise her arms, and exclaim, "I knew he couldn't resist me!"

It was Hipparchus Gorgon.

A floodlight from the craft shown down on her. Static from the light beam made her hair pull up and stand on end. Gorgon's staff bearers clapped and jeered as the copter's windy undertow made Sofia's skirt ride-up.

"You want to see a really, really cool trick that I learned in the Mysticus?" she hollered.

The helicopter lights flickered. The amassing squadrons from both sides readied their weapons.

"You should take them all out with a Conus magus, Sir. The charm. Nip it in the bud," Victor nudged.

"Yes, I should, shouldn't I," Leo replied, but he watched the maga twist her fingers into a mudra—a magical hand gesture—instead. Her index fingers gnarled around middle fingers and other digits bent and wove so that her hands made a triangular shape that was perhaps meant to resemble a clitoris.

As if cued, The Crazy Professor, evil staff in hand, bounded from his perch on the embankment in a dash toward her. The girls who had been frantically prancing around him as if stricken with St. Vitus dance collapsed into faints.

Leo ordered Victor to hit the ground. He himself was going to charge in toward Sofia and Gorgon's people but was blown back by the rut of monstrous phantoms that had risen up around the saboteurs. They were ragged hermaphroditic humanoid creatures clad in animal skins or even human remains, red-eyed, fanged, tentacled, and covered in blood and ash. It was an unexpected encore of Sofia's earlier performance, but these hobgoblins were not from the pages of Hindu myth. but another paradigm.

The earth quaked with the footfalls of the monsters. The weapons they held flashed sharp with blinding sparks of light as they incandesced and swirled to resolve into gyroscopic arcs of light that boomed into sound. It was a drone that became a roar like the reverberation of a mass of symphonic gongs. Relentless swells of light and crescendos and polyphonic timbers surged to such intensity that dematerialization occurred.

Staff-bearers of all persuasions and allegiances, Sarin's girls, de Lux, and any loiterers in the area were swept up in a storm of motion, light, and thunderous sound. Groundless and bodiless, they would only experience themselves as awareness without will or motion, haplessly arrested in a blinding and relentlessly reverberating sound field. It was a preview of a vortex at the end of Time that sucks the remnant of existence back into undifferentiated mush in a matrix.

It surely did not last as long as it seemed, but its cessation was abrupt. No helicopter was in sight, neither was Sauros. Any person who could not manage a quick getaway before the maelstrom peaked was collapsed, shivering, shocked in faint or sapped of breath and motion. Only Leo de Lux had managed to hold his ground, frozen and weighted in place lest the slightest twitch throw him off balance.

Sofia was in the distance, placidly taking in the sight of the devastation. Bodies, not dead but shuddering, were heaped about. That Leo and she were still standing presumably meant that they had "won." There was no hint of The Crazy Professor.

Leo reeled as he gasped for words. He thought he should call out to Sofia but *"The unmitigated gall,"* was all he could muster. With eyes reddened and bulging in fury, he bellowed at the sky as if Hipparchus Gorgon were still *there: "I'll not be defied by your mules and lackeys! The Eschaton* has come!" he announced. With his staff, he cast out a sweeping metal net over the mutineers. Most were still collapsed and struggling to revive. "Round them up," he ordered those still on his side, themselves yet struggling to recover.

"Where are those little bitches," he added. The consul scanned the area for Medea Sarin's girls. He found them scrambling to flee. *"Out of my sight!"* he shouted. A lightning bolt, shot from his staff. It made them freeze and collapse again. "I'll put you and that hag out for good!" Struggling to compose himself, he breathed deeply and ruefully muttered the word "plagues" a few times.

He turned to Sofia, who had approached. Beginning in a plaintive tone, he said, "I had hoped to have much more time with you. You were an answer to me. A line has been crossed and I am weighted with impossible choices. The end has come too soon."

"This puny weakness and sentimentality doesn't suit you, Leo de Lux," she replied. "You got what you asked for. You can either ditch it and go back to being a self-serving prick or you can stand up and fight."

"There's no going back," he rued without giving a second thought to Sofia's insults. He was simply peeved at the lack of options. "What happened to your 'partner'?" he snapped.

As if startled, Sofia glanced around to catch sight of Zosimo, but he was not to be found.

"Casualty?" Leo asked.

A perplexed pallor overcame her. "He must've gone home," she uttered

Leo froze at the ridiculous response. "Who is he to you?"

She turned dumbfounded and defensive just as she had that night when Leo accused her of overstepping her bounds with Leonard and Pyr Sacra empowerments. Tense, guilt-ridden, and guarded. Found out but about what this time?

"Match point," he said.

Instead of speaking, she moved toward him. A lost and helpless expression overtook her. Leo realized that in her concern about Zosimo's welfare, she had something pathetic to confide.

He softened. He allowed her to draw very close until they were in embrace, her electrical pulse infused him and her mouth was braced against his ear.

"I'm not ready to say, but you'll find out," she sulked. "He's not my lover, okay? He's just got to be away and not dead though."

Leo motioned toward Victor and, in a biting tone, requested that he "go find out what's become of that Zosimo-character."

"Right away, Sir," Victor replied with a polite bow as he took a step backward and translocated away to fulfil the task.

"Thank you," Sofia quietly whimpered to Leo.

It strange to have her trembling, teary-eyed, and cleaving to him now after she had spent the afternoon battling monsters and thwarting a coup in a bombastically ripped show of force.

"Today's threat is just the beginning, despite your excellent show," he said. He felt her give a nod of agreement.

"Rough magic and intrigue. I may be up for it," he said.

He suddenly felt excited and elated about the adventure that might be in store. Intrigue and risk and utter reinvention. It spiked his ardor.

Sofia was wilting and shivering, though. The tingly aura she let off wasn't happening much.

Leo drew her to arms' length to see that she had turned quite pale. Her glazed eyes were observing the colorful clouds that blind the eyes and accompany that airy, vertiginous lift one feels flying up from the throat before fainting.

"Are you alright?" he uttered.

"Power outage," she eked before her consciousness fizzled into whiteness and void.

XIII
The Daughter

Mirelle was flabbergasted by the sedate and antique opulence of the de Lux estate. She had never been anywhere near a patrician's home. People said that the consul's residence was eccentrically modest for a person of his stature. It was very small and sparse compared with other villas. Sofia had told Mirelle that even Dr. Bruno lived in a futuristic industrial-chic monstrosity on a cliff overlooking the sea.

Mirelle looked straight ahead into a huge park in the center of the house. It was stuffed with tropical plants as if were a portal to a Cost Rican rain forest. She watched Leonard walk in, sit down cross-legged on a divan, and materialize antlers, as if he were the Lord of Beasts. Mirelle shook her head and sullenly flashed her spooky eyes at him. She wasn't going to give him the satisfaction of seeming too amused or impressed. Then Leonard displayed how he could balance stacks of butterflies on each of his fingers all at once.

"He's making remarkable progress as a side-show act," the consul muttered good-naturedly and winked. The cordiality surprised Mirelle. The consul handed her a petite stem glass of port and asked her if she liked sweet drinks like her mentor did.

"Brandy is better to put fire in your belly on these sorts of days," he said.

"I could do a brandy," Mirelle replied.

"Good!" The consul took the stem glass away and coaxed Mirelle to follow him along a walkway around the perimeter of the house's atrium. They passed through one of many porticos and through dark, ornately antique wood-paneled doors to a room that looked like the study of a Victorian-era aristocrat.

Dark, perfectly seamed and varnished wood-panel walls framed long, leaded, carnival glass windows and spanned up to a high and vaulted ceiling on which was a fresco of a virile deity with ruddy hair. It was Jupiter whose eagle was shown screwing a swan among storm clouds and lightning. A thin ring of images encircled Jupiter. At first glance, the ring could be mistaken for a floral motif, but it depicted Roman warfare.

Tiffany lamps peppered the room, and classical music could faintly be heard. Three lounge chairs made of thick leather and mahogany were set around a table on which teaware and stacks of papers sat. Consul de Lux motioned for Mirelle to take a seat there. He wandered to a liquor cabinet that was embedded in the wall. It contained fancy decanters, tumblers, snifters, and brandy warming contraptions.

"You don't smoke cigars with all that?" Mirelle called out.

"Billowing smoke is distasteful to me," the consul replied. "Contrary to rumor, I'm not a dragon. And you, Lady Soleil?"

"No. Not in the habit of smoking cigars...and not a dragon," she told him.

"Because I would indulge you, if you like," he said.

Mirelle shrugged. The mere fact that the consul was talking to her in a cordial manner and about to give her a snifter of a very high-grade brandy was so indulgent that it was frightening. In any other circumstance, she would've thought the man intended to drug and eviscerate her and use her body parts for wicked sorcery.

Dr. Bruno and a bunch of other people were at the house, including Raphael Magus. The consul had invited them all—all these magi and magian sympathizers—to his villa. Indeed, Dr. Bruno was in an adjacent room. He was on the phone. Mirelle could hear him mouthing off forceful words that sometimes sounded jolly, sometimes threatening. Mirelle didn't know who or how many persons he was talking to at any given moment.

Sofia was supposedly sulking in the early moonlight on the turret of a tower that was attached to the house. Word was that she had blown a gasket during a magical skirmish with Hipparchus Gorgon that afternoon. With a grave and determined manner, the consul had removed her from the parking lot of the H. Trismegistus campus and carried her in his arms, like a shining knight rescuing a damsel, step by step, to the top of that tower. He remained out of sight—presumably in Sofia's embrace—until his guests grew tired of fretting and instead turned their attentions to ogling the Villa de Lux. They mingled and sampled finger foods and wines that servants brought around.

Mirelle was hoping that the consul might let on about what had occurred earlier that day. He seemed to want to do so. Why else would he be acting like a pal? Then she noticed that the stacks of papers on the table at which she sat were about her: her immigration papers, her academic file, her medical records.

He handed Mirelle a warmed snifter of a highly aromatic cognac. The smell was always better than the taste, but Mirelle knew this drink would be smooth and make her gut delectably toasty.

The consul placed a chair directly across from her. He sat very close and pulled the whole movement together in a menacing way: the grasping of a thick, smelly leather chair, the placement of it within inches of her, the setting himself down on it with drink in hand. Then he leaned in to speak with hot white eyes. His tone was low and hissing.

"I am a highly distinguished patrician magistrate. You

are a lowly immigrant neophyte. The lowest of the low. Dimidium Pleb. Under other conditions, you would not even be fit to serve as the slave of a person like me. Furthermore, this proximity between us would be highly defiling of my person. That you look me in the eye or speak freely is a grievous affront," he said.

Mirelle squirmed and lowered her gaze. Holding the snifter of cognac seemed like a mockery.

"Audacity can be a useful trait for a sorceress," he continued, "but not if it isn't tempered by a keenly discriminative faculty. Subtlety and deviousness make better weapons for the weak than hostility. If I were your foe or if I were a threat—as it seems a whole brood of dark sorceresses and their mother hen have become for you—it would be no good for you to display pique, nor to be abrupt or even to-the-point. Another strategy would be required."

Dead silence ensued. Mirelle didn't know quite what the consul was getting at or whether she was allowed to speak.

"Is the aperitif disagreeable with you, Lady Soleil?" the consul asked.

Mirelle mutely shook her head. She reluctantly gulped the drink and went back to being silent.

"Do you not have any questions for me?" he asked.

She strained to think up one.

The consul winced and rose from his chair. He laughed in a scoffing and private manner. Leonard appeared in the doorway, presumably to stare down his father in case anything prickly was going on between him and Mirelle. The consul ordered Leonard to check on Sofia. "Go cuddle with her, why don't you. I hear she's not feeling well after her big day," he said.

"With pleasure," Leonard replied defiantly.

The consul sighed out a laugh. He motioned a finger

toward Mirelle then upward as if pointing to wherever Sofia was, and then toward Leonard: "The moon revolves around the earth and the earth revolves around the sun—or the son, in this case." He pouted at Leonard who grinned as if having won an arm wrestling match. Then he flecked a hand at the youth that he should go away to fulfill his task.

"Why did she choose you, Mirelle?" the consul then asked.

"She didn't choose me exactly. I was kind of foisted on her," Mirelle admitted. "But she doesn't treat me like what I am. She treats me like a real magical person and wants me to stand up and act like one, even before you. She is all and totally great."

The consul smiled. "La Maga Magus' powers are extraordinarily subtle, impactful, and profound, and she is extraordinarily self-effacing and tender about her abilities. I am glad to see that her levity and familiarity with you—her display of ordinariness—has not dulled your awareness of how precious she is as teachers and magical persons go. In any case," he continued, "you are a 'real magical person,' Mirelle Soleil. And my son—and the aerie little girl Miss Mirabilis, who your precious mentor has just taken on— must be extraordinary persons to have caught La Maga Magus' attention and endearment. It is for this reason that I can put aside certain . . ." the consul hesitated for the right words, "prejudices and models of mental conditioning to recognize you. Do you understand what I'm saying?"

Mirelle wasn't sure. She again felt the surrealism of the glass of cognac in her grip. She had to take another sip and savor the heat infusing her esophagus and running along her back and chest. She nodded demurely.

"Do you have any questions in your mind about me or questions about our circumstance with La Maga Magus?" the consul asked again.

Mirelle mused on it and told the consul that she did

have a question "in a way. You went through this metaphor about the sun and the moon, but what are you in all this, do you think, Lord Consul?"

He became thoughtful before wistfully smiling. "I'm beginning to think that I might be the galactic space within which these relationships and intrigues thrive." He told Mirelle that he had an elder brother who in his youth—when the consul himself was yet a very young child—envisioned that the consul would grow up to herald a new golden age.

"Can you imagine that? I turned out to be a terrible disappointment to him—the consul of the North Atlantic Sovereignty, an art dealer, and a forger," he smirked. "I understand that he thinks I'm the enemy now and also rather decadent even if a person's life, death, and overall well-being are in my hands. He's right about what I've become, but I'm beginning to think that he might be right about what I have yet to be. I haven't seen him since my father, who was a man driven by saturnine expediency, banished him to an insane asylum when I was . . . oh . . . about the same age that Leonard was when he became motherless," the consul confided. "My brother is my only warm memory of childhood. I was never allowed to admit this to anyone—not even myself for a long while. He runs an apocalyptic Illuminist magi cult called the 'Lions of Light.' That's my name, you know—and Leonard's. 'Lion of Light.' As you can guess, the name commonly recurs in my family dynasty."

As the consul brooded, his eyes were misted over in melancholy and relief.

"Of all his offspring, my father chose me, the last and final product of his ejaculatory spillage, to be his successor," he continued. "Emmanuel and I are the man's only surviving sons, the other two murdered by magical means that almost claimed me as well. That story will perhaps make it into a history book someday."

Mirelle was well aware of the story, but she dared not admit it.

The consul smiled wryly. "I executed a full true Conus magus maneuver on the assassin of my brothers and cousins. I was 22 years old. After that, my father regarded me as a superior. He retired from public life, leaving my hands full of it. What about your father, Lady Soleil?"

"Absentee," she replied hastily to add, "What about the Conus magus?" because although she knew the story of the consul's family drama, she was quite surprised about the added detail.

"Well, it is a secret, my dear," he said. "I am entrusting it to you."

Mirelle blinked, perplexed, in wonder, and not knowing how to respond.

"Perhaps you can share a secret with me? I'm curious about the exact relationship between your mentor and that professor from the Bythos Academy, Aurelio Zosimo Sortiar."

In response, Mirelle forced her mind to become as empty and spacious as she could possibly muster to fend off any mind-reading ruses that the consul might try. She wasn't going to tell what she had recently discovered.

"They're friendly," she shrugged. "They're not lovers or anything like that."

The consul smiled with that odd, knowing grimace he displayed sometimes — a flicker of the eye, a tic at the corner of the mouth.

"Very good," he concluded.

Mirelle wondered whether he already knew and was testing her.

"We'll not mention it again until and unless it suits La Maga Magus to do so," he said.

Mirelle nodded very subtly, unsure whether such a

gesture had betrayed her vow of silence about it.

"We're going to talk in more privacy now," the consul announced. "Take your drink."

He led Mirelle into the ground floor studio of his tower and closed the door. It was a round, well-lit work room with a circle full of shadows of histories of chalk markings on the floor and work benches with patens and shelves full of potions and various implements. An alcove to the east had a small altar with images of Babylonian and Greco-Roman deities and emblems derived from what had to be very ancient mysticism. He showed her a staff that was different from the thick, obsidian-topped staff he had been wielding earlier that afternoon. It was more slender but nearly as menacing. It was topped with a citrine figurine of a winged lion leaping from a flame. "Oak," he said. "Your staff should be oak, perhaps holly. Never mind the precious metals. Wrap it in iron. Obsidian, diamonds," he said.

Mirelle told him that her staff was made of wood from an ash tree.

"Excellent," he said. It was another kind of warrior wood wielded by kingly deities: Poseidon and Odin.

"And garnets and malachite," she told him. They were stones that had protective and strength-enhancing energies. The two together balanced male and female energies.

"Very good."

"And nickel." It was a resonant metal once only acquired by smelting meteorites.

"That's fine," the consul said. Then he proceeded to grill Mirelle about her encounters with Medea Sarin Sortiar and about her history with the three harpies who had put a damper on their afternoon before Hipparchus Gorgon's people turned the screws. How many times had Mirelle been in the company of Medea Sarin? What was said word-for-word? Were any pacts or agreements made? Did the warped sorceress pass along anything that could be interpreted as an empowerment?

Mirelle had only met the woman twice. She didn't like her, but her friends were excited at the prospect of learning coercive spells, establishing reputations, and getting back at persons who had slighted them.

"My family background is in Hoodoo. A lot of Hoodoo is about coercion. It wasn't an ambition for me to study that on this side of the divide," Mirelle told Consul de Lux. "I wanted to do something else even though I didn't think I was going to get the opportunity. I met one of the girls, Karen, because I was selling potions through the Black Magic Market. She bought stuff from me, and we started smuggling things into the Outer Plane and then the operation expanded," Mirelle explained.

She was actually admitting a high crime to the consul, but in the moment, it didn't seem as if she would be taken to task for her confession. "I didn't think those girls were dark. We were just, you know, surviving. We had to be edgy and fuck the system. My mother didn't give me up to cross from the Outer to Inner Plane so I could be some senator's window washer or sex slave; she wanted me to be *powerful*," Mirelle said.

"So you became an apothecary of sorts—and a spell-dealer," the consul said.

"I just knew how to make stuff, and I sold it, and people who knew I could make stuff capitalized on it and expanded the operation to the Outer Plane, just like every sovereignty-sanctioned patrician businessman does. That's just business, but when someone else besides you people are making a profit on it, suddenly it's not business; it's a crime."

The consul glared at her as if the ramble was very rude, but she continued.

"No sweatshops, environmental pillaging, or genocide were involved in my little cottage industry," she boasted.

"Medea Sarin Sortiar," he enunciated. "Continue."

A wide smile grazed across her face, and she giggled, "K," just as Sofia might. She told the consul that Medea Sarin was mainly interested in Mirelle's seizure experiences. "Because I used to 'see' people when I went under, and sometimes they would tell me things. Other times, I would tell them things."

"Did you tell 'things' to La Maga Magus when you alighted into her midst years back when you were a seizure-addled child and she in exile in the Terra Mysticus?" the consul asked.

"Probably."

"What do you think you might have told her, Mirelle?"

"I probably told her things to make her feel better. Things that other people I met told me," she replied.

"You know, some persons in this realm go to great lengths to contact entities in the Deep Inner Planes," the consul commented, "and there you were, a Commons, penetrating those territories. The word is that you've been unwittingly empowered by entities far more powerful and distinguished than persons like myself or your mentor. What are you going to do with that? Or what do you think a person like Medea Sarin Sortiar would do with that?" he questioned.

Mirelle shrugged. "When you have a key to something, there's nothing to 'do' about it. You don't even have to know you have it, and if you do think you have it; well then you probably don't," Mirelle said. "I've been told that I have keys," she smiled demurely. "I don't know what that means, and Sofia says that, for now, that's good. I have no clue what Medea Sarin Sortiar thought she was going to get out of me or how she thought she could exploit me, but she seems to think I'm a trophy."

Mirelle finally got around to telling the consul that she was supposed to meet with Medea Sarin a third time, presumably to discuss initiation, but Mirelle delayed the encounter and confided in Professor Waite. In talking with Waite, it came to light that Mirelle had a connection with Sofia La Maga Magus. That was how Mirelle was redeemed.

"Because this sorceress has been quibbling about you. Giving Sofia lip. She's been a nuisance for many years. After today's dramatics, I might have to put an end to it. That's the least of it," the consul said. He paused for a while. They sat quietly. He brooded. Then he said, "A coup attempt was lodged against the Sovereignty today. This hag, Medea Sarin, and your erstwhile 'friends' appeared to be colluding. Your mentor and her 'friend,' the good Professor Zosimo Sortiar, took matters into their own hands."

"Really?" Mirelle beamed in anticipation of how that story played out.

The reply caused the consul to flinch.

"I mean, what did they do? La Maga Magus and Zosimo Sortiar?" Mirelle asked.

"They ended the world. Momentarily," the consul admitted. "It was extraordinary. Unparalleled perhaps. This creates a dilemma for me. On the one hand, to seemingly have La Maga Magus's allegiance and for her to apparently have Zosimo Sortiar's devotion is encouraging. On the other, if the two of them went renegade and on a rampage, from what I witnessed, it may be beyond control. Can you grasp what I'm attempting to express?" he asked.

"DAMN! that I missed it," Mirelle exclaimed. "Time bomb. 'Weapons of mass destruction,'" she grinned. "That's not what they're about, though. Definitely not," she assured the consul.

"Definitely."

"Totally definitely not," Mirelle insisted.

"What is he to her?" he asked again.

"They're friends," Mirelle stammered. "You said we weren't going to talk about it again."

Leo eyed her.

"It's kind of obvious," she relented, "but I'm not telling."

He nodded. A bit of a clue he would have to chew on. He sat quietly. Then, he thanked Mirelle and told her that she could address him in a familiar way going forward. "If anyone asks, you're a member of this house," he said quietly and glared at her. "Understand what this means," he snapped. "Do not cross me. Do not interfere with my designs or my momentum. Can you manage that, Mirelle?"

She nodded. The consul huffed and grimaced. He stood up and approached his altar. "Alright, then. Stand here," he commanded. Mirelle complied. The consul grasped a highly polished diamond-shaped dagger from the altar and lightly pressed it against Mirelle's breast bone. With his free hand, he gripped the back of the girl's head and arched her neck into a taut and choking posture. He glared into her eyes, white to white. Mirelle felt her blood drain from fear of what he had in mind only to feel the rush of an empowerment initiation: a hot, scintillating, and heady pulsation.

"'Magic is potentiated when the self is effaced by pleasure or pain,'" the consul lulled.

An electrically erotic sensation flooded through the dagger into Mirelle's chest and through the man's eyes into her brain. She relaxed into it. The searing stare and torturous grip became softer, until they seemed like a caress.

The consul gently released his hold. He placed the dagger within inches of Mirelle's brow. She focused on it past the light that was flooding her mind. The platinum grip had a ruby and citrine inlay of gems that spelled "de Lux."

The man grinned as if he didn't think Mirelle would believe what she would next see. A miniature angel with a lion on its breastplate and a flaming sword in hand emerged from the dagger and flew into her head. It made a peculiar tickle as it snaked its way to her chest where it settled like a glowing ember.

He placed the dagger back on the altar and announced, as if commanding the spirits there, "No one dare touch this child with malice! She belongs to me."

He took up the staff he had shown her earlier and holding it horizontally in both hands, presented it to her. Then he bolted from the room. Mirelle scurried after him, suddenly breathless with teary-eyed love-feelings for him.

They returned to the turret of the consul's tower where Sofia had been recuperating, but she was not there. Night had fallen by then, and most of the guests had departed.

The consul and Mirelle tracked down Leonard, who was with Thetis Mirabilis. The two were sitting in one of the outdoor patios. They were buttressed against each other, heads inclined toward one another, hands and fingers sensuously intermingled and all-in-all resting in each other's quiet and budding infatuation. The girl was startled when the consul came upon them. Leonard acted as if he were expecting his father's intrusion.

de Lux senior didn't pay any mind to the young couple's courtship behavior. He only wanted to know Sofia's whereabouts.

Leonard cocked his head toward the estate's driveway turnabout in the distance. There Sofia was leaning against a middle-class sedan. It was Raphael Magus' car. She and Raphael were sweetly speaking. They were holding hands. Their silhouettes in the shadows of night bespoke compassion as they gently nodded at each other's utterances. They hugged each other. He kissed her forehead, got into his unremarkable car, and departed.

"She may not be long for this world, but I want her to stay," the consul said. He seemed unable to verbalize whatever else he needed to express. He clenched his jaw and looked distant.

Mirelle grinned wickedly and winked at Leonard and Thetis. "She really does move you, huh?" she remarked.

Leo made an affirmative gesture with his eyes.

"Like, in what direction?" Mirelle quipped. ". . . does she move you, that is."

"Toward myself," the man replied stiffly. "But I'm not prepared to be a pawn in Chaos or Clarus Principle eschatology if that's where all this is going."

"Nothing bad is happening," Mirelle said.

The consul gasped out a rueful snicker. "If the world is to be renovated, it's going to be on my terms," he announced, adding, "Say, 'good night,' Leonard. It's time for our guests to depart. Little Miss Lady Mirabilis-Almost-Magus can stay over another night some other time when I'm unaware of her presence in the house."

The youth scowled.

Thetis meekly sidled next to Mirelle, expecting that the older girl would know the appropriate way to leave. Mirelle waited for the consul's cue.

"Leonard, can you page Lazar and ask him to take the girls home?" he requested. "Why don't you just go, Leonard? Take a ride with them—but no 'lingering' tonight. You know what I mean. It's not the safest night to play about." The consul eyed all of the young people. They all obeyed and were quite happy and relieved to do so.

*

As the week began anew, it seemed that things had settled into their usual pace. Mirelle felt confident that her ex-friends Karen Brevis, Tina Hamadryad, and Silvie Puck would keep their distance after what Zosimo Sortiar had done to them. She didn't know what would happen if they did get bold enough to try anything—or what she would end up doing in response, what with whatever hidden abilities La Maga Magus and de Lux Sortiar had woken up in her through their doting attentions.

Consul de Lux Sortiar had warned her to keep her cool. The "take home" message seemed to be that she should use her lowly role as a shield behind which she could slyly fuck people over and get her way. It was Hoodoo all over again but scaled up a bit.

On a Wednesday in the early afternoon, the Consul tracked her down on the Academy campus. He had her board a huge SUV. In addition to de Lux and the driver, five other persons were in the vehicle. One was a mature gent named Emmanuel de Lux Magus. He was the brother that the consul had talked about. Another was Vinca Blanco Sortiar, a petite woman with pale skin and a jet-black bob. The consul's attendants were also in attendance—Victor and a butchy platinum blond woman named Lou who was even pricklier than Mirelle. Also among the entourage was a gorgeous, dark-skinned man who Mirelle otherwise didn't officially know but ogled whenever she visited the Bythos Academy of Magical Sciences. He was an assistant professor named Michael Camael Magus.

They drove to the seedy side of downtown, which was called Limbo. It was where storefront art galleries were nestled among "chop" shops where controlled substances and organic materials could be acquired. It was where bootlegs of anything could be bought and sold, and where, if you knew the right table to approach in a café, you could trade in wacky worts and prohibited spells and then go to a back room or downstairs or next door to ingest the stash or have sinister strangers assist you in diabolism or else exotically fetishistic or erotic encounters with players and sex-magic workers.

It was a place where things got very loud and wild at night in clubs that had no windows. It was a gritty demimonde.

Mirelle was not unfamiliar with it. It was where the wilier among the marginalized thrived, made decent money, and lived on the edge and off the vices and vulgarities of patricians instead of being cannibalized by them.

"I was saving up to open my own botanica here," Mirelle mentioned. She smiled whimsically and pointed out a tiny gallery with a red construct in the window that kept exploding. It was some artist's interpretation of extreme sexual overstimulation. A person could not look at the image for too long without feeling hot, breathless, and ecstatically on verge of lifelessness.

"That space was for rent a year ago," she sighed and placidly watched one of the two men who were gaping at the contraption in the store's window mess his trousers and faint.

The consul casually asked if she had ever seen Leonard in these parts. Of course she had — frequently — but she told the consul that she had never seen Leonard outside of the bounds of the H. Trismegistus Campus Pavilion. The consul made a tsking sound because he knew she was lying.

"Just being polite," she said.

The consul did not respond.

The vehicle slowed as it approached a club called Homunculus Tongue. The consul was in the habit of raiding it at least once a month. The place, which was named after a heavy metal blues-rock band that was the rage when the consul and Sofia La Maga were young, was frequented by college-crowd rabble and magical iconoclasts, extremists, and mavericks, including Professor

Aurelio Zosimo Sortiar and his entourage. The band had played there a few times back in its heyday when they toured the Terra Novit. It also was where Mirelle's gang hung out.

"Is this it?" he asked her.

Mirelle gulped a "yes." She used to sit at table in the shadows and take Hoodoo orders while Karen and the other girls drummed up business and shook down people.

They parked. Lady Vinca Blanco Sortiar pulled out a black scrying mirror. She spritzed water on it and turned it toward the light. She and Professor Camael Magus gazed into it intently. Mirelle leaned in to study it as well. She had to push up close to Professor Camael to do this. She smelled his cologne. It was something with vetiver and sandal and torturously titillating to whiff.

"Are these the girls?" Lady Blanco asked Mirelle.

The mirror held an image of the inside of Homunculus Tongue. It was a dingy, rustically wood-paneled place that had tables scattered around facing a stage.

"That's Tina—Serpentina—Hamadryad." Mirelle pointed to the wiry girl with the dark, pin-straight hair. "That's Karen." She pointed to a more imposing and husky young woman with red hair and ruddy, freckled features.

"*Karenia brevis,*" Professor Camael snickered. The others in the SUV turned quizzical glances at him. Then the white-haired man, de Lux Magus, shook his head and tapped his brow as if something very stupid had occurred. He seemed to be even more grave and snobby than de Lux Sortiar typically was.

"Karen Ea Brevis. You know her?" Mirelle asked.

"The affectations of young magical persons never cease to amaze me," the consul's older brother quipped.

Lady Blanco was smiling smartly but sort of compassionately—or maybe it was pathetically. The consul was clucking and shaking his head. "Does Karen Ea Brevis sound like a magical name to you, Mirelle?" he asked.

Mirelle simply blinked. It didn't except for the "Ea" part.

"Karenia brevis is the name of toxic microscopic algae, the proliferation of which causes a phenomenon known as Red Tide," the consul announced. "Do you know what Red Tide is with your ties to the Creole South—the Gulf Coast of the U S A, Mirelle?"

Professor Camael and the others gaped at her, as if hanging on to her answer.

"Red water that kills everything in it and can kill you if you eat anything fished up out of it and takes your breath away and makes you wheeze if you stand on the shore near where it settles," Mirelle recounted.

"What kind of person would choose such a name for herself?" the consul asked bitingly.

Lady Blanco told the consul to stop picking on Mirelle. "So she's got an adversary now. That's the spice of life. A little excitement. Every young sorceress should have an adversary. Otherwise, she might as well get a job as a radiology technician or something in the Outer Plane, don't you think, Leo?"

The consul simply nodded distractedly.

Lady Blanco turned back to Mirelle. "Are you a maga or a sorceress, Sweetie?

Mirelle told her that she hadn't decided.

"Yes, why do people have to be one thing or the other? Why is that, Leo," Lady Blanco quipped.

The consul didn't reply.

Lady Blanco grimaced. "He's 'distracted,' Sofia La Maga. Who knew," she uttered to Mirelle. "Then she said: "First, we want to keep track of these girls, especially that one." Lady Blanco pointed to Karen in the mirror. "Them and their fearless leader."

"'The Wicked Witch of the West,'" the consul piped in.

"Yes," Lady Blanco smirked. "You didn't know he had a sense of humor, huh?" she remarked to Mirelle. "Only his very intimate close friends—like Sofia La Maga Magus—know that," she snipped.

Again, no comment was offered by any of the men, but Mirelle imagined that the consul was peeved.

"Second," Lady Blanco continued more soberly, "know that something more problematic is unfolding. We don't know how it will play out exactly."

"The smallest, truly volitional shift in the paradigm makes the entire world spin out of kilter," the consul exclaimed.

"It's time, Leo. It's been time for a long time," de Lux Magus announced.

"Wholly unnecessary turmoil," the consul muttered as if pushing the words through his teeth.

"You could either make it happen or have it happen to you. It is supposed to happen—and you're the one it's adopted for the cause—or adapted to it. There's no blame for what has transpired over these long years. The methods of coming full circle are mysterious, but you have to come to who you are now," the brother announced.

The consul shushed him with a hissing grunt. "Damned or saved," he remarked.

"Foolish dissipation—and profligacy," the brother scornfully muttered.

Mirelle watched the consul seethe, wince, and display an attitude that ever so slightly hinted at shame.

"I don't remember you being this noxious as a child," the younger de Lux told his brother.

"You're no longer a child," the elder replied.

"I am the Consul of the Sovereignty and you, technically speaking, are an Enemy of the State, Brother," de Lux Sortiar snapped.

The older man shrunk back and brooded. Mirelle did

her best to keep a poker-face through the repartee and then turned her attention to Professor Camael, who was asking Blanco Sortiar if she could locate Medea Sarin within the scrying mirror. She only managed to hone in on people with the same last name.

"Oh, Leo, you should see what Marina is doing now," Lady Blanco remarked. "Ooh, baby, look at her go." The woman chortled impishly. She nudged Mirelle as if they were sharing an adorably mean inside joke about their good friend, Consul Leo de Lux.

The svelte blond woman in the mirror was merely retrieving a child from the Little Cherub Day Care Center. Mirelle watched the shapely woman scarp a happy little girl into her arms and plant a sweet kiss on her cheek. She carried the child to a vintage convertible car, the back seat of which was loaded with bags from an apparent high-end shopping spree.

Leo de Lux and his entourage lingered in the vehicle in front of Homunculus Tongue for about 40 minutes. There they scrutinized the activities of Tina Hamadryad, Karen Brevis, and some other characters. They saw Silvie Puck enter the café and then, through the mirror, they watched Karen scold her.

Silvie was toting a paper bag that Karen snatched. She peered into it and hollered in an accusing manner. Silvie protested. The young women yapped fiercely but then diverted their wrath to a group of young men who were egging them on.

In all, the girls seemed to be making appointments, relaying instructions, and dealing out substances. Mirelle saw envelopes and packets change hands.

"Are they dealing out spells?" the consul inquired.

Mirelle shrugged. Of course they were, and intoxicants and what not.

"Dark illicit substances for antisocial effects, I'm sure,"

the consul mused in a sly tone. He eyed his two attendants who in turn nodded in agreement. "They never found out who was responsible for that trough of decapitated cats some weeks ago. Victor himself has been particularly protective of his boxers lately because of some reports of attacks on dogs. Isn't that right?"

Victor nodded and smiled slightly, as if entertained by the consul's dry humor.

"Who knows whether the macabre vivisection of that unidentified folkie discovered last year wasn't tied in with this rash of violence against defenseless animals for their parts?" the consul continued. Smirking as if something devilishly satisfying had finally occurred that day, he instructed the attendants to call in a raid of Homunculus Tongue.

"We've received a complaint that profiteering and some other illegal activities are being perpetrated at the Homunculus Tongue club . . . Trading in prohibitive organic substances . . . IMMEDIATELY," Lou, the lady staff-bearer, gruffly enunciated into her communication device. "By order of the consul." She cupped her hand over the contraption. "Do you want a sweep of the strip?" she asked.

"I'm only interested in this one establishment," the consul replied.

The staff bearer repeated the news to whoever she was addressing by phone. "Do not wrap it up without detaining a young woman named— What is it?" she asked the others.

"Karen Ea Brevis Sortiar. A little zaftig and freckled," the consul said. "Incarcerate her for a few hours. Fingerprint her and start a dossier. Ask her about those black cats. Charge her with something troublesome that incurs a large fine. Why aren't they here yet?"

"I DON'T SEE ANY BACK UP YET!" Lou roared a husky shrill into her mouthpiece. "What does

'IMMEDIATE' mean if it's not immediate?"

Victor and de Lux winked at each other as if their manly female compatriot was a rip and the intrigue was fine entertainment. Then a slew of municipal staff-bearers, clad in protective clothing, converged on the place. The consul's attendants joined them.

The consul watched the drama from the sidelines for a short while. Then he sullenly announced, "Enough," as if the fun were over. He ordered the driver to depart the scene.

They took Mirelle to The Magistrar and told her to stay there with Sofia. She was not to go back to the dorm or school.

"You're under house arrest," the consul said firmly, but Mirelle knew he was just being smart with her.

"Michael will help you move your things," Lady Blanco lilted. "What? Tomorrow? Or when can you do it, Mikey?" she asked him.

"I can do it tomorrow," he said and smiled at Mirelle.

"He's one of my apprentices," Lady Blanco quietly confided. "He'll be quite suitable for protection and other things," she told Mirelle. "You can thank Leo if and when you get around to those other 'things' with Mikey. The consul thought it would be good for you two to, you know." She wiggled her fingers around each other and winked.

XIV
The Screw

"Are you kidding? We can't have someone like that running around the North Atlantic Sovereignty — or running around anywhere for that matter. What I mean . . . what I'm SAYING," Reggie Solaris stuttered.

"You're having no trouble saying what you mean," Leo griped. "And we know that it is about me, not her."

Reggie sighed mournfully. He pushed his drink to the side. "I'm not the messenger. I'm telling you this because we're friends. We've had times. I'm not the messenger, alright."

"Get on with it, Reggie."

"They want you out. Get rid of her at least," he complained.

"I can't do that," Leo replied.

"Exactly!" Reggie snipped.

Leo slammed his drink onto the counter where they sat at the Orion Club. He seethed. He had meant to reason with Reggie, his closest friend. But in doing so he would have to say things that he wasn't yet ready to admit.

"She's a powder keg."

"She's on my side, which is a lot more than what I can say for the rest of my associates," Leo griped.

"Your side? Seems the other way around and that's the fly in the ointment. What did she do to you anyway? You need intervention. Stop this, Leo," Reggie implored. "When you wake up again, everything about her is going to look very different, and you're going to be as livid as the bottom of hell for what she did to you. But sooner than later means victory instead of utter chaos and ruin. Absolute ruin, Leo. It will be on your head forever."

"Nothing bad is happening," is all Leo could manage to say. He didn't have words. He had resignation and a scintillating silence in his mind that was very vast. He wanted to fly away in it, but he was sitting at the bar at the Orion Club with his closest friend, Reggie Solaris, who was working himself up to issue threats.

"You've lost your mind," Reggie announced.

"I have to think about this," Leo said softly. He stared into the glass display on the other side of the bar. He watched the reflections of persons dining and chatting among the palms, carp ponds, and gazebos behind him. He caught sight of his own severe appearance, his own eyes: frozen steel and Reggie beside him, head in hand, looking panicked and morose.

Leo placed his hand on Reggie's and let heat ride through. The gesture caused Reggie's eyes to tear.

"I love you, buddy. I don't want to see you or your kid get fried. I'm telling you. So you have to do the right thing."

"Leonard's marked?" Leo questioned.

"What do you think? They say he's her lineage holder. How could you do that, Leo? They're probably going to sail that kid. What a freaking mess," Reggie lamented. "It's suicide. Hell, you'll have to off yourself out of honor when you come-to anyway if this situation blows up the way it pretty much is looking like it will."

"The Deep Inner Planes will take us all," Leo muttered.

Reggie sputtered and seethed. *"The maga and your lunatic brother — and that FREAK Zosimo Sortiar — are all in this together!* I can't believe you fell into it. Man-oh-man, they pulled some heavy-handed binding spell on you! For Jove's sake, let me arrange an intervention," Reggie pleaded. "It will be very discrete. Just do it, Leo. You're spellbound. Everyone knows it. They don't really fault you for it so much. They just want you back, buddy."

"Do you know the particulars about Leonard?" Leo asked matter-of-factly. "His demise? How it is supposed to go?"

After glaring confoundedly at Leo, Reggie pointedly reminded him that some magical persons can perform a lethal Conus magus charm.

"Assuredly," Leo replied and laughed to himself.

"What are you going to do?" Reggie insisted.

"I'll give it some thought," Leo repeated and told Reggie that he had decided that, while he was still head magistrate, the sovereignty should rid itself of the sorceress Medea Sarin. "Could you get someone to arrange that, Reggie—while we're on the subject of assassination plots."

"I'm talking about THIS thing here," Reggie protested. "Now you want to talk about offing some bitch who put a dent in your car?"

"I'm changing the subject," Leo insisted.

Reggie huffed and finally snipped, "Maybe you could arrange for a sports event where Sarin could have a wrestling match or duel or something with your 'girlfriend.' That would kill two birds with one stone."

Leo rolled his eyes on the sarcasm. "Well, I'll have to speak with the gaming commission about that," he spit. "With any luck, these two noxious women will kill each other, and things will be as right as rain. So that's it, Reg. It's all sorted out. Thanks so much."

Reggie was stuck for a reply. After sitting with jaw agape, he gritted his teeth and uttered, "It's a plan." Ablaze with pique, he dismounted his stool. "Get rid of her, Leo. Get back to life. Save your kid and yourself."

He stormed out, leaving Leo with the bar tab.

Leo laid out the situation and its implications in the serenely wide expanse of his thought-field. He thought it peculiar but not troubling that he didn't feel particularly emotional. It was as if he were investigating how the saga between him and Sofia La Maga had evolved. He pondered where and who he was within the drama and what its fruit consisted of. Which was the more authentic life? Had he ever been his own man or had he always been a tool? Was his life now spiraling out of control or just spiraling like a circle expanding across limitless space?

On the heels of Sofia La Maga's insinuation into his life was the reunion with his brother, Emmanuel. Leo could not say that it was as satisfying as he imagined it would be. It was tense, awkward. His brother had the aura of a Rumpelstiltskin collecting on a pact. Thus, it was not a stretch to conclude—as Reggie Solaris had—that Leo's lover and his brother were colluding and that he was being set up to fulfill their messianic designs.

He didn't feel particularly spellbound, though, and he still didn't care about whether he was. Up until a few days ago, he was the happiest he had ever been. Nevertheless, he was being coerced into making life and death decisions about the greater good. Two wildly divergent paths opened before him. He knew which one he preferred to take.

Leo contemplated his childhood mentor Lumiere Sortiar, the warrior archangel Michael, and patron deities such as Ea, Jupiter, and Saturn. Then, he decided he would stir the pot. He would indeed arrange a public spectacle—a sports event in which Medea Sarin and Sofia La Maga would face-off just as Reggie had sarcastically suggested. It would be explosive, and Leo would use the event as a set up—a diversion in which a surprise attack could occur. Sofia wouldn't much like the plan but would go along with it. She might even sabotage it in her own ingenious way. That would be okay, all things considered. No one would touch her in the run-up to the event; they would be too busy calculating odds and placing bets and plotting other intrigues.

Not losing his position, his life, his lover and especially

his son would be an impossible task. What was the point of involvement in the maelstrom? What was it to wake up from the idea of oneself? What was the life beneath the mechanisms of the mind and body? As a man who had mastered the nature of illusion such that he could be a creator and destroyer, Leo knew that there was something "made up" about him. He did not believe that he—or hardly anyone—truly had free will. No; his actions were driven by a program. The program was an artificial personality that was dreaming a dream.

The personality called Leo de Lux Sortiar was the product—indeed, the side effect—of circumstances and experiences that preceded and manifested as him. He was not a being of his own making. How could blame be laid on him or anyone? He and every other person were simply interdependently arising aggregates of circumstance.

Becoming truly real, conscious, and willful began by realizing the whimsical nature of one's own being and then detaching from that personality and its momentum. The momentum wouldn't stop; the personality wouldn't become truly conscious, but the person who was the life beneath the mechanism would open his eyes and watch himself go through the motions of daily life like a dreamer watches a dream and sometimes manages to exercise control over it.

Having left the Orion Club, Leo called Sofia from his car. He told her that Leonard had to be hidden and that she should scheme with his brother about how to do that. He also told her that if Medea Sarin challenged her to a public spectacle—a magical duel or something of that sort—it would be best to humor her. "Play along. Bide your time, and endure what I'm asking. I have a complicated plan," he told her. "Can you do this?"

"Sure," Sofia replied.

"Also," Leo braced himself and uttered steadily,

"Circumstances being as they are, we have to part."

"What do you mean?" she questioned.

"I can't go into detail. Let it be. Don't let them kill my son. Do something so that he doesn't hate me," Leo said, thinking that the request was ridiculous. Then he slid the hood of his phone over the display. Leo glared at the device for a while. He expected Sofia to call back to protest, but the phone did not ring.

Leonard was not in the house when Leo returned home. Leonard was not to be seen the following day or the next. Sofia would not let any harm come to him. Who knew how and for what she had outfitted the youth. Whatever it was would be placed on a fast-track now, considering the uncertain state of her own lifespan. She was on shaky ground: there would be an exacting fallout for besting Gorgon out of a political coup attempt and putting the elite of the sovereignty into a snit for whatever she had done to de Lux. He had been rendered into a ruined lame duck because he had fallen in love with her. Yet, he didn't think it was so bad, considering. Leo had been longing for a profound, life-changing event, something extraordinary. Now, he was in the pit of it.

Medea Sarin challenged Sofia to a "magical efficacy match" — a duel — through the Gaming Commission. Leo approved it. Sofia took two suspense-filled weeks to answer the challenge. Bythos and H. Trismegistus both submitted bids to host the spectacle. Bookies calculated odds and took bets. Reggie Solaris confided to all of his compatriots that it was Leo's warped and passive-aggressive ruse to purge the sovereignty of two plagues — the troublesome sorceress and the noxious maga.

The general gossip was that Sofia La Maga had been spurned and was going to use the spectacle as an opportunity to put on a breathtaking but ultimately harmless horrific show before publicly apportating to the

Deep Inner Planes in a spitefully bombastic transfiguration.

Leo's actions and motivations now confused those on both sides of the skirmish, and chaos abounded as everyone took matters into their own hands, each in his own deviously magical way.

Leo's brother even got into the act by appearing, unannounced, at Leo's estate late one evening and neutralizing every security safeguard — magical and otherwise — to do so. The mage had the wherewithal to alight onto the consul's property and rap on the front door. Lady Poinsett had alerted Victor. He detained the quietly brooding mage momentarily and searched the home for Leo.

The consul, inofficiously clad in a mauve velour bathrobe, was in the dungeon of his tower, a locale that even Victor had second thoughts about entering. The night happened to be moving into Sunday. The moon was nearly full and in the eighth lunar mansion, called The Gap, 0 degrees Cancer, ruled by the Sun, and entering the sign of Leo. Thus, it was reasonable, given the circumstances, that Victor should find Leo engaged in talismanic magic. Planetary hour charts were tacked about, strangely fragrant fumigations infused the dank atmosphere, candles flickered, and a bloody patent was in view on which a small creature had been dissected in defiance of the sovereignty's blood-letting laws.

Victor found Leo muttering and tracing sigils over a small pot of bubbling wax and called to him from beyond the doorway of the chamber.

"Excuse me, Sir. Your brother is here," he officiously announced, and had to repeat himself a few times to catch the consul's attention.

"How is that?" Leo replied.

"Tripped security, Sir. I have no explanation."

Leo placidly poured his bloody yet aromatic wax smelt

into a clay mold on which was engraved the image of an eagle with a man's head. The wax would cool into a talisman for victory in war. Without banishing or any other ritual fanfare to close his sorcerous activity, he left the dungeon to greet his brother. They went to his study.

"Tea?" Leo uttered.

The brother made an equivocal gesture with his hands, which nevertheless sent Lady Poinsett to the kitchen to brew something—a teapot of a sweetened lemongrass and chamomile infusion with a shot of limoncello liqueur, a rather soothing and sedating evening toddy, but it would not put a damper on the tension between the brothers.

"Popping in and out of high-security areas is unwise, Brother. The Sovereignty is already in riotous straits now that word has gotten out about your presence and our interaction. That is not to say that I would not have received you in the spirit of great hospitality had you called ahead about your visit," Leo said.

The brother simply smiled in a wizened way. He was clad in white garb. A woolen beanie on his head, sandals on his feet, cotton trousers, a wide-sleeved dalmatic, and a thin woolen cloak. When Leo looked at him, though, he saw himself aged by 12 years. Emmanuel's eyes were a watery, tropical blue, his face was bonier, and his nose pointy, but the resemblance was unmistakable.

"But you've come here to tell me why you are on the rag, hmm?" Leo finally said. "Was it that pressing? Or did you simply happen to be in the neighborhood?" Frankly, Leo would have liked to embrace his brother with warm grins and giddy back slapping except that the elder de Lux's manner was prickly. It was cold, like his father had been. It would take some time for Leo to discern whether that was the way his brother really was or if it were a sneaky glamour.

"I'm trying to wrap my mind around where you stand

in all this and whether we are meant to be reacquainted," Emmanuel said, which was suspicious, because that was exactly how Leo was feeling about his brother. "By the way, I don't need to dissect a frog or know what stars are about to work magic. Did you know that?" the older man remarked.

Leo felt his temper pique but tamped it down. "Well, we are both unique among men," he lightly replied, adding in greater solemnity, "You were once a kind of a father to me — and a kind one at that. It's not been forgotten."

The brother's manner softened with the hint of smile and an agreeable nod. Then he began a discourse that seemed to be something of a test.

"I suspect that your initial interest in La Maga Magus was carnal and streaked with spite," he said. "You wanted to break her and yet each of you fell into the designs of the other. Mutually corrupted, as it were. From that sprung a kind of love. But if things don't go well, your son will be lost," Emmanuel said. "Our bloodline ends with him. Not that I care about perpetuating the lineage..." his voice trailed off.

"Leonard will thrive. I have faith that he will be vouchsafed from harm and aspire to great things. A man need not have affection for his father to do so. Look at us," Leo replied.

The elder de Lux huffed out a wry chortle and went on. "And your behavior with this this duel-thing between a diabolic sorceress and your lover — it's more like the posturing of an inchaote than a distinguished high sorcerer. Can you enlighten me on that, Leo?"

"The maga has a soft spot for inchaote sorcerers," Leo snapped. "I'm trying to impress her. The games of courtship. Not that you would know, being a white-coat mage and all."

The brother huffed out another derisive laugh and

said, "She spends a great deal of time with that character from the Bythos Academy."

"'The Crazy Professor,'" Leo muttered. "Aurelio Zosimo Sortiar, a controversial professor given to Expansionist politics."

"And you have no qualms about this rival liaison?" the brother questioned.

Leo was about to say that Sofia La Maga and Aurelio Zosimo were "just friends," but thought saying so would sound stupid. "Is it my place to police who else the maga is in relation with? Am I so pedestrian?" he remarked instead.

"Are you sure she is not scorned and plotting some odd and terrible revenge against you with her other man and your own son? Signs are that she may want to sever her attachment to you. But not to fret just yet; a magical item through which she can accomplish this has gone missing," Emmanuel stated.

Leo's draw dropped a little bit here, not so much because he was surprised that Sofia may have worked a spell to grab his devotion but because he was realizing that his long-lost brother had a rather impish streak.

"Yes. An item through which she enchanted and bound you to herself," Emmanuel continued. "Missing. But not missing. Stolen by the rival—the mangy inchoate--or so the Deeple seemed to think when she appeared before me a few nights ago. Interesting feat for a Deeple half-Commons...masquerading as a ghost and interrupting my evening meditations to inform me of your romantic ado," Emmanuel said in a roundabout discourse.

"Mirelle has some interesting talents," Leo replied in step but winced. "What did she tell you?"

Emmanuel repeated that the "Deeple" had "rudely" materialized as an apparition in the safe house he had been inhabiting and told him that a magical item that Sofia had used to romantically attract Leo to her had been stolen by

Aurelio Zosimo Sortiar. "She seemed concerned about the consequences should the spell be broken. And you?"

"I am not alarmed," Leo replied, although he was. He added that Zosimo Sortiar was of no consequence. "I am not bound to La Maga Magus by a spell that can be interrupted by another. Ridiculous. At any rate, both Sofia and Zosimo are on my side and have inscrutable designs," Leo declared. "I leave them to it and rest in trust. Perhaps you should, too."

Emmanuel harrumphed yet again. "She is the apprentice of that Bruno Sortiar, a 'wise guy,' as they're called in the Outer Plane."

"Part of her charm," Leo griped.

"Insidious," the brother hissed. "And that Deeple has no manners."

"The 'Deeple' does not act casually," Leo barked. "Something of great importance spurred her actions. That you are standing here, she must've achieved her ends. – *Why are you tormenting me,*" he finally said.

"I suspect saboteurs in your redemption. I fear that you have been tempted to plunge from a cliff to unduly test angels to catch you and carry you aloft," Emmanuel replied...but that wasn't true.

"No. You're playing Devil's advocate with me to find out what I'm really about," Leo announced.

With an impish sneer that mirrored the one Leo wore when he was feeling randy, the mage nodded reassuringly. He urged his brother to snatch the magical item from its thief. Then he dissolved into a golden mist.

Leo, though clad in a fluffy mauve bathrobe, immediately translocated to the home of Michael Camael Magus who was asleep, atop a large cushion, nuzzled cock to butt under sheets and quilts with Mirelle. The cushion was sprawled on the floor of a large, mostly bare room meant for magical operations. It contained a large fireplace with yet glowing embers. Protection charms abounded, but, like his brother, Leo was resistant to such things.

Leo abruptly yanked the quilts and sheets from the couple. The two scrambled, shooting off defensive flares that had no effect on their target. Leo's sullen face could be seen in the lightning flashes of the discharges. Michael and Mirelle composed themselves.

"It's me," Leo scolded.

"So what?" Michael shouted. "What are you doing here?"

Mirelle was matter-of-factly cloaking sheets over her body when a lamp incandesced. Leo charged at her, staff in hand, forcing her to bunch up into a cowering huddle on the floor.

"It is *criminal* to steal the magical activations of others, Mirelle Soleil," he hollered. "What is it? Why does he have it? How did he get it? Why is it my brother's business and not mine?" he questioned. "You know what I'm talking about."

"Yes, Sir," Mirelle gasped.

"And it's a?" he insisted.

"A screw," Mirelle announced.

"A what?"

"A screw. A nut and bolt, but she calls it a screw," Mirelle stuttered in speech that was pressured and surly. "She used it to get liked by you."

Pondering the silliness and innuendo, Leo let out a wizened laugh, but decided to grip Mirelle by her matted dreadlocks for good measure. Fending him off, searing staff in hand, he hollered at Michael to keep his place.

"But what is he to her?" he raged. "Why does he have it?"

"She gave it to him to protect her," Mirelle hollered. "Just in case."

"In case what?" Leo questioned.

"In case YOU TURNED ON HER with the bullshit you're pulling," Mirelle yelled. "But I told your brother that he stole it so he'd tell you and you'd do something about it. Do the right thing."

"Take it up with Zosimo Sortiar, Leo. Leave her alone," Michael Camael protested. He tried to overpower the consul's violence, but instead got pushed repeatedly across the room as if battling a gale force wind.

Leo felt a bit craven in that moment. He was not sure whether he was mildly peeved or threatened or perhaps riled at being insulted. Betrayed. Groundless maybe, as if an investment had gone sour and it was the fault of these two people although he knew it surely wasn't.

He shook off the tension and composed himself. "I don't mean to hurt either of you," he relented. "I want answers — and loyalty, some semblance of it. Everywhere can't be a mutiny, can it?" Leo allowed Michael to grab a robe and seat himself in a nearby chair.

"I want to be the herald of a new aeon. I want to take hold of my own freedom by embracing it. I want you to trust me, and I can't have her crazy dark knight or troubadour or whatever he is in possession of an item that binds us. I can't have it," Leo insisted.

"Yeah. That's the point," Mirelle snapped. "But what are you doing? Because if you end up hurting her, you are going to be so fucked by Zosimo Sortiar."

"Is she threatening me?" Leo asked as he continued to tug at the ropes of her hair.

"Yes!" Mirelle screeched.

Leo laughed and giving Michael a suggestive glance, he gently folded himself over Mirelle's tawny and slender form, curled up and half-exposed in whorls of the blankets she gripped.

"Listen to me, my tattered and faithless child," he hissed. "I love Sofia La Maga, and I hate everything else."

Then he drilled a Sweet Surrender maneuver into Mirelle. Tears of strange guilt and relief flooded from her eyes.

"You don't have to do that," she choked in resistance.

"My Mirelle is a great and powerful sorceress, Camael Sortiar. If you ever lose sight of this, you are a sorry being," Leo said.

"I understand that, Sir. Could you get off her?" Michael replied, but Leo held on in a mildly erotic embrace. He said, "A confrontation with Zosimo Sortiar would be explosive and compromising. I prefer to avoid it, but I want that thing in my hand. How do I best achieve my ends? I need you to be my spiritual child and diplomat in this matter, Mirelle."

"I'll fix it. I think I can," she said breathlessly.

"Good," he replied and stroked her head and neck as if calming a shuddering animal. Michael crouched beside them, and it was as if they were all sitting in a cuddly enclave then.

"I need Sofia to best them. To leave no room for doubt. To strike in anticipation but defensively with ease again and again and again," Leo explained. "I will be the secret support underlying her actions. You will understand my meaning in time. She is going to show up for that match, isn't she?"

Mirelle stressed and blinked.

"Is she off to run away with The Crazy Professor then?" he asked.

"She'll show up, but then what, I don't know," Mirelle admitted.

Leo grimaced and nodded solemnly. "You do know that you will be acting as her second in that match, facing off against Medea Sarin and your good friend *Karenia brevis.*"

Mirelle dropped her jaw, a bit stunned.

"Because this role would ordinarily go to Leonard but

that is not possible at this point in time. I believe you can rise to the occasion. Do you?"

"Me and Sofia will kick the shit out of them," Mirelle declared.

"Good," Leo replied. He stood up, brushed himself off, and tidied the immodest skewing of his mauve bathrobe. "Apologies for intruding on you nice people," he said. Bidding them goodnight, he translocated from their sight.

XV
Nature in Its Entirety
Is Regenerated in Fire

He bided his time as a politician fallen from grace, watching his back and planning a mixed up and perhaps diabolical scheme to turn the tables on his one-time compatriots and the whole Terra Novit.

He spent long, morose hours away from the Senate, mostly tending to hobbies and busy work in the Outer Plane. He was selling off things and surveying new acquisitions and properties. He once had ambitions of ascending to deeper, more sublime planes of existence, but he was planning to exile himself to the world of Commons. It would be an outpost from which he would scheme and manipulate what went on in the Inner Plane, like Zeus and other Olympian archons dicking around with the fate of mere mortals from their post on Mount Olympus. He would be an Illuminati secretly wreaking havoc for the sake of a great vision. Sofia, he hoped, would remain his accomplice.

He was trying to wrap his head around how to deal with the Zosimo-fellow. Whatever the link was between him and Sofia, it was closely guarded, impenetrable to divining and bespeaking the formidable nature of his — or her — art. But how threatening could he really be? He was saintly by all accounts — a Lux Clarus expert, a sappy champion of and spiritual advisor to Deeples and DeeVees and not particularly politically engaged. He practiced magic that was careless and trendy and made art in his spare time.

He was the son of a foreign dignitary — a Corps General named Massimo Zosimo Sortiar of the Terra

Principalis—and an eccentric artist named Dorrie Auriel Magus. This pair had long parted ways, with the wild artist claiming that Aurelio Zosimo was not General Zosimo Sortiar's flesh and blood but either the miraculous product of parthenogenesis or the offspring of the lead guitarist of the rock band Homunculus Tongue. She toggled between these delusions depending on her mood and didn't quite care that she was contradicting herself when she did. In any case, Dorrie Auriel Magus was not Aurelio Zosimo's birth mother. They looked not a whit like each other, one all smoky dark and the other a pale, rough-and-tumble blond with a hook nose and sharp, brassy features. Still, "mother" and "son" were said to have an endearing and enduring relationship despite "Daddy's" departure.

On a day when Leo might otherwise have been soberly strolling through the Mercury Gardens in between important matters of State, he was, instead, sitting on a bench gazing at the reflection of willow trees, swans, and gazebos in the pond of the Public Garden in Boston. The bright and cheery sun made the landscape look almost as bright and green as landscapes looked in the Inner Plane. Crisp, lucid, present.

He was enjoying a sleepiness brought on from the release of tension and was gazing downward at a patch of grass that he was watching himself make greener. Glowing, as if the whole landscape should glimmer jewel-like as it did in the better parts of the Inner Plane. Leo looked at his hands as if for the first time to see whether he was glowing, too, but he couldn't tell. He only knew that Outer Plane people sensed his importance. He turned heads. People made way for him, gave him preferential treatment, ballsy women threw themselves at him. He had taken the privilege for granted, but he began to ponder why right then as he sat on the bench.

He realized that a man with an outstretched hand was

standing before him. Leo briefly mused on whether to ignore or repel the beggar, or else "miraculously" fill his girly red trouser pockets with cash. Before looking up to meet the fellow's gaze, he noticed that the trousers, which were a bit baggy for the man's physique, were held up by a thick belt that had bones and small amulets dangling off of it. The blue plaid shirt he wore was buttoned askew beneath a dingy, orange sweater vest that Leo thought he saw patterns of strange creatures within.

"You're not a Commons," Leo exclaimed as the item in the man's outstretched hand incandesced.

The widget resting in the palm of his hand was a screw—a brass bolt saddled into a copper brace.

Leo's eyes darted up to meet those of the man standing before him. Aurelio Zosimo Sortiar. Zosimo smiled rather widely and sweetly. He had an aura that was as soft and subtle as the lightness of the day's breeze, and he had a delicately masculine and familiar face that was somewhat swarthy. His eyes were smoky, bright, and as if given to pondering, and his long, dark hair fell past his shoulders in frizzy waves and ringlets. Leo wondered whether this disheveled, docile being could've been the same rabidly, transmorgraphic creature he saw, clad in tight leather and brandishing a wild and phallic staff, weeks before.

He stood so as to be on par with the fellow but was put off by Zosimo's height. Despite the careless slouch, he was taller than Leo.

"Consul Leo de Lux Sortiar," Leo officiously introduced himself.

Zosimo gently nodded. He jutted his chin slightly toward the gadget in his hand. "My Sofia's screw," he announced in a melodic, slightly Roman accent. It was the first time Leo had heard the man's voice, and he wasn't completely sure whether his words were referring to the gadget or Leo. The two men shook hands anyway. The copper and brass widget lay nested in their shared hand clasp and then it was in Leo's palm. He gazed at it as if the acquisition were far too easy. The head of the bolt had numbers and letters on it that hinted at planetary magic.

"Who are you, Zosimo Sortiar," Leo asked, even though the answer was now obvious, just as Mirelle had said it would be.

Zosimo flashed another wide smile. "I'm the *brother*," he gloated. "They took the boy, not the girl." He winked and smirked as if the joke were on "them" for doing so. "I want to be a Lion of Light," he added. "Are you one of those?"

"I've assumed my namesake," Leo replied. "I don't know what I'll become for it, living in exile as it were," he muttered, adding, "Sofia's brother?"

"You're going to be a cult hero, like Jesus — or maybe Lucifer. Something like that," Zosimo said in childlike verbal gambol.

"A fallen star. Fallen from grace in humiliation," Leo lilted.

"The same as the rest of us," Zosimo consoled. "The dust of a falling star fallen. Matter, a cinder, volatile ash poised to be ignited and transformed into its latent potential in pure, fiery light. *Ignus natura renovatur integra.* You wanted Deep Inner Planes. But they don't come out of a gum ball machine."

"I'm not complaining. I'm prepared," Leo stuttered.

"'Nature in its entirety is regenerated in fire,'" Zosimo softly lilted. It was an alchemical adage about the nature of transformation. After going awkwardly mute for a while, Zosimo said, "I'm the brother" again.

Leo nodded. It was indeed obvious. "Will your sister stay near after the deed has been done?" he asked.

After letting out a quirky giggle, Zosimo assured Leo that Sofia would follow him to the ends of the Earth. "We were one and became two. Maybe you two will become one now. Eventually. The one in the two, the two in the one," Zosimo rambled. "I don't think you will hurt her," he added distantly. "But if you do, you will be very sorry." He flashed his black, jewel-like eyes and smiled assuredly just like did Sofia in her more impish moods.

The threat seemed reasonable enough, so Leo said, "Okay." He shook Zosimo's hand as if a gentleman's agreement had been met. They took a stroll. Leo explained his plan to The Crazy Professor, figuring that despite the fellow's strangeness, Leo ought to acquire his trust. In exchange, Zosimo told Leo how he and Sofia had serendipitously crossed paths through their respective teaching posts at the Bythos Academy and, in the course of becoming fast friends, figured out their shared history.

"Our mother accidentally aportated to the Deep Inner Plane after reading a tiny little note written by a magic bird," Zosimo said rather plainly.

"A casualty of *The Beauteous Consorte of the Mirour* of Luna document," Leo affirmed.

"Yes. And our father was the Romano Corps General Massimo Zosimo Sortiar—or else he is a minstrel, a guitar player. You may have heard of him?"

Leo blinked and realized, plain as day, that Zosimo did resemble a younger—albeit spaced-out in a completely different way—version of the lead guitarist of Homunculus Tongue.

"So, it's true," Leo replied.

"No. Everything is in question," Zosimo responded. "Truth is what you consent to believe."

Leo grunted in agreement at that piece of wisdom and turned the topic to the screw. "And the screw is now in my possession? And what does it do?" he asked.

"It does whatever you want," Zosimo harrumphed. "It's a program. It's *programmed*. You know?" he said pointedly, as if Leo should know what that meant.

"It's a talisman," Leo replied.

"It's an amplifier of the missile of magical will," Zosimo declared.

All Leo knew was that it was a piece of Sofia's desire. Her desire for him. "But it's a talisman. Right?" Leo repeated.

"Yes. Okay," Zosimo shrugged agreeably.

"There is some concern that Sofia wants to modify the 'program' or entrust the task to another," Leo said cautiously.

"So that's why I'm *giving* it to you," Zosimo announced. He glared with his dark quizzical eyes as if Leo should perfectly know what it all meant. "I don't think you will hurt her, but if you do . . ." he reiterated.

"I mean to work through her in battle to restore the order of the universe, as gods do through their goddesses," Leo explained.

"Okay," Zosimo grinned and seemed satisfied. The two sorcerers then managed to shake hands yet again.

They bantered as they sauntered through the park, traded a few magical tips and techniques, and then, Leo, inspired, returned home to his villa to work on a nasty glamour and gaze into the crystal-lined tank in the dungeon of his tower. The tank had a pump and a drain so that it could be purged and refilled because, sometimes, nasty substances—toxins and body fluids—had to be deposited in it in the course of spell casting. Leo had taken to using it as a scrying device. He was scouting out everyone he knew and documenting data related to Hipparchus Gorgon's assets and the assets of others of Gorgon's ilk.

He also made compulsive attempts to locate Leonard during his scrying sessions but was unsuccessful. Whenever Leo tried to hone in on Leonard, he was confronted with images of Phaeton maneuver matches that seemed to be memories, or narratives at least. They always celebrated how Leonard had deactivated the helios. Reggie Solaris's son, and too many other familiar faces made up the teams. The images seemed to be Leonard's way of saying, "Hi, Dad. I'm alright," but Leo regarded them as incriminating evidence about the delinquency of certain patrician children.

He had resisted scrying in on Sofia, fearing it might be too distracting. After the encounter with Zosimo and acquisition of her magical device, he couldn't resist. He dribbled an oily, aromatic concoction into the scrying pool and peered into the patterns of bubbles and debris. When her image emerged, her eyes were closed, as if she were meditating. When he uttered her name, she opened her eyes, put her hand to her mouth and drew out a snail with a banded and dappled shell like one of those in Leonard's collection — a marine cone snail.

The image of Sofia in the scrying pool flung the cone snail at Leo. Spurting out of the water, the thing struck his chest. Leo watched Sofia repeat the same action. She drew a cone snail from her mouth and pelted him with it. She continued this behavior until one of the creatures finally stung the hand with which Leo was shielding himself.

A searing, spasmodic burn seized the hand. It leeched, as if piercing the bone, up the arm. It gave way to searing prickles and then numbing paralysis. The sensation flooded up to the side of his neck to his ear, around his head, spidering across his body. He collapsed in a spastic twist.

He lay on the cobblestone floor. He could not feel a thing. He did not know whether he was breathing or whether his heart was beating. He was simply two eyes that could not blink. He did not feel inside himself and didn't seem to be outside either. He could not sense the presence of any special guiding lights, in the case that he was dying. He was only aware of the swinging bare light bulb overhead and the faintly fetid odors of the jarred contents he kept in the dungeon.

Was she killing him? Or was it the wily brother? A bitterness veined through the panic and made tears that he couldn't feel flood his eyes. It was a sensation that was both horrific and exquisite in its intensity — to feel as thoroughly as he did and to wonder whether this was his miserable end. How long would he lie there as just flooded eyes before there was no breath, no smell, no sight? Silence or darkness. Wouldn't that be the thing that followed, or would he slowly waste away there? Wrecked and mocked and then gone.

Leonard appeared in his view. He was camouflaged in a black sweatshirt and jeans. His hair, which had grown out, was tautly tied back. He was holding a gold- and silver-sheathed staff. A chunk of amber carved into a winged figure that had the head and upper half of a lion and the tail of a dolphin crowned the staff. Leo wondered if the youth might strike him with it.

"Get on with it," Leo's mind hollered.

"Now, you're being an idiot," Leonard said. He crouched down and put his hand on his father's head. A scintillating sensation spread through him. It was like the feeling of slowly coming to wakefulness from a dream.

Leonard sat on the dungeon floor and cradled his father against him. The youth breathed as if the respiration were meant to melt the man's frozen arrest. He had an electrical pulse like Sofia did. It was giddy, as if Leo should laugh under its influence but he hadn't the nerve.

Leonard drew his father into a tighter grip. "You don't even know what that feeling is, do you?" Leonard said sadly.

"Yes, I do know, Leonard," Leo uttered. It was love. He managed to reach around to pat the youth's arm. "It's very dangerous for you to be here," he added.

"Looks like it's more dangerous for you," the boy snickered.

Leo did not have words. Only pique.

"She's not out to hurt you or anything," Leonard apologized. "She was just being dramatic. Otherwise how else would you end up here crying in my arms?"

Leo cringed. "She thinks I've abandoned her or that I'm in the way—either her or the brother. Have you convened with the brother, Leonard? Received any tips to apply to your magical pursuits from The Crazy Professor? Hmm?"

"He's not what you think, Dad," Leonard replied.

"Oh, yes! That, I know," Leo exclaimed in rueful sarcasm. "I've only been stricken down once before, Leonard—and you know that story. To think a folkie maga and her crazy brother gained my trust to nearly put me out of my misery." He let out a nervous laugh and attempted to get to his feet.

"You can't get up yet," the youth announced. With that, Leo's legs went numb.

A panic welled up. Leo flailed against the youth, struggling to lift himself but couldn't. "What are you now?" he hollered at the boy.

"Why can't we just sit here for a little while," the youth replied. "We haven't talked for a really long time."

"Why did she pick you, Leonard?" Leo growled. "What is she up to?"

"She 'picked' me, because I asked her to help me, and I think she really wanted me to ask her that. Why did you pick her?"

"She 'picked' you because she has an agenda, Leonard. She 'picked' me for the same reason," Leo griped.

"She 'picked' me because she likes me," Leonard remarked. "She likes you, too," he added. "The fuck if I know why."

"Think whatever you like," Leo shot back. "Have you bedded her, Leonard? Do we have that in common as well?"

The youth made a scornful huffing sound. The giddy scintillation of affection that he had been passing to his father weakened. Even though it made the room cold and hellish, Leo couldn't resist pricking at the issue. "I'm guessing that's a 'no,'" he drawled condescendingly.

Leonard told Leo that he was an asshole. Leo found humor in the guff.

"She loves you because you are in her vision," Leo relented. "You perpetuate a mission that is like a vital organ that controls her life, like a heart or a lung. She is keenly aware of this, but the knowledge does not rule out her tenderness for you. She's taken you as her child. A mother's love is the fiercest. This is why certain persons revere the Divine Mystery, not as 'Father' or as 'Lord' but as 'Mother'—as she has been known to do. Then, again, the Mother is the iconic throne on which the Son, who represents the victory of life, reigns. The Father is merely the bed out of which it all emerges. I became fond of her because she was the only person who was fond of you, Leonard. She saw you and saw your soul and gave you back what my negligence and cold-hearted self-involvement robbed you of.

"At first, I thought she was trying to show me up—trip me up—but the results of her intercession were life changing. I wanted that experience, and so I did 'pick' her. She strangely saw something noble and desirable in me, or so it seemed." Leo's voice dropped into a windy sigh. After a while, he perked up and announced that there were no two greater feelings to revel in than awe and gratitude. "It's only natural that a person would crave the persons and things that spark those emotions," he said.

Leonard rested his head against his father's and hugged Leo more firmly. He said, "Thank you."

Leo had no response for the remark.

"She misses you, you know," Leonard added. "She's kind of depressed about it, actually."

Again, Leo refrained from comment except for a thoughtful grunting sound. He took solace in the news but decided to chat about Leonard's staff. The wood core was holly—a wood with fiery, creative, and martial energies associated with establishing new orders. Gold expressed the active, masculine energy of the sun, and silver captured the receptive, feminine energy of the moon. The amber out of which the winged aquatic lion was carved suggested the merged energies of the sun and the watery creative feminine. The figurine, Leonard explained, was his idea of himself pervading the elements. "From the heights to the depths, but like the great lion of the sun instead of a saturnine sea-goat."

"You've become a great man, Leonard," Leo exclaimed. "You're precious to me. I've not expressed that. I'm the seed of something bitter. Don't perpetuate it."

"I understand you, Dad. Everything is alright," the young man consoled. He muttered that slogan about nothing bad happening, although his tone lacked conviction. Then Leonard told Leo that Sofia wanted him to pass on the "'keys to the car,' so-to-speak. You know what I'm saying."

It took a few moments for Leo to catch on. "The Conus magus charm is a myth, Leonard," he sighed.

"The youth made an airy, frustrated sound. "I need the key," he uttered in an anxious tone. "Call it, whatever-the-fuck charm," he said. "You have to open it up. Hipparchus Gorgon is not going to take me out."

"Can I get up and walk now, Son?" Leo uttered. He had had enough with being a hostage.

"Will you do it?" Leonard threatened.

"Of course," the man agreed.

Leo flexed his ankles and slowly grappled to pick himself up off the cold, cobblestone floor. He assured Leonard that he was working on a rather complex strategy and that, although he could not make any guarantees, he intended to lose no one. He stood, leaning against a work table, squeamishly grappling with his son's request. The youth wanted an empowerment that would enable him to perform the deadly Conus magus charm.

Leo and Leonard scaled the steps to the second-floor of the tower. Initiations . . . empowerments . . . mind transmissions. Leo had been stingy with all of it.

"This key is difficult to absorb," Leo told his son, even though he was sure that Leonard already had the talent in his genes. "It brings on a mean temperament and a lust for diversions that can separate you from the reality of illusion—the illusion of yourself. If you cannot grasp the key to illusion, you cannot grasp the key to creation and destruction," Leo lectured. He knew that there was no way to "transfer" or "initiate" someone into the Conus magus charm. It wasn't a magical empowerment; it was a strange inherited trait. Leo would go through the motions of an initiation procedure in the event that the theatrics would wake the kid up about what he probably was already capable of. "Be prepared for an unpleasant effect," he warned.

He uttered a few exotic invocations and drew the celestial light through the energy vortices of his body. He consecrated his tools and acknowledged his tutelary deities, angelic hosts, daemons, elementals, and mentors. He drew the ritual circle, exorcised the elements, and banished spies and obstructive energies.

"Do not resist," he instructed his son. He forcibly yanked the youth backward into a choking posture, arms hyperextended in a lock behind him. "Surrender to being overwhelmed and think of nothing but that and what I tell you," he said.

Leo gathered the key and the intention in his mind-field and prepared for transmission. Leonard was panting in the pain of the unnatural stretch. His eyes widened and his expression became breathless and marked with dread. Leo gently put his dagger in place against his son's thorax. It was an awestruck moment for the boy, no doubt; a tender one for the father, bonding in this way after seeming aeons. Then came the surge of fiery light that is both thrilling and terrifying. Leo watched Leonard wince, close his eyes, and absorb it stoically. A long tear dribbled from the boy's right eye as he relaxed completely, as if released from his body.

"Ignus natura renovatur integra," Leo muttered caustically. "Nature in its entirety is renewed in fire." He caressed his son's head, acknowledged the deities, the angelic hosts, the daemons, the elementals, etcetera, and dissolved the circle.

"Stay alive," he commanded Leonard and saw him out of one of the back doors, through which the youth blended into the night.

XVI
She Who Is Fierce

"Please do not do anything weird with my screw," Sofia told her brother

He simply began drawing circles in the air that took on the phantasmal forms of ouroboroi—serpents swallowing their tails. The phantasms, in turn, inflated into iridescent soap bubbles that softly popped.

"Circles, circles, circles," he began to chant like an 8-eight-year-old child.

"Really, Aurelio. It's my screw," Sofia said.

"Yes," he drawled in agreement.

"I know you want to protect me and that I gave it to you and all, but you should give it back," she said.

"Your screw is safe with me," Aurelio replied.

He and Sofia were shamelessly snuggling, just as if they both really were 8 years old siblings, on a high, grassy knoll remotely situated a 1.5-mile hike within the wild acreage that was part of the Bythos Academy compound. A person had to trek through forest, bramble, and inclines to get there, but it was worth it. It was a breezy clearing, high and bright in the sunshine, and the grass was soft, parched and speckled with buttercups and wild strawberry. If a person kept on walking westward along a tiny dirt path through the hills and brush, he would come to a housing settlement of cottages built on a woodsy incline beside a wide river. Aurelio lived in one of those cottages.

It was good tor Sofia to snuggle up against him—someone she had snuggled with while in a womb, someone who she perhaps had been stuck to for aeons in the realm of timelessness before being born in this life.

"If I can't be there, I just want to be here," Sofia sulked.

"If they don't kill me tomorrow."

"Not good talk," Aurelio chided and continued to chant "Circles" while tracing ouroboroi in the air that took on the form of bubbles that popped except that the pops started to sound like farts, but that was to make Sofia laugh, which it did.

"He wants to get off the wheel. Really really," Aurelio said.

"What's with the rigmarole then," Sofia complained. "Can't even defend his own son straight out because it's easier to stab his good ole boys in the back so they don't know what hit 'em than step on their toes and make them squirm. Cowardly lion."

"The devil is in the details. Gods like to play," Aurelio replied.

"I did the wrong thing getting attached. When I first saw him, I wanted to get to him so bad," she admitted. "'Sweet to the taste, burning in the stomach,'" she added — an adage among ascetics about the dangers of desire.

Aurelio hissed in disgust. "You will have all eternity to be 'illuminated.' Be alive now."

"*No eye, no ear, no nose, no tongue, no body, no mind, no form, no sound, smell, taste, touch, modes of thought; no basis for vision, leading to no basis for mental perception; no wisdom, no ignorance, no end to wisdom, no end to ignorance, leading to no old age and death; no end to old age and death, no misery, no accrual, no extinction, no path, no attainment, no realization,*" Sofia rambled. It was from the *Prajnaparamita Sutra*.

Aurelio clapped his hands.

"I really need you to give me that screw back," she said.

"I am not," he replied.

"I am going to take it back," she exclaimed and attempted to get to her feet to leave. Aurelio held her down, his body tented over hers in too curious an embrace for grown siblings. His hands were clamped on the top of her head and thorax to keep her from translocating. *"'You sit tight right there, La Maga Magus,'"* he mocked because, unlike Leo de Lux, he could overcome her.

"You have to help me with this!" Sofia cried.

"Yes. No," Aurelio rambled. "You are going to finish what you started and like it."

They tussled like children in a rumble until Sofia began to cry.

He was straddled on top of her. When he realized how agonized she was, he relented, lying down with her beneath him, not snuggling kiddies, but a man and woman pressed together.

"The one in the two, the two in the one, the one in the two, the two in the one," he gently chanted as if it were a lullaby but also as if he maybe was really having a hard time adjusting to be being "two" in the particular way he was with Sofia.

They may have been just one person in some distant past or else two that became one in one way or another but now they were twins who seemed to be meant to disengage to merge into unions with others. There was a dangerous resistance to circumstance. The Fates might have deemed it wise that the twins were separated during infancy. They really weren't supposed to be running into each other and falling in love later in life, which was what Aurelio at least had sort of done.

"Nothing bad can ever happen to you. Not ever," Aurelio said. Then he kissed Sofia in the way lover's do. She let him but then wriggled away.

"You're going to give me that screw back or what?" she snapped.

"The screw is coming," he uttered in his cheeky way.

"That's just 'great,'" Sofia replied and went back to bitterly brooding.

Aurelio went back to chanting "The one in the two, the

two in the one . . ." while inching back into a tight cuddle with his twin. Then he said "Don't be weak. It is not very becoming of you. You should abandon this puny faintness of heart and rise to the occasion, La Maga Magus." The quip was actually a line from the Bhagavad Gita, uttered by Krishna, a famous incarnation of Vishnu, because a warrior named Arjuna was back peddling about stepping to the plate in a civil war. Aurelio recited the statement in a quirky sing-song, though. "Trust the Lion-of-Light man," he said. "He wanted to be saved, and you heard his prayer. Now, he wants to save us. Let him, Sofia."

And so they rested in that thought. Upon returning to Sofia's apartment, she and Aurelio performed a brief Lux Clarus rite for themselves and for Leo and Leonard. Then, before departing, Aurelio zapped Sofia with a sleep spell so that she could pass the night restfully before her big day.

As the spell took effect and sedation set in, he told her that it was no use badgering him about returning the screw. She would be hard-pressed to retrieve the widget since it was now in the possession of Leo de Lux. Then, he laid his body against hers in a tight and sensual grip.

Sofia was too anesthetized to protest. Yet, with that, despite the sleep spell, slumber was rife with dreams. The two in the one, the one in the two, the two in the one droned deliriously on top of hearing her old guru Prakash Shaami speaking to her. Preaching . . . chanting. It was gnawing, distant, and tinged with dimness and delirium.

"Go to sleep already," her brother's voice hollered, but a dreamscape emerged anyway, and, with it, the ancient holy man Prakash Shaami. He was a tall, bald, sturdy fellow with leathery skin, big piercing eyes, sunken cheeks, and a slightly amused smile. *"Joi chun-deem bhavotee,"* he deeply uttered: "Victory to she who is fierce!"

Sofia's heart flip-flopped with elation because the holy man said "is" instead of "will be." He pointed to a cave.

Sofia entered it. The inside was like one of the spaces she had lived in during her exile in the Terra Mysticus. A hearth was near the entrance. A pot to cook gruel and another for tea were suspended above it. A bookshelf, lantern, and mat furnished the cave. She sat down and observed the cool and musky space. A lion with a huge mane gently sauntered out of the gloom. It pressed its snout into the back of Sofia's neck and nuzzled hard against her ear. The animal's breath was windy and piercing, stinking of musk and mulch and fetid vapors that were remnants of its appetite.

The animal bore down with a weight that became crushing. It rolled Sofia forward and straddled her as if poised to either snap her neck or mount her. She eked a brief whine, but held steady, remembering that she was in a dream after all.

The animal became a man but the weight didn't ease. "I have resigned myself to the momentum of the Chaos Principle," the man said. "It is the Reality; we two are the part of its dream that is about to cause its whole projection to turn inside out."

"de Lux, you are an amazing person," Sofia whimpered beneath the weight.

"You are the life beneath me, the agency of my action," he said and recited what seemed like a spell: "'I set my seal on you. Love as strong as death.' By my will, no one crosses it."

A searing sensation sliced into the space between Sofia's shoulder blades. She yelped. The word "Syzygies" pierced her ear as if a bumble bee were stuck in it.

She startled awake and lay there feeling tender and afraid to move. She called her brother's name, but he had gone. The shadow of the dream yet pulsed in the form of a burning pain in the pith of her back. She muttered a prayer, tried to feel safe, and lapsed back to sleep until 8 AM when

Mirelle barreled into the apartment. She hollered up to the loggia. "Get up!" the girl scolded. "GET YOUR ASS UP! Dr. Bruno's here."

Mirelle alighted at the top of the stairs and gasped. Sofia heard a slushing sound, like that of a person wading through fallen leaves.

"What does this mean?" Mirelle exclaimed as she gazed upon what she was sloshing through.

Sofia stirred from her covers to find herself buried in red flower petals—tulips mostly—but roses and chrysanthemums too. The room was piled with them.

"Are red tulips good?" Mirelle uttered.

"Leo de Lux is in love," Sofia griped. "What a pain in the ass."

By then Mirelle had caught sight of a mark on Sofia's back. "Holy shit!" she exclaimed. She ran to the banister of the loggia and hollered down to Dr. Bruno and Michael Camael: "de Lux Sortiar put a big mark on Sofia's BACK!"

"Is it a love bite?" Danny Bruno asked.

"He branded her," Mirelle announced.

"Yeah. I heard he's a little B and D," Danny quipped.

"What does it look like?" Sofia asked. She stepped to the bathroom mirror to inspect herself. Sure enough, her back was seared with the consul's family crest: the sign of Leo set in a sun circle. "Isn't that sweet," she grumbled.

"You got him in your pocket, Baby," Danny announced. "What's the deal with the son? The kid isn't dead yet, is he?"

"No," Sofia replied nonchalantly and turned to Mirelle. "I thought it was a dream."

"I got a lot of money riding on that you'll take her out in the third round," Danny hollered.

"Yeah, well, I don't think there's going to be any 'rounds,'" Sofia said. She hung over the banister of the loggia despite that she was disheveled and half-naked.

Danny leered. Michael didn't seem moved.

"Could you all leave now?" she said.

She handed Mirelle her wallet. "Go buy some vestments already. You have to look really spiffy for the match. It's a 'public display,'" she said. "If you don't come back, I'll know you cleaned out my bank account, eloped, and fled to honeymoon in Hawaii or some other 'Commonality.'"

Mirelle pouted. Her eyes went all rabbit pink and mirror-like and began to tear.

"Hot and crunchy on the outside, soft and gooey on the inside," Sofia quipped. "Like a piece of fried okra."

"You never had a piece of fried okra in your life," Mirelle cried woundedly.

"Sure," Sofia asserted and materialized a morsel. "It's the vegetable that cums in your mouth." She took a bite and made her eyes bulge as the mucinous, horn-shaped morsel squirted out its sap.

"Now you're acting more normal," Mirelle sighed in relief.

"Yeah, well," Sofia shrugged.

The women held hands and put their foreheads together.

"Someone is going to try to kill me today," Sofia confided. "I can't guarantee that she — or he or them — won't succeed, and you can bet that everything will go shit-faced ballistic Armageddon if it does happen. Professor Zosimo and Leo and Lenny won't let up if it rolls that way. I'm not going to intentionally disappear on you or anything," she promised. "No matter what happens, nothing bad is happening," she said.

*

Later that day, at the Bythos Academy Stadium where

the extravaganza was to take place, Mirelle strode onto the field among cheers and jeers—most particularly jeers accusing her of being a Deeple. She was armed with the lion-topped staff that Leo had given her and was dressed in a brilliant violet alb covered by a lightly embroidered crimson dalmatic with a coral-pink stole embroidered with red roses and golden leaping lions. She wore amulets crafted especially for her by Camael Magus, and her hair was loose except for a wide headband that matched her stole.

She stood across the field from Karen Ea Brevis Sortiar, who was wearing a dark green dalmatic with a matching, hooded chasuble embroidered with red and dusky serpentine designs.

Upon being introduced, Medea Sarin Sortiar materialized in her signature billowy plume of red smoke. Her chasuble was black, violet, and crimson, and her matching cone hat was tall with a wide brim. Her frizzy, platinum hair was woven into three braids that framed her face and ran down her back.

Medea and her girl preened and posed. They jeered at the spectators. Mirelle stood her ground despite being occasionally pelted with items thrown about by the rowdy crowd. Over-ripe tomatoes and other fruit, eggs, and weird thought-forms of small reptiles, vermin, skull-less heads, and that sort of thing were already being launched at her and the sorceresses that she and Sofia would duel. This would continue, according to tradition, throughout the entire match.

Unlike Medea Sarin, Sofia was not quick to appear on the field. The referee, a short, wiry man, announced her twice before asking Mirelle if the maga was going to show up. Mirelle shrugged while pockets of people in the crowd began to holler "Forfeit!" Quickly then, the young woman pointed to a tremendous pink soap bubble that was hovering above the stadium. "I think that might be her now," she smartly quipped.

All focused on the bubble. It was the appropriate complement to Medea's red-smoke. It slowly descended, touched down, and transformed into the apparition of Sofia La Maga Magus. She was clad in her raw silk vestments, including a long, white dalmatic; a rose-embroidered chasuble; and a matching, hooded cope. Embroidered on the cope's back was the Rose Mystica—scarlet on the perimeter and brilliant white at the center. It was overlaid with an inverted triangle—a symbol of the Goddess—in gold brocade.

The stadium was raucous with cheers and jeers and factions holding banners advertising their allegiances. A band of white-coat magi held aloft a banner with the message "Pride Goeth Before a Fall." Some banners proclaimed, "SUICIDE!" and one banner, held by a bunch of kids who were barely teenaged read: "Sarin, Look Out for Falling Houses, You Wicked Witch!" Thought-forms and nuisance projectiles abounded, all making for festive chaos.

Sofia performed a trip on her long dalmatic as she approached the referee, who rattled off some rules of etiquette that no one ever abided by: animal materializations were within the guidelines but animal transfigurations were prohibited as were incendiary devices. Direct, martial strikes through staff discharges or other weaponry would be considered fouls. The match would go up to seven rounds of 8 minutes each in which the opponents would spar, like in a duel or a boxing match. The aim of the duel was to try to trip up the opponents through sanctioned magical spectacles until one of the dueling teams did not recuperate from a 10-count.

Generally, during these fetes, the field would be chock full of wild materializations and attack charms. Sofia had something else in mind.

She turned to pace back toward her station. She glared at Mirelle. "Hold firm to that staff," she instructed. "Where did you get it?" she asked and then mouthed, "Where's Bruno and de Lux?"

Mirelle gestured her head toward the box seats where all the big shots sat. Sofia was surprised to see an entourage of politicians from other sovereignties seated with the consul. It angered her to realize that she was now the butt of something like a gladiator melee where slaves and war captives were butchered for entertainment purposes. The consul smiled faintly at her. She gave him the finger.

"Are you ready to roll, La Maga Magus?" the referee impatiently asked.

As Sofia turned toward him, and before she could speak, she ducked from a discharge from Medea's staff. It shot straight toward Mirelle, who had the wherewithal to block it.

Ricocheting off Mirelle's staff, the shot dispersed into sparks that flew yards upward like a bottle rocket. The sparks fanned out to the perimeter of the field. As they touched down, goofy creatures with the torsos of circus clowns and the heads of lions, tigers, and bears materialized and bumbled about. They mindlessly collided into each other and dissolved on impact.

"Oh my!" La Maga exclaimed just like Dorothy kept saying in the Wizard of Oz whenever she was surprised. She clapped her hands and gestured toward Mirelle, praising her before the crowds for how well she had blocked the attack on her.

"Get on with it," Medea screeched. She stood at the ready, moping at having been reprimanded by the referee for premature engagement.

Sofia fussed with her cope and appeared distracted. The referee had to ask her, again, whether she was ready to proceed. She said yes and uneasily steadied herself, only to delay.

"Wait! Wait!" she urgently requested. Looking earnest, she stepped back and handed her rose-topped staff to Mirelle. Then she shook her hands as if relieved to be free of an annoyance.

"OPEN-HANDED. OPEN-HANDED," the crowd roared.

"No weapon, La Maga Magus?" the ref inquired.

Sofia displayed her right hand. The index and middle fingers were extended and the other fingers were folded into her palm. All magi knew that this was the mystical gesture called The Hand of God.

"This is my weapon," Sofia announced.

Magi and a slew of Expansionist Party sympathizers rose to their feet, chanting "MA-GA! MA-GA!" and "HAND OF GOD!" while other persons hollered bitterly, "STOP THE BULLSHIT. GET ON WITH IT!" Fiery lights of mischievous attacks that the audience launched against itself spun and collided overhead. Sofia stood poised with her mystical gesture. Medea insisted the maga throw the first shot. Sofia stepped forward. She had barely extended her arm when Medea's staff bucked, emitting a farty spark. The sorceress teetered backward from the impact.

Sofia shrugged and faintly sneered while.

The women faced off and, again, Medea simply lost her balance upon engagement again, inscrutably blocked by the Sofia's subtle arte. Those few spectators who were aware of what they were actually witnessing, genteelly clapped and cheered. But there was no color, no drama for the rabble..

"WHERE'S THE SHOW!" the crowd hollered angrily. They began to scream "FIX!"

The round had ended, at which time the referee scolded the audience for its rowdiness. A group of staff-bearers was summoned to hem in the perimeter of the field.

The referee then asked Medea whether she was equipped for the match.

The question caused the sorceress and Karen Brevis to so verbally abuse the petit man that he produced his staff to keep them at bay. The Commissioner of Fetes and Games calmly motioned from his box seat beside Leo de Lux, that Medea Sarin Sortiar would be fined for her conduct. He also told Sofia that she had to use a traditional staff during the match and would do well to expand her repertoire of dueling techniques.

After unnecessarily curtseying, Sofia retrieved her weapon from Mirelle to turn to find herself limbs snagged in a mass of tethers. With a tug, Medea Sarin dragged Sofia a few yards along the loam of the field. Materializations of demon-ish bat-like creatures began to swarm to keep her bound and down.

But Sofia let out a sonorous chant of foreign sounds, the tenor of which caused the tethers to snap and whip at the spooky-bat hoards, which popped into thin air like balloons.

She scrambled to her feet, placed her fingertips together and then drew them apart so that a silvery line, like the thread of a spider, stretch from one hand to the other. With a thrust of the arms, she sent the line skirting through space toward her foes, who were forced to stumble back against the weight of an invisible wall flying toward them. Medea and Karen found themselves squeezed between the barrier and the stands before Medea managed to shatter the barrier seconds before a 10-count was up.

After making a bravado of resuming her place on the field, she lobbed a helios at Sofia, who turned up the temperature before lobbing it back.

The ref skittishly dashed into the fray to yelp that helios-playing was strictly PROHIBITED. Medea had already volleyed the thing back, aiming the now combustibly ripe orb at Mirelle. All the young woman could do was point her staff at it and recall all the things that Leonard had ever told her about the Phaeton maneuver.

The orb turned flat, silvery, and disc-like before fading into the aether. The crowd went wild at that impressive feat. Irked, however, by the Medea's assault on Mirelle, Sofia swiped out an electric line from her staff that whipped the sorceress's ankles and felled her.

"Next time, it'll be your head!" Sofia screamed as Medea pulled herself up.

The women ignored the ref and gaming commissioner's insistence for a time out and shouts about fouls and fines. Indeed both women menaced the staff bearers who approached them. The gaming commissioner even turned to the consul for support, but Leo simply waved him off dismissively and could be heard saying, "We're all here to see them go at it, aren't we?"

The women paused and paced to face off for another round. Medea insisted that Sofia make the first move. So Sofia clipped the sorceress again, as promised, in the head.

Medea fell back hard, flat, and too befuddled by the blow to rouse herself. Her supporters cried "Foul!"

Sofia turned toward Leo, the gaming commissioner and all the hoity toity seated with them and shouted in disgust, "We're done!"

Danny Bruno's voice was then in her head telling her that something threatening was about to hit but that she should play it cool. And he said that Aurelio Zosimo could not jump in; he was across town being detained by staff bearers because Leo de Lux didn't trust him.

Before Sofia could react, Mirelle forced her lion-topped staff into her grip. "It's above," Mirelle gasped.

Overhead, flashing like a pulsar high in the sky, was

the diamond-encrusted staff of Hipparchus Gorgon. It gleamed like a flashing beacon as it twirled head over tip, threatening to take aim to impale its target. Sofia gaped at the weapon and then sharply turned because Medea was back on her feet.

The sorceress sneered victoriously as she cocked her head to assure Sofia that she, too, had noticed the thing in the sky. "You're going to the other side, La Maga, but not so fast," Medea announced. The sorceress produced a small, red bird that she abruptly smashed with the head of her staff.

A crushing pain seized Sofia's chest. She collapsed while Medea struggled against Mirelle to pull the lion-topped staff away from Sofia. Staff-bearers fell upon the sorceress. She fought them as spectators gaped and hooted or fixated, as if mesmerized, at the pulsar in the sky.

Once Medea had been yanked away, Mirelle threw herself over Sofia as a shield. When not screaming at people to keep their distance, she was muttering prayers about taking refuge in the "great lion of the light" and avowing in heart-rending whimpers that she would go with Sofia into the next plane.

Gorgon's staff continued to pulse but failed to plunge into its target. Sofia wondered whether Mirelle's staff was keeping it at bay.

"Whose is this?" Sofia wheezed.

"The consul's. He gave me an empowerment," Mirelle confessed. "Why is he allowing this?"

"The age-old question," Sofia huffed. She bid Mirelle to help her up. A robust burp alleviated her chest pain. She excused herself for making the sound and hissed because the sear on her back was stinging.

Motioning for Mirelle to stand back, Sofia raised her right foot to balance on the left. Aiming Mirelle's staff at the sorceress, she transfigured into the Goddess in her destructive form. Her complexion turned blue-black, her eyes red, and the tips of fangs peaked from her lips. She was waiting for Medea to charge her once she broke from her stand-off with staff-bearers.

The sorceress scoffed at Sofia's posturing. She raised her staff, cackled derisively, lunged, and abruptly disappeared in a burst of flame. Meanwhile, the staff that had been hovering overhead exploded. A hale of cinders and diamonds rained down hard, pelting Sofia and the others manning the field. When the rain of shrapnel subsided, all that was left in the air was a wisp of brackish red smoke.

"Where did she go?" the referee asked bewildered.

Karen, bruised and burned from the rain of debris from Gorgon's staff, scrambled up from the ground and began screaming "MURDER!"

Victor was then on the scene. Sprinting spryly onto the field, the matured and husky fellow scooped up Sofia, hoisted her over his shoulders, and raced across the field. He crunched over a gravel of diamonds and ash, dodged and fended off marauders, and did not stop running until he had entered a remote salon within the Bythos Academy where he deposited Sofia on a couch.

Many of her familiars were in that room, including her brother who stood brooding in the shadows and patiently watching others adjust Sofia's limbs, dress her wounds, minister magical healing routines, fuss with her hair, and try to get her to come-to. Pierced, bruised, and seared, Sofia was too out-of-it to acknowledge them.

Then the consul appeared. He affixed cool compresses to her head, primped her hair and rouged her lips and cheeks.

"It was stabbing me. It was coming all the way into me," she whined.

Leo winked at the others to assure them that Sofia was

coming around.

"Hipparchus Gorgon's staff," Sofia sulked.

"Nothing bad is happening. Don't be weak, La Maga Magus. It doesn't suit you," Leo lilted.

Sofia flinched and gestured that Leo lean in closely. "Aurelio Zosimo is my brother," she gasped. "Where is he?"

"Not far," Leo smiled, finally satisfied. He gestured to where the fellow stood a few feet behind him. "He and I had a nice chat some days ago," Leo admitted. "In fact, he gave me a screw."

Grinning with a silly nod, Aurelio waved and made his fingers fleck back and forth from two to one with the one being the middle finger sometimes.

As Sofia's gaze toggled between Leo before her and Aurelio some yards away, she listened to Leo relate that she would have to endure a brief inquiry. "It will seem officious and grueling but it will be relatively brief, and nothing will come of it. Look about. You have to be put-together," he said sternly. "Let them know that your actions were calculated and controlled and purely defensive. Don't babble too much about the 'staff in the sky' or Gorgon Sortiar."

"Why do I have to do more now," Sofia huffed. "I'm finished. I want to go."

"Just a little bit more, La Maga Magus," Leo coaxed.

"*Fuck that,*" Sofia exclaimed and attempted to translocate but was far too spent to manage it.

Leo sighed hard. His diamond-like eyes welled up and turned pinkish. "Listen to me." Grasping the sides of the maga's head, he continued pointedly: "You defended yourself. I am a conniving bastard who will avow that I have hidden my son away from your subversive company, contrary to rumors about disappearances and assassination plots. Whether or not Hipparchus Gorgon Sortiar had a hand in the violence against you today is open to inquiry. However, La Maga Magus, don't confuse things. The story is that you were attacked by a death charm cast by a notoriously deranged and violent sorceress. You killed her. You had no other choice. This is your circumstance. Endure it. Forty minutes more . . . an hour. I'll make it up to you or your brother can kill me."

He may have meant to kiss her, but it felt more like a bite. In the midst of it, he startled and abruptly vanished.

No sooner, a cadre of staff bearers barreled into the salon. They escorted Sofia to a moderate-sized lecture hall like that of her classroom at the H. Trismegistus. Instead of students, the tiers of seats were occupied by senators, tribunes, censors, praetors, and other such dignitaries. A committee-table of seven such big shots sat at the head of the room. The consul was not presiding at the center of that table; he was sitting at the far end to the left. At center was a mature and royally imposing maga named Alba Sandalphon Magus. She was a member of the Imperial Cabinet of the Terra Novit. She was a dark-skinned woman who was arrayed in a blindingly white alb, dalmatic, and ornately brocaded chasuble all of which were particularly striking against her complexion. A tall, impeccably wrapped, cone-like turban was fastened to her head. The veil she wore with the turban was affixed with a pin of iridescent moonstone, baubles of craggy uncultured pearls, and platinum.

Mirelle was escorted into the room and positioned next to Sofia. The women clasped hands. Her Excellency Lady Alba Sandalphon Magus flecked her wrist dismissively, however, to command that Mirelle be excused from the proceedings. Protests went out about the girl's menacing conduct on the field. Senators also stressed that the alleged murder weapon happened to be the staff that the girl had been holding until she thrust it into the maga's hands.

"She's an accessory," they shouted and someone even hollered, "Deeple."

Lady Sandalphon scowled and ignored the dissent. She instructed the staff-bearers to escort Mirelle from the room, despite the girl's objections.

"I'm staying with my mentor," the young woman declared. But her voice changed from being insistent to emitting shrieks and sobs after staff-bearers hauled her, struggling, to the corridor. The door shut behind her. Her protests yet resounded and the thud of her body bolting against the door could be heard as well. After she stopped pounding on the barrier, she cursed, and then piteously pleaded in wails until someone picked her up and carried her out of earshot.

Tissues and hankies were handed to Sofia because she was moved by Mirelle's plaintive outburst. She daubed her eyes while Lady Sandalphon Magus announced, "Professor La Maga Magus, it is my personal opinion that you came to this fete quite reluctantly, taunted by public pressures and some underlying circumstances the investigations of which are delicate and complex. I wonder who and how many are at fault for what I suspect occurred today?" Lady Sandalphon pouted and glanced around the room. "We need to be clear, however, about the present condition of Medea Sarin Sortiar. Murderousness is not taken lightly in this realm."

"Respectfully, Your Excellency, given that the event was witnessed by hundreds of persons, I want to note for the record that, in my opinion, this hearing is unnecessary. Medea Sarin Sortiar's fate is obvious as is the reason for her demise," the consul interjected.

"Recuse yourself, de Lux!" senators heckled and uttered *"Shame!"*

"You're best to keep silent, Lord Consul. You yourself are not above investigation," Lady Sandalphon griped. She took the occasion to poke into Leo's own questionable circumstance. "La Maga Magus, before we become submerged in the proceedings, have you information about the condition and whereabouts of the consul's son? Word is you are his mentor and also that the boy has been disappeared. Is this not so?"

Before Sofia could reply, the consul heatedly announced that there would be no talk about his son and that he took offense at the rumor that the boy was missing, which he insisted was wholly untrue.

"Did I miss some legislative petition insisting that no child be allowed to travel outside of the sovereignty? Is every child who spends his summer with a noncustodial parent who lives in another terra considered 'missing'? Don't you think I'd act swiftly if my son were 'disappeared'? Not only is it ludicrous; it's defaming, and it will desist."

A lull ensued before Lady Sandalphon tersely commented, "Duly noted, Lord Consul." She turned to Sofia: "La Maga Magus?"

In a meek voice and despite the consul's outburst, Sofia confessed that Leonard de Lux, Junior—the consul's son, who was within days of his 17th birthday—had been disappeared on account of his liaison with her. "He is probably dead or worse," she added in a grave and gravelly voice. "Furthermore," she went on, "what 'hundreds' of people saw today was an assassination attempt against me, orchestrated by certain persons in government and business. The attempt failed."

A cacophony of jeers erupted from the senators and other magistrates in attendance. Lady Sandalphon shot a lightning rod from her staff that loudly sizzled across the ceiling. It quelled the noise. Then she turned an eye toward the consul, as if coaxing him for a rebuttal. He flecked his eyebrows and smirked as if Sofia's allegation was as humorous as it was preposterous.

"The maga should be assured that my son is quite alive and safe," he snipped in a scoffing manner. "The young man has been removed from her influence, and she is understandably perturbed. I will excuse the grandiosity and paranoia given the maga's trying ordeal and will concede in fairness that she was clearly the victim of a death charm at the hands of Medea Sarin Sortiar. The maga retaliated against the sorceress, albeit defensively. Alternative defenses might have been enacted by a more sophisticated magical person. However, the maga appeared to be in extreme and life-threatening duress and acted accordingly. Her only crime may be lack of finesse and perhaps delusional thinking. This is my observation," he said smoothly.

"Now, I wish to dismiss the committee, reestablish public order, and conference about La Maga Magus' fate in relation to the many 'complexities' of her provocative presence in a closed-door session at a later date," the consul said and stood up as if to depart.

Rather than adjourning the hearing, Lady Sandalphon requested that the alleged murder weapon—the lion-topped staff—be presented to her. The magistrate assessed it. A wave of annoyance crossed her face. She handed the weapon to the other members of the judicial panel. Each also looked dismayed and scoffed after inspecting the piece. When the consul's turn came to examine the object, he declined. Thus, it was handed back to Lady Sandalphon. She flung it onto the table before her. "This weapon has not been discharged today," she announced.

The audience hissed but was abruptly silenced when Lady Sandalphon shot another thunder bolt from her staff. She glared at Sofia and then down the table at the consul, who simply matched her sullen gaze.

"Are we done?" he snapped.

Lady Sandalphon sneered slightly. Excluding Consul de Lux, she briefly conferred with the other judicial panel-members before announcing:

"The judgment is that the sorceress Medea Sarin Sortiar met her death at the hands of the defendant on whom she had cast a death charm. We deem that the defendant acted in self-defense, and we hold her harmless. However, a substantial fine—to-be-determined–will be imposed for her provocative behavior during the fray. You're free to go, La Maga Magus. Good luck to you. No doubt, you are in dire need of it."

Without prompt or adieu, Lady Sandalphon disappeared in a sparkling haze of white light. The audience of senators was then free to group into cliques to express whatever comments they had to squelch in the presence of Sandalphon Magus. They slowly filed out of the room. The consul already had departed through a side exit—or perhaps he had translocated from the area as well.

Sofia stood frozen in place. She was unsure of how to depart or where to go exactly. She observed the faces of the senators who passed her. Some eyed her with awe or adoration, some with fascination, and others with dismay or disgust.

"I would've been a much better catch than ole' White-Eyes, sweetheart," an unfamiliar man muttered with a wink as he grazed by.

Someone slipped her an address of an underground organization that assists persons who need to go into hiding. Another gave her a card with the name of a high sorceress with a slash through it and the memo: "Can you take care of this? Excellent compensation." Then there were the few folks who, from a distance, caught the maga's eye to make throat-slitting and gun-shooting gestures.

A petite woman with a pale complexion and a perky bob of black hair sidled beside Sofia and squeezed her hand. The woman was the mediator Vinca Blanco Sortiar.

"Don't disappear," she said. "Follow me. Don't worry. I'm helping." The woman pulled a gold medallion from her blouse on which was embossed the insignia of the Lions of Light in a thin ribbon of platinum. "You know what this is, don't you?'

Sofia followed Vinca through a door that led to a small office, out another exit, through a private corridor. They descended stairs and then passed through more desolate hallways that held the echoes of the women's silent thoughts and hurried footsteps until they neared a door with a frosted pane glass window. Sofia assumed that it led to the outside.

"How did you get Leo?" Vinca finally asked. She had to repeat herself a few times because Sofia was addled by the question.

"He just came around," she finally replied.

"'Coming around' is one thing; staying is another," Vinca griped.

Sofia simpered and nervously pawed at the frosted-glass door. She rubbed her hand against her brow. It had been a very long day, and day's end was nowhere in sight.

Vinca sourly informed Sofia that a silver SUV was supposed to be on the other side of the door. "It's okay to get into it but only if Victor is at the wheel. You know who Victor is? Right?"

Sofia asserted that she did.

"I mean, you can just disappear if you really want— but they rather you get in the car with Victor," Vinca continued.

"Alright," Sofia said. She abruptly materialized a staff for each hand: the rose-topped staff in her left and the lion-topped staff that had become state's evidence in her right. Vinca jumped back from the shock of it.

The maga smiled kindly at the sorceress. She thanked

her before bolting through the door to an enclosed formal garden of symmetrically designed plots and topiary. At the end of the main path was a wrought iron gate with gilded accents. It was hemmed by marble pillars that had leaping lions mounted on the cornices. A silver vehicle was parked beyond the gate. The set-up seemed rather confining, and who would actually be beyond that gate where the silver SUV was parked anyway?

Sofia turned around to look at the frosted glass-panel door behind which Vinca Blanco was sniveling and scorning her. Then she looked back at the gate.

Vinca appeared beside her then. "Alright," she gave in. "I'll go first."

She lightly sprinted, like a flying pixie, toward the gate. She held a hand out behind her urging Sofia to keep a cautious distance. When Vinca got just beyond the gate, Leo came into view. He peeked into the courtyard and encouraged Sofia to make haste in coming forward. As she neared, she watched Leo hug Vinca and hold her tenderly. He kissed her in a long embrace and continued to hug and console her until Sofia got within range. Then he embraced Sofia robustly although his mouth was full of the taste of Vinca's heart-broken tears.

"Take a little drive with Victor," Leo grinned and told her that she didn't need the rose-topped staff. Sofia watched it disappear as he laid his fingertips on it. He urged her to hold firm to the other one. "I'll see you in a bit." Then he disappeared, leaving Vinca and Sofia to gaze at each other, both looking tearful and soggy but for different reasons.

XVII
The World Within the Mind

I t was fascinating to see her display such pique. It was perfectly understandable. Leo had been walking a thin line all these many weeks. In any other situation, it would've been foolish and sadistic to submit a love interest to such ruses and trials. Resentment would breed hate and repulsion, of course. Leo would soon find out whether he had been overreaching in assuming Sofia would understand his method.

Victor had been instructed to drive around for an hour. The butch staff-bearer in Leo's entourage was supposed to keep Sofia company and keep her from translocating—or apportating—or otherwise escaping. The vehicle was some minutes late in rendezvousing with Leo, as instructed, in the brush at the far end of a field that Leo had learned, through his scrying endeavors, was an adolescent Phaeton maneuver arena—a rather secret place.

Besides the length, tedium, and uncertainty of the ride, the last leg of it would have to be particularly uncomfortable, what with the 4-wheel drive SUV clamoring over barely cleared dirt trails and raw terrain. It surely wouldn't have been as entertaining for Sofia as the jaunts depicted on television commercials for car sales that were fed to Commons.

When the vehicle pulled into the brush, Leo passed through the side of it. He was joyful . . . excited. Sofia was livid and weather-beaten. She put her hands up to keep him from embracing her.

"I don't get the monstrousness," she scolded.

"Of course you do," Leo replied. The response only made Sofia cry. Leo testily ordered the staff-bearers out of the car. Then he told Sofia that things wouldn't work without complexities, intrigues, and noxious effort. "They have a delicate course, after all," he said. "It's far from over, but the line has been crossed. I'm bringing it all down," he said, as if she should be proud of him. He nodded reassuringly. "Things will change. We'll be able to live in our own peace then, and let the momentum of this mayhem ride along on its own." He cupped Sofia's chin in his hands and peered at her apprehensively. "Are you still with me, Sofia?" he asked.

She faintly nodded.

"You expect me to go on with this, don't you?"

She mouthed the word, "yes."

He held her and let her sulk and tremble for a while; then he spread her out on the seat and rolled himself upon her. He toyed with the position momentarily, the pillow of her beneath him, before pulling her from the vehicle and lifting off the ground into a whirl in the interspaces of the atmosphere.

They set down on the rocky shore of a placid sea. The sun was setting toward the left, casting a tawny orange glow on the ground paved with tumbled white, orange, and pink stones and coarse gravel. The sea itself was very clear so that schools of fish could be detected streaming within the shoals off the shoreline. Moss-covered boulders loomed from the shallows, and gulls bombed the rocks with shellfish to puncture their armor and get at their meat.

The beach was cut off by a steep incline covered in scrub brush, dog roses, goldenseal, ground-hugging cacti, miniature pines, and then, at the top, wiry seaside shrubs and trees, and the hint of houses nestled in woods of maple, beech, and pine.

Having set down in that scenic and desolate spot, Leo and Sofia lost balance. They stumbled over the pebbly terrain as they tussled in an embrace. They fell over, Leo first, and then Sofia crashed down onto the stones.

She lingered, crouched, hands pressing against the cool, jewel-like pebbles as if she meant to clamp into the earth and root there. Her eyes were still tearing and her attitude was contemplative.

Leo grappled at her. He turned her front side up and clamored on top, peeling down a sleeve and the slit collar of her dalmatic. He fondled a nipple with his mouth and nuzzled into the now robustly musky sweat and pheromones of her armpit. Sebum and grit coated her skin from the tension of the long day, but it was as delicious as a holiday roast to Leo's senses.

He threw off his jacket and freed the buttons of his shirt from their holes so that he could touch his skin to hers. His belt buckle . . . his trousers . . . The couple maintained an arrested gaze, eye-to-eye, as they maneuvered over the folds of fabric and the restriction of clothes, and then Leo thrust himself in. He had to. Reddish light behind his eyes and enthrallment overcame him.

They pressed into it but briefly. Sofia gasped too passionately. Her insides hugged him tightly in a sustained and pulsing grip. It caused a scintillation to fizzle over Leo that made him feel as if his head didn't have the confinement of a skull.

He nuzzled and incoherently muttered words about sweetness as if he were a toddler describing a cupcake. Composing himself, it suddenly occurred to him that Sofia couldn't have been very comfortable pressed between him and a bed of stones. He hauled her up and asked her if he had caused her pain.

"Yes," she replied, "and I have to pee really badly." She lurched up and stumbled toward the edge of the tide. Leo was startled to see that the back of her dalmatic was rather bloody and that the blood made a smeared imprint of the crest that he had magically marked her with.

He watched her squat in the tide and then wade in. She howled as the salt sea stung into her wounds. Then she submerged. She managed to float for so long that Leo thought she might have been waiting for him to take a hint and go away.

When she stumbled back to shore, drenched, Leo uttered that he never meant to cause her pain. "Your back... I—"

"You did, too, you lousy bastard," she hollered.

"It was to keep you from getting killed," he remarked.

"The whole thing was stupid. And Blanco Sortiar. What's up with that?" Sofia said.

"Vinca's quite heartbroken," is all Leo replied rather wistfully, "but she'll get along."

"I mean her Lion-of-Light thing," Sofia remarked. She stoically shivered in her bruised condition and shreds of bloodied wet clothes.

"Our actions—you and I—and what I have been up to during our separation have given certain persons license to be bold and subversive," he replied. He began to produce layers of garments that, each in order, he re-outfitted Sofia with: a silken alb, a red dalmatic, and woolen chasuble and cope. He laughed. "That shot you gave Sarin to the head was excellent, La Maga Magus, but then you lost it. You crumbled when Gorgon arrived."

"I was ambushed," she huffed, "because 'things don't work without complications, intrigues, and noxious effort,' you know. If it weren't for that lion staff it would've be all over, wouldn't it?" she griped.

"You are cherished, La Maga Magus, but you already know that sorcerers like it rough," Leo replied.

He smiled and subtly motioned his jaw toward the top of the incline where hints of houses could be seen. "Do you know who lives up there?" He laughed as if profoundly self-satisfied and whispered in a snicker, "Us—after we kick Leonard and his groupies out."

They did not ascend the steep wooden flight of stairs but, translocated from the shoreline to a rustic tiered garden at the top of the cliff that led to a large stone house with big, stained-glass windows that opened out like double-doors. Trellises of roses spidered over its granite walls that were illuminated in orange light from the setting sun and mirror-like sea.

A dim light shone in the upper-most room that perhaps once was where an anxious wife of a sea-farer waited for whaling vessels to return to port. Otherwise the house was dark and quiet in a way that felt more like a hush than a vacancy. Leo and Sofia wandered up the path, their footfalls making musical sounds their on the multicolored gravel stones.

"We might be in trouble if he doesn't know it's us," Leo said as he rapped on the back door. "He never pays attention to my mind transmissions," he lamented. Leo knew a host of people were hiding in that house. They were waiting for Sofia's triumphant return.

Some rustling was heard. Leo smiled and waved, imagining that Leonard was using some special power to see through the door. The door opened. He expected Leonard to be joyful and enthusiastic about the reunion, but his eyes bulged and his face fell when he saw how bruised and disheveled Sofia looked even in her change of clothes.

He turned a murderous glance at his father before briskly shepherding Sofia through the house into a large and rustic kitchen. Leo wanted to boast about how he had saved the maga, but Leonard's scornful manner prevented him from getting into it.

The youth was clad in a tunic and pants made of a thick, hand-loomed weave of raw, unbleached cotton. His hair had grown out so that the ends, which fell over his shoulders, curled into loose ringlets, and he was sporting a thin and rakish goatee.

"My, aren't we beguiling these days," Leo quipped. "Where's Goldilocks?"

He observed Leonard briefly wince and shift his eyes in the way Leo tended to when he was privately annoyed. The youth jutted his chin toward a doorway where stood the alluring big-eyed girl, Thetis Mirabilis. The girl seemed worried about smiling too cordially at Leo lest Leonard take offense.

Leo watched the teenaged couple embrace, console, and dote over the maga as if they were the parents and she a young child who had wandered home from a schoolyard fray. In an anxious but controlled tone, Leonard asked her about the outcome of the match.

"She got mad and exploded," Sofia remarked. She wandered from the kitchen and entered a large parlor furnished with Victorian antiques, a fireplace, and a wide staircase. "Well, actually, your dad made her explode . . . into a stinky puff of smoke. It was very romantic," she said.

Leonard looked puzzled. The admission allowed Leo to feel vindicated. He grinned and nodded.

"And then your dad told Hipparchus Gorgon where to go," Sofia continued.

"We'll talk later, Leonard," Leo urged haltingly. "The maga needs to wash and rest and get a good meal— including perhaps a glass of . . . scotch whiskey. Do you have something around or will I have to make it?" he asked his son.

Even though Leo had never actually been in the house, he directed Sofia up the stairs and around a curve to the right to the far end of the hallway. To the left she would find a large suite with a high canopy bed, a bay window facing the sea, and a private bath. "And what would you like for supper, my darling? Perhaps a plate of tagliatelle with a wild boar ragout; a large, stuffed artichoke cooked in butter and a robust Argentinean wine."

Sofia shrugged agreeably.

"I'll think about something Bach in G for the sound system," Leo said.

She muttered "bubbles" as she limped up the stairs.

"Champagne?" Leo questioned.

"No. In the bathtub."

"Done," he promised, and with an urgent wriggle of his finger, he ordered Thetis to sprint up the staircase in case the maga needed an attendant.

Leonard gaped at his father. The frivolity in the man's demeanor was unsettling. Father and son watched the women vanish into the recesses of the second floor. Leo commented that Thetis was an okay starter for his son. He winked and smiled approvingly, but Leonard continued to scowl.

Leo looked around at the antique maritime abode, but he wasn't interested in the décor. He glared at his son who pointed to a darkened room just off the main entrance.

"Don't tell me your 'Lions of Light' are hiding in the dark, Leonard?" Leo snapped. He peered in to find the lot of them—nearly all strangers to Leo—huddled in the gloom.

"They want you to tell them the story," Leonard said.

"Oh. I'm on trial now," Leo snickered. "Where's my brother and Sandalphon Magus and my other people?'

"They're out on a boat," Leonard said flippantly.

"Do we have a boat, too?" Leo grinned.

"Uncle Emmanuel has a boat." Leonard rolled his eyes. "They went out on the boat when you didn't show up when you said you would."

"Mmmm. Faith," Leo boasted. "Enjoying the sunset on a boat instead of sitting in the dark waiting for someone like me to turn on the light."

"They're waiting to see whether you really are going to

turn on the light—metaphorically speaking—or if you're going to fuck them over," Leonard snapped.

Leo laughed. "You're going to turn on the light 'metaphorically speaking,' Leonard. I'm just going to provide the electricity." He waltzed into the room and announced, "Hello, boys and girls."

In a hushed and confidential tone, Leo related the day's events from his perspective. Yes, everyone was faulting him for subjecting Sofia La Maga Magus to a fierce ordeal, but it was a necessary subterfuge, he insisted. Besides, what would the unfolding of the Chaos Principle be without chaos?

Leo—no thanks to the Lions of Light cult—had discovered the renegade allegiances of consuls in three other sovereignties. Not only had Leo established diplomatic rapport with them but also with not one but two members of the Imperial Cabinet who had designs on overturning the corporate power structure. One of those two Imperial Cabinet members was Her Excellency Alba Sandalphon Magus.

"You are no longer an underground fringe group of apocalyptic wingnuts," he told them. "You are a movement that is moving rapidly and forcefully. Thank you." He grimaced as if slighted. "Insidiousness—virulence—is the key. An up-swelling like a nest of red killer ants that devour a sleeping Goliath," he glossed on.

Leo was attempting to be inspiring. He thought it was working alright. The faces of the young zealots in the room seemed placated—enthused even. Leo would have to tell Leonard in private that the shift he was ushering along would be long and fretful. It would leave martyrs left and right in its wake. Once achieved, a new paradigm would ever so slowly turn banal and corrupt before another revolution was ushered in to purge paradigms again. Back and forth it would go, and it would be the senseless activity that was life itself.

"All these nice people aren't staying here, are they? The house isn't that big—and I've sworn off orgies," Leo blurted. "Feed and send them home, Leonard," he bantered audaciously.

By then Emmanuel and his entourage had returned. Thus, another series of conferences ensued. It wasn't until very late at night that Leo and Leonard could speak alone. After they had both passed through the first shift of a night's sleep and had awoken too alert to rest, they gravitated toward each other in the gloaming dark of the stone house.

"We can't have all these people in the house again, Leonard. It's a security risk," Leo uttered without pause or greeting when he encountered Leonard along the staircase.

"K," Leonard replied.

"Do you have a minute?" Leo asked and watched the young man purse his eyebrows.

"It's 3:30 in the morning," Leonard said.

"And this means . . .?" Leo replied.

Leonard glared at his father before materializing the bottle of whisky that Leo had been musing on. He led his father though the second floor hallway to a flight of stairs that wound up two more short staircases to the room where the colonial sea-farer's widow who first-ever lived in that house must've spent hours moping.

The room was wide with a pitched ceiling. It was furnished with cushions and mystical and magical accessories and a telescope that looked out to the sea and stars.

"My new studio," Leonard announced. "No one's allowed up here."

Leo thanked him for the privilege of admittance and finally asked about the reason for his ferocious pique.

"She looks too beat up," Leonard said.

Leo sighed hard and, producing two tumblers out of thin air, proceeded to indulge in the whiskey. "She'll be alright. It was tricky, Leonard. I did what I could. She came through for me—and I for her. They were going to hit her no matter what if she stuck around—and I couldn't have her leaving, after all. The brother, Zosimo, was okay with it. I was going to make the 'witch' just disappear—Conus magus and all—but Bruno thought it might be fun to have her 'explode.'"

Leo explained that he had put a seal on Sofia—the family crest. "It was supposed to be armor. The force of the attack on her had to have been profound because the mark I put on her ruptured and bled."

Leo explained how Gorgon Sortiar made his presence known and told his son that, although the spectators saw two magical women acting badly and indeed witnessed a death-by-sport gone awry, the spectacle was merely a ruse. It really was a battle between the consul and Hipparchus Gorgon played out by proxy between the two women.

"Have you used the 'car keys' at all?" Leo asked. "There's been gossip about 'disappearances.' You haven't had any troubles with it?"

"I hit on a few nuances," Leonard replied cryptically. Leo let the boy keep his trade secrets. He complimented him on how put-together he looked, how nice the place was, how juicy 'Goldilocks' seemed to be, and how smooth and uniquely smoky was the choice of whiskey.

*

Leonard and Sofia stayed in that house mostly quietly and alone. The Crazy Professor showed up on occasion, and Thetis came and went at leisure. Mirelle breezed through too, although she had become more aligned with Leo. Dignitaries that he dealt with had no qualms about interfacing with her on his behalf. Her association with La Maga Magus and clash with the late Medea Sarin Sortiar made her something of a legendary character in Terra Novit.

Leo wasn't sure what they all did in that big house by the sea—whether they were cowering or conspiring or whether they merely lounged by the surf and took boat rides with "Uncle" Emmanuel. Perhaps Sofia, arrayed like a contessa in a flouncy skirt and broad-rimmed hat, and Leonard, dressed in starched white, lolled about the area's tiny tourist towns, pawing at antiques, grabbing coffees in the cafes, and indulging in ice cream while loitering on gull-infested docks. It seemed idyllic and droll, but Leo liked the thought of it.

He continued to labor at his job. The Senate was stirred, of course, as his duplicity increasingly came to light. It had made him much more popular on the one hand and much more endangered on the other. Persons kept trying to kill him, but couldn't. Rather than burdensome, it was thrilling, like an extreme sport. He came to understand the levity and impishness of other expert high sorcerers— like Danny Bruno. He had learned what it was like to play with fire, crack the code, and realize that he was virtually untouchable.

Overall and despite all, he felt rather joyful. He could certainly count reasons to be grateful, but he was grateful inexplicably.

He felt light as a feather. He felt he understood what the term "Headless" meant as a name for the top of the Cabbalist Tree of Life: Kether . . . the Crown . . . the Vast Countenance . . . the White Head . . . the Headless . . . whose God-name was the sound of the out-breath and in-breath. How did he get to this place, and why did it take so long?

He had been dreaming of lights. The dreams were

vivid. They were full color, texture, and tactility, but most of all, self-awareness.

When the lights first began to appear, Leo would find himself in a pitch-black darkness — an abyss. Curiously, he would not panic. A voice would say, "Look up." Directly overhead would be a distant, small, and icy orb that would beam down on him like a watcher. Then he would be gazing at a brilliant and ominous full moon. Then, instead of the cool moon, Leo would see a cheerful sun at dawn on the crest of a flat horizon of a peachy pastel sky. From there emerged all sorts of stars and scenes and episodes.

In time he knew what these lights were. Space to Luminance, Luminance to Radiance, Radiance to Immanence. It was happening to him. It was no longer a conceited idea. It was no longer something he had been taught or had read about in a manual or treatise. He was approaching the supreme illumination — the culmination of the Great Work.

He was going to that place. He was apportating, but it wasn't the way he imagined it would be. It was neither disorienting nor odd. He did not experience a separation or extraction from the pleasantries of his ordinary environment. Everything seemed pleasant. Everything seemed delightfully different and even unfamiliar even though Leo knew "things" weren't different; he was.

He met with his own conspirators in the apocalyptic mayhem in which he had become embroiled; he studied the forecasts of the stars, the seasons, and the phases of the moon. He plotted out the auspicious moments, performing sacrifices to the corresponding angels and daemons. He gave over to it. Then, under cover of night, he went for a little visit to the Outer Plane to the stone house by the sea.

The house was dark and quiet . . . empty. As if a ghost, Leo passed through the door and alighted to the top of the stairs. Curiously, he found Leonard and Sofia together in bed—she under and he on top of the covers. Leonard was fully clothed and unruffled in his off-white tunic and pants.

Leo gently grasped his son's head. "Don't you have your own girlfriend to sleep with?" he hissed.

The youth startled. "It's for protection," he protested in a hush.

"A quilt is not a form of protection, Leonard; a condom is. Were you AWOL the day that lesson was presented in school?" Leo flecked his thumb, gesturing that the boy should scram.

Leo was about to remove his shirt to commence with what Leonard was apparently not brazen enough to manage when he figured he ought to deal with business first. He followed Leonard to the hallway and told him that it was time he returned home and got a handle on his ministry. "I think you'll be alright. You've become a household word, and you're meant to 'be' anyway." Leo paused before he said, "You're precious to me, Leonard. You are my savior."

"I'm going to far surpass you," the youth uttered defiantly.

"Of course," Leo replied. "That's the point. Now go away," he said gently. "I want to fuck my wife."

Smiling kindly, Leonard wandered up the flight of stairs to the upper-floor garret of the house.

Leo called up to him. "You've become a great man, Leonard. A great man." He felt an upwelling of warmth flood through him as he mused on what a soulful and adept magical person Leonard had become. "Great," he repeated under his breath.

"Thanks, Dad," the youth replied in a tone that sounded cajoling.

The chatter had roused Sofia. Before anything, Leo gasped, "I think I'm apportating to the Deep Inner Planes. What will happen to us?"

"What do you want to happen?" she replied.

"Things will change if we become too aetheric," he said. "Don't do that yet."

"I think we're still a ways off from what you're worried about," she assured him.

"You think so?"

"'The world is in the mind like space in a jar,'" she lilted. It was a saying from a treatise called the *Yoga-Vasishtha*. "That's what Queen Chudala told her husband King Shikhidhvaja, when she saw that he was approaching enlightenment. The queen told the king that the world is a projection of the mind and that the mind is the Creator. When it looks outward, it creates the world but sees it as separate from itself and interacts with it. When it looks within, it sees the Source of things and merges with it.

"We go back and forth between the inner and the outer traversing all its many planes just as the drama of life sways from one extreme to another over and over. All mere entertainment, like you once said," she reminded him. "Perhaps you and I have played this game many times before and will again."

"What of the king and queen," Leo asked.

"They reigned for a thousand years as enlightened beings before merging into God. We can do that, if you like," Sofia winked.

Leo reflected momentarily before nodding slightly. The suggestion was agreeable enough. He figured, Eastern mumbo-jumbo aside, that after several dozen lifetimes, he and Sofia would just become the same person — "the two in the one." Leo just hoped that when and if the "one" that they would become then split into two again, he wouldn't be the disheveled, crazy, idiotic side of the pair, like what happened with The Crazy Professor....

In the morning, he and Sofia were already sitting at the kitchen's rustic wooden table when Leonard descended from his studio. They were drinking tea and spreading jam on scones. Leonard was wearing a long white dalmatic over which he had donned a crimson chasuble. The chasuble was thickly embroidered with deep pink roses on which were marked, in fine gold stitching, the insignia of the Lions of Light.

"You're not going out dressed like *that*, are you?' Leo said.

Leonard pouted and gaped at Sofia who smiled her impish, lopsided, and amused grin. Leo himself was clad in white—all white—with a Popish white beanie on his head.

"Don't listen to him. You look just like Jesus with your hair and outfit, honey-bunny," Sofia told Leonard.

"Don't encourage him, La Maga Magus," Leo chastened. "Are you ready, Leonard?" Leo asked his son.

The youth smiled and shrugged.

"Well, sit down and have some breakfast," Leo said windedly. "Then, we'll all get out and get on with it."

Finis

Afterthought

When thy spiritual eye is opened, and thou shalt begin to see to what end thou wert created, thou shalt want no necessary thing either for thy comfort or support; only keep in rules we have prescribed in the being of this little treatise—Fear God, and love thy neighbor as thyself; be not hasty to reveal any secrets thou mayest learn, for the good spirits, both day and night, will be thy instructors, and will continually reveal thee many secrets.

–from *The True Secret of the Philosophers Stone; or, Jewel of Alchymy. In The Magus A Complete System of Occult Philosophy Book I* by Francis Barrett (circa early 19th century).